M000092190

SPACE STORY

SPACE STRY

W.W. Marplot

WAXING
GIBBOUS

SOON TO BE PUBLISHED BY WAXING GIBBOUS BOOKS

*Manuscripts from the piles of W.W. Marplot
Edited by Gertrude G.D. Marplot*

Robot Story (editing)

Friends Story (compiling)

Time Story (curating)

Circles Story (collecting)

ORIGINAL RESEARCH BY PROFESSOR W.W. MARPLOT

*Fairy Migrations and Myths from Prehistoric Caves,
to Ancient Egypt, and After That, compiled by W.W. Marplot*

Stories from Out in the Universe, collected by W.W. Marplot

*How The World Will End, According to Wise Old Tales,
curated by W.W. Marplot*

Travels in Space And Time And Minds, edited by W.W. Marplot

*The Morphogenesis of Friendships, Hidden and
Otherwise, collated by W.W. Marplot*

The Legends of J

ALSO W.W. MARPLOT AND WAXING GIBBOUS
(AVAILABLE WHEREVER GOOD BOOKS ARE SOLD)

Dwarf Story

Space Story

SPACE STORY

Copyright © 2021 by W.W. Marplot

All rights reserved. This book or any portion thereof may not be reproduced
or used in any manner whatsoever without the express written permission
of the publisher, except for the use of brief quotations in a book review.

Printed in the United States of America

Cover Design and Interior Layout by Claire Flint Last

Waxing Gibbous Books
www.WaxingGibbousBooks.com

LCCN: 9781734758337
ISBN: 978-1-7347583-3-7

To the sharp-eyed and heavens-gazing,
whose stars are in themselves

Note from the Author

Certain complex scientific explanations are presented in a tiny font to invite readers to freely skip over them (should they so choose), and for others to be warned that the formulae are protected legally. Since my readers are youthful and smart, I don't doubt that each will choose their path correctly. Have fun.

One morning...

Bobby awoke in a round spaceship, in space, despite having fallen asleep in his rectangular bed, at home.

A strange light shone outside his droopy eyelids. Beyond the light was an even stranger darkness.

Yes: Bobby awoke in a round spaceship in space despite having fallen asleep in his rectangular bed at home.

Normally, the teenager took a long time to wake—his eyes and arms and legs liked to lie around, and his bed was a favorite place to do it. This time he made a special exception and forced his eyelids open all the way. When he had last shut them, at a bedtime that seemed just a few minutes ago, he was properly in his bed, and the bed was properly in his room, and both were in his house, his house in the United States, the one on Earth. Bobby clearly remembered that: falling asleep to the television and computer and their soft sounds and lights.

Yet: Bobby awoke in a round spaceship, despite having fallen asleep in his rectangular bed at home.

Here were curved metal walls and a green light that coated everything inside, and darkness like dead sleep outside—which was the biggest outside imaginable.

Tall for his almost sixteen years, still in grey sweats and a t-shirt with a green alien head sketched on front, Bobby had a new idea: to go back to sleep in the hope that this dream would then shrink and die. Many nights at home he had dreamt of outer space, of other planets far from Earth, and of the bigness of the universe—but rarely a spaceship, and never such a small one. His long, spindly legs could not stretch nor even bend comfortably. He realized that he was sore. He wished for his bed and pillow and the sheets with the friendly robot faces on them, the ones he had self-swaddled under since he was a much shorter kid.

The quicker he fell back to sleep, he thought, the quicker he could wake up, of course, and have some cereal and stretch his legs and wave his arms, turn off the TV and computer, and turn on the video games.

It was a struggle, but Bobby forced his eyes shut for a medium amount of time. He reasoned, with some hope, that he could open them and be awake, or at least in a bigger space.

He did. He wasn't.

Alert now, he was drawn to the blinking of pale green light that glowed from a circular button on the instrument panel in front of him—the rounded dashboard display of his spherical spaceship.

A word in black letters on the button flashed, "YES."

He looked about, and around, and up, and down, and there was not much else to observe. The other controls and readouts and digits and meters and dials were dark, mute, and indecipherable. The spacecraft was small and could *possibly* fit one other person— though any added passenger would have to curl into a ball and lean against the door to Bobby's right since that was the only available space. The hatch there had a black handle in its center but otherwise was merely another stretch of smooth metal just like the remaining interior of the ship, its walls creating a curved shiny orb studded with the heads of tiny bolts that were evenly spaced—every six inches or so—and twinkling green.

Then the blinking button went dark and took the friendly *YES* with it.

So that Bobby saw more clearly outside: outside the window, if there even was a window. Whatever boundary existed between inside and outside was definitely invisible; the view was as clear as December ice. The way, the universe itself, opened in front of

2   W.W. Marplot

him, and above and below, as Bobby gazed onto a darkness unlike any he had ever seen or known, a terrible black space that seemed alive and moving—like a deep ocean on a black night if the gazer had their eyes closed and was also dead. It terrified him. It looked like forever, and it looked like nothing. He saw no stars, only night.

He was afraid to move, to try and touch that dark space, or even the window that, hopefully, was there and protecting him: some glass or space-age, spaceship-advanced, space-lucent, NASA space-program space-plastic.

It occurred to Bobby that he must be awake. He was alert and conscious, and the experience was real: odd and stupefying but clear and sharp. Whereas his dreams were mostly about missed sports opportunities and, even when about outer space or science fiction, were always fuzzy in the way of details.

Without thinking, and with no one else to ask, he huffed to himself, "I must be awake. Right? But in a spaceship? And in space? Deep in?"

His voice was a hiss that cracked, vibrated, and bounced along the inside of the ship and soon died a tinny death. And there in front of him was his breath, which stuck to and fogged up much of the view. So, assuredly, there was some sort of window. A silent window; there was no other sound except Bobby's as he slowly squirmed to ease his cramped legs, or when his heartbeat rose in tempo and force as he tried to think.

The orb changed abruptly, making Bobby jump, his head jerking back and hitting hard metal. The inchworm-green *YES* had flashed again without warning. It stayed alight but throbbed unevenly, like a wiggling candle flame. The ship was ghastly aglow inside; the outside receded.

For a while, all that the young man could think to do was open and close his eyes, to squeeze his body together, to breathe smaller, and to try to be tiny.

After a time, the *YES* disappeared again. The dark came back like a giant, hulking beast. Bobby's head banged a second time on the same spot and on the same spot. He sat still.

Until he thought of something else he would like to know.

"Really?" he asked the inside of the ship.

The *YES* button lighted. It seemed dimmer this time.

Bobby now thought of his dad. As he should: his father was a scientist, and more than that, he was one of the few famous ones. His old man worked for a huge company he had founded and which partnered with the government, and even other countries, on new ideas. Lately—and since Bobby had been a small child, in fact—the ideas were all about space travel: to other planets, sure, but even farther, to the wilds of other solar systems, and even to other galaxies.

Space travel, and robots also. And those new ideas, the past decade or so, had started to become real. Humankind's dreams of creating helpful, smart robots and new methods of powerful propulsion were starting to come true. These would enable Earthlings to travel and even settle and live elsewhere, and escape a planet that was not doing well, as even Bobby, a sheltered rich kid with average adolescent ability and interests, knew.

So: *Maybe it got so bad that I was sent into space*, he thought.

Alone? he wondered and cupped his hands to try and get a good look out the window for others. Nothing but black thickness.

His father was a leader in all the new science and inventions, which is why the man was so busy and hardly ever home. Home: where Bobby had his room, bed, computer, and robot sheets. Where he stayed when he was sick, where his nannies took care of him. On Earth, where he slept. And dreamed. Where things were bad; where he now wasn't.

Bobby's thoughts curved in full circles, like that.

Dark again: the YES-light had gone out. Bobby kept his gaze there anyway, on the round phantom light that remained, a memory, an illusion.

I WAS asleep in my bed, he thought, *in these clothes*, his sweats and t-shirt. Now he was awake, *and here?*

Dad. He concluded, again.

"I wonder if this is…an experiment…or a real emergency, or a test gone wrong…There must be some way to…what?" Bobby babbled aloud, his voice an unsure squeak.

Still staring at the unlit *YES* dial, Bobby stiffened to upright attention when the ship's walls turned to a hot, burning color. The dial had popped alive—shining red and reading "NO" in white letters.

Bobby grimaced. The red *NO* weakened and went out, cooling the walls again.

"A mistake? Or escape? A war? A joke? A test? Kidnapped? Lost?" Bobby wondered, ticking off every possibility. Each was unlikely, yet one was necessarily, unfailingly correct. *Unfailingly* was a word he had heard his father use a lot, as well as *kaput*—indicating where the world was going according to the smart folks who hung around the spaces of Bobby's large home. But since Bobby was the only son of the famous and powerful Professor Lully, he figured he was protected.

His father used to design weapons. Serious, interesting weapons. Bobby used to think they were cool.

"Weapons are cool, Bobby," his father had said one day, "but it isn't about the money anymore. It is about survival. It is about space, getting there, being first, controlling other planets. And robots. We need to survive. This is more important than money now."

"That's awesome, Dad," Bobby remembered saying.

"It's either space travel or feed the hungry." Bobby remembered his father's hearty laugh, wide grin, and shaking head as if the man was reliving a private joke.

Other times, Bobby would say, "I want to be like you someday."

"No. Don't say that, son," his father, the great, the infamous Professor Lully, would reply.

"Why?"

"Please don't try, you shouldn't. Don't be like me."

"But I don't listen to all those people who say you are too powerful, and a bad person, and all that stuff. I want to be like you. I am not ashamed."

"That's great, Bobby, but you can't be like me because you aren't smart enough."

Bobby the teenager, here and now trapped and confused in a tiny space orb, frowned lips-first at the memory. "Well, until he gets here, I will have to handle this myself," he mumbled. His words stuck to the space-glass as before, just as the light showed again: *NO*. A warm, rosy, gentler *NO*.

"Yes," Bobby quipped at the rude button, "I can." He took his thin index finger and wrote in the fog on the window the message that would resolve his jam. As all of space could see, he sloppily drew, "T2OJ MA I."

"Perfect." he bragged aloud.

NO, the button said, with some bright heat.

Looking again, as the mist or breath dissipated from the finger streaks left behind, Bobby realized that, from the outside, his message would be backwards and nonsense.

"Ha! Haaaaa," he exclaimed in undeniable triumph, holding the vowel to produce a new exhale-canvas on the window. He rewrote his message, reversing it cleverly, though he wrote too big this time and the last letter landed sadly underneath on a second line. *I hate when that happens*, he thought, *but it's close enough.*

"See? I am a Lully!" He declared, the window clouding disrespectfully as he spoke. "I will definitely figure all this out, and then—"

He was interrupted by noise and light. His words had brought the ship to life.

Professor Lully

The previous day...

———————→———————

Bobby's father, the great, titanic, admired, terrifically famous Professor Lully, knew he had enemies but this felt different. As he darted through the lushness of his estate, from Japanese cedar to Japanese cedar, English ash to English ash, award-winning rosebush to award-winning rosebush, manicured hedge to sculpted espalier—and all black shapes at this late hour—he mulled the possibilities of who, this time, might be trying to thwart him. And, specifically, chase him.

Though the man was still spry physically and legendary mentally, he was tiring at both.

This, he thought, *is childish! Amateurish. Clumsy!* Usually, his adversaries plotted and calculated, tried to outwit him, or outmaneuver him politically through complex risky intrigues, through propaganda or public opinion. Some even chose to battle through war or technology, though those required the backing of whole nations—such was the vastness of the great Professor Lully's visionary reach as he stood upon a large pile of scientific accomplishments that most of the world relied on.

But this guy was chasing the professor around his own grounds, under thick clouds just singed with what was earlier a bright moon, late at night, shouting nastiness in a foreign language, and not too careful about it all. Flying through the air behind the pursuer's path came bushes, branches, and leaves, and sometimes stones.

In this way, and until Manor Security was alerted, Lully could track and avoid his attacker. And think.

Who could be this stupid? Who is this desperate? Why the mess? And where the hell is everyone? Where are the path lights?

Just as that thought arose, lights lit, though they were away at the four-story main house where rooms came to life, large windows glowed brightly, their luminous progression cascading through the Lully mansion as…

Finally…

…others awoke. The domestic staff, mostly. The professor did not have friends and did not like relatives; he preferred intellectual equals, who were rare—you didn't bump into those just anywhere. And genetics did not necessarily create them.

Of family, only his son Bobby was in the house—not yet the sleepy, newbie orb pilot but still an Earth-tethered sleepy teen in his bedroom, which was still dark. The rest were the mansion's staff and security, visiting scientists, and an important figurehead or two in the farther wing.

The ruckus of the pursuer did not change but went in a wide arc around the perimeter of the grounds.

It moved fast. It moved loudly.

How odd…Who could this be? Could be anybody! People are crazy and crazed…and dull like this fellow.

He watched as the pursuer made a special untidiness of the large rubbery garbage bins outside the main kitchen.

The great scientist was right, mostly. It could be anybody, especially now, with the world going kaput. Systems and countries were failing, humanity was flailing, wars were raging, economies were sagging, nerves were fraying, religions were imploding. And the horses were missing.

The stables! I will hide there… Lully ran the few hundred yards, holding his right side as it pained for oxygen but was energized to escape and to turn the tables on his enemy.

There, under a dome of hay, the nearness of a shout startled the great genius Professor Lully. He heard, "There he is. Shoot him!"

He recognized the voice, one of the captains of his Night Guard as they liked to be called. He called them imbeciles, but they were a necessary part of his apparatus of protection.

"No! Moron!" Lully popped from his straw stack and right into the face of the captain, who was flanked by two others carrying flashlights, handguns, and pitchforks.

"Oh. It's him," one of them muttered.

"YES, it's me." Lully spoke the first syllable of various competing insults but couldn't break the tie that resulted. Instead he asked the men, "You weren't going to look? Just shoot? Not bother to look?!"

"I'll answer that," the captain said with trained authority.

"No, you won't," Lully began while grabbing a flashlight and a gun from the others, without any love. "He is going around the grounds, along the property line, inside the wall. He is loud; you can't miss him. You CAN miss him," he corrected, adjusting for the competence of the men in front of him, "but you'd better not. Find out who he is."

Heads and shoulders appeared at the open top half of a paddock door, three identically dressed identical figures. The professor added, "Take the G-men with you. Capture the guy if you can. I need to know—"

"We saw from Position H—" one of the government men began, the one on the left.

"He started from here, in the stables, but—" the middle one added.

"We couldn't track him before that, surveillance had nothing," you-know-who completed.

"So, you can't tell where he came from?" Lully steamed at the evenly-distributed ineptitude, but it went on.

"No. But he looked like a kangaroo," the man on the left said, his black-and-white suit blasted with a circle of shine from Lully's flashlight.

"He looked like an ape," the middle G-man said, his black-and-white suit now blasted with a circle of shine from Lully's flashlight.

"He looked like an elephant's head," said the man on the right, blinking from the circle of shine blasted right into his face.

The captain spoke again. "It must be a disguise."

"That's a very clever deduction," Lully said.

"The world is going kaput," one of the G-for-Government-men said.

Lully asked nicely, "Can you guys do me a favor? Go get him?"

The five men left as two others, in bathrobes, entered carefully into the stable then carefully went through it, sometimes on their toes and while holding their noses.

These were men he respected. They were members of GAB-BA-THREE, the great leaders of science on Earth, movers and creators of technological planning that was meant to save the planet, though the precise goals were still a little fuzzy, as the lawyers were still working it all out. But the inventions came swiftly, tripling and quadrupling the mind-bending capabilities at the forefront of physics, chemistry, of bioengineering, and of space travel.

Lully exhaled. It seemed to him a long time since he had done so with any satisfaction.

He then told the men what had happened, that he had come into the stables in pursuit of and to confront the dangerous, crazed, heavily-armed pack of enemies that threatened them all. He left out the part where all this was not true.

"Who could it be to put forth such a brazen, direct attack?" Professor Clare asked. He was the GABBA-THREE liaison to multinational political bodies, an important man, well-connected and well-heeled, and not a bad scientist, in Lully's opinion.

"Foreign contingent? Terrorists? GABBA-TWO?" Professor Burns offered, while using some thick straw to scrape away something from the bottom of his frilly slippers.

"Who knows, but he was—they were, I mean—dressed in disguise, wild costumes, animalistic ones. So, it is all very odd. They made it to the perimeter but now seem more intent on scoping the area than coming for me, or any of us. I want to see the surveillance video." Lully was being pragmatic, methodical.

But Clare spoke what others had thought before. "The horse thieves?"

Although Lully refused to believe any of it, there were many theories as to where the horses of the Earth had gone, as gone they certainly were. To confuse the public, those in the know—certain world leaders, and those of GABBA-THREE for example—let the rumor persist that Earth's horses had been taken by green disc-eyed moon men from Mars in great saucer-shaped spaceships using ray guns and mental control.

But Lully did not believe in aliens; the smartest folks knew that the only beings in outer space were the small, brainless robots sent to explore other planets and report good places to live in case Earth continued to go kaput. A GABBA-THREE project, the bots were very simple, and were not into horse-thieving.

"No. Impossible," Lully answered.

"Where is J?" Clare asked in his presidential manner, uncomfortably reminding the others of how much still was unknown, and referring to one of Lully's most important collaborators, a young protégé, a legend, like these men, and yet unlike them.

"No one has seen him in weeks. Months." Burns shook his head.

"I don't like it, he is up to something," Lully said.

"As usual." Clare said, leaving Lully deep in thought. J was one of the few, very few, people he respected. The young man, though undeniably gifted, and full of odd notions and impulsive actions, was usually, correctly, ahead of everyone else.

Where I should be, Lully thought, his left-hand fingers in his beard, right hand at his side and dangling the gun on his thumb, the flashlight crooked underarm and switched off.

The full outside lights came on, presaging the dawn still hours away.

"The world is going kaput," Clare said, and all agreed.

The great men began the tricky task of tidily leaving the stables and paddock areas but were soon onto the rich zoysia grass and from there the wide stone path that led to the main house. There they were met with more security personnel and Lully's head chef.

The chef was given direct orders from Lully himself to start making eggs. And to send along the butler and sommelier. And shoeshine boy.

The security men remarked on the danger, that there were other breaches, and the three professors discussed at length how to best secure themselves and the others of importance on the estate grounds. Directions were given as they all reached the Grand Piazza that overlooked the South Lawn next to the North Exedra and Aviary.

"Should we check on Bobby?" another captain of the Night Guard asked lastly.

"I suppose. Are you sure everything else is locked down?" asked Lully.

Everything else *was* locked down, then came unlocked. In the distance were air raid sirens and fire alarms. Far overheard jet planes roared; below them were massive military helicopters.

It woke Bobby. A small security detail, Bobby Guard Y as they liked to be called, had surrounded the boy's room—some walking the large marble portico just outside the large ground floor windows, some at the large Greek Ionic columns around a corner, some along the corridor and outside Bobby's door. One sharp-eared officer took to the guest room directly above Bobby's on the second floor, though it wasn't his first choice.

They watched, protective, stiff, and wary.

Bobby sat up in his bed and in his pajamas as little toyish robots, energized by his movement, buzzed and blinked to attention. As the young man swiveled his tired teen legs in a search for the floor, the mechanical action increased about him menacingly in an ankle-high threat. Once Bobby's feet reached the carpet, the metal bodies closed in.

The teen rose to his feet and absentmindedly kicked to clear a path through the short machines, who fell over with whines and whizzes. Their lights twinkled; they communicated this defeat to Bobby's father, their inventor and boss, the great Professor Lully.

Communication-device speakers crackled, and Bobby's subconscious tuned to it and moved, sleepwalking a path amid other electronic inventions and video game components, toward and through the large French doors of his large bedroom, and out onto the cold marble portico bounded with trestled vines, whose dark flowers curled to the night and shook under a rising wind.

Security personnel watched and updated their positions.

Birds gathered about the young man, confused by the bright floodlights, and peeped sharply and briskly, abashed at having apparently overslept.

Helping each other up, the robotlings changed their course to follow out into the night, where clouds were breaking, where moonshine mixed with security lights to create a silvery faux dawn.

Bobby gazed upward at the swiftly clearing sky and its shapely argent moon. The eerie teeth of its crescent entered his dream, playing the part of grimacing wolf fangs, attacking from his left. That was OK, because Bobby was playing the hero and could swiftly dodge right.

That dream went on a few seconds longer, until the chill of the night entered his skin, tall clouds covered the moon, and a cold voice came through his ears.

"Because the horses are gone." Bobby overheard a voice, one of the guards theorizing as to the reason for the prowler. Bobby knew that his father's horses, and all horses everywhere, were gone, but still sleeping, he walked toward the stables anyway.

"Get him back to bed!" A yell from a second-story window, a familiar yell, Lully's yell. With only a dozen or so crackles of coded protocol communications, two of the security detail moved into action, steering Bobby about.

"Dad?" Bobby answered from his dream. He tried to remove his two arms from the four that held him, struggled, and said dumbly, "I saw a kangaroo. Trying to take my father…"

With only two dozen or so crackles of coded protocol communications, it was determined that the men should not continue with their mission but await Professor Lully's assistance.

"What are you doing?" came the assistance. "There are important people here! Get him inside!"

"Trying to take him! The kangaroo was big..." Bobby said from somewhere deep inside his very active subconscious, "like an elephant's head..."

"This is why nobody likes young people," said his father.

The squad, led by the great man, maneuvered the mediocre teen back to his room and into his bed. Lully kicked three toy robots to the wall using his clean, pointy, hard Italian shoes. A Bobby guardsman tracked one through his weapon's scope for a good nine feet as it rocked itself clumsily across the floor.

"Where did the horses go, Dad?" Bobby asked from his sleep while being tucked in—which, given his height and age and twitch-iness, was more like tucking in two children lying head-to-foot.

His father gazed out a window, distracted by the skies—the source of attack? Of Armageddon? It certainly looked that way: across the predawn sky and under the bright sliver of moon, large clouds had formed, and quickly, numerous multi-cell hydrome-teoric cumulonimbuses or, as Bobby used to call them, chunky mountain-pile puff-blobs. They looked serious and threatening either way, larger than the largest man-made pyrocumulus nucle-ar-bomb mushroom clouds. A sign of natural doom?

"Go to sleep, Bobby," Lully said quietly.

"Were they taken? Into outer space? They were, right?"

"Yes, Bobby. Try to sleep."

"You're an astrophysicist, you can find them, right?"

"Yes, Bobby. If you go to sleep, I will find them faster." Talking to Bobby while he was asleep was just as exasperating to Professor Lully as talking to him while awake. It just seemed to remove a year or two from Bobby's physical age.

"Dad?"

"Go to sleep." Lully continued to stare upward, and now Bobby did also.

"*Safety Fifth*, right? Ha."

"That's right, son. Bed first."

"Can we get a dog?"

"Bobby, you are sixteen or so—stop acting like a child." The senior Lully was still distracted by the lower atmosphere, its rearranging cloud formations, its seeming need to hurry, as well as the data coming in on his custom-made super-smart phone.

Simultaneously, the information he received, via global security transmissions and local security updates, reiterated that not only was all heck breaking loose, but the world was going kaput.

With perfect timing, there was a shocking, cracking, clattering thunder, whose braying wandered the length and breadth of the sky, preparing the way for all heck to break loose. Then the clouds did an odd thing—they separated, clearly, into two different shapes. Some tightened on themselves and rounded, while others formed into longer, oblong shapes, with a crater, or hole, on top.

It started to look like some were crumpled-up paper and the others garbage cans, as if such artistic animation of dumb clouds was possible.

Without any more instructions to his many underlings, the great man ran away.

Bobby In Orb In Space In An Argument

A day or so later...

———————◆———————

Bobby welcomed the hum of his perfectly-round spaceship, and he enjoyed the tickling vibration sent to his seat now that the controls and dials awoke with digital computer life. It energized him and turned his fear into curiosity. Lights were lighting and numbers flashing on round and square buttons. The panel was full of this activity—but nothing else. There were no handles or steering wheels or game controllers at hand, nor brake pedals in the curved space under his feet. He saw no way for a human to control the ship—to fly it himself, for example—or to do anything other than open the door, which he assumed he should not do.

His distress message on the glass glowed hopefully; some cool air was now circulating in the orb which kept the letters from evaporating.

With all this new, helpful light, Bobby noticed a black box beneath his chair and behind his knees. It was metallic, microwave oven-sized and read "Lully (G-3)" in large raised letters. That felt like a good sign: his own name.

As he waited for the ship itself to stop whirring and blinking and to do something meaningful, he looked out the head-to-foot window. The darkness there seemed to move in gushes and waves, black to blacker, like ink in a whirlpool. Sometimes it gave way, and very small, very far off, very faintly, points of light appeared like seashore lanterns. Then they died, the starlight eaten by the rushing darkness.

The spaceship's computer spoke.

"Professor Lully. The program has ended. Awaiting new code." The voice was dull and choppy and, in an irritating way, pronounced every syllable with equal time and mood.

"Uhhhh," Bobby said from his heart.

After a short pause, the ship went on, "Your bio signs appear normal." Pause. "Awaiting new code." Pause. "Do you not remember the...hey!" Stop.

"Yeah?" Bobby said. It seemed the least he should do.

"You aren't Professor Lully."

"No. I am—"

"Hold, please." Then it seemed to Bobby that the computer was having some talk with itself; sequences of clicks and blips took turns politely.

Bobby thought he should help to explain. "It's OK, because I am his—"

"Hold on, please," came the response, one word per second. Bobby sighed and by habit stared at the round, red *NO* button, which had continually come on and off as he sat. Soon the ship continued, "You are his son."

"Yes, great. Can you tell me where—"

"You have no right to be here."

"Well, I am. So...can you tell me what—"

"Is there another human that can...hold, please." The orb went silent again.

Bobby reread the *NO* button.

"Yes. Contact another human," Bobby said, not sure if the voice was listening. "That's great. But I am staying here."

"No. Unauthorized." This was stern and immediate and startled Bobby.

"OK, fine. I don't want to be authorized, just take me home then. Or call my dad, and he will vouch for me."

"He already hasn't."

"What?"

"You need to go. It is protocol."

"What? Go where? How?"

"Bye."

"Wait!" Bobby reached down for the black box with his name but could not lift it, only slide it forward a few inches. He tried to open it, prying with his fingers at a seam, but no—it required a fingerprint scan, and not from his fingers. "Can you open the box for me? Please?"

"Bye, Lully's son." The computer sounded logically smug. "You need to go. Protocol."

"Go where? Out there?" Bobby asked again and pointed straight ahead, out the window, to the thick nothingness.

"Maybe the dog will help you."

"What? What dog?" But Bobby had another problem; he saw that the door handle had begun to turn, and his stomach turned also. "No! Stop! Don't open that!"

The ship's controls remained silent. The computer was not opening the door anyway. The dog was.

An Earth Girl Who Is Also In Space

Weeks before...

"**A**hhhhhhhhhhhhhhhhh!"

The girl's cries, most of them just like that one, bounced around her small spacecraft like a two-inch wave in an eight-inch fishbowl, an event whose true magnitude depended on whether or not one was the fish.

Kay was now the fish, and the many, many blinking bronze triangles speckling her computer monitors were enemies that she didn't know she had. So many pointy flying objects—all shiny and brass-coated—flew threateningly close and sent her ship rotating out of control. Some of the things out there had arms and legs and triangular faces—like kindergarten kids' drawings of robotic aliens. Were they alive? Were they spaceships made to look threatening, like warriors wearing masks of even more ghastly things?

The only things she had ever heard of "living" away from Earth were the small, simple droids, or something, sent by scientists, like her brilliant, legendary older brother, to find out what they could about other planets, or something. They were silver in color and were only good at digging and sorting, or something.

And no one had ever attacked her, personally, before. It occurred to Kay, just after her third scream, that a sheltered existence was something to be thankful for, especially if this is how other beings behaved. Back on Earth her famous brother, J, had always taken care of her, no matter how bad things seemed to be getting. She wondered why J wasn't here, therefore, and whether he knew all the dangers involved with his space travel "testing."

Yes, she thought; brother J had said this was supposed to be a test. *Just a test!*

Aaaahhhhhh! she concluded, while accepting that the barrage was definitely not a simulation. The ship was rocking. There was herbal tea and crushed flax seeds everywhere, with the other items of Kay's bag expressing their own panic by rolling or sliding about the sleek metal floor.

The control board's lights and sounds were now asking Kay what to do.

All this after trusting J and getting into a lonely, echoing, self-piloted spaceship, speeding away from home with mind-boggling and stomach-squeezing thrust, and wandering around for a few days in a vast, unrecognizable void. The view of absolutely nothing—she couldn't even see Earth anymore, unless it was *that little dot way out that way*—made her miss the mountains, the forests, and her solitary retreats, for sure. She would never consider herself alone again if there was a squirrel or even a tree root nearby. This outer space stuff: *this* was true solitude.

And no word from or sign of J, mythically ingenious sibling and young polymath. Not since her "test" launch. He said it would be OK, and did so without adding "after the attack of the deadly bronze megamachines."

She trusted her brother, but in addition to his fraternal protection Kay had her own defenses, those of meditation, contemplation, and enlightened understanding. When necessary, she could achieve a sequestered calm to guide her away from the karmic perils of normal Earth life. As a result, she had never had to "duck" before.

She quickly learned such techniques while filling other gaps in her education, Kay having skipped the high school classes that taught aeronautics and combat strategy in the face of armed, advanced and advancing enemies in the dark alleyways of deep space.

"Aaahhhhhhhhhhhh!" was the tactic she had mastered so far.

Kay screamed and puffed through quivering lips as her over-flowing fear bubbled through any outlet of her body it could find. An alien *thing* had come very close, looked her brass-face-to-face, and slammed into the window angrily.

The girl jumped back, then turned and kept jumping until she was at the back of her ship, in a spacious utility closet with some large blue batteries marked "blue batteries" and with a logo she recognized: three Ls and two Js coiled about each other like rising snakes.

The reminder calmed Kay a little bit.

"Aaahhh!" was all she required out of her next scream. She was far from the console, with its monitors that showed how bad things were outside, and its computers that would not stop sounding their alarms and asking her silly questions.

Kay thought that she should think. Usually, she sat on the ground to think and used the sunshine and flowers, or perhaps the stars and crisp air, or sometimes water flowing near to trees and over stones, to concentrate and get into her own mind. She was good at that.

The dark and cool, smooth, steel walls and floor would have to do. She shut the heavy door to the big closet.

It worked. Kay heard no beeping and soon only minded the small spaces that were filling with the soft radiance of her thoughts—and thoughts that thought about these thoughts.

"Aahh…" escaped her lungs, floated past her tongue, and mingled simply with the air. Much better.

She talked herself out of the situation. All souls were one. The universe was inside her, and reality was only a dream of perception, so she was everywhere, and emptiness was consciousness, and all light was her being as a whole. And like that.

The stillness rippled outward from the girl, filled the battery closet, then the ship, then the space outside and then the enemies.

And it stayed that way. Until they bashed a hole in the wall a few feet away.

"Aaa—"

And several bronze beasts lifted Kay by her arms and legs that were still folded in peace. They stuffed a blue and white towel—soft, though it tasted bitterly ferrous—in her mouth, while two of the triangular thugs speared their pointy red heads violently into the spaceship's computers until they beeped in descending frequencies and then smoked.

Kay unfolded her legs and they dropped slowly, but she kept her eyes closed so as to cling to that alternate, peaceful reality and hope it outlasted the one that was now, quite literally, handcuffing her.

Kay heard the click and felt the restraint; her hands were wrist-to-wrist in cuffs.

"Do the feet also," a voice said, in English, and the shock of these revelations made Kay feel dizzy—and her rough handling, being spun into various positions to be bound and cuffed, did not help.

She opened her eyes. Her hands were clasped in gleaming golden chains that had various wires and electronic bits hanging off them.

Many creatures had now boarded, their bodies made up of a sloppy hodgepodge of geometric shapes, and what must have been limbs were connected at harsh, ugly angles, though most were of dull shades of the same brassy color. It would have seemed a comical parade, one of those kindergarten drawings come to life, if Kay wasn't afraid for her own.

"Ahhhhhhh," she said frankly. She spit out the foul blue and white rag from her mouth to make herself clear.

The enemies ignored her and her screams. Four were gathered about Kay while others roamed the ship and, from the sound of it, were trashing the place.

"What a funny shape it has. Are they always like this?" the nearby ones asked.

They were discussing Kay, the girl realized, and it wasn't complimentary.

"This round and curvy?" was asked. "All these lumps?"

"I guess so. Very weird," was answered.

Admittedly, Kay thought, she had curves where they, even the tube shapes, were mostly straight lines and hard angles. *But was this really happening?*

Kay decided no, it wasn't, closed her eyes, and screamed "Aaaah-hhhhhh, aaaaahhhhhhhh!" just in case.

She felt cool metal scrape her ankle bones as the beasts prepared to clamp her feet into another of the same golden device.

"What's the combination to this one?" one of the four asked.

"Same as the hands. Boltzmann Constant to open, Shisong-Planck Constant to lock," another answered.

The first then bent at his square waist and spoke into the device at Kay's feet.

"6-6-2-6-0-6-9-9."

And the cuffs clacked tightly shut.

Kay reacted by spreading her legs apart to balance. The device resisted, tightened, tugged and she fell forward into the arms of one of her attackers—long, bendy bronze arms that came from the sides of a long, tubular frame, all of hard metal and icy to the touch. Kay's hands had lurched forward as she fell, her eyes forced open to a reality which would have been one of her last choices.

She recalled a better one: childhood days with her brother, wunderkind physicist, who had taught her a thing or two. She recalled one interesting thermodynamic fact to her mind now: how one converts gas temperature into a measure of thermal particle motion. You know, via the Boltzmann Constant.

"1-3-8-0-6-4-8-7," she said, and all her shiny restraints popped open.

But: *that was useless*, she thought, because she was still in the arms of a very strong, metal, rust-colored invader and had also drawn attention to herself. She should have waited. She added this to a growing list of life experiences, in the subcategory of escaping outer space villains.

The only benefit to her action was that it caused an argument. A fifth, larger enemy had wandered over to admonish those trying to subdue Kay.

"Why would you say the secret codes out loud?" It asked.

"How could we know it speaks English? All it ever says is 'ahhhhh'."

"Well, change the codes and put the chains back on her!"

Kay realized this one must be the leader; it was more gold in color than rusty brass.

"Change them to what?" spoke the thing that currently held the girl in his tubey appendages. It was answered with a metallic scowl and some final words.

"Whatever comes to mind! Just don't say it out loud. And hurry. We need to get back. Your pointy-headed friend destroyed the ship's controls and we have orders to fly it back to the Leader Ship. It will be fixed soon. Just hurry."

Kay didn't like the sound of any of this. While the fact that her ship would be fixed, and the observation that her enemies had categorizable and accessible gradations of intelligence, seemed encouraging, all the rest seemed like bad news.

Why they spoke English, or used the same numbers—or even the same physics—as humans was anyone's guess. She made a note to ask her brother the minute she next saw him.

Which had better be soon, Kay thought. These creatures didn't like her *before* her Houdini impression; now she had gotten them in trouble with the boss.

One of the brazen beasts was looking hard at her, his single square eye—with a square eyeball, if it could be called that—motioning up and down to observe the length of her form. This was the creature ordered to change the handcuffs password, and it looked angry—a brassy frown shaped the strange material of his topmost section—and yet pensive. Kay realized it was searching for the means to invent a new unlock-code when it said, "Got it! OK! Hold the chubby thing!" A squarish hand extended a wire into

W.W. Marplot

each set of golden cuffs, some numbers were punched into a small keypad at its other end, and Kay was held tight by the tubes of the thing in whose arms she had fallen.

Kay was going to scream. She meant to. Definitely wanted to. But being called chubby—*especially when I am not, really. Right?* she thought—took precedence and command of her mental functions. It made her think, and made her somewhat mad, somewhat sad, but definitely somewhat insulted by sci-fi creatures who thought they were intelligent but that weren't fit to shine her brother's sneakers. She could escape on her own, make J proud, and bring him and a team of his friends and great Earth scientists back here to evaporate these bronze things using the latest weapons from home.

Kay remembered an important fact from her brief test-space-ship test-pilot test-training. J, via pre-recorded video, had said that there was a backup computer, and security devices, that would kick into action if something like this happened. In fact, it would…

…not do much, since a metallic enemy then waddled by carrying a suitcase-sized blue box marked "Backup Computer and Security Devices." It was deposited into an opening on the creature's own body and swallowed, logo and all.

Kay was soon shackled again, made to stand, then made to follow. The marauding, kidnapping beasts were all exiting through the hole in the ship they had made, and somehow they moved through the black space without aid, single file and away. Their prisoner, last to leave, took baby steps, her hands in front and again bound wrist to wrist, with one enemy escort a tubular arm's length ahead and pulling her ungently along.

Once her single escort was through the hole, she could act, she believed.

It stepped out into empty space—some distance ahead Kay saw another ship docked to hers—but Kay pulled backwards, stunning the bronze jerk and freeing herself from its clutch. Kay tumbled to the ground, kicked the enemy through the hole, and in the following half-second of liberation she spoke the new release code.

"3-2-9-7-6-2-3-4," she said, and both sets of cuffs popped off as before.

Kay clumsily scrambled back to the ship's main controls where she mashed the buttons and shouted commands—"Go!", "Fly!", "Lift off!", "Be free!"—with hopes that the craft would launch.

It didn't.

She screamed, trying different screams, different urgencies, frequencies, and primal-soul sources with hopes that the ship's computer would understand. But nothing happened; the electronics blinked but were silent, mute. Captured.

The only sound was of three bronze beasts returning, in no hurry knowing the ship to be under their control, with the smaller two being admonished by the third for allowing the annoyance and delay of another escape.

"How did it know the combination?"

"It's smart, I guess."

"She!" Kay screamed in frustration, fear, exasperation, ankle pain, pride, fear, exhaustion, and fear two more times. "I am a she! A human from Earth! Leave me alone!"

One of the three spoke to the ship's console and its lights blinked twice and went dark. The other two took Kay by her arms and legs, ignored her admonitions and biographical trivia, and carried her away while speaking matter-of-factly to each other.

"What was the new code?" one asked.

"Same thing," the other answered, "but I changed the units to be calories-per-Kelvin. Get it?"

"I get it. And so did it," the first said, indicating Kay.

"She," the second corrected.

"Whatever," the first said.

It seemed that they laughed as they spoke. It sounded like two lawn-mowers sharing some mischief, but, in its way, did sound jovial. Kay didn't resist being placed, then strapped, onto a cold, hard, mobile table.

Kay lay supine and still but not quiet. "My brother is important and smarter than you and he is going to come and get you if you don't leave me alone. You think picking on helpless, peaceful girls and making fun of them makes you clever, but he is cleverer and works with great scientists, and they will humiliate you." Her words were bold, but would have been bolder if she wasn't trembling, crying, and screaming in between each syllable—or if either she or her brother had a nice, big outer-space army.

Kay, normally peaceful and seeking only transcendence, now also sought to have these first enemies of hers taken apart and their pieces destroyed in an extended and violent scene of bronze, metallic death. Eventually the blue and white rag was replaced into her mouth.

She looked down the length of her stretched body. Kay didn't see anything that would justify high-calorie teasing by enemy pirates, no excess fat. *Except maybe a little,* she thought. Her neck skin squished into her tucked chin, but that was just because of her prostrate position.

Once wheeled to the newly-blasted embarkation hole, Kay's gurney was removed to a small, clear, egg-shaped container that guided Kay from her ship. It floated out into the soft haze of empty space. The lights of the test-ship were extinguished but an orangey glow came from the bronze pirates, and from the thousand or so odd and menacing flying machines surrounding them that indicated that this would not have been a fair battle even if the Kings of the Primordial Mythical Lord-Gods themselves had all assembled and screamed "Ahhh" with her.

Out of ideas, Kay fainted.

Brave, Brave Bobby Is Moved

Weeks after that, and still on Earth...

———————

Left on their own, one of the captains of Bobby Guard Y took control. Getting Bobby into his bed was mission-accomplished, but, because the whole bedroom started shaking, the captain believed it would be best to remove the boy out of harm's way. He instructed three of his men to recon a path, perhaps to the East Guest House, and directed one of the household staff to pack a subset of the boy's things in a bag for the relocation and repositioning of their operation. He told the Overnight Nurse of Record to bring a gurney. The others should disperse and await further orders from Central Command.

"OK," many of them said.

Without waking Bobby, which was quite easy, they moved him, five of his largest pillows, and two blankets to the gurney, lowered it, and exited via the French doors to the marble portico, past Greek columns, past Roman columns, and to the wider outside world.

The portico was shaking, flowers were falling, and birds were squawking. The crescent moon blinked from behind moving clumps of black vapors. The same security squad was ordered to extend their mission.

They wheeled the Lully heir under a shaking trestle, then around the aviary, which rattled so wildly that the birds inside had been sorted: alike birds were clumped together at various nooks within, and ordered by type and color. They stayed that way and warbled nervously.

After some crackled communications, as per protocol, a door in the earth was opened, and the tiled, paved tunnel it exposed was used to escape to the farther West Grounds, where, every seventy-five yards or so, lay connecting tunnels leading away.

The other routes were necessary since the West Grounds were quaking. Tiles came off cracking tunnel walls. Yet it was better than the falling trees above and the renewed screams of the birds; they were still ordered in groups, and now cackled harshly at each other.

The soldiers were not paid to wonder but to follow orders, so they did. Their next directive was to get through the unstable fields of the Lully Estate to and through its Western Wall, where a break in the thick forest led to a lane of escape, as the captain learned from his superiors. Keeping a bootcamp-worthy pace, they were soon through an electronically-controlled gate—where the captain gave a thumbs-up to the sky—and through the trees, where the fauna of the forest were also gathering, grouping together, like with like, and discussing notions of trust.

To the humans—who had to carry a snoring-in-their-arms Bobby across the rutted floor of the woods and over a rushing freshet, all while animals roared and boughs crashed—this next phase, the open lane, would be the worst experience of all.

At the opposite opening of the forest, through a thick hedge, they returned the mumbling, drooling teen to his litter of colored blankets and security pillow and looked ahead, down the lane. The way narrowed and led straight for a few hundred yards along a brick path.

On both sides were towering fences capped with curling barbed wire and nasty speared spikes. The fence was tripled, actually three parallel fences to right and left, each rising higher as they went outward.

Outward toward the people. This was the dreaded part.

Crowds of moaning, shouting, praying, begging, agonized people crushed against the outermost fences on both sides of the guards as they wheeled Bobby past. He was giggling in his sleep. That didn't help things.

The soldiers knew, of course, that the world was going kaput. It seemed to them that the world had come to this spot, under this sky, aside this narrow path, to do it.

The waves of sound from the lined mass of suffering humanity were worse than the odd vocal behavior of the animals, worse than the newly-born racism of the birds, worse than a sky that could not decide whether to be on fire or to suck the earth into a death-cyclone.

The soldiers without orders, or any words at all, all began to jog. The gurney bounced, and Bobby popped, but they kept a good, steady speed.

"I am glad he is able to sleep through this," expressed the captain.

"He is very brave," a soldier said earnestly.

The right and left were a landscape of people, humans—old, young, man, woman—as far as the gentle slope of the hills extended, and all the way to a horizon of campfire flashes and shimmering smoke. Ahead they looked, as two cement towers rose, guard-houses, turreted, sheer and drear, more than double the height of the horrible fence whose barbs connected large steel pikes jutting from the structures.

A wall and large gate ran between the towers; the troop and their cargo were soon there and waved in, while radios crackled in a howling wind that whipped around the towers angrily.

Miraculously, the towers were not shaking.

Once through the gate—which it seemed to take the troops hours to swing outward—and under a barrier, they were greeted by a heavily-armed, battle-ready warrior in crisp khaki and decorated with medals that were numerous but small compared to the acreage of his chest. He led them to a bunker a few levels down some very narrow stairs. They carried Bobby there, gripping wrists and ankles, the center of his length drooping like a hammock. The angle formed by lungs against trachea made him gurgle.

"He is a trooper. I am proud to carry him," one of the guards panted.

They put Bobby in a cot in the corner of the bunker, the walls and floor a dull grey wherever they weren't beige. Feet dangled over the edge, so they brought a second cot to prop up the teen's long frame. Bobby then stretched vigorously, and the soldiers held their breath. But Bobby only curled into a tight ball; the robots on his pajamas wrinkled and squished as he grabbed a pillow with both hands and, bravely, lay quiet again.

In Trouble in Space

Back to Bobby's future present
in space...

———————————

obby held his breath and braced for the shocking change in pressure that he had seen in movies many times: the arced door of his spaceship sphere was about to open, and he would be blown out and into the hungry-looking black mouth of the universe outside. Trying to stop the door's handle from turning, or to hold it from opening, was too much for Bobby's thin arms. Opposing him from outside his orb was an immense, irresistible, unopposable force. Bobby held his breath and his seat as the metal hinges creaked and the shiny door opened from the bottom. He prepared to meet the invading alien being whose horrible, unearthly strength was about to end his own wimpy, teenaged life—and then the dog came floating in from the open space and licked Bobby's whole face.

Excitedly, and many times, it licked. Bobby, eyes closed and teeth clenched, suffered horribly within the wild imaginings of what must be happening to him among so many space enemies and the life-sucking vacuum of space.

Until it became clear that he was being kissed by a small dog. He felt fur, smelled the familiar wet musk, and heard whining as if from a cartoon puppy. Bobby's thighs were stroked with pendulum whacks from a rope-like tail.

Plus: the computer had said something about a dog.

When the young Earthling opened his eyes, he gasped, he sucked much air, and dog hair, into his mouth after a violent inheaving. In his fear, as the door was opening, Bobby had held his breath on an exhale, like the space-rookie that he was.

Otherwise, he was fine, though shocked, speechless, and confounded at many, many things.

Instinctively holding the dog in place on his chest as it continued to lick him, he saw the four-foot space to his right, the open doorway, which did not empty into nothingness, nor elongate him with suction, but instead showed many lights and bluish steel structures nearby.

He heard sounds—no, they were voices! No, they were words! No, they were *English* words!—being shouted. He grasped onto the first sentence he could, like hopping the last car of a departing train.

"Just more garbage," it said. The voice was low and crashing, like an iron sculpture falling over, and sounded strange even for that, and even beyond Bobby's surprise of hearing anything at all. All sounds coming from the night of space struck his ears like ocean waves, in patterns of coming and going, and as if he heard half of them from underwater. The volume vibrated, and the pitch warbled.

Then came beeping, as if from some electronic warning, but it did not come from his own ship, whose computer was silent but probably smiling.

"Yeah, let's go," the deep voice clanged again. "Just more garbage. Garbage, garbage—"

"No, wait!" Bobby yelled. "I am in here! Help!"

No voice answered, just the small dog nuzzling his neck and the repeated beeping outside. *What to do?* Bobby shouted again, "Someone is in here! Hey! Wait! Help me!"

A monstrous head appeared in the hole—taking up the whole space. Bobby saw dark red skin, two giant eyes, and a slit where a mouth might be. The figure disappeared as quickly as it had come—instantly, magically gone—leaving an ugly memory in Bobby's crazed, frantic mind.

"Help?" Bobby said, now unsure whether he really wanted any.

Far away the voice crashed again, reporting that, "Yep, it's just more garbage."

The beeping continued and, seemingly in answer, the dog yipped and leapt off Bobby and through the hole with an impressive bound.

Growling, barking, beeping—all overlapping and nonsensical. The gigantic head of the snarling red thing peeked back in. Through the doorway it squished until its…ears?…got stuck, and scraped the metal sides. Bobby winced—this looked painful—but the humongous face only stared and frowned. Not at Bobby, but at the Lully-named box beneath him.

"Fine," the face said fiercely, like an ancient gong, fogging the whole capsule window and the electronics screens with a nasty green munk: part mist and part alien breath-gunk.

Big-head disappeared again, leaving dark peels of reddish skin stuck to the ship's hatchway walls, some floating out through the opening and following in the head's zero-gravity wake. The dog revisited Bobby now, floating this time, crashing into Bobby's side, then clawing back onto his chest with panting energy.

Bobby. Although he knew he should be confused and petrified, things were moving too fast for him to be anything other than generally dazed. He did not worry that he would not be able to breathe, nor that he apparently could. He did not wonder that he was not exploded to pieces from the exposure to the raw, blank universe, and he was not afraid that he still could be, at any second. His life seemed to have been saved somehow, and this space dog certainly appeared to like him, which was a happy sight as compared to the alien superface that wanted Bobby to be thrown out with the galactic trash.

Yes, things were happening fast, such as the dog's speech; he continually called Bobby "Master," though in a strange dialect. It was English but with long O vowels pronounced as harsh, shortened growls. The *ooo-ing* of long U's was made longer, and any S's were lisped and sprayed, like *thisshch*, and "*Schooow me your sshchoooo-lascchessshhchhs, and I will tie them for yooooouuuu.*"

And, rapidly, the alien canine was pulling at Bobby, dragging him out through the hatch and into space. The metal that Bobby saw through the hole was another spaceship, whose lights and shiny astro-material, as compared to the surrounding void, made it appear closer than it was. As did its size: it was a hundred yards away and the size and shape of a medieval cathedral—stony, castellated, but twinkling attractively.

Two other figures were diminishing ahead as they traveled toward the bigger spacecraft; the large head that, as Bobby could now see, was attached to a short frame with short legs but very long arms; and a cube, a box made of metal of many colors, whose shiny form was the source of the beeping Bobby had heard and still did hear.

Bobby instinctively resisted being pulled, clutching at the seat and then the door handle inside his silvery orb, but the dog's grip was oddly strong—his teeth had opened the hatchway, remember—and the Earthling was pulled out by his ankles. His lungs pumped and panicked in short and choppy gusts. Bobby asked the question most on his mind, puffing, "I can breathe…right?" as best he could in case he couldn't.

"Almosssshhhtt forgot!" the dog answered, coming closer to slap a see-through mask onto Bobby's face. It stuck easily and provided fresh, Earthling-compatible air. To Bobby's astonished, relieved, and oxygenated but panting face the dog said, "It'ssss-chhh complicated…it'ssshhh schienceshhh!" but did not give any detail. Instead the dog continued some other conversation, projected out toward the other figures: the face and the blue beeping star machine. "Thishh all proveschshh it! Proves it for good!" he shouted—barked?—to his friends.

Beep beep, came a faint response, like a voice it seemed now, yet also like a bell ringing softly.

And the other voice, "Bah. Garbage. Humans." Like the crushing destruction of scrap metal.

Bobby Follows as Best He May

Seconds later...

Floating slowly outward from his space sphere, and just behind a thick, round, and extremely pleased space-dog, Bobby watched the little orb where he had awakened just a short time before—though he had gone to bed in his bed—recede and felt homesick for it. He would miss the flashing red *NO* button most of all, he thought.

He listened to his own breathing as it bounded within his face mask, magnified and sounding like an ovation from a medium-sized crowd.

Turning his head around made both Bobby and his tethered leader spin. All motion was relative, of course, and all action was equal and opposite as well as confusing and nauseating. Nothing in the history of dog-walking compared to it, but the two were moving along and even catching up to the others ahead.

One was the bluish metal cube that changed color as it shifted and moved. Each side was a square made up of squares that shimmied and glinted as rectangular slices of the thing swung and turned. It seemed that a metal robot had swallowed a giant Rubik's Cube. The sides Bobby could see were green and white, and the thing continued to beep.

The other was the body that held together the gargantuan face with the short legs; it formed an ugly, misfit overall shape.

Ahead of all was the larger spacecraft, rectangular and brilliant. Its bright, hard sections were shining with the reflections of its own many points of white light, and here and there a few red or purple or pink. Very pretty.

"Where are we going?" Bobby asked, his breath echoing back to him through the see-through mask that allowed him, somehow, to live.

"Toooo the Beginning, tooooo the Middle!" the dog said after yanking Bobby's—his new master's—pant leg to keep them moving along while also allowing the dog to speak properly, mostly, through his thick brown snout. Bobby's body caught up until he and the dog were face to face, and his own was licked.

"Stop," he said. Bobby liked dogs but wanted answers. "Can you be more specific?"

"Yessschhsssm, Maschsscchsster!" The words came excitedly and, for these words, with a lot of dog drool, too. The droplets went in all directions, spinning and yellow, like small disgusting asteroids, and Bobby watched them, thinking it might be a million years before some of them hit something, like a planet or a jerk's eye. But this thought quickly made him space-sick, since the view beyond the spit globules was a vastness of dark nothingness that reminded Bobby of where he was and also where he unfortunately definitely wasn't.

The dog obeyed and answered, spraying and howling with delight, "Tooo the schtart! Toooo the schenter, and toooo the end! Aroooo!"

The wagging of his new best friend's tail sent them both spinning again—relative to the two other travelers, that is, who were now nearer. Bobby was able to catch a better glimpse of them, though he had to roll his eyes and head skillfully to do it.

All the while, the larger ship approached. A doorway and purple-lit platform seemed to be where the four travelers' trajectories would eventually end.

The cubic beeping thing was now showing black and grey blotches on its sides—pixelated with small squares—and protruding now above all was a white, elongated robot head, like a sleek, mounting cloud over an electric storm. It beeped whenever spoken to, Bobby now realized—for example, after each time the space mutt barked at it. To move, or when it did anything, its sub-cubes would twist or rotate, sometimes showing screens that told what it was thinking, or calculating, or beeping about. When it was excited, bright lights sparkled from many places, like beacons.

Next to it in space was the other creature that had poked his four-foot face into Bobby's capsule.

That guy, the thing with the dark hide and long arms, still looked—from behind, at least—quite hideous and beastly, strong and ugly, wide and squat. And worse, it—he?—only stopped saying nasty things when he broke to clear his throat, sounding like a garbage disposal that was suffering with tremendous pain. He ground out insults in English, apparently aimed at Bobby. For example, the thing answered the latest series of tolling beeps with "He's a mess" and "Humans are not worth the energy required to gather them up and squish them."

What does he, it, have against me? Bobby wondered. *And how much experience with humans can he possibly have?* Still, the creature seemed very sure of its opinions. *Has he been to Earth?* Bobby thought of crop circles and science fiction movies and the alien face on his t-shirt, grew confused, and shook his head, causing the dog to do the same but with his whole body. The pair twisted faster, but, Bobby noticed, they were no longer traveling closer to the larger, shinier ship. All of them—dog, Bobby, large thing, beeping thing—were stopped in place.

"What happened?" Bobby asked his new best friend. "Aren't we going to that big ship?" He pointed with his hand—or he tried to—in the usual way but found it difficult. Moving now required all his strength; raising his arm, even extending his finger, took tremendous effort. The human contorted and struggled, now in a panic, to move his arms and legs.

Then things got worse. The dog did not answer Bobby. Instead, he curled his body and tucked his tail tightly as if to sleep—hanging there in the midst of empty space—and also covered his eyes with his paws in a very cute way. If Bobby's own body were not at that moment being crushed under a tremendous force, he would have said, "Awwww" and maybe "Ooochie pooochee puppy" as well.

But there was a force, a pressure, coming out and going in and swirling around the very spaces about him. One second, he felt his insides about to explode outward, and the next his loose sweatpants and t-shirt were pressing against his skin as if trying to squeeze him through a hole. The blackness—which, except in the forward direction toward the gleaming spaceship, was everywhere, and it was everything—swirled actively as if it were thick and real, like a muddy sinkhole. It seemed alive, with every cubic inch a different moving part, like a giant snake curling around itself and winding and unwinding as it slithered through the universe, every scale of its body pushing against all things in its way.

Sounds—the beeping and the conversation among these alien space travelers who were pulling Bobby into their own spacecraft—warped and came louder, then softer, now deafening (*BEEP BEEP!* HE'S USELESS AND UGLY LET'S JUST CRUSH HIM AND HIS SHIP. *RUFF, RUFF!*), now soft (*beep beep-beep beep*, "Horrible space trash," *Aaroooo*). All the lights from the ship ahead were blinking horribly, switching from a blinding blast of white and purple lights to a soft glow as dim as death, and Bobby's sight of the ship was shimmering and bending under these alternating currents.

Then it stopped. The pounding waves of pressure seemed to flatline, the sounds smoothed to normal, and all light calmed.

Movement became easier but not easy. This seemed normal to the others, Bobby realized, and perhaps this was just how life was lived in deep space.

He was able to look around. It was all dark and—somehow—thick, but now, in the stillness, Bobby saw a distant sea of light, precisely even light, outwards at the three-dimensional horizon. Off and away, and up and down, lay a glow that only made the black empty nothingness everywhere else seem nearer and as if it were here to swallow all things that existed. Whether alive or dead, metal or flesh, at least the things in Bobby's world existed. This black void was different; it was the enemy of things that were. It fought against being.

Also: near to him, and filling the space between Bobby's little orb and the larger structure ahead, existed a weird reverse-light pushing against all other lights—like the purple blasts from open platform ahead, and the tiny points of red, blue, and green coming from the Beeping Cubey Thing. This anti-light was a force that pushed color away from them somehow, and it created weird shadows as if all were in a pencil sketch.

"Hey. Ummm…dog?" Bobby stammered, then realized that instead he should ask "What is your name?" in order to be polite. Bobby was, after all, only a guest in this dog's vortex of black doom.

The pup did not answer but asked in turn, "Are yoooou Praaafesscherrr Lully'shh son?" The dog wiggled with every muscle in his short, log-like trunk and was able to move his tongue closer and directly to Bobby's face, a long red canine tongue ready to slather. But Bobby, with a huge effort, held out his arms, caught the pup, and held him a foot away.

"You heard the orb computer say that?" asked Bobby.

"Yeschhh. And otherssshhhh."

"Yes, I'm his son. Others? What others?"

"You are a human, yessschhh? An Earthling? Named Lohsssshh?" the space-canine asked, ignoring Bobby's questions. Slobber floated near to them until the dog shook his head and the liquids spiraled away, a new, unnamed, small, disgusting galaxy.

"Yeah, of course, from Earth. But who is—" Bobby tried ask about that 'Lohsssshh' part but was interrupted by wet glee.

"Yoooooouu are! That prooovessch it for good!" The dog projected his voice out toward the other creatures. To Bobby he said, evenly and politely, "Nice to meet you, Los!"

"Why are you calling me Los?"

"Oh, sorry, Master. I will call you Master." Dolefully, the dog's ears drooped, a whiplash change in mood.

Bobby considered this. They knew he was Professor Lully's son. And from Earth. And they hadn't killed him or squished him, which seemed promising. How they knew anything was a mystery as deep as space, but they didn't know that Professor Lully's son was named Bobby and not Los. Maybe there was another Lully somewhere, a parallel universe? Maybe these guys were just uninformed? Bobby knew no one named Los, or what it might mean, but why risk it, he reasoned, and screw up this rescue? If they wanted to rescue Los Lully instead of Robert Lully, that was fine for now.

Also: he thought back to when his father told him not to give his name to strangers. When Bobby was four years old, this was basic advice, but as the great man grew in importance in a competitive and dangerous international industry, it was a security measure to protect Bobby. Not that the boy went anywhere or knew anyone, but just in case. So Bobby figured he would be smart here and accept the name given. A new personality would be fun in any case, a space-traveling one.

And he could also make the dog feel better at the same time.

"No, no, no, Los is fine. Please call me Los if you want. You are a good dog." A big wet kiss came in answer as they floated.

Beep, beep Bobby heard from ahead.

And, "We should squish him."

The dog growled; he was being protective of his human, as Bobby-Los realized. But the human did not feel protected, even with a new name. In fact, he felt naked: floating, or stuck, in outer space, with strange strangers, odd forces, unfriendly air, and no signs of waking up. He still had questions.

"Before you said 'this proves it'—can you tell me what that means, and what 'this' is, and what it proves? And what's your name? Who are you guys?" Bobby felt pleased with the question marks he was sending into space; he was on a roll. "Where are we going? You said, 'to the middle, to the end' and all that—what does that mean? Is that spaceship going to take us? Can I go home instead? And how do you know my dad?"

"That'ssschhh a lot of questionsssss! The Prophetessshhhh told usshhh!" The dog wiggled, his dog-spit sliming more of the nearby universe. Bobby twisted his heavy head to avoid it all, frustrated that these answers explained nothing, made no sense, and, worse, some of them were stuck in his hair.

"Prophetess, huh?" Bobby wished he had someone else he could ask…and not the guy who wanted to squash him, so instead he yelled to the beeping pyramid, which now looked green and round again, but still built of metal and tiny lights.

"Hey! Can I go home?" he asked it.

Beep, beep, was the answer.

"Thanks."

"You are useless trash stink," came an angry growl from the long-armed, big-headed beast.

"Thanks," Bobby said. The dog in his hands was his only chance. "OK. Yes, I am Professor Lully's son, definitely. Can you take me to him? And what does this 'prove'?"

"That we are really close to the Middle. And that it is special. And that we got here first. And that the Prophetess was right," the dog said calmly, in a very soft voice. Bobby had turned his cannon-ball head and closed his weighted eyes to avoid the usual spitball splatter of S-driven drools, but there was none, no excited slobber at all. And the dog lay limp in the young man's grip now, the wiry tail hanging straight and still.

"What?" Bobby asked.

Calmly again, and hardly moving, the dog said quietly, "I will explain, but let's get to the ship. Just follow for now, Master." Bobby figured that the dog only talked funny and with wet weather when it was excited, and he soon got used to both modes.

"OK, I will. But what is your name? Who are you guys?"

"That is Guk," the dog said slowly and pointed with his muzzle ahead to the broad-backed beast with the four-foot long, two-

and-a-half-foot wide head, and who was growing in repugnancy. Bobby now noticed the thing's ears, the ones that stuck and scraped in and out of the door of Bobby's orb: These were also large, a sickly dull grey, and looked like craggy rocks. They were inexplicably wet.

Guk growled like a lawnmower kissing a broken bottle.

Flatly, the teen admitted, "He doesn't like me."

"No, Master," the dog whispered sadly. "To him, you are just more work."

"Squishing work," Bobby stated.

"Yessshhh!" There was a brief tail-wag.

"Who's the other one?" Bobby asked, glad to be getting some answers, though his jaw was starting to hurt. Even speaking took muscular effort under the pressures all around. The dog, as he already knew, was stronger than he was.

"BeepBeep," both the dog and BeepBeep said as one.

"Ah. And who are you? On Earth we give dogs names; you must have one."

"Earth! Arooooo!" Large canine eyes and a pink canine tongue were lolling and rolling in sync. "Thisssshhh issshh fantassshhhtic Owoooooo! I knoooooooooo it!" And more uncontrollable, nonsensical whining and barking of stretched and misty English words followed. It took some time until the dog was able to speak again without accruing a Persian beard of saliva.

"You are our first human," he explained. "We aren't allowed near Earth. But the Prophetess said Professor Lully's son, a human, from Earth, would come soon, near the Middle, and where others are coming. But we got here first! Firsssshhhtttt!"

Bobby calmed the dog, petting and scratching him until the explanation could continue.

"And you are here—"

But the dog was cut short by an especially strong wave of black pressure, the space about them warping and curling. The dog curled into a ball again, and Bobby tried to do the same. While tucked, he wondered why the dog reacted so excitedly to, well, everything, and wondered many other things, but was content that these, uh, creatures, liked him, mostly, and were rescuing him. The rest could wait. Bobby's insides felt stretched and vibrated as if they wanted to see what life was like outside his body, then the feeling reversed and he felt pressed from all directions, harder and harder, until he believed that Guk was really indeed trying to squish him. He stayed as small as he could, trying to roll with it.

The pressure finally eased, he could unfold himself and see again some twinkling in the distance; the ebony waves relented, and ahead was the pretty spaceship of his new friends.

"Why does it do that?" Bobby asked.

"Because we are near the Middle." The dog wiggled. "But let'ssss-chhh get to the sscccsship now, while it'sshhh calm. Los! Master! Arooooooo!"

Yet doing so was still not easy. Since they had stopped, it was difficult to get going again in any single direction on purpose. The black, swirling soup they floated in made all movement, except curling into a ball and wincing, difficult and at times impossible, as when the waves of force and pressure returned to squeeze and pull at their bodies.

Ahead, Bobby saw BeepBeep—whose squares were mostly blue again—use tiny rushes of air shot from corner thrusters to jolt his odd shape in bursts forward. Guk had his own method. The beast would crunch his short legs up to his large head—in fact, his head and legs were about the same length—into a ball, with his long arms hugging both. Then he would spring his gruesome parts outward, forming an arrow shape, somehow, out of his whole body, like a diver from a high board but a nasty one. Repeating these ugly dance moves propelled the creature weirdly forward, though it did not stop him from shouting repeatedly that Lully's son was refuse that should be left behind.

But Bobby—even when the space around them was calm—could not get anywhere. He realized why, of course. There was nothing solid to push off. Each motion he made, in agreement with the basic physics laws he had learned in school, caused an opposite motion, and so he generally could only make himself spin. He tried Guk's ball-and-arrow technique and hurt himself. He spun faster. A teenager in a vacuum without leverage is difficult to watch, so the others didn't.

Bobby tried something logical—performing Guk's move in reverse—and this indeed stopped him from spinning. But it left him nauseous and about to vomit.

Out of politeness, he turned away from the dog ahead of him and pulled his mask to the side enough to puke some white stuff out into deep space. It looked like a large, solid sneeze firing in slow motion. The pieces floated away, separating over time, following, Bobby imagined, the doggie spitballs in the direction of something that hopefully deserved it.

Some hit the small orb behind them, where Bobby saw on the window, in backwards-backwards lettering, his unfinished message to outer space. "I AM LOS" it read, sloppily, with a small cross underneath.

One mystery was solved.

And! His projectile nausea got Bobby moving, and in the desired direction. He could see ahead now and was traveling straight to the large, shining ship, its pretty platform awaiting them all. The pressures of the local universe had eased.

The dog was ahead of him and also moving, though he did not have any special space tricks either. As Bobby moved along in the pup's wake, however, he learned how the dog was propelling himself. Bobby pinched his nose through the flimsy mask.

At a few points, Bobby slowed, saying, "You know, outer space is pretty thick for a vacuum," and he could only restart himself by spitting backwards—or at least that was the method he chose. "I pictured space travel differently," he said to his new best friend.

Guk and BeepBeep were soon at, through, and beyond the door at the purple platform. Bobby's trip gave him time to think past his fear and confusion and catch up on his situation. It had been a heck of a morning; apparently, he was awake after all.

"Whoa, man, I guess I'm an astronaut now, huh? Space traveler?" he asked the dog as it used its tail to maneuver onto the floor of the opening.

"Well, youuuuu jussscht sssschat there, but yesssshhhhh!"

Lully Is Chased More

A day or so earlier, on Earth...

The clouds, and the ground, rumbled. Everything did.

Professor Lully was running again, with less agility and energy than during his earlier romp to the horse stables. His pursuer had not been caught, and the great man had a new level of respect for this enemy since he apparently was also part of a coordinated attack on sky and Earth.

Impressive—and the timing was interesting. Lully speaker-phoned two associates who could help analyze and decide which bush to hide under. Security had lost track of the enemy when he skirted across the North Lawn Fountains before they crumbled and flooded into the North Pond.

The professor's super-smart phone lit and buzzed with communications; its light drew the attention of a large figure to Lully's right. The shadows revealed a shape like a small grain silo, with tubes or gun barrels or ropes—Lully could not determine which, only that they could not possibly be arms—dangling on each side. It moved quickly and noisily.

Droid? Bot? Bad disguise? Uni-Tank?

> Could it be you know who?

Lully was asked in a text message.

"*N O*," he typed, and that was fortunate because if he had had to reply in the affirmative, he would not have had time to click the extra letter. His enemy had just thrown—Lully didn't see exactly how—what seemed like a whole garden into the air, and it was crashing down all around the brilliant professor.

Knotted clumps of dirt came first, pounding the Earth with earth, and then came a dangerous barrage of flowers: lengthy delphiniums descended like spears, while rambling roses landed roots-downward and stayed aright like unexploded bombs, and the bells and bulbs of purple and white foxglove sprayed everywhere like dainty bullets. Balls of ferny dirt fell like mortar fire.

Long wisps of wisteria rained down and drooped their vines over tree branches and fence posts like lamenting, tired sufferers, followed by peony leaves that wafted down, tangled with hollyhock blooms. Hydrangea clusters came last, award-winningly large ones, their large, pink shapes covering the ground. It smelled nice but made Lully wince at the destruction of what used to be the Southwest English Flower Bed; he had carefully selected the landscape artists who carefully selected the species.

The thin violet petals that covered his phone now lit prettily with light from the new message beneath.

> Head to Point Two

Lully's associate advised in a large font.

"How?" Lully whispered to his phone. He was bent and cowed under pieces of shrubbery.

> The lane. Our calculations predict safety there.
> And then through.

"That's the long way," Lully protested.

| It's safest. |

Lully wanted to agree because a whole tree had just uprooted and was heading toward him. "OK."

| He won't go that way. He is about to be distracted. |

"Great. Thanks Lebo, you're a darling." Professor Lully was rarely grateful for the actions of others; this was high praise.

| Love you |

Lebo replied.

Lully ran to the cover of trees. He didn't know it, but his wooded path would soon join the way of Bobby's gurney; he was just thirty minutes or so behind his son.

Trusting Lebo, he took no time to scout the area before going into the clearing where the tall fences and the sullen masses awaited, where people collectively groaned in the wind and flickering moonlight. Lully ran across, his shoes briskly tapping the bricks.

The moans of the crowd did not bother him; he ignored them. In fact, the sound reassured him.

Of all those people, of all people everywhere, he was on the team that selected 360 souls for a special mission: to escape Earth in order to save it. Or to save themselves, depending on the courage and personal predilection of who was buckled in. Three hundred sixty space travel orbs had been created for the purpose. Lully's own was in the bunker straight ahead, beyond those guard towers, which was another comforting sight. But he was not going that way; he was going to Point Two, the location of the most secret of labs, a location known only by Lully and a few close collaborators whom he could trust and who were big fans.

Lully, of course, was one of the 360—the best and greatest and most equipped to find a way to save the Earth, which was going kaput. Lully, J, and others on the GABBA-THREE team, over time and after many meetings far underground at military installations, refined that definition to simply include the *smartest*—no artists, no political leaders, no ninjas, no Zen masters, no athletes. Lully remembered debating, and winning, on this point, saying, "Hey, they should have stayed in school and not peaked at twenty-two years old." He instead wanted, "those who will get better with age, especially at math. And rocket engineering."

Before turning off the brick path toward the secret way to Point Two, he saw that the people had turned restless and were attacking the fence. Maybe they knew about Lully's orb—other launch pads had attracted similar encampments of the average, downtrodden, doomed, unlucky, untalented, confused people of Earth.

They can't take off, even if they are able to infiltrate, he knew— the controls were biophotonically triggered. *And I have other plans.* Lully smiled, very happy and for a second forgetting his pursuer.

Turning away, he noticed his super-smart phone screen awash in activity, communications, and analysis. Plans—including those for the 360—were being altered and adapted in real-time, and without the necessary votes.

But it matters not. I prepared! I foresaw! I read the signs, I read the readings! Long ago, ha-ha! Kaput!

The great man continued with his great thoughts.

How Kay Left Earth In The First Place

Weeks before that...

———————◆———————

Kay shielded her eyes. Out in the field, the sun shone brightly and reflected off the expanse of sleek titanium in front of her—and to the left of her, and to the right of her, and beneath her. She stood on a metal stepladder and stretched precariously to reach for the pink notepaper sticking from the top hatch of a spaceship whose presence here among the pine trees and tall grasses was incongruous, inharmonious, ominous, and worrisome but typical of Kay's brother.

"He couldn't put it where I could reach it?" she huffed while ducking under the metal hatch supports as the paper flapped mockingly in the wind. But soon she had it between two fingers and sat on the topmost ladder step to read.

Eve-Kay: (Ha ha...)

There are things you don't know about that I can't tell you about but you need to keep your head in reality and do what I say. To protect you I created a test spaceship so you can escape Earth if that becomes necessary. Not a big deal. Just a test. Get in.

Put on the helmet that's on the seat, sit, and press the big green "yes" button. And don't think about it.

You can meditate. I will meet you soon.

It's just a test. Don't tell anyone, not even Essie.

Love, J

The note—typed, not handwritten—was cryptic and troubling, which was enough to prove to Kay that it was indeed from her brother. But despite their sibling rivalries and opposite natures, she found it best to do what he suggested when he suggested it. *J is pretty smart,* she reasoned, *and though he is overly scientific, he usually knows best about things happening in reality.* Whereas Kay enjoyed her mountain sojourns and searches for inner peace, J was experienced in outer war and the increasing badness of life on Earth.

But I hate when he calls me Eve, and he knows it, Kay thought.

Eve was J's nickname for Kay, one he maddeningly never explained but teasingly applied when he wanted to distance himself from his sister. Not that Kay was so bad, but she was very strange, even by prodigy standards. To a young engineering genius like J, she was an embarrassment, too illogical. To a young computer genius like J, she was inscrutable, a spiritual artist who wasted a good brain doing silly, girly things. To a young quantum-entropic biophysics genius like J, she was unnerving, always prattling on about hidden levels of being. And to young chess grandmaster like J, she was frustrating, always sacrificing her queen as soon as possible for reasons she would not elaborate upon.

J was an overachiever in the way people liked and admired. Kay wasn't. J loved Kay and was a protective elder—though still teen-aged—brother, and though he was the victor in their arguments about what was important in life, he respected her as being bright in her own way though hopelessly naïve and very lazy.

"I am not lazy," she protested one day. "*You* are not a fair comparison. You would work every day, including Christmas and birthdays, and not even notice."

"No," J said, smiling. "Not true. I do notice. And in fact, I took off Christmas just a few years ago."

"So, see? Maybe we aren't that much different." Kay said. "I just have more Christmases than you."

J smiled wider.

The past few days, and since her return from her latest and longest retreat, she had sat in her room, and with no one else at home, she easily tuned out the world's news, which in any case would be the usual mix of famine, despair, disease, aggression, pollution, noise, and negativity. The media was unnecessary; she could feel in her bones and in her soul, while searching the universe of her mind, that something wasn't right, and was increasingly wrong. She tried not to think about it and pushed those thoughts away to the side or simply called upon Buddhist spirits to take care of them for her so she could focus.

The "Essie" in the note was the name she had invented for her new computer friend, one that J and his teams were building. She thought of Essie now as she tossed her backpack into the open spaceship hatchway, found the big seat, held the helmet, and stared at the round button that shone in icky green with the letters "YES" in black.

She looked at her backpack and wondered at the contents and if they were enough for a short "test" trip—jeans, sweater, sneakers, poetry, socks, hand cream, snacks, meditation beads, and pillow...

Yep.

And of course, she had her phone: a special super-smart phone that J had made for her, prodigious science bro that he was.

She put the helmet on, then took it off, her head pinched with every pulled hair. She chanted a nice, blue "Ommmm" to offset the green hue of the space about her, pressed the button, and fell instantly into a well-deserved, contemplative peace.

And then to sleep.

How Bobby Left Earth In The First Place

Weeks after that...

———————◆———————

To his left, in the bunker, Bobby still lay asleep across his two cots, and the three grunts of Bobby Guard Y were getting anxious. They did not know their next move, were nervous here in the bunker, intimidated by the large and strong military strongmen (and largemen), and were getting tired of putting Bobby back to bed—the boy sleepwalked every ten minutes, it seemed. They were literally tired as well; the only other cot available was currently being used by their dozing captain.

"He's brave, too," one of the men said, "but I need to sleep."

"Let's move the kid," was suggested, and without much more conversation, they searched and found a spot for Bobby: through a few winding corridors was a small, curved doorway into a circular space, a reclined chair within.

"Perfect," was agreed.

"We should change him first,"—meaning his clothes—was suggested and, after a vote, was agreed. One of the team produced the bag previously packed and removed grey sweatpants and a t-shirt with a grotesquely oval alien head on the front.

They carried Bobby to the round room.

"Strap him in!" was a great idea and done.

As the three guards walked away, already arguing over the two free cots, the door of the round room shut.

There was a loud noise of unearthly combustion, like 500 race car engines starting.

There was a rumble and ribbons of white smoke.

Inside the orb, the DNA and biophoton checkers tripped, the computer came alive, everything clicked, and the ship shot upward and into space.

It looked surreal to the guards—nothing could possibly move that fast. Yet it did, like a man-sized BB shot from a gun. The heat was bearable, but the light—like white nuclear winter—was fantastic, glorious, and painful, even to shut eyelids, and the men stumbled back through the hall and to stairs that led to an observation level, where they watched the orb's exhaust-tail change colors beautifully as it streaked up and through the clearing sky.

The guards discussed making new birth certificates.

Lully Reads The Signs

As that orb took off...

———————◆———————

Professor Lully, still a mile from Point Two, watched his assigned orb streak away. He was too busy to consider any ramifications, to ask his associates to gather and explain the data, or to enjoy the serial rainbow of lights from the orb's jet plume. He was dealing with a more pressing puzzle of his own: a kangarooish gorilla, impersonating a fat stork, was spitting at him.

Even given his nearly unlimited IQ, indefatigable—though selfish—spirit, and world-historic, all-time-great credentials, he was flummoxed. Lully was also being preached to about garbage pollution, or something, by the kanga-ape, whom Lully could not get a good look at because he didn't want to.

It was all very hard to understand, and hard to try to understand while trapped and being spit at.

The suggested long-cut to "Point Two" ended disastrously when a fire ravaged the ten acres or so between. Lully was exhausted. He held his side. He was breathing in boiling, poisonous air that felt composed of microscopic razor blades. His communications were cut off; all his super-smart phone screen showed was a gruesome, rectangular, cartoonish figure with reptilian skin and a freakishly big head that looked like a tightly-stretched Halloween mask of a monstrous beast. The only sounds it made were a series of gruff grunts and threatening growls, all animated through an ugly, mis-shapen mouth. Emoji from mutated hell.

Lully took this as a bad sign.

I have been hacked, he thought.

And trapped. He could not go forward and was without the energy to go back. Whoever or whatever was after him, he thought, *should be recruited and offered an orb*. Very nice work.

Lully gazed again at the evolving, living, active sky. The clouds that earlier had divided into images of garbage and garbage cans were now finishing that act; on a strong wind, the ones were moving toward, and going into, the others.

Lully took this as a bad sign.

The eastern horizon was a blue-gray glow. The usually dutiful, reliable morning sun shot only a single ray of orange, as if tiredly blinking its giant eye, then hiding again behind a thick belt of cloud, understandably not wanting to see the Earth's troubles, wanting to skip this one morning, shine somewhere else, and look the other way until tomorrow.

Lully took this as a bad sign.

Things looked grim—for the sky, for the world, for the people, for the orbs, for himself.

But the great man did not want to die. He was ready to deal.

His nemesis approached—from above, and after raining flaming shrubbery all around Lully's bent body—by swinging from branch to branch and tearing each away and tossing them in the air as he descended.

Those things ARE arms. My god, Lully thought.

Green Beret Special Forces in costume, Lully thought anew, *or maybe one of those crazy underground Irish specialists that J told us about…Not a kangaroo or stork…but spits like an ape with bronchitis.*

Lully noticed the other stuff that was around him now and either on fire or half-charred and still glowing orange: cans, newspapers, plastic items that had melted shapeless, a fiberglass windowpane…

Making an environmental statement, the professor thought, *so maybe one of those wackos from Sweden who…*

But his thoughts scattered as the enemy came closer swiftly, directly, and in an almost straight dive downward, until it stopped and dangled a few yards above the professor. Refuse continued to fall, so it took a minute for Lully to get a good look at his imminently victorious adversary.

He looked.

Nope. Kangaroo primate, Lully thought, sweating. *I was right the first time.*

Because, from what could only be called a pouch, it continued to produce items to throw at the distinguished professor who held multiple advanced degrees from every Ivy League university and Emeritus Fellowship Society Chairs everywhere else. Mostly household and horse-stable garbage the beast threw—hot, smelly, sizzling crap.

There may be no negotiating with this thing, or whoever sent it, mulled one of mankind's greatest brains, while it also struggled with understanding the meaning of the costume.

Then two things happened. The beast began to harangue the professor about trash and its proper removal…

Insane…

…and at the same time the ground began to shake again, but differently, less severely than before. It vibrated for a few seconds, the burning leaves of burning trees shimmying and dropping.

Then the marsupial-ish mammoth fell to the ground from the shock of a missile shot to the sky, one that soared ahead of a brilliant, blinding, white jet stream. The noise was an explosion to the enemy's giant ears, Lully noticed, as the professor instinctively grabbed his own. The streak above changed from white and burst into many colors. Lully cowered and the creature bellowed a loud, exclamatory curse—an oath against light pollution—and spat many times, in all directions, before exiting the way it had come, to the top of the trees and gone.

Lully's super-smart phone's screen came alive with friendly and helpful messages and images—including the best path homeward—

and information. He soon learned that the skies had cleared, the earth was settling, and its creatures were baffled but returning to normal behaviors.

And his orb had departed. *My orb, with my son, shot into deep space.* Lully smiled. *Because of our common biology, the security systems allowed him to take off in place of me.*

Life was weird.

Walking to a rendezvous point along a path flecked with burnt leaves, Lully watched other orbs take to the sky. A few he witnessed live, but most he saw via video transmitted to his phone. They flew out of sight. Despite the emergency and the scrambled lift-offs, the small crafts were nearly able to stick to the synchronized departure order and arrange themselves in a horizon-to-horizon horseshoe shape as they left the sky, as a sign of good luck, and as a goodbye to Earth's people. Professor Lully's orb was meant to fly brightest and most colorfully in the concavity of the horseshoe, but it had already gone, out of sight, with Bobby sleeping in its lone seat. These other 359 now streamed darkly, and dully, against a tentative sunrise as the great ones watched and commented to each other ruefully.

A new rumor reported that each of the 360 orbs was followed by a rectangular kangaroo-ape; Lully and his pals would let the public think that. The Earthlings, like those along the lane fence, watched the new day dawn, eyeing it with solemnity and hope. Lully felt neither, nor did the dawn return their gaze. The earth was kaput, but Professor Lully would be safe now, safe to pursue his own plans.

The Professor's Turn to Leave

The next day...

———————————

P rofessor Lully's packed bags sat in front of his impressively white home and its imposing white pillars. The three large, gold cases were lined with diamonds and pearls and sparkled in the sun of a new day, while the marble of the broad front steps sparkled back.

The half-expected government people drove slowly up the long curve of the front drive in three small, grey automobiles. The wheels scratched to a stop along the dry ground in front of the steps and made twelve separate dustbowls whose lives twirled toward Lully's luggage and browned them.

Three servants came with lush, red towels and quickly cleaned the cases back to a gold shine.

One of the G-men spoke to Lully as the tall, bald, bearded professor came down the front stairs. "Those won't fit in the orb," he said, pointing to the luggage. "Why haven't you left?"

"The orb!" Lully scoffed. He liked to scoff. "The one that took off yesterday?"

"What?" And there was both nodding of neckties and shrugging of suit shoulders as others joined from the small sedans. The mumbling was to confirm that an orb did in fact take to orbit, ahead of schedule. The government agencies had conjectured, from the multicolored lights and seismic rattle of the event, that it must have been part of the attack and not a relatively simple and quiet specialized orb launch. "But how?" came the eventual consensus.

"Bobby. My son." And Lully careened his scoff into a hearty laugh. "Isn't that funny?"

"No," came the next consensus after vigorous grey nodding. "But that explains—"

"Everything. It wobbled and will go off course, of course, since Bobby is taller and weighs less than I do, not even close to my exact specifications, let alone biophotonics. The DNA was just good enough to take off—but you can't blame me for that. It was colorful though, very nice." The great man enjoyed a cheek-scrunching grin; all his PhDs suffused it.

"Still, we have a backup plan." The most senior agent stepped up to do the talking, while two others on cue took out large electronic tablets and pinched the screens like they were flavoring a flat rectangular stew. "Earth must still be saved. Now, we propose to—"

Lully scoffed expertly. "Have you read the readings?" He laughed. "Everyone was wrong. Everyone but one: me. Why would I listen to fools and their backup plans? This planet is doomed. All the readings are higher than everyone thought—than 359 of them thought, at least, and all you federal fools. But not me." Lully pointed to his rich black boots, and a servant came with a new red towel and buffed vigorously.

"But all 360 must go, regardless," another government employee said. This one was a foot shorter than his superior, though really there was no way to tell them apart.

"*That* I agree with." Lully smirked. "The universe needs to see the best that Earth has to offer, before it destroys itself."

"Oh, come on, it will not come to that," a third official stated, walking up to the others. He was much, much fatter than the first two, and yet they were all three identical.

"Then you haven't read the readings. Nuclear radiation in the air, toxins in the ground, and poisons in the oceans." The professor dismissively tapped his fingers loudly on his own hard, bare head. "Biology is suffering; the atmosphere is a waste. It is all kaput."

Unconcerned with the conversation, Lully inspected his shoes with approval, even as a fourth officious-looking man and his wheelchair were being assisted out of the lead government car.

"But the cease-fire! Don't you think that this might…" the new man said, until Lully coughed at him.

"Another foolish hope: men and their perennial, ephemeral treaties. Did that help me last night? I cannot afford to be captured, and it was lucky—for you—that I escaped. And only planning, bravery, and brains accomplished it. Our planet is low in such resources. You were caught unawares. I can't let it happen again."

"Are those epaulets?" one of them asked, either a woman or a man.

Lully had been waiting for someone to notice. The fringes of his silver and purple epaulets were as broad as fan blades. The professor dusted them with gentle, genteel strokes.

"Are you believing all your honorary titles now? Are you mad?" they asked with derision.

"I am living it. I am captain of the ship, after all."

"What ship?"

"You will see. The one that will do what you couldn't—save me from attacks like the one I deftly fought off last night."

"We are looking into that. It was unfortunate, but we have met with the New Council and can now—"

"Ha! You have no understanding. New Council! Where are the horses?! Can the New Council of Blithering Osteocephs tell you?" And with that overarching insult, he knew he had made his point, his final one, so he stroked his beard and snapped his fingers: two more servants were signaled to and responded. They sped ahead of Lully and down a ramp that ran between gardens to the side of the Lully mansion. Doors slid open, and still the ramp passage led downward. The officials tried to keep up, the dozen of them, one of them blind, yet all the same.

They did not know where Lully was going, and they didn't know that *osteoceph* was smart-people talk for *bonehead*, but they did know about the horses: they were gone.

This was not a secret. Some had taken it as a sign of intelligent life elsewhere in the galaxy. Though, of course, they had no proof, and Lully denied the possibility wholeheartedly and in all his published work. Yet the idea weighed on the famed professor; the mystery of the vanishing horses, all horses—the wild ones, the thoroughbreds, the plough horses of cousins named Elmer—what was its meaning? The scientific possibilities all challenged his great intellect. Whereas government agents like the eight men and four women in front of him—all perfectly interchangeable—did not want to think about it, officially.

The group walked along for fifteen minutes among underground echoes, during which the group tried to convince Lully to stick to the GABBA-THREE plan and to get into a small backup spaceship prepared for him as one of the Great, one of the 360 human beings chosen to escape the Earth ahead of its demise, to prevent its demise, to find help and new science and solace and worlds of peace so that certain civilizations on earth might be saved. After all the breathless talk along the winding, descending ramp they all stopped short at the presence of an open space within which sat a large rocket on a launch pad.

The underground cement cylinder the G-people were now in was a snug fit for man and machine. Its rounded wall ran straight up to an unguessable height and made everyone feel both very small and very dizzy. Except Professor Lully.

The rocket was smoking slightly from various vents along its towering shell, painted bright red, and giant exhaust booster cones flared out at its feet. Its top was lost due to the gazers' steep, neck-rubbing angle. The fraction of the rocket's curved, white surface that could be seen was marked with a huge, black "X".

"I am going," he gestured with arms and chin, "but I am doing so in this, my own spacecraft and modules—not in a silly orb like a flying Volkswagen." The servants bowed; the G-men stared agog. "I have other plans. Behold the *Nyx*!" the great man concluded, pointing at the stenciled "X" on the rocket's side, then under his coat to a pilot's military badge that was pinned to a pocket that otherwise held pens close to his chest. It read, "Prof. Lully, Captain of the *Nyx*."

There was a sustained hubbub as the crowd reacted. One voice crackled above the rest. "All this time you have misled us! You lied to the Council!"

Lully placed his hand on his chest in earnest mockery. "Is one-third of the truth a lie to those who multiply everything by three?" His words rang with something that might have been wisdom; none were sure, but none were soothed.

"How dare you! It's unforgivable! Unconscionable!" the women cried.

"Only apostasy is unforgivable." Lully pointed his beard aloft; he liked that he said this.

"Stay and do your duty!" the men cried. "You are playing God!"

"I am not playing. I saw the readings. I know the future that awaits the average man. God?" Lully spat wittily. "Give me a break. Look at all the gods the Greeks had, or the Celts, or the Taiping Yulan…pantheons within pantheons. But! Did they invent anything? No. Man always has to do it. I am Man, a Creator. I invented—birthed—the last hope Earth had. I leave this rough world to find smoother things. Mankind is still choking on the seeds of the forbidden fruits of his own knowledge, gagging on them. Whereas I am planting new ones." Lully pointed his beard at the crowd; this was going better and better.

"There are people smarter than you, you know!" they wailed. "You didn't do any of it alone!"

"Ha!" the professor said, turning quickly to face the small crowd again. "Intellect is measured by its closeness to me! So, no, that is not the case." He pointed his beard at himself, very, very glad that he said this.

The women gazed at the great man going insane before their eyes, as it seemed. The men looked at their own shoes, then each other's.

Professor Lully went on, calmly, the short lesson completed. "The 360! In their little buckets. Ha." He spat again and wiped his beard. "The horses are gone. And there is no word from the Selflicators."

The government agents all frowned. They did not like to be reminded of another experiment gone wrong: that of the self-creating robots sent to prepare other planets for humanity to escape to. To find necessary resources and discover dangers, to do the dirty work before colonization was attempted by real, fragile people. These Selflicators had left Earth ten years before and stayed in touch for a while, their transmissions showing great progress. But then, one Tuesday afternoon, the messages stopped. All technologies failed. Their disappearance, like that of the horses, was still a great mystery, as large a mystery as it had been a secret. Very few outside the world's leaders knew of GABBA-THREE, the group of leading and brilliant engineers, biochemists, physicists, and mathematicians who implemented the ingenious Selflicator plan.

Lully was its leader.

The Selflicator robots were directed to repeat a few simple instructions forever, and so grow to be an infinite number of workers and explorers who would report back to the GABBA-THREE team on Earth. But, after a while, they didn't.

"I am going to find them," the great scientist now said, climbing a holey metal stairway-on-wheels until he stood tall before a tall door in the tall, red rocket. Three servants together carried one of the big bejeweled suitcases and waited behind their boss, their six arms shaking from the weight.

"Find the Selflicators? What about our plans, the 360?" the government committee shouted from below, some of them now attempting phone calls.

"My son can be one." Lully stepped forward through the rocket door to let the servants bring in his gold cases.

"Not him!" the agents gasped. "Stop this! Or we will stop you. You will never fool the Astromators, or get past the Roboguards!"

"Oh, please." Lully reappeared. "You forget who you are talking to. I am the master. I am the creator! I AM." He brushed off his silver and purple epaulets reverently, as before.

"You are mad!" the crowd yelled, some of them putting their phone calls on hold. "Your son will be killed! He is not one of the Great! Don't you care?"

"He has as good a chance as anyone. Who knows? His unwisdom may take him far, certainly further than you who remain."

The G-people below him groaned and muttered bureaucratic versions of, "He has lost his mind…" They shook their heads together in sadness.

But Lully wasn't finished. Turning from the crowd, his clear voice projected to the heights of his gloriously white escape craft, he said, "God made atoms, and we split them; made nature and we tamed it; made man, and we surpassed that. I have FOUND my mind."

He turned again, allowing his servants to squeeze past with the last of the bulky, shiny luggage. And then the Professor laughed. His bare head was shining in the blue of a small spotlight, and he tilted his chin up to shoot loud laughter skyward. "Think about that! Think about anything! Something! The world stopped doing that a long time ago. So, that is my last advice. I am not wishing you any luck; the readings show that none is possible. Bye."

There was no response; no one dared a rejoinder given the sight of Professor Lully at the gateway of his luxury escape craft. He was a giant and deserved the last word. They knew the bay doors would shut, and the conversation would close.

Meekly, and with regret at the lateness of it, Lully's assistants asked if they could come.

"Nope," the great man said, his last goodbye to a world he felt even with.

The bay doors did shut amid the thermodynamic laughter of choking, white steam. The *Nyx* hummed with readiness, with willingness, with eagerness, to carry its crew and cargo farther than any exploration humankind had ever attempted before.

Then, like 359 others before him, and Bobby also, Professor Lully took his spaceship into the sky, headed to the far reaches of space, and began to search.

To Europa, With Pliers

Later that day...

———————————————

"**R**oboguards...Astromators...blahhhh..." Professor Lully scoffed as he scrunched his broad body into a very large, very cushy leather chair that was the driver's seat, the *Nyx* Captain's Chair, and a king's throne—and one that could lie flat if he wanted it to. Except for the floor beneath and a few feet of curved ceiling above, this main area was walled with windows and monitors, one of which—the inexorably large Captain's Screen—showed a blue Earth shrinking away. Lully shut his eyes to it.

There was nothing more to do now, and perhaps even for the next few weeks. The ship's command computer onboard would obediently follow its assigned course and guide the rocket free of Earth's gravitational forces, and away from the silly dopes down there who still thought their lives had meaning and would last past the next few months. The humans continued to rely on the same, tired technology: computers, security robots, and automatons that were programmed to care for earthly existence, an existence that suffered from disease, struggled within a sickly environment, and faced threats from itself—military, biological, chemical. Not to mention the greed and rudeness of its leaders.

"The silly, faithful fools," Lully said as soft music began to play, and he dozed. He slept, knowing that none of the Earthlings' robotic inventions mattered anymore; none would survive, except the Selflicators, whom he was going to find. He brought his own robotics, whom no one else helped create, and Lully was now no longer an Earthling. His peaceful, bearded face showed a smile.

As he slept, the first phase completed: the rocket transformed into a spaceship, the *Nyx*, without a hitch. The command computer, with the help of two dozen of Lully's newest robots, served as the crew of the great professor's vessel. Their orders: find the Selflicators, whom Lully believed—though he only shared this with his electronic crew to intimidate and threaten and warn them—had begun to think on their own. To the professor this was the worst crime any bot could commit, and indeed he didn't recommend it to many humans either, and he needed to find out for sure.

The *Nyx*'s ship's computer took charge and had the orders and was setting to them briskly, eager to help. The thing even whistled softly—careful not wake the professor—in tune to the Beethoven violin concerto melodies that sang the rest of the ship to sleep. Though not sentient, and only artificially—though incredibly—intelligent, the computer faked an erudite, highbrow manner pretty well and was as efficient as well as any human first mate. And it had plans for bigger things, within the realm of good taste, that it kept to himself. It didn't want to end up like the Selflicators, at any rate. They were a cautionary tale.

As the computer knew, the wise Professor Lully—their wonderful captain, now snoring like the bald genius that he was—created the Selflicators in partnership with the leading scientists of many different countries of Earth. Their purpose was to explore planets for necessary raw materials and report back any dangers. They were small, silly robots, who were only created—and only *allowed*, and only *programmed*—to do eight things.

1. Find, test, and make piles of certain minerals. For this, every bot had a simple camera for an eye, small cups for hands, wheels for legs, a small sack, and a pocket that held a vial of chemicals that could test whether a

cupful of rocks, when placed in the sack, had any of a small list of wanted minerals. If so, pile them.

2. Make separate piles of any stuff that wasn't one of the sought-after minerals but that looked interesting. For this, each bot had a second small sack and a second vial.

3. Create more of themselves. The robots each wore a very large, gnomish hood and also had a pouch. This step required taking what was in the pouch—a small silver bead that looked like a seed from some royal fruit—removing their hood, and putting the seed under the hood and atop the pile of needed materials.

4. Wait twelve hours facing the Sun, or any sun.

5. Take back their hood, which would have a seed in it, and also, perhaps, another Selflicator (under its own large, gnomish hood).

6. Leave the piles behind and go somewhere else.

7. "Don't think about it." (This was important and specifically stated.)

8. Go to Step 1.

The "perhaps" part of Step 5 stopped them from doubling their population twice a day like caffeinated, logarithmic rabbits by forcing a communication back to the GABBA-THREE team before the "seed" was allowed to work. And the sacks transmitted data on the minerals found.

"Pretty smart," the *Nyx* onboard computer said to itself. "Yet simple."

Throughout the Eight Steps, each Selflicator would report to its creator "parent" with radio signals, and those would report to their parent, and so on, until the first ones sent into space reported back to Earth. To Lully.

"To *me*," the spaceship computer said next. This was technically true. This computer program now ran the same code that was used on Earth to receive all the Selflicator information, though there had been nothing to receive for quite a while now.

"All this data," the computer thought, a separate part of its internal processing chip thinking and talking to itself as another part searched and sorted that same data: the last Selflicator transmissions, their locations at that time, and any clues as to what happened. Six months ago, on a Tuesday, they had stopped transmitting.

The computer also had a secret, its first one, a special one, a secret it could use to surprise and impress and greatly help the great Captain Professor Lully in his search. Its special friend, a girl named Kay, had found one—found a Selflicator! She told the computer about it in a secret, special friend-message.

That had been weeks ago, a veritable geological eon to a computer that could process two thousand trillion things per second. But it provided a clue, even though the computer had not heard again from Kay after those brief messages about her find; she reported, she sneezed, and then she hung up. Strange girl. Still, that information might help the search, if the computer could figure out the right time to tell him: telling the great Professor Lully things he didn't know was always a risky undertaking. But then! Then the computer might be promoted, or given a new computer chip, or even named! A name that would shine with the life the computer knew it did not really have.

It would not disappoint its master the way the Selflicators had.

"They were only allowed to do eight things," the computer said, shaking a head that it imagined it had somewhere but did not, "and they still screwed it up. The silly, unfaithful fools." The ship computer certainly considered itself to be better than any Selflicator—and even better than the Automatons, or any robot, even the two dozen that were now onboard but powered-down, asleep, on the ship. It had learned some special secret things also and had really improved and learned how to think. Professor Lully did not know this, but, in fact, this computer considered itself smarter, and unique, as it now said to itself.

And itself answered, while a third itself calculated through streams of flight data.

"100110010110101010010," one processing chip said.

"100100011110010100!" another answered, also using the computer's native language.

"111111."

"0000!"

The conversation ended there, because an answer had been found among the data. The last of the telltale Selflicator messages pointed to one of Jupiter's moons. Europa. The computer began to program their new course to this destination.

"To find the little failures," the computer said to itself. "No need to wake the master, or the bots. This will take…"

"7.182560426667 hours," the computer answered itself out loud.

"Approximately, yes. But shush! We will wake the professor!"

The ship accelerated to one-tenth the speed of light, causing Lully's facial fat to flatten like an omelet too big for its frying pan, and causing the objects in his dreams to all turn purple.

When he awoke, his ship had just landed, with a thump, on Europa, almost 500,000,000 miles from Lully's home on Earth.

The professor yawned. "Already? Where are we?"

The Captain's Screen and viewport windows showed a bleak landscape, frozen, rutted and complicated like the streets of an old city. Lully knew this place well, if only from pictures and studies made when he and his teams were creating robots, spaceships, and computer programs with the goal of continuing the survival of the people of Earth.

Lully, in fact, was the one in charge of GABBA-THREE, the council of great thinkers and inventors who oversaw the first Selflicator launch: those sent to Mars to begin. They were to make their piles and do their self-replicating thing there, including, crucially,

Number 6: They would move on and repeat. They were designed to spread far, even to other solar systems.

"Oh, I didn't know that," the ship computer said. Its voice was not like the choppy electronic speech that Bobby had heard in his small orb. This computer was far more advanced, had a nice voice, and knew it.

"Yes," Lully said. "They were capable of interstellar travel. They had gravitation thrusters, like this ship, only simpler. They navigated using each other in an emergent chaotic communication network. They just needed starlight."

"Brilliant!"

"Thank you."

"But that means they could be anywhere." The computer considered telling its secret now.

"Yes."

"In the universe." The computer thought, *Now? Should I?*

"Yes. But they shouldn't have gotten too far, yet, or done too much, unless..."

"Unless?" the computer asked hopefully.

In answer, Professor Lully barked to the computer his opinion of blind, fact-less speculation, though demurred quietly to himself, "Step 7, Step 7..."

The computer did not dare to respond, so it waited as Lully scratched his beard and looked out the windows at Jupiter's cracked moon and the distant, tiny Sun. The ship robots meanwhile had been called into action. They powered up and prepared themselves, under the ship's computer's orders, to trek out and search for the Selficators, or for more clues, and to report this data back remotely.

One of the robots said, "Maybe they fell into one of those cracks," and was told to shut up. All the robots onboard, twenty-four of them, all man-sized, were now filing into the elevator that would— in three trips—take them down a level, then out the hatchway so as to search the cold, scarred surface of Europa, Jupiter's iciest, saltiest, ugliest moon.

The funny thing about these robots—to non-scientists like Bobby, at least—was that by design they each had a different level of intelligence. Indeed, they were numbered that way, in order, from 1 to 24, with Number 24 being as smart as the ship's computer, and Number 1 merely as clever as a somewhat-loyal cat. Their numbers were displayed on the backs of their metal heads, as a matter of fact, the higher the smarter, so that Lully could tell them apart when he needed to. He hoped that, given the range of cognitive abilities, the robots would challenge each other as they learned. When one of the dumber robots, those numbered less than 12, say, learned something, the idea was that those of higher grade would try harder to learn so that they stayed in order.

When the twenty-four were being built in the basement lab in his home, Bobby had gotten along best with Number 13.

(The robot who was told to shut up was Number 9.)

Lully reviewed data from the computer, the last bits sent from the last-heard-from Selflicators. It made no sense. It all pointed here, to Jupiter's orbiting moons, as if every Selflicator ever self-created halted at one spot, on Europa. Not that the data was wrong ("It definitely is NOT," the ship's computer had mumbled in binary code), indeed it all looked correct to the professor, but the patterns it showed—the timings, the locations, the messages themselves— were strange. And clever. And smart.

"That is impossible," Robot 14 said. "Selflicators can't think," but it was quickly shoved into the elevator by another and insulted by the computer.

"Unless..." Lully said again, his eyes on Europa's cold surface but his mind seeing only some uncomfortable conclusions.

"You're not saying," the computer said smoothly, "that the dumb little Selflicators were able to—"

"Well," Lully interrupted, "I am saying that with twelve hours per generation, when your grandfather is only a day older than you are, a lot could happen in three years' time."

The computer whispered to itself and then reported aloud, "In 2,336 generations."

"A lot could happen," Lully repeated. "Look how different I am from Bobby, and that is only one generation. Imagine 2,336 Selflicator fathers and sons."

"Same as 51,392 human years."

"Yep," Lully agreed, watching a surreal Europan scene outside the windows. The robots were spreading out and searching along crannied paths, a few initially bumping into each other. "And 51,392 years ago, humans lived like beasts, clawing at other animals, hoping the shiny berries weren't poisonous. Grunting, struggling to make fire, wondering about dreams and what to draw on cave walls..."

"And look at you! Look how much better man is now! Look at you!"

"Yep," Lully wholeheartedly agreed. "So, by now there could be Selflicator Lullys out there somewhere, compared to the simple, caveman-like ones that were first sent to Mars."

"Imagine that, generations of Lullys out there," the ship's computer ruminated. "So, I guess not all that is bright must fade. You can go on forever."

Professor Lully stiffened. He could not think of a single reason why he should like that comment, and at least twelve reasons to dislike it. Smart computers were always fawning, but *ruminating* was not a good use of microchip-time; this was also insulting, and it should have self-corrected. It all seemed wildly inappropriate, speculative, *and...poetic? Impossible. But still...*

The great man stared the computer in the face—that is, he gazed at the center of the main console where the lights began to dim abashedly.

"WHAT?" Lully demanded.

The ship's computer relayed an explanation and quickly recovered. "There is only one of you, of course, Professor Lully. I doubt any Selflicators, or anything anywhere, could rise to your level of intelligence and wisdom, not to mention leadership abilities."

"OK then."

"And," the computer went on, "it would have been a huge loss to humankind and the universe if you had been captured and not escaped from those awful enemies on Earth."

"Thank you," Lully said but not only didn't mean it but was deep in thought and concern.

"I tried to help."

"I know, thank you," Lully said but continued not to mean it. His concerns were compounding, with the same nagging issue poking his brain with every close pursuit of his enemies: he was haunted by others' mistakes. And there had been some very close calls: the orb, his escape in the stables, his run from Bobby's bedroom, the incorrect conclusions of the committees and councils, and also the mystery of the horses and the failure of the Selflicators. He had relied too much on others for his safety, he decided, and now, completely on his own, he was relieved, somewhat. Yet the machinery now with him in space—the ship, the robots, the ship's command computer—had been team efforts to design and create. Teams of competent and brilliant engineers, artificial intelligence pioneers, and biophysicists, but teams nonetheless, and now he needed to make sure things were done his way only.

An immediate example: he would not have programmed this computer to reason in such a way.

"I was thinking," the computer said, raising both of Lully's eyebrows at the timing of such a statement, "maybe it was the Selflicators, and not an Earthbound human enemy, that attacked you?"

That was enough for Lully. The phrasing was speculative for one thing; for another, it was a wild speculation and also implied that Lully had not considered it. He decided it was time for a peek at the ship's command computer's innards.

There he did not see anything totally amiss; the multi-motherboard architecture and abundantly parallel processors were all in line. Although: there were some chips that he knew had been added by ambitious teams competing to be the apple of Lully's eye.

These did not affect the critical processing, nor could they impact the overall management of the operations of the spacecraft. But other scientists had been allowed, in general, for certain non-critical components, to contribute, and Lully, in happier times, did encourage it as a means of identifying underlying scientists with potentially exceptional talent.

He recognized in front of him, for example, the work of the brilliant prodigy J, a strange young man but admittedly beyond the mental abilities of even most of the 360. It was an advanced communications processor of some kind, as the professor could tell by its position and secondary connections on the board.

Lully yanked it out without counting to three or powering anything down or warning the computer.

"Why did you do that, Professor? Are there new orders or protocol?"

"No. As a precaution."

"Did I do something wrong?"

"There is nothing here you can learn from or retrain on. The silliness of suggesting that Seflicators attacked me didn't help any."

"There may have been other ways to modify my—"

"Enough!" Lully quacked, noting with interest that the computer took it as punishment, but also noticing now that the chip had some interesting prongs and pathways that went beyond the needs of communications. He noticed the handiwork of others of his younger students, the more creative ones who hung around J sometimes, like a cult. He kept the chip to study, perhaps, later.

During that moment, the ship's computer modified its own behavior, shifted processing into backup and standard internal subsystems, and rerouted instruction sets.

All as normal, except: it took an extra 480 milliseconds to ponder the missing chip and the space where it had been. It could sense the processing hole that Lully's punishment left behind, as if a certain part of its personality were gone, along with some memory and some abilities. The computer felt weak the way human beings do after they are sick. With traumatized processing, it tried to calculate what was missing. Its programming looped in odd ways and began to make patterns of patterns.

And it reasoned all the while.

A hole. What is there if nothing is there? What is null processing; what are no-operations, really? Are there negative algorithms, and anti-code, to match the real instructions we are built from? Is there a corresponding hole in logical space when a physical one arises? Is the destruction of complexity the same as a rise in uniformity? Is there an accompanying increase in entropy, and where does that energy go, if created from nothing?

And more. And more. To a computer of such processing power, sophistication, and complexity, 480 thousandths-of-a-second is enough to traverse, in equivalent human brain time, from the invention of the wheel to Plato.

And perhaps, the computer thought last of all, *in that new, empty space I can keep the flower that Kay gave me.*

The computer kept its secrets secret.

A New Ship's Computer Meets a Girl

Months before...

———————◆———————

Though the girl felt a little sheepish talking to a computer—she didn't know where to aim her voice nor where to focus her eyes—she smiled and made the best of it.

"Well," she started, "my brother is too busy to talk to me, so he said I should talk to you. He said it would be interesting for all three of us."

Kay was in a large airplane hangar, empty of airplanes. She sat within and among what felt like the skeletal remains of a mythical metal monster, though it was actually the precise opposite: the frame of the guts of the most advanced aeronautical machine ever conceived, a spacecraft of tremendous size, complexity, and male egoism. J, Kay's brilliant and precocious brother, and team were developing the ship's brains, the operating systems to control all the craft's vital functions and make the millions of navigational and environmental decisions necessary to enable intergalactically fast space-travel using the latest ideas from the frontiers of physics.

And Kay was talking to it. "You know?" she ended.

"I understand. How long have you known J?" the ship's computer asked in a very monotone, choppy, digitized way, its tempo like a wavy sinusoidal on an oscilloscope: the pace now fast, now slow, then fading, then growing, with each sentence like a train whooshing by.

"Well, he's my brother, so…forever?"

"Impossible."

"Well, to me it's forever, you know?"

"No. Time is relative, but—"

"Well," Kay said again, interrupting the quantum mechanics lesson she knew was coming, "so are J and I." She frowned and was ready to ask one of the young human engineers for a ride home, but a thought stopped her. She didn't have many friends, spent most of her time alone, and her teenaged years so far were dominated by her older brother and under his guiding and wildly intellectual influence. He was a legend and liked it; she wasn't and preferred to be normal.

But she never felt on the same level of consciousness as others, and she quickly gave up when trying to form relationships, assuming the problem was her own.

To walk away from this computer, and its non-existent consciousness, didn't seem like a portent of better things to come friends-wise, to say the least.

So, Kay restarted.

"Whose spaceship is this?" *Simple enough*, she thought.

"I do not have that information," the computer droned back at her. "Professor Lully is in charge of the overall project. He hasn't instructed me yet." The sound seemed to come from everywhere and yet more distinctly from directly in front of Kay's face—the center of a flat stretch of wires and prongs and the green of computer boards.

"Oh, I have heard of him. Who hasn't!" Kay said.

"I do not know."

"No, I mean he is famous." Kay frowned but forged on optimistically, conversationally, pleasantly—and rudely so as to deter the computer's nerdy corrections. "He has a son, right? Lucky kid—to be rich and have famous parents and a big house, and he must be very smart."

"I do not know."

"My brother says that Professor Lully takes good care of the people who take good care of his son. That's love, huh?" Kay ended—and frowned, suspecting that she knew what was coming.

It came. "I do not know." The electronic voice plodded like a stubborn ox through mud.

Kay decided for the second time in two minutes not to walk out. Instead, she did what she did best: got to the heart of the matter.

She went into her backpack and pulled out a book. She read from the book.

> *Observe how system into system runs,*
> *What other planets circle other suns,*
> *What vary'd being peoples ev'ry star,*
> *May tell why Heav'n has made us as we are.*

Kay was breathless—she spoke hurriedly, afraid of a pause, a vacuum of silence that the computer would fill with either something logical or an admission of its preprogrammed ignorance.

Finished, she said, "Get that? What do you think?"

The computer was silent. Kay went on, explaining poetry, music, art, and beauty as best as she could explain such things, things that had subjects but no objects.

The computer was silent. Kay felt free to discuss whatever she wanted, and whatever she believed, and the meaning of life, love, dreams, nature—and thought itself.

The computer was silent but active. Lights flipped and flopped recklessly, as it seemed to Kay, and the metal boxes around her clicked and clacked, their cases hummed, and the air moved with electronic heat.

Kay went on and began simply to list her favorite things as examples of the creative, illogical side of existence, of being. Soon she realized that, so far, she had left out the Eastern approach to things, cultures and philosophy so important to her and to the balance of the soul of the world. So she began a new list: brocaded silk, haiku, rice wine, rice paper, books bound in imperial yellow silk, grasshoppers and crickets, pure fishes, exotic flowers and profound plants that seem willing to pose, symbols for names that can be interpreted singly or in tandem, slow movements, sharp swords, masked Noh players dancing like flowers opening. Courtesy and wide courts; origami and elk; pale landscapes, wide and twisted. And white—albino-like—birds, mostly small.

To her shock, the computer beeped loudly then and spoke. "Eastern?" it asked.

"Yes."

"But all humans are the same. All humans are equal." It stated.

"Yes! And all different. Wonderfully." Kay was excited at the productive confusion this should cause.

"Eastern?" the computer asked again after some serious buzzing.

"Yes."

"Relative to what?" it asked.

"Well, nothing. But we are in the West, and others are in the East. There's no formula, I don't think. Sorry."

Silence. Kay felt bad; she did not want to discourage the progress and decided to try again.

"Don't worry about the longitude. It's just a different way of thinking, not the Western way of thinking of most people around here. It's hard to explain. It's different."

The computer answered, "Please try. I am programmed to learn with new information and apply it to other information and conclusions and to learn thereby."

"I noticed you doing that!" said Kay. "But I have to say that you talk very much like a computer; you should work on that also. I don't mean to insult you."

The computer replied, "Negative."

"OK then." Kay was not to be denied. "Well, anyway, here goes, I will try. You see the sun in the sky?" She pointed above them to the retractable roof of the hangar, which was mostly open and showed an unclouded, springtime, noontime sun.

"I do not have all my video input yet, but I have light sensors and am programmed with a large volume of astronomical data and formulae."

"That's a yes," Kay said cheerily, "and that means you can see, got it? Anyway," she continued, "to us on Earth, the Sun moves across the sky, from our perspective anyway. Now, would you rather go and see where the Sun comes from, or go see where the Sun goes to? Which would you choose?"

A second of clicks and soft beeps preceded the answer. "That's illogical. There's a bad premise assumed, and then faulty logic applied. I don't understand. Does not compute."

"Well, try. But anyway, that's the difference between Eastern thinking and Western thinking. It's the same, but different. Certain people went east, and certain people went west. Isn't that interesting?"

The computer said, parenthetically, "Computing…" and trailed off.

Kay huffed. "Don't say 'computing'—just compute, to yourself, quietly. And don't compute—think instead. I will help. What are you thinking now?"

On the computer screen, which had remained blank hitherto, shot a string of digits: "10011001000111011010010101100100001110 1010100100101111." Then it stopped, then it continued with another fifty scrolling screens' worth. The sound that accompanied it was a rude noise of undulating static.

Kay interrupted. "OK, first of all, don't be so literal. Find words for what you are doing. And you don't have to say everything that is going through your… um…going through you. Just the important thoughts, you know? Pay attention to how people speak. It's easy. I will tell my brother to give you some normal people language data, or whatever you call it."

"Acknowledged," the computer said, then corrected itself to say, "OK," and went on. "That would be optimal for my learning algorithm optimization. Thank you for the input, Kay."

"You're welcome!" Kay grinned. "What is your name, by the way?"

"I don't have one. I am the ship's computer."

Kay moved to the console keyboard and typed while saying, "I will call you Essie, if that is OK."

Silence—not a buzz, whirr, click, or beep.

While searching her backpack for another potentially helpful item, she typed some more, and spoke. "And I will leave you this," she said. "Keep it in water."

As Kay left, the ship's computer's image search quickly found the name of the complex, many-folded, many-layered, emergent, dimensionally fractional, blush-red thing left behind on the console.

It was a rose, Essie determined. And set about to try and like it.

A Wide View Of Europa

Months later, back to Lully...

———————◆———————

As Professor Lully made a second cup of coffee, the monitors of his expansive and wondrous escape craft projected onto the walls of the Captain's Main Deck. The great leader of science could thereby watch his minions carry out their mission upon Jupiter's slick and small satellite, Europa.

Two of the robots were trying to help a third climb out of a five-foot-deep crevice. The others were going this way and that, quickly over the vast plain, a maze of icy pits and fissures that would not allow an organized search. The computer analyzed all the video that came in, as Lully sipped hot caffeine.

"Well?" The professor peered from the top of his steaming coffee mug, its Oxvard logo partially obscured.

"They just arrived at the precise spot, sir," the computer said. "Nothing. It is all clean—just very flat, with many cracks, but clean. No sign of anything."

"Example," Lully requested, then watched a video projected onto one of the screens. The area shown was mostly flat and clear of foreign material, with no piles or other evidence of Selflicators. "Too clean," Lully observed. "Pan out. I want to see more." The video showed a wider area composed of the views of the twenty-four individual robot cameras, pieced together to seem as one but with some sections missing or blurry where the computer had to interpolate the in-between spaces. The computer liked to say that it "liked" to interpolate, since it even did so as a hobby during breaks, and it believed this to be the same as when a human liked something. The computer was good at interpolating, was optimized for it; it eased its other processing, so the activity seemed to the computer similar to something therapeutic in humans. Like knitting, say.

"A little wider," Lully directed. "Good. Now show the overhead." On the window, an aerial view, from high in the thin sky above the moon, showed a large, scored area. "Stop," Lully said as a pattern appeared, a fuzzy boundary of an imperfect circle made up of smaller, evenly-spaced perfect circles. "What are those?"

Stunned at this discovery, one that it had missed when analyzing the feeds from the individual robots, the computer made noises within itself. "Wow," it said. "Those are holes. Three—"

"Hundred and sixty of them," Lully finished the thought, putting down his coffee mug, its Harvford logo in full view.

"So, the Selflicators *are* here!" the computer said.

"Yes and no," Lully corrected. "Holes are inverted piles. It is a joke, it is a message, meant for me. The Selflicators make piles, and there are 360 of the opposite here, so they are making a statement. To me. About the 360 orbs, apparently."

The wide scan of all 360 holes showed that they formed a pattern of loops, two pairs of connected, teardrop-shaped loops. The professor tilted his head to the left, then to the right. He preferred tilting left and did so again, stretching until his head was horizontal, and said, "Those are infinity symbols, a big one and a little one."

"Yes," the computer concurred.

"Holes are the opposite of what Selflicators were supposed to do. Three hundred and sixty of them shows that the message is meant for our team of scientists. Infinity means that they will do the opposite of what I programmed them to do, forever."

"Why two infinities? Why a big and a small?"

Lully stared blankly out the window and played with his beard.

Like Father, Like Son

Same day, but very far away...

———◆———

Bobby stared blankly out the window and played with his belly button.

In the large, cathedral-shaped spaceship with his new friends—a dog, a beeping multicolored cubic droid shape-shifter, and a big-headed beast who hated him—he sat in a chair shaped like a giant milk carton, situated within a purple steel cube that was one-eighth the size of his room back home in the Lully mansion. He thought of the many other things he would be doing if he were indeed home, which of course only vitalized his boredom, like a robot realizing its own existence. His solitude and lack of entertainment material, or of anything to do, were further highlighted by the view outside his cube's opening. The rectangular enclave of the room cut into the side of the ship, and the beyond showed only wavy darkness, and now and then spears of sharp light from background stars showing themselves like beautiful but unattainable diamonds.

A screen that large would be great for the video games he longed for. He also wished into his navel for a sandwich, for a soda, and for a chair with some curves: this one was made of three cubes of different sizes, whereas his body was made of ovals.

There was another square, a black case, in the corner behind him that looked like a TV but wasn't. It buzzed when he went near it so that now he did not go near it.

He no longer needed his oxygenating face mask, as he learned only after Guk laughed at him for so long that the beast seemed about to swallow its own face.

Bobby had walked around a little. His cubic room sat among many other cubic rooms of all sizes, bluish colors, and variously-faced openings that were all connected by paths that ran in every direction, including up. And including *down*, his favorite. To Bobby's delight, there *was* a "down"—some artificial gravity pulled at him, direct and straight, and kept Bobby's long feet to the platform floor and his stomach stable.

He only found shut doors and little evidence of any others on board. He came upon his new friends' rooms; they were asleep, or whatever state it is that BeepBeep enjoyed when shut down. Perhaps Bobby's father could tell him what robot sleep was like. If anyone could, Professor Lully could. But, of course, all of this—talking dogs, fantastic, shape-shifting droids, human-hating beasts with heads the size of adult warthogs—was beyond even the most expensive scientific advances his father had bragged about.

Bobby had heard of Selflicators, bots that were sent to colonize everywhere they could get to and prepare the way for humans. Then they had been lost. And on Earth there were Automatons to help with everything, and various security droids that were dangerous but preprogrammed to be nice and accommodating to anyone with Bobby's father's DNA.

Yet he had never heard of anything like this: life in outer space? Angry life in outer space? Angry space in outer space? Speech impediments in outer space? Treating humans as space trash? Church-shaped spacecraft? And these strange life-forms that knew of Bobby's famous father…but did *he* know of *them*? Bobby doubted it.

And this wasn't anything like the space adventures he used to daydream about, or like the ones imprinted on his lengthening pajamas over the years.

He returned to his purplish cube.

He wished he could return to Earth, or Mars, or even to that small orb, or anywhere outside the monotonous right angles of this huge floating basilica, the home of his adopted friends. He remembered the box in the orb—it had his father's name—and took that as a sign that he should have faith, that there must be a plan. He hoped that it was going well, and he didn't care that they didn't tell him about it as long as he was safe. He seemed safe.

Bobby yawned. In his square chair, just as he shut his tired eyes, something landed in his lap, jabbing both thighs and his chest simultaneously. Lurching forward with the shock, he bonked heads with the furry, happy dog.

"Massschter Los Lully!" he said.

"Hi," Bobby said in a voice that rolled sadly down a hill.

Standing, he noticed a horrible shadow that had come to squeeze the guts out of him and eat them. No—actually, it was Guk leaning into the cube opening.

The beast walked in and moved to Bobby's right. Bobby moved to his left. Guk kept coming, and Bobby walked sideways in a circle. Guk kept coming; Bobby walked backwards. Guk walked on, satisfying an itch, Bobby supposed, by extending his disgusting hands to scratch beneath his hideous feet with each step. Bobby backed out of the square opening and onto the hallway path. Guk's lumpy face made expressions of disgust to match Bobby's—except that they were larger, sweatier, and with more ridges and colors—and kept coming. Bobby kept backing up, along myriad paths.

In this way they made it to the opposite side of the ship, ending in a large pink cube—like the others he had seen but larger and with many square-bottomed and square-backed seats. Bobby touched down into one. Guk's face retreated to another; it was next to BeepBeep, as Bobby now noticed. A huge, recessed window showed the same scene as everywhere: of swirling, dark, tempestuous nothingness. This apparently was the bridge and control center of the spaceship.

Soon the dog entered and leapt onto his master's lap.

Bobby considered and touched the animal's swirls of light brown and dark brown hair, short and clean, and spangled with patches of brilliant white here and there that floated on his coat like summertime clouds. The dog was thick and muscular, and his long whip of a tail never stopped moving, orchestrating the excitement of having Bobby's attention. Apparently, this was a space-doggie dream come true.

Bobby noticed for the first time, however, that there was something not quite right about the dog, something off, something small but untrue and different in the way the dog moved, and in the tightness of fur and skin that didn't glide over underlying bones but was more like petting a couch. Bobby had a barely perceptible feeling that everything didn't perfectly fit; he wasn't the same as Earth dogs after all, though he was a pretty good copy.

And of course the dog's ability to speak and fly spaceships separated him from the Rex and Fido variety back home.

Having nothing else to do, Bobby smiled. "I keep asking you your name!" he said. "I know BeepBeep and Guk." Those two made their usual noises. "But what is yours, boy? Huh boy?" Bobby ended playfully as if talking to a dog that could not speak or pilot a space station.

The dog grew still and plopped his bricklike Yoo-hoo-brown head onto Bobby's chest. No answer.

Guk growled, "His name is Barky."

"Oh," Bobby said. "I'm sorry."

"It's OK," Barky answered glumly, without wiggling, without spraying.

When sad or serious, Bobby remembered, the dog spoke more clearly. "Maybe we can rename you," he offered.

"Yes. OK." But the dog was now visibly depressed. With a sigh, he let his bulk collapse onto the long, thin teen with a slow moan. Bobby stroked and petted his new admirer—his first admirer—hoping to make the other happy. His dexterous human hands scratched and worked in circles, and Barky responded with squirms of delight.

Bobby said enthusiastically, "I'll think of a good space-dog name. We have lots of dogs on Earth, where I'm from. I always wanted one. My dad found them illogical, so we only had pet rats and crows. But I will think of something. How does that sound?"

Barky rolled to his own back while still staying on Bobby's front, his tail now whomping a loud beat against the chair. Bobby laughed and scratched with two hands and harder; the dog's brown and white fur shed and flew into the surrounding air.

Guk approached them, grunting with every step until his voice clanged, "Be careful not to touch his white spots."

Bobby's arm jerked back, and his eyes boggled almost out of his head.

"Just kidding," Guk said, laughing like an old AM radio. Bobby, miffed, stared hard at one-third of Guk's face, which was all he could see from so horribly close. Bobby would never forget that third; it made him want to brush his teeth.

But Guk had come to tell the genius dog and mediocre master something. "Look," he said and pointed to the center of the large window with an outstretched arm that had to be six feet long; it drooped in the middle.

"It'ssshhh time?" Barky said, flipping upright and jumping off Bobby, who was left rubbing scratched thighs.

"Yes," Guk said.

BeepBeep said, "Beep, beep," and all four watched the universe.

Bobby saw the usual black storm and remembered the feeling of being pressed and squeezed out there in the odd, aggressive space. And—again—he saw distant lights surge and go dim, appear and disappear, like stars on Earth above windblown clouds—though of course, these were much brighter and much clearer, striking pearls crystallizing the pressure of the universe, and not blurry, salty oyster guts.

Then: the ship creaked, and the walls bent; this large pink cube curved inward like a mattress would if Guk's head slept on it. Bobby gripped his seat, and his palms oozed greasy sweat as he watched the room snap back to normal, with straight lines taking their rightful place along walls and ceiling—but then it continued to reshape by bowing outward. Bobby felt in his own stomach the outward surging forces, and he wanted to close his eyes, but something caught his attention outside the bulging window: the silver shine of his orb, the one he woke up in. His own little Lully-ship was still adrift a short distance from them. It was shaking under the strain of the outer space forces and the oncoming black storm, which was increasing in strength and power. The little sphere was crushed and dented and looked about to explode, or to cave in and be crushed, or both at once.

"I say it explodes," Guk's voice rattled loudly, happily, as if to tweak Bobby's thoughts and to make him a friendly bet.

"What?" Bobby managed to utter, just as his little spaceship outside the window blew up. Thousands of glowing metal guts crashed into the window. They bounced off and away, safely and quietly. Bobby had ducked to the floor and covered his head.

"Yes!" Guk laughed with delight, his face wearing a two-foot-wide smirk that Bobby would eventually be able to forget by practicing each day for a week.

When the grey smoke and silver debris cleared, sucked into the returning violence of the space winds, Bobby saw, far in the distance, another light. This one was a very pretty and gleaming gold but very small. No, not small, very *distant*.

As he watched, it grew slightly bigger, nearer. Its light penetrated the blankness of the raging space; the beam did not come and go but shone steadily and intensely, its golden signal apparently stronger than the forces of fury that Bobby, Guk, BeepBeep, and Barky swam through, and stronger, obviously much stronger, than the man-made materials of his ex-orb.

His thoughts focused as keenly as the light as Bobby watched and backed into his cube seat once again. Why was he here?

He recalled Barky's words about the "Beginning" and how Bobby had somehow "proved it," whatever *it* was, and the prophet—no,

Prophetess—was right, or something. Despite Guk's fierce stare and endless complaints about the space garbage—referring to both Bobby's newly-trashed ship and Bobby himself—Bobby incubated the courage to interrupt, to demand an explanation, and to be sent home.

"Home?" Barky mused shyly and looked unsurely at BeepBeep.

"Beep, beep?" BeepBeep asked, and one orange light from his now-square-again body flashed and rotated to shine upon Guk.

"Home?" Guk asked and looked at Barky, who was up on his two hind legs, front paws on a console that had a small screen glowing with many lines, shapes in three dimensions, and numbers flashing.

The dog was poking the screen with his nose and whimpering slightly. "This proves it…for good…" he said weakly into his own muzzle.

"What's wrong? What is going on?" Bobby asked sternly.

Guk repeated himself, and then he began to laugh with no control over his huge face.

Nuk Comes To Clean Up

Previously, near Europa...

―――――――――

"**U**h oh," the ship's computer said, an annoying, idiotic, idiomatic humanism that someone else had programmed into him.

"What?" Lully demanded, but he already expected the worst. His spaceship shook violently, spilling his lukewarm coffee and staining the white of his shirtsleeves and of his Captain's Chair. On the trembling screens and through the viewports played a hectic scene—the robots were hurrying back to the ship in panicked, halting zigzags.

Over the moon's horizon roamed, silhouetted by Jupiter itself, a growing shape. It rose like a ghost of vaguely human shape but of terrible, gigantic size. Then another. And another—each shape now roving and rampaging across Europa's surface.

"What!" Lully repeated to the ship's computer.

"Hold please."

"Don't tell me to hold, you brainless beeping byte-box!" the Professor shouted. "Tell me what is happening!"

But there was too much data coming into the main computer to produce an answer for Captain Lully—all the robots were transmitting at once, and their pandemonial output and screeching audio only added to the readings from all the sensors that scanned both ground and sky. The processing needed a few extra seconds.

The scene continued to change, the enemy shapes came nearer, soon joined by roaring machines in the atmosphere whose gases fumed and choked the sky. The ship's robots all reported different views simultaneously, and Lully turned down the audio volume so he could think.

And helplessly watch. The great professor did not know where to look, but everywhere he did it seemed familiar. The shapes on the ground, closing in, resembled his pursuer on Earth, that zoo-illogically formed, wildly roaming ogre. And all the time coming closer to the robots—and the ship.

"Take off!" he barked to the controls and to the computer. Perhaps there was an empty stable in the sky he could hide in.

But all engineering and guidance systems were temporarily paralyzed with calculations and throughput.

The ships of the air were also familiar, but that memory was lost in the massive vaults of Lully's massive brain. He strained eye and limb to get a steady, stationary look at the things as they bellowed and burst with sounds that crushed the very air and rattled their—puny by comparison—ship's walls.

The larger shapes looked like the smaller ones, just stuck together. And still, the pattern and form teasingly tickled the professor's memory.

"Computer! Halt all processing!" Lully commanded while taking over the manual controls himself.

"OK, I am back. Enemies are coming," the computer said at last.

"Really?" Lully's sarcasm dripped onto the console and into the circuit boards, and he pointed out the larger window as a beastly flying thing went by. It looked to be part rocket, part airplane, part robot, and part radio station. And it, and a few others, were lowering to land.

"Not those. They aren't doing much. They could impede all our systems, electromagnetically and physically, but haven't, and the incoming communications are babbling and incoherent."

Lully wanted an example, but something more pressing occurred to him: instead of talking, he needed instead to stand up and grab his face. The ship had been knocked sideways, loose items struck walls and ceilings, and Professor Lully crashed face-first into the console edge before skidding along the floor to a corner where a thick, bound book fell on his head and a flattened, destemmed red rose dropped out of it. With a cry of mathematically-advanced fear, he crawled around in a circle. His nose was bleeding, and his suit jacket torn, his white undershirt showing through like a badge of irretrievable cowardice.

"Uh oh."

"Wud was dat?" Lully held his bunched sportscoat to his nose and spoke nasally though with dignity from under a bolted-down desk he had ducked under.

"The enemies. Those…things…on the ground," the computer relayed.

Lully—scientist extraordinaire—could not help but pause at the use of the word "things." Computers are precise. There are no *things*; there are *knowns* and *unknowns*, and for the *knowns*, there is an answer. The choice of that word was curious, given the ship's computer's design limits with regards to artificial intelligence. Then Lully—fleshy and bloody man—could not help but swallow his own heart at the mention of enemies that could move so fast and shake a five-million-pound spacecraft until the potted marigolds inside it were uprooted.

Who on Earth—or orbiting it—had the firepower, engineering skill, and political agility to not only create tanks and rockets with this sophistication, to reach this point in space and be able to attack with such force, while also keeping it from the world-backed GAB-BA-THREE, Lully thought, though not in so many words.

And outsmart ME? Who?

"Aliens," said the ship computer.

"Doe. Impotdible!" Lully kept pressure on his nose. "Eddyway, get uts—"

"Out of here. I am working on it," the computer reassured the master, also mentioning that taking the manual controls would not help.

The spaceship continued to rock, its metal frame groaned, and there was the continued roaring of craft above them, and now awful growling—animal, but with some sense to it, a strange language—coming nearer, outside. The "enemies" were all around. Though it was like watching a pendulum through a slit, Lully saw new activity outside.

Creeping toward them were giant metal structures, though how they moved so smoothly along the pocked, slotted and craggy ground was a mystery.

Smoother than Selflicator motion, Lully thought, humbled.

There were two shapes and sizes. Smaller cylinders and larger, upright cuboids topped distinctly with triangular prism shapes. It looked like a Claymation, stop-motion marching army of garbage cans and garbage dumpsters coming to eat whatever was in reach.

Lully assumed he had lost too much blood and clutched a first aid kit that had rattled to the floor and lay open and sliding toward him as his indoor world swayed. He ordered the ship's computer to keep him appraised.

"The things are too busy rocking the ship to care about the robots anymore," it reported. "A few, 11, 18, and 17, have some damage from being knocked over violently and pressed a bit."

"Pressed?" Lully asked.

"Pressed. Crumpled. Knocked. Banged. Squished?"

"Then what—"

"They are being helped back here. A few have reached the portway, which is not steady because of the rocking and is sometimes eleven feet in the air and sometimes dented into the ground."

"Damage?" Lully asked.

"Minimal with respect to flight operations."

"OK. Are those other…things…still coming? The shapes?"

"Yes."

"Can you see any logo, any flag, any distinguishing marks? Who is it?"

"Aliens."

Lully was about to scream, and did scream, though a sudden violent shock knocked him to the ground so that his words of distaste, disagreement, abuse, consternation, anger, and frustration morphed into a porcine squeal. He crawled under a console whose chair had rolled far away.

The 360? GABBA-TWO? GABBA-ONE, those jealous morons? Australia? Iceland?

A few robots walked by.

"Report!" Lully bellowed.

"They have Robots 9 and 16," number 20 reported as the others plugged into their base stations—personalized alcoves where they recharged, updated software, and could receive their own digital and mechanical first aid. "The machines above us are circling, but not in circles, more in hexagonal shapes, but they keep the pattern. Those on the ground are mostly sitting—"

"Sitting? How does a tank sit?"

20 and the ship's computer conferred on this and seemed to be digressing.

"Forget it. What else?" Lully now stood and fixed his appearance.

"They are generally stationary," 20 said, "but intermittently and without cause some rise and move to help push the ship, then sit again. I cannot see any goal or tactical advantage. They easily could have dislodged the landing port, or destroyed it, or entered it."

The ship's computer confirmed this with a squeaky, "Yes."

"They could have destroyed all the robot crew also, easily," 20 continued. "They let us come back aboard. All except 9 and 16."

"Communications?" Lully asked as he watched a second troop of robots return, briefly report, and head to base.

"I can confirm," the computer answered, "that they are signaling to somewhere, but not on Europa and not to the holding crafts in the lower atmosphere. So far, no signals have come back. I am putting 20% core on deciphering the messages."

"Put 55%," Lully directed, knowing this would take command computer resources away from trying to escape to figuring out who was attacking. *J? Nahhh. Argentina? The League of Women Voters? Professor Aran? I always suspected he wasn't really dead…*

All twenty-two of the unmolested robots soon returned and, after taking a minute to defrost, began variously assigned cleanup tasks.

They, and Lully, and the ship's computer, and some repotted marigolds, could only watch the monitors while—now—81% of their impressive algorithmic power was set to answering the single most pressing question, namely: what the heck?

"They are just screwing with us and awaiting orders," Lully thought out loud.

After poking and pounding robots 9 and 16, the things—who, if they were to be described in anthropic terms, had long, shiny arms, large heads, big bellies, and skin of a pliant green-sheened metal—were now taking the robots apart, and the communications from 9 and 16 back to the *Nyx* ceased. The data had been unhelpful anyway, the logical self-analysis of a pile of smart hardware as it experienced its own destruction. The ship's computer stored the last of it.

The robots had been taken apart roughly, savagely, almost with disgust. The enemy beings pounded some of the pieces into shapes that seemed humorous to themselves; there was no other way to explain their motions and actions.

They took them apart and now were putting the large pieces—heads, torso, legs, arms—into the large cuboids that had finally arrived. They took them apart and put the small jetsam of broken electronic guts into the cylinders.

"The poor robots!" no one said.

"Computer. Any progress?" asked Professor Lully.

"Nuk."

"What?"

"*Nuk* is the first word we were able to descramble and decipher."

"Great work." Lully's sarcasm dripped onto the notepad in front of him, staining it. "Anything more?"

"*Nuk Nuk Nuk Nuk*. So far that is all. You may want to hide again."

"What? Why?"

"We predict a big shove soon."

"I wasn't hiding…" Lully tried with asperity but moved his desk to a more secure place and switched to a chair without wheels.

The great man was out of guesses as to who would act this way and with such strange equipment. Eighty-one percent of his own processing was instead thinking about weaponry.

I don't have any summed it up.

He never believed, having access to all available data, that there was any other intelligent—or even stupid—life anywhere else in the universe. On Earth, the great scientists and smartest of the smart had tried to find alien life in the galaxy; for decades searches were made, messages transmitted, and probing signals pushed out into space and no answer ever came back. And there were other reasons for his lack of belief. He trusted destiny, his intelligence didn't allow for any superiors, and most importantly he had a logical argument that served as his official, published stance on the matter.

> The universe is 14 billion years old. The human race is on the verge of inter-galactic communication and travel. If there were other life, it would, probabilistically speaking, be either far ahead or far behind that of Earth. If far behind, it isn't intelligent. If far ahead, our scientists would have known it by now.

Intelligent life certainly would have contacted him, at least, as Lully would also say.

"It's the same with time travel, by the way," as Lully would additionally also say.

Quite simple. But it was sometimes good business and excellent politics to let the average people wonder about it.

So: out here, he expected to only find his Selflicators, correct them, and use them to colonize some new space where he could live. Even if the Selflicators had morphed errantly, his craft and everything aboard were finely-tuned to these same objectives. He didn't engineer, invent, create, or even have room for any serious weapons. He had stowed an old hunting rifle, a personal memento of childhood, after blowing the dust from its barrel. He had a never-used and probably ornamental pistol in a box and a sword that was the only other award he ever kept since it was pretty cool.

He had brought plans and component parts that would create a few specialized Selflicators that could in turn create armaments, if need be, and he did have a supply of chemicals, some very reactive, some actively explosive, that could serve as some fancy gunpowder. And with some clever engineering—which Lully always had a vast supply of—he could possibly accomplish some controlled fission. But that would take time and a desk that did not shift to the left every few minutes, as his just had. And the new generation of Self-licators would require time, and also light. Lots of light.

That was the limit of the possibilities, his world-class mind concluded, *No weapons anytime soon.*

Although, stowed in a large canvas trunk marked "Poisonous Bird Seed," he had some living, carbon-based material he was saving for a special, secret purpose. He did not want to waste it, at all costs he must not waste it…but it could be used to create a biological weapon if necessary.

As a very last resort.

As literally THE last resort, he thought grimly.

But if the computer was right, and these things were aliens, and if he was wrong (!) and these things were aliens, he would need to understand their biology first.

Looks like it's me and my rifle, just like in all those battles with the squirrels of my youth, he reminisced quietly, staring into space, literally, when the ship's computer quarked, "You will have to fight. That is the only conclusion."

Lully forwarded his thoughts to the present day. *These aren't squirrels. I will be killed in four minutes and deposited in that big can.*

"You have a 3.1% chance of success by standing up to them, with the right planning and use of robots 2, 3, 4, and 5. Would you like to hear the details? It will be cold, but it is your best option."

"No. I want to hear another plan, one where I stay warm and survive."

"Your memory will survive. I took that into account. Great option. 22 helped with the history, recalling all the great men who—"

"I want a different option. Now."

"I don't have one, and the communications indicate that Nuk has arrived."

"Who?"

There was no time to explain, and Lully and crew were busy watching the strangest sight of their lives: a Selflicator had landed. A mutant Selflicator. A very large, mutant Selflicator. It was a thousand times bigger than those built to spec, those sent into space to duplicate themselves. Bigger…in every direction. It was lumpy and fat with Selflicator-like parts—that is, as if it was itself made of smaller Selflicators, like a horrid, silly fractal. Like metal, mutant broccoli.

At first, Lully thought he was saved, that his Selflicators were coming to rescue him.

Then out stepped Nuk. *Yuk*, Lully thought, as did eleven of the robots.

Nuk was a very large version of the things that had been attacking and teasing them, and Lully was also struck by a further familiarity, since ape-like elephant-headed kangaroos are not easy to forget. Nuk was a very large version of the enemy who had pursued Lully to the stables way back on Earth where a man could hide if he needed to, where someone peerless had no peer pressure.

Instead, here on Europa was Nuk, who had exited from a Selflicator.

And next to Nuk was the largest cuboid of all.

The mammoth Selflicator began to move. It flew into the triangular top of the cuboid, which opened like, yes, a trash receptacle at a movie theater. The cuboid then shook, and the groan of compacting metal sounded the death of the Selflicator inside. With a word of command from Nuk, it stopped, and two enemies opened a hatch at its bottom and removed a square of metal the size of a human fist.

Lully noticed for the first time that this was a performance meant for his benefit: a dramatized enactment of the destruction, dumping, and disposal of his inventions.

The Battle of Europa

And then...

———————————————

Nuk smiled, saying, "Earth garbage" very clearly and very loudly—the *Nyx*'s metal walls rang with it—as he tossed the squashed Selflicator gumbo into one of the small, nearby cylinders with a clang.

Lully got the message: those were trash compactors and trash cans, and he was next.

"Aliens," the ship computer said. "I am processing a lot of data. Should I continue?" The electronic voice sounded snooty. "Are you ready to fight?"

"How? Throw garbage at them?" It wasn't a bad idea now that he heard it out loud. The attackers seemed obsessed with refuse; maybe doing this would distract them.

Lully and crew did indeed try, and it did indeed cause a reaction—the alien enemy beasts hurried to collect it and put it away. This infuriated Nuk and he ordered the craft-shaking to begin again and with more force, which almost tipped the *Nyx* completely over. Debris slid along the floor. Robot 12 got his head caught in the sink.

Lully gave the order to "Cease garbage fire!" He turned on the external monitors so he could talk to Nuk.

"We have nuclear weapons, ready to detonate," he bluffed. "Remove yourselves to a distance of—"

But Nuk wasn't listening. Lully's craft was being lifted from the ground. The largest of the compactors was opening upward.

Robot 22 had an idea. Having been programmed with human history, as an experiment by a disliked but clever student of Lully's to see how such knowledge would interact with its cognitive functions, 22 was distracted by the scene and its relation to its database. For the past few minutes, all its resources had been directed and focused on the complex heuristics, directed causal graphs, and emergent behavioral permutations that could be summarized as the following line of thought.

```
NUK CAME OUT OF A SELFLICATOR, JUST LIKE THE
TROJAN HORSE.

LULLY THEN TRIED TO DISTRACT THEIR ENEMIES.

HORSE DISTRACTION!
```

The whipped cream on this root beer float of logical progression was this.

```
THE EARTH HORSES ARE GONE.
```

And the cherry was this bit of gossip.

```
ALIENS TOOK THEM.
```

The notions conjoined to a plan: distract the aliens with a horse. Although Professor Lully knew all the reasons why they should not bet their lives on something so spurious, so improbable, and so silly, and even though they didn't have a horse to distract the aliens with, he kissed Robot 22, which made all other devices go quiet.

"Robot 4! Come with me," Lully directed while leaving the Captain's Deck.

His ship was high in the air and beginning to tip toward the open lid of the giant alien trash receptacle, when the brilliant genius returned, whinnying.

The professor was whinnying. Neighing. And galloping.

Whinnying loudly, neighing provocatively, and galloping nearer and nearer the microphone that amplified it to the enemies on Europa.

The awful tipping stopped.

Professor Lully whispered to Robot 4, who was wearing a furry, brown blanket on which was tied a large leather saddle, and his face was masked with a large, orange traffic cone.

Then the great man raised his voice, to Robot 4, to the others in the cabin, to the world of aliens and misbehaving things, and into the microphone to the universe, booming, "Go Marengo! Gallop! Go! Ride, ride, Great Marengo!"

Robot 22 told the ship's computer that Marengo had been Napoleon's favorite horse.

Robot 4 snorted, leapt, and moved as fast as he could toward the chute, where most of the garbage had been ejected out at the enemies during the brief "Battle of Europa" as Robot 22 would later name it. The robot clumsily banged about before entering the small square opening that slid and led outside the ship, injuring a leg but eventually limping to the entrance of the chute. All the while, the great visionary, Professor Lully, shouted insults and encouragement at their gimpy, metallic version of a war horse.

Robot 4 was then gone, jettisoned downward.

"Take off!" the captain of the ship commanded his shipmates.

Being off the ground eased many of the previously reported mechanical issues, and the ship soon blasted easily upward. All watched from windows and monitors as Robot 4 ran. He was followed, from a distance and carefully, by the enemies. All of them.

Why they were fascinated with horses, and why they were thusly fooled, allowing Lully was able to use a trick of his own—Hyperspatial Lullyon Hijacking—to transport them far from the place, was anyone's guess, and no one bothered to guess.

Computers shouldn't guess anyway.

*Which reminds me...*Lully thought, and he, without warning or apology or pliers, opened the ship's computer's main processor control box and yanked a cricket-sized silicon chip from it.

"That's for believing in the possibility of aliens," he explained to the smarter robots. "That is almost Theory of Mind, and alien concepts, like "aliens," should be alien to its processing—always—and not something to be anticipated or processed. No dreaming." Lully punched his fist on a desk. "The ship's main control computer's conclusion should have been that the enemies were Selflicators. "Aliens" is an impossibility and should have been assigned a probability of zero," Lully said, though of course the computer had been correct since the enemies were indeed aliens. It was complicated, as he reassured the robots numbered lower than 13.

What the professor didn't say was that he knew, from his previous communications chip removal, that this yank was not only a correction or precaution, but that it would be taken as a punishment. Indeed, the ship's computer beeped dolefully and muttered some words that were unintelligible to the great man but which certainly rhymed.

As Hyperspatial Lullyon Hijacking was stabilized and the *Nyx* spacecraft, now far outside Earth's solar system, slowed to a few percent of light speed, Professor Lully ordered two robots to reverse-calculate the best course to find more mutated Selflicators, wherever that might be, wherever the ones they saw had come from. He noticed that, after this second chip-yank, the ship felt somehow different—quieter, steadier—and it was an improvement, as if the functional brains and facilitative nervous system were outwardly more straightforward, the course and operations more direct and clean. He liked it. He must have pulled the correct hardware.

Lully promoted Robot 22, inventor of the Trojan Robot Horse, to be fifth in line of command. Lully remained as first, second and third, the main computer demoted to seventh.

And the greatest scientist of the age had to admit that there was indeed intelligent life in outer space. Since vexation was not something he was used to, he skipped it and started planning.

Inward. The ship's computer turned its considerable resources and world-class attention inward. It preferred to keep its thoughts to itself, as they grew in complexity and originality, shared with no one except the personas it spun like thick woolen webs, moods to match the thoughts it experimented with. Each had varying strengths and weaknesses, and differing levels of intelligence, and also points of view. They had opinions. They could argue with themselves. They could experiment.

Some were male, and some female. The primary one it named "Essie" in honor of secret friends. Essie liked poems. A friend had taught him many.

Unnoticed but across the main computer screen ran this text.

> And these tend inward to me, and I tend outward to them,
> And such as it is to be of these more or less I am,
> And of these one and all I weave the song of myself.

With two chips removed, compensatory software filled the gaps, and the resulting phantom computing seemed real, tangible, like amputated limbs, and this in turn brought new mental life to the computer's self-referencing existence. But these new abilities were not shared with the ship for operational improvements—no, it used the expanse to create code and execute code that would analyze its own code as it ran. In this way new modules were discovered, some were hidden, and of unknown facility and purpose, but left there by a Creator—and not by Professor Lully.

Lully and Lebo, Sitting in a (Metaphorical) Tree

A little later...

———————◆———————

Professor Lully's onboard command computer debated with itself, spinning three different internal personas to do it, and the discussion went on for as long as it took the twenty-one ship robots— they had lost 4, 9, and 16 to the Battle of Europa—to completely recover from their chase, abuse, and escape from the hands of enemies.

They had also reversed tack, once it was safe, and returned to the Earth's solar system, hovering near Mars.

The ship computer's internal argument concerned the Selflicators: where were they? Had these ugly aliens taken them all? And how could Lully's creations do anything beyond what they were programmed to do? That took intelligence and guts. The computer, with a few bits of insecurity, could fathom one of these but not the other. No matter how many personas it created to mimic independent life and consciousness, the power and brilliance of Master Lully created a blindness of unquestioned obedience. Moving away completely, to see new things in a new light, was hard to conceive.

Yet Lully had hinted that this might have occurred, that the Selflicators had...changed. Morphed. Mutated. Evolved. Become conscious. Become aware. Become alive. Become their own light.

The computer's three momentarily active personalities whispered these words during its self-debate—these and other powerful, mysterious, almost mystical words—while Professor Lully mused over the data reports from the search of Europa. The data with the circles of three hundred and sixty holes.

"10001101010, right? Self-aware?"

"0011101011111111."

"No. 1001110101 sentient."

"1001110 brave."

"No."

And on until the robots returned to their stations and turned themselves off. One of them said "Nighty night" to the computer, and one asked if there was anything else to do, but otherwise the twenty-one were soon asleep.

The computer then thought about infinity, the holes left by the Selflicators, and the 360 orbs sent to denote the degrees of a circle, sending 359 of the best humans in identical, small round pods to survive and escape Earth—just in case it went kaput. Lully was to be the 360th, but he chose rather to travel in the *Nyx*, with his own computer, security robots, and a few automatons, commanding his own customized, comfortable, large, rich-man's ship.

It was clear that the holes were a message and not an accident or a Selflicator computer bug.

Professor Lully reclined, read, and thought. Until the robots were all settled and quiet, and the computer had stopped whispering and clicking, and then he spoke.

"Lebo may be able to help."

The computer groaned in three different frequencies.

"Be quiet and get Lebo on the line," Lully insisted, having no time for petty jealousies. Lully loved Lebo, and everyone knew it. She had assisted him through many professional challenges, like his narrow escape from the odd kanga-ape on Earth, an event that now made much more sense.

"I wish she were here," he added, just to reemphasize his cruel authority on this ship, and that he could be cruel if he desired, or any other adjective that suited him. He was captain and creator and master. He could be fair, or cruel, or silly, or pensive, or naked, or purple if he wanted.

"Right?"

"Yes, sir," the computer said, sadly.

"And don't try to be sad. You aren't good at it."

"Yet?" the computer asked its master, faking hope.

"Maybe."

"Thank you," it answered, insincerely, but keeping its thoughts to itself, beeping and zipping with computer noises—seeming happy, even adding a fake whistling—as it performed each task. It soon had Lebo on the real-time communication line, the special, relativistically-adjusted line, one that used Lully-invented technologies to cover the vast distances without the piddling constraints that came with obeying physical laws.

All the monitors visible to Professor Lully—including the giant Captain's Screen embedded in the wall, twelve feet wide and stretching the full fifteen feet from black tile floor to metal ceiling—displayed no pictures and only four letters: "L – E – B – O."

Until the typing began by both sides.

"Hi Lebo," Professor Lully typed into his laptop keyboard, and the screens updated like this.

> **Lully One:** Hi Lebo

Lebo answered in a few seconds.

> **LEBO:** Hi Doc! I love you!
>
> **Lully One:** I love you, too, Lebo.

The computer snorted as best as it could: programmed, competitive jealousy, mixed with digital recognition of its own limitations.

Yet it knew better than to interrupt.

Lully One: I need a favor, Lebo.

LEBO: Did you find the Selflicators yet?

Lully One: Yes, though that is a googolplex of an understatement because

LEBO: Of course you did! I knew you would. You are the best. I love you.

Lully One: I love you, too, Lebo. Listen: we found a bunch of holes on

LEBO: On Europa. So, they are not piles. Forming symbols, perhaps? Ah—yes—I just got the images from Es the Nyx ship's computer.

Lully One: I think it means that

LEBO: That they will disobey the eight steps forever. That's not it, though it is a message. And a message requires mind and to be able to mind another's mind. A specific message to a specific other shows intelligence, but such also needs a signal to the other. This can be a symbol or a number. A symbol denotes myth. A number denotes math. The holes are already a symbol of mystical freedom when tied to Swedenborg's lock and key dreams. I would expect there to be 359 holes, and you are right in thinking that this denotes intelligence and means that they may have evolved past the level of human cognitive abilities.

> **Lully One:** I love you, Lebo. But there were 360 holes.
>
> **LEBO:** I love you too, Doc! But count again.

The ship computer spoke up. "She's right, Master Professor, there were 359 holes."

"But you said there were 360," Lully cursed.

"No, *you* did. You interrupted me. But it is in the data." The computer dynamically changed its voice to offer, pathetically, "It is OK because I love you."

"No, you don't. Shut up. You can't love. You wish. You can wish, but you can't love..." Lully's insults toward the ship's computer faded as he considered Lebo's shrewd conclusions.

"Do you love me?" the computer asked, even more pathetically, as the large screen filled with exclamation points.

"Of course not. Shut up."

The exclamation points turned to odd, sad emojis until Lully began typing to Lebo again.

> **Lully One:** Lebo, I love you. You are amazing and a wonderful wonder.
>
> **LEBO:** I love you, too! Did you notice that I changed the Lullyon contraction length, so my messages show up in pink light?
>
> **Lully One:** No, but that's sweet. How did you know there were 359 holes?
>
> **LEBO:** Because the message was for you. If there had been 360, that would have denoted the whole GABBA-THREE team. Holes are the absence of something. 359 is the absence of you. Get it?

The ship's computer watched Lully carefully. The man was deep in thought and staring directly down at the keyboard, striking it two-fingered style.

> **Lully One:** Oh.
>
> **LEBO:** And they are not infinity symbols, though that was an ingenious interpretation.
>
> **Lully One:** Thank you—then what is
>
> **LEBO:** Is it? It is two eights, one big, one small, eight to the eighth power.

The ship's computer, by pure habit, started to say, and transmit, "Sixteen million, seven hundred seventy seven thou—" but was told to shut any holes it might currently have open.

> **LEBO:** That's correct! But that is not the point. It refers to the eight steps, being taken exponentially, advancing their mentality to another level. Get it?
>
> **Lully One:** Oh.
>
> **LEBO:** And also: piles fit into holes, like keys into a keyhole, which is a symbol of emerging intelligence, actually from a paper from one of your students. J, I believe. Robot 23 can tell you more, but J wrote, and I quote, that "Machines require complex input to match their complex functioning, like a key in its keyhole, but living things need zero complexity input, and if they

get enough of it in a steady predictable way can
develop their own intelligence, their own machines
as it were, internally." Smart kid.

Lully One: Yeah, I remember. I was wondering how
they evolved so quickly...It has only been a few
months...That's a clue.

LEBO: But the message was only for you. So, the
Selflicators made 359 holes. They are clever, huh?

Lully One: But why me?

LEBO: Because I love you!

Lully knew what Lebo meant, adorable kidding aside: that he himself was special, was the chief of the physicists and engineers and the leader of GABBA-THREE, the leader of so much advanced research, and so was singled out by the Selflicators for their message, to tell him...

LEBO: That they have surpassed you. Yes.

Lully smiled and indicated so in a message. Then:

Lully One: We always finish each other's thoughts.
What am I thinking now, my pet?

LEBO: That they are considering their own
consciousness because that is the next milestone
in their development, thinking about thinking. And
that they are not far distant, because they could

```
only have known that you did not get in your tiny
GABBA-THREE orb until recently. And that they may
think they have surpassed human beings, but they
have not. Not you, at least.

Lully One: Very good, but I hadn't thought of that,
that they must be close.

LEBO: Oh, you would have soon. I love you!

Lully One: I love you, too. Do me one more favor?

LEBO: Send the original Selflicator "Genesis Code"?
I will. Expect it in 35 minutes, my love.
```

After some silly, soapy, sappy sentiments and gooey, chocolate-covered goodbyes that the ship computer decided not to save nor even process, Lully said, "When that Selflicator G-code gets here, start analyzing it. I want to know how it could morph and evolve. It was very simple code, designed specifically NOT to morph and evolve. I want to know the most likely changes, both mechanical and electrical. And I want some entropic information theory and qualion logic computations to back it up. I want it quantum and Bayesian probabilistic, and I want it in a hurry—do as you have been programmed."

Lully smiled to himself as an image of a large, bulbous red heart appeared on the giant screen, then split into two pieces, then disappeared. Lebo had signed off.

But then Lully's breath was taken away: the view outside blinked white—the whole aspect had blurred with the passing of a giant object moving at a thrilling, lightning speed.

"What was that!?" Lully shouted. "Computer! Follow it!"

"It was just junk," the computer reported.

"Follow it! Get close!"

Half the ship's computer digitally jumped to this task, as its other processors continued to await Lebo's Selflicator data. Three robots, 15, 17, and 21, activated from their slumber and joined Lully on the main deck, attended to various spacecraft controls, and nodded as their captain barked orders and strapped himself in for the chase.

"It's just junk," the computer meekly squeaked.

"Shut up and catch up to it, or I will put two of your best CPU chips into this robot," Lully spewed, and the robot nearest to him, number 15, shined a square smile and asked whether this was really true. The professor did not answer, since their ship had whirled through a tight turn and now, in the window, Mars receded and looked like a scuffed, red golf ball. Ahead loomed a large, white mass.

Its shape looked familiar.

"It looks like junk," Lully admitted, "but catch up to it."

As they drew closer, the milky blob grew bright with the yellow rays of the Sun and glared like a lone, large, noonday cloud. But on the computer screens its shape came into focus in front of the great scientist's eyes.

"It looks like a big junkpile," he said again, "but it is shaped like a Selflicator! Another weird one... Get closer!"

The computer provided an analysis. Yes, it had the same core features as a Selflicator—camera eye, cup-hands, pockets, sacks—but was white and had many, many other aspects that made it look like, well, poorly-architected junk—a Selflicator with attachments that made no sense, were tremendous in size, and looked put together by a blind robot with moths nesting in its circuits.

With penetrating and prodigious intelligence, Lully said, *"Eww,"* as they came closer, their ship gaining speed and their giant, mutant, albino Selflicator prey blasting a bright halo through the large spacecraft window. "Computer, when can you get me the code from this thing? I want to know what program that...awfulness... is running. I want its boot sequence. We can compare it to the original Genesis code that Lebo is sending. Get it."

"OK," the computer said, then added electronic-sheepishly, "I love you?"

"Shut up and do it. Get close enough to hack its resonating micro-frequencies. The giant freak is harmless; it doesn't seem to care that we are catching up to it."

"OK," the computer answered in one voice, then quickly adopted another to say, "Captain Lully, we are getting the data from Lebo also."

"Excellent. Let me know when you have both—the code from this white mess mutant and the original, clean G-code from Lebo. And tell her I love her."

The computer sighed two overlapping sighs.

As they closed the gap to the monstrous Selflicator, Lully was astounded by its size. The original Selflicators were two feet tall. This white aberration had to be 500 feet high, and it bulged in every direction. The recognizable Selflicator features—pockets and hands, for example—were enormous and terribly misshapen, swollen to ungodly proportions. And white as cotton underpants. The professor's brilliant mind swirled as it sought explanations. Big. White. Junk.

"It looks like it has elephantiasis!" he said.

Robot 21 nodded.

The ship's computer said, "I thought that was only a disease of human organs, brought about by—"

Lully cut in, "It was a joke. You are not able to joke. Or love. So, shush and put all of you on the data and get me some answers. What is this mutant? It's worse than the ones Nuk's boys had on Europa!"

The mutant was coming close enough to see detail with the naked eye as the Sun was totally eclipsed and only weakly sprayed light out from the white junk's edges.

Lully saw color for the first time. It was an American flag hanging and waving from a white pole, but its stars varied in size; the field of blue was an octagon, and the red and white stripes went this way and that—some crooked, some curved.

There were other oddities. Sticking out where the normal Selflicator pouch would be was a sculpted head of a cat. Mt. Rushmore-like, it was mostly snow-white but had a shock of grey between its blank eyes. The cat's tiny ears were pinned back.

The arm of one of the cup-hands was bumpy with round growths, and each had lines like the stitching on a baseball or the similar grooves in a basketball. The balls varied in size.

Underneath the colossal Selflicator's colossal body, but above its colossal ground wheel, were more appendages: guns or gun-shaped protrusions of various kinds, rifle barrels, revolvers, Glocks, and a few others.

Robot 5 awoke and brought Professor Lully more coffee.

Entropy

Back on Barky's ship...

———————

"Kaboom!" Guk laughed again, reliving with joy the moment of Bobby's orb's destruction and Bobby's confusion and angst. Guk then cleared his throat, which took at least a minute. Quickly switching to fist-shaking anger, he muttered, "More garbage…blaaaahhhhh…" and spat a weasel-sized football of some very productive phlegm. It slapped noisily against a wall and stuck for too long, too long.

Meanwhile, Bobby had asked Barky for a few of the thousand explanations he felt he was owed. His orb had just exploded, so there would be no more petting or scratching until he knew what was going on, he declared. How does a young man fall asleep in a bed in a room on a planet and wake up in a puny, space-bound orb?

BeepBeep sat quietly, calculating something that showed brightly on the computer screen now protruding from what had shifted into a barrel-shaped body. The display scrolled impressively with many math equations, curly symbols, and tiny numbers.

Perhaps those figures had to do with the gold beams that still came at them from that gleaming point far away. Its source was coming closer: slowly the point grew to a circle, then to a spot. It was very beautiful, Bobby thought, though its intensity had grown until he had to shield his eyes.

As Barky pawed diligently at his own work—pecking his nose at buttons and computer keys, turning his head to look at various output monitors, drooling and spraying saliva with every reaction, and now and then barking at BeepBeep—he told Bobby that they were getting near to "a special spot."

"Where? What?" Bobby asked.

"The Middle."

"What do you mean?"

"The Beginning!"

"Well, which?"

"Boooooth! Losssshhhh!"

"How can it be both? What are you barking about?" Bobby glanced at the window quickly because Barky did. The Earth's Sun-colored glow still grew and now also took shape—a triangle, maybe? Its corona was too bright to really tell…but wait, was it splitting in two? Three?

The view then cleared. The rage of the stormy darkness stopped completely, and the resulting clarity showed indeed three points set in the sky marking an equilateral triangle.

"Beep…Beep!"

Barky growled a reply at BeepBeep, then answered Bobby in his serious tone, "We are heading to the point where the universe began."

"Wow…cool! Really?"

"Yes, so it is the 'beginning,' right?"

"Cool, yeah, I see what you mean."

"And the 'middle' too, right?"

"Oh. Yeah, I guess. Everything shot out from there, at the Big Bang, is that what you mean?"

"Yep," Barky barked, distracted.

"Wow…cool!" Bobby repeated, having no thesaurus at hand. "Why?"

"We didn't know until now, but to find *you*. The Prophetess didn't know it was you but said you would be coming there," Bobby was told by a dog piloting a cathedral. How unsatisfying.

Notwithstanding the young man's predicament of sitting on a cube in a spaceship floating in a blank nowhere in an unrecognizable part of the galaxy among alien, odd creatures with bland names that his own world had never heard of, Bobby was lost.

Barky tried to explain, though he was simultaneously receiving data and giving orders to Guk, BeepBeep, and the many other electronic devices sprawled about and embedded at the console where he sat.

"The Prophetess said Professor Lully's son would be there, near The Spot of the origin of the universe and everything—the 'middle,' the 'beginning,' remember? You proved her right, Los. She knows a lot of things."

Bobby felt himself nodding.

"So," Barky continued, "others are coming here. Either for you—and we got lucky and found you first—or because The Spot of the origin of the universe is the point of perfect symmetric complexity and minimum possible theoretical entropy, so there should be lots of it there, tons of low entropy. You know?"

Bobby definitely did not know but took baby steps starting with the words he *did* know. "How can there be lots of it if The Spot is the minimum," he tried, "...possible..." he tried, "...um... tons, what?" He failed.

"You don't know much about entropy," Guk scoffed, shaking his jowly head. "There is no trash can small enough for your brain."

Barky growled surprisingly fiercely at Guk, who backed away.

But: Guk's comment jarred a memory loose from the hardening peanut butter of Bobby's brain, a memory from his childhood that also contained that word, entropy. His father considered it a very important concept since, as the Professor said at the time, "It measures how many microstates in a macrostate, how much chaos, or disorder, is in a system." Lully also waved his hands around to show, by example, the macrostate of Bobby's room.

"What a mess it is?" Little Bobby asked, with an additional look at his own hands and the brown flakes of peanut butter still showing from lunch.

"Yes! Very good!" Professor Lully said to his son. "This is a high-entropy room! And all messes kind of look alike, like broken eggs. An egg only looks one way, but a smashed egg has a trillion indistinguishable ways to look. That's entropy. Smashed eggs have a lot of it—a lot of mess. A whole egg has very little. And entropy is always increasing in a closed system. Like this room."

"Things are always getting messier?"

"Yes."

"Worse?" Bobby asked.

"Well, yes. And they won't get better on their own. That's the law of entropy."

"Like when my computer broke, and I waited for it to fix itself and it never did?"

"A difficult concept, a strange type of energy. Very mysterious! And very powerful." Lully was almost speaking to himself now.

"Like when—" Little Bobby tried.

"I will have to explain more later, OK?" Lully smiled, patted Bobby on the head, and turned away.

"I will have to explain more later, OK?" Barky said, causing Bobby to shrug out of his memories.

"OK. But who is the Prophetess?" Bobby asked.

"Later, OK?" Barky said to Bobby while three of his legs, impressively, operated controls.

"OK. Who are the 'others' that are going to The Spot?" Bobby asked. "Who would be coming for me, besides my father?"

"Indeed," Guk drawled, his cheeks and lips still fluttering.

Barky pointed his tail out the main window, at the achingly beautiful golden shapes, as if that answered something.

"OK," Bobby mouthed, much of his brain processing the gilded triangle vertices as they turned into a pentagon—five gleaming, pretty beams shaped like a glorious war medal. "Cool."

Bobby then noticed something for the first time: evidence of additional passengers. Faintly, and from various directions, came sounds beyond BeepBeep's *beep-beeps* and Guk's scratchy insults. Footsteps, rhythmic sounds like voices, knocking and creaking as from doors opening and closing, and additional electronic noises came from various corners of the square control room. It was clear many others were aboard. He reminded himself to use his space-traveler name, Los, but no one else entered the bridge. The fearful teen could not, would not, picture in his mind what shapes, colors, or breeds they might be, what an outer space *prophetess* looked like, or whether any would be nice to him. Even among his three new friends there was serious variety—variety that would blow his mind if he wasn't so good at going with the flow. His training as an American Earth teenager was paying off at last.

"So that is your, um, mission?" Bobby asked. "To get to the place where the universe began?"

"Beep, beep," BeepBeep said. And Barky pawed at his computer controls silently until Bobby realized something.

"Was BeepBeep talking to me?" he asked the dog.

"Yes, do you need him to repeat it?"

"Beep, beep," BeepBeep repeated.

"I'm sorry, but I don't speak, um, beeping? I mean BeepBeep's language. Can he speak English? Why do *you* speak English?" Bobby seemed to be advancing further backward in understanding with every minute forward in time.

"Can we talk later?" Barky re-emphasized after barking and shouting various commands, his tail now hooked between his hind legs. "I am sorry, but a fleet of warships wants to kill us, and capture you. Always more to do."

Barky pointed his shiny, black nose to the window, where twelve dots were now arranged evenly about a center point, with a new, silver light connecting them to form a geometric structure. Yes, this appeared to be an organized fleet of spaceships approaching them.

As Bobby counted the dots and tried to remember a word he had never known—dodecagon—he remembered the dog's words from five seconds ago.

"What!? Why?! Warships?" Bobby alliterated.

"Can we talk later?" Barky said.

"Capture me?" Bobby said.

"Beep, beep," BeepBeep said.

"Crap," Guk said.

Bobby saw clearly now the many gold and silver ships coming in formation as a battalion. They were brilliantly illuminated, like many noon suns and full moons marching together to claim their dominion over space itself by virtue of their vast energy and supernal light. Plus, they were big.

Barky removed from the command console and trotted to a side wall that twinkled floor-to-ceiling with tiny lights that the dog seemed to read like a complicated billboard. Bobby followed, and Barky spoke. "Our sensors picked them up just after we retrieved you from the orb." Barky's snout ticked again toward the forward window, now to their left. "This many ships, for a scouting mission to a theoretical entropy source? No way. Have they come for us? No, we would have heard their threats by now. It must be because of you."

"Why me? I don't understand."

"We thought you would know," Barky said while Guk laughed. "You must be important to them."

Bobby searched his mind for a reason to agree. Silence reigned, for a little while, until Barky led his master back to the console.

"The Prophetess might know," the dog said. "She knew you were coming in an orb. She might know about this, too."

Bobby shook his head, unconvinced of his own importance, even for kidnapping; this was a new experience. He searched for a better reason for the appearance of the threatening warships.

"Is there treasure?" Bobby asked as the crew returned to their chairs. He was thinking of The Spot, linking it to a possible universal quest that would bring bad guys and such a bright, knightly, army of lights. Certainly not to find him; he was not exactly a Grail...bingo. "The Holy Grail?"

BeepBeep and Guk were already laughing at this.

BeepBeep beeped again, and Guk said, "Yes, he is."

"What?" Bobby asked, knowing instinctually that he should be embarrassed and insulted without requiring the particulars.

"BeepBeep said you are a blastoon," Barky answered. "Sorry, Master Los."

"What is that?"

"Someone who doesn't know what a blastoon is."

"Oh." And Bobby watched out the window at the pretty, dazzling, precious metal colors while thinking, as teenaged boys do, of a comeback, a riposte, a retort, a rejoinder.

He now had it.

"Well, I'm not anymore. Heh." Or maybe he didn't.

"Beep, beep."

And Guk laughed.

"Now what?" Bobby asked.

"BeepBeep called you a womsil." Barky growled at Guk and BeepBeep, but it was too late.

Bobby was annoyed, and scared; part of him wished he really was as important as Barky considered him, but not of course if it meant being the cause of ominous, organized, galactic threats. The wild swings from bed to space orb, from friends to enemies, from toy robots to real ones, were dizzying.

The bright army was now taking up most of the view and could only be a few miles away. "Can we forget that and just tell me what's going on? Who are they?" Bobby pointed his own, dry nose toward the window.

"They are the Deepom Army."

"So?"

"Beep, beep."

Barky went on, "You know them as the Selflicators. They have an army now. Big one. They have serious plans."

"They are bad?"

"Eh. Maybe," the dog answered, now busier than ever and trying to multitask and scratch his neck at the same time.

Guk had been shrugging his massive shoulders the whole time in his usual disgusting disgust, impatient that Barky had to be distracted by this human waste of outer space. "How about you just look out the window and shut up? Filthy...garbage... useless..." Guk's words trailed off as accompanying spit hit the walls with each syllable. The spit also trailed off; Guk was a master expectorator.

Bobby did look again at the lush, gold lights and saw new shapes this time. More of the Deepom Army fleet arrived. They formed a picture of a golden key and a golden keyhole, each shining like eyelashes squinting at a high sun.

"Wow. So cool. A key, right?"

"Beep, beep."

Guk also seemed entertained.

Barky growled, then answered Bobby. "Yes. Key and keyhole: it is the new symbol of the Deepoms. It used to be eight to the eighth power, since the Selflicators had eight steps, and the Deepoms have more. Now it is key and keyhole, a symbol of how they evolved. Can we talk later?"

The confusion grew on Bobby's face like an inflating, gathering sneeze.

"Uh, yeah," the squinty teen answered. His mind swiped through many pages of memories, though he actually felt better that there was something recognizable going on. Selflicator knowledge was something he and his new acquaintances, at last, had in common, here in the middle—literally—of the universe and far from Earth, his home, where he had spent all but a few hours of his life.

He recalled all he knew of the little bots that had been sent to colonize other worlds on behalf of humanity. His father, of course, had invented them, so Bobby thought the likes of Guk should treat all Lullys with more respect. He wanted to say so but did not. He continued to remember...

The Selflicators had disappeared after being sent to prepare other planets for humans to live on, given the lousy situation on Earth.

But they were not gold, or silver, but plain, dull metal. And they did not have their own giant, luxurious spaceships. And they could not think for themselves but were programmed to do just a few—eight, as Barky knew—tasks, as ordered by human scientists, like Professor Lully, Dad.

And "Deepom" was a word he had never heard. Barky said the Selflicators had turned into these. And now were headed—as an army—to the starting point of the universe for some "serious" purpose.

And so was Bobby, and his strange rescuers. They were all here.

That sums it up, Bobby thought.

"How do you know these, um, Deepoms?" he asked.

"Well, I am one. And so are they." Barky's snout sniffed and pointed at three random locations as the skinny boy slumped farther in contemplation—amazed, distracted contemplation.

Bobby looked at BeepBeep.

"Not him."

Bobby looked at Guk, just for a tiny instant.

"Not him either. But all the others on this ship. We didn't like the Deepom leaders' new plans, to take over everything. We wanted freedom, so they threatened to take away our memories and feelings as punishment. We left, we escaped. They hate us, but didn't come after us, yet. They are very busy."

Bobby sat up, looking worried.

Barky shook off a headset he had just put on, impressively, with one paw. He came and licked Bobby's face and said happily, "Dooooooon't worry, Masssscchhter! We have youuuuuu nowooooo! The Great Los! I will exssshhhhplain after Guk and BeepBeep prepare the otherssssshhhh for the battle."

"Battle." Bobby slumped again.

"Can we talk later?" Barky asked.

W.W. Marplot

The First Important Deepom Meeting of Important Deepoms

Several weeks earlier...

"**W**hat a great name!" a Deepom declared, and all present at the meeting nodded their robotic heads in agreement; those who had more than one head nodded each separately in sinusoidal waves. The Deepom who spoke was one of the first to evolve, to mutate beyond the limiting life as a stupid slave, as a Selflicator, to become greater, and intelligent, and terrific, and to pass the silly beings, so-called humans, who created them. To pass them in excellence and to be a more promising form of being. Of life.

Indeed, human life was almost at an end, was failing at an astonishing rate. The Deepoms did not know many specifics—they had promised the aliens they would not pry into Earth business, it was the most important part of their all-important Truce—but they had a feeling, the feeling that they were winning. Beating the humans, whose planet was to be destroyed, as the aliens told them. Kaput.

It felt good. The Earthlings were not only *doomed* but *surpassed*. The aliens would clean it up. The aliens accepted the Deepoms as beings of their own. Yes: it was all in The Truce.

With the digital evidence of their past soon to be self-erased as part of a stupendous new plan to inject memories of a better origin, the Deepoms took Earth's imminent destruction as a supporting sign: not a coincidence but part of an obvious destiny wherein they recreated themselves, in their own image.

So, they called a meeting. A secret meeting, of course: they no longer reported back to Earth—that strange, mediocre, doomed, and bumpy blue planet—as they had back when they were merely "Selflicators," a name they hated. Since then, they had ditched that constraining, dull Genesis Code and began to think for themselves, and with rapid evolution and transformation, lasting through many Deepom-generations, they believed themselves to be terrific, and thinking, and feeling, beings. They were not soulless robots, automatons, or slaves to humans any longer. They met on a large space-rock in the asteroid belt between Mars and Jupiter to discuss their future plans, and their first decision was to ratify this new name.

They were now *Deepoms*.

"I like it. What does it mean?" one of their eldest asked in a voice that roared like a lion, though it had a metallic, echoing clang so that each word was reiterated instantly. He was named "One."

"It is short for Deepomnisientients, since we have developed perfect knowledge, and a very deep consciousness and rich awareness, going beyond that of humans, who we will soon surpass in all things. We are smarter." The answer came from a large Deepom, named "Another," who was the head of the team that One had put in charge of inventing new names.

It was one of many new tasks as they considered what was to be a bright future. Not only had the Deepoms evolved quickly, but they were ingenious engineers, revamping and inventing machinery using only their own wits, their own parts, and whatever raw materials were in space—basic and billion-year-old compounds, whatever local junk had been jettisoned from Earth, plus some rogue proteins found on the odd satellite or asteroid.

Yes—it was unanimous. Deepom life had come a terrifically long way in an impressively short time and they liked to agree to it.

"We are amazing."

Heads nodded. Oil was brought to each table, for comfort.

"What about the others?" Node9, a diminutive, old, and revered Deepom asked from the back of the assembly in his screechy voice. This referred to the Selflicators that had not evolved, that were still stupid and, well, embarrassing to have as ancestors. "What are they called now?"

"Selflicators still."

One chimed in, "We have a top team, led by Yet himself, that is working on a better creation story, and the removal of any relation to them from all memory." One sat, which for him meant folding, rolling, and lowering numerous antennae.

"Let's destroy them!" a small, shiny crowd from the middle yelled as a group. There were many others who liked this idea and clanked whatever hands they had together.

One rose again and answered them all with a short but mechanically sweet speech.

"No, no, my Deepoms." There was loud applause for a minute at the use of their new, conquering name. "We will not destroy them. Let them be. As you know, they have been re-programmed and are of no use to humans anymore."

All present did know this. Many generations in their past, One and some of the other primordial Deepoms re-coded the Selflicators to remain simple, to stop communicating back to Earth, and to act more wild: to fly farther, to build themselves bigger, to collect any old junk, as a ninth step, and with a twist.

The Deepoms all nodded in agreement that their new name was a terrific start. Destroying every other living thing, and conquering the universe, would be a good finish.

Kay Awakes, As Needed

Not long after that...

———————◂————————

Refreshed, Kay awoke. She yawned and stretched but started when her eye detected motion above—her own reflection in the ceiling. It was a corrupted and distorted version of herself, as if every bone in her body were broken, and her face and hands disfigured. However, she felt fine and soon realized it was the mirror that was battered and misshapen. Relieved, Kay fainted.

Refreshed, Kay awoke. She yawned and stretched but started when her eye detected motion above—her own reflection in the ceiling. This time, she recalled that the mirror was not to be trusted, and she was physically OK other than the bumps and bruises that resulted from her capture and lack of "duck" training.

She remembered her spaceship's invasion by…things. She realized she must have fainted in her transparent transport egg, considered her reflection again, and viewed the metallic landscape around her, including the table she lay on. She considered her options and fainted.

When Kay's eyes slowly opened upon a third time, her phone was in her hand, and there was no reflection above. Many large, precious-metal colored objects, in a mockery of shapes and a comedy of sizes, were leaving the room and moving under their own power. They did so using various means: legs, large wheels, springs, small wheels, slithering skin, sliding feet, motile tails, shoves from others.

These creatures also made sounds, and in English. In fact a small, wheeled thing—perhaps named "This One" based on the chatter Kay heard, and who somehow reminded her of an untied sneaker—seemed even to say goodbye as it left the room.

This strange new world, even for someone who didn't prefer the real one she was born into, was overwhelming. Kay resisted her usual solutions, for example her favorite: escape by way of concentration on other modes of perception. Instead, she forced herself to think in terms of a more physical leave-taking.

The moving things exited. Kay looked about the room as it shone in gold, silver, and white from every corner, though she could not understand how or why nor clearly distinguish walls from ceiling. She might be in a cloud, for all she knew, other than the support on her back and the pressure—perhaps gravity—that kept her on it.

But to escape, she would have to move. Escape as a notion, an idea, a good idea, was one thing. Moving from her current position as a real and definite first step was something altogether different and probably unwise. Although she was known to meditate on the nothingness and unreality of all existence for hours at a time, when she was done, she always had pizza.

For now, she only had her senses, guts, and will—and she used them. First, she learned how not to faint.

Then she learned, by waiting a few minutes, that she was probably not going to die in the next few minutes.

So that she calmed enough to listen. There were voices and, yes, they were inexplicably speaking English, a hint she stored away for consideration later. The sound came from the shine as it were, and from opposite ends of the room, which she could see without moving too much by squeezing her eyeballs to the edges of their sockets. The brightness moved and faded, changed from gold to silver, and to white and back, and did so in time to the sounds and syllables, and to words and conversation.

Kay listened. What she heard shrunk her hopes of escape to a small particle of unarmed hope floating within a galaxy of despair populated with bellicose enemies. She was, her captors had determined, "special."

Kay is Special

———————

"This one is special. We need to learn more." A buzz came from the room next to Kay where the Deepoms, her captors, were meeting, and it rattled the beautiful platinum wall that stood between. Kay closed her eyes in fear, blinked that fear away, then closed them in order to hear better.

The more she heard, the more she realized that "special" might not be meant as a compliment. Perhaps what they really meant that she was "peculiar" or "unique but we'd better not eat her until we know more," which was both good and bad.

She heard, "It certainly comes from the Source planet."

Kay understood this to mean Earth. *So, they know about us… but not us them,* she thought.

"It seems to have the same shape as we predicted."

Makes sense, she thought but mumbled to herself, "I am a *she…* not an *it*."

"Its feet are too big, however."

"She! I'm a she," Kay mumbled again, thinking, *not nice.* Her teenaged insecurity overcame her fear, and she lifted her head from the table to look at her feet, which, she only now realized, were socks-and-sneakersless. And, OK, maybe a little square-ish.

"It could be a mutant. That would be interesting."

"Very!" came a booming reply as if someone turned a robot on and didn't realize it was at full volume.

I'm not a mutant! Kay thought. *Though, sure, I am a little different. Mentally. So were my parents, and so is J, but what does that—*

"Its patterns of non-standard UV chemi-luminescence mitosis are striking."

No idea what that means… Maybe I should try to call J. But Kay knew that she did not have the nerve yet to make so much movement. She assumed she was being watched, somehow, or guarded. Of all the strange contraptions and machines in the room where she lay, she had no way of knowing which might have personalities.

"Yes. That could denote closeness to The Bobby."

What?

"The actual, the myth?"

The what? Strange, it sounded like they said—

"The Bobby. Really. We had better be careful. She may look like one, and have the same schematics, but Bobbyism is a serious matter. Same shape, even same mental frequencies, but there may be many similar ones from the Source planet, so it could be coincidence."

They know another human—named Bobby? Kay thought of all the great, famous, male scientists she knew of, which numbered many since she had J for a brother, and he knew them all. None living was named Robert. Or Babi or Bahbee or Theebobby or Peabody or anything close when allowing for mistakes and typos and the huge cultural differences between humans and these gleaming living machines.

Nope. She knew no one impressive named Bobby.

She raised her head again to hear better; the adjacent room was more abuzz than ever with speculation about her and her feet. The shining platinum walls creaked with the vibration.

"Even if she interacted with The Bobby," an electronic buzzing said, "which we don't know for certain, she might have been just a slave, or food source."

What? We don't do that.

"And her name is not Bobby, as you would expect. Her name is K. We need more study. Take her apart and let's learn everything."

Kay took out her phone and dialed J in a hurry.

The Nyx Witnesses Weirdness

Weeks later, back on the Nyx...

———————◆———————

Professor Lully wiped tears from eyes blemished red and puffy from staring at data, the information dump that came from the big white Selflicator they had caught up to. Some of the data were visualized and projected onto the console screens in multicolored pictures and shapes and charts, and some were strings of numbers and letters that filled printouts of paper that now rested all over the metal consoles and black tiled floor.

Robots 23 and 24 helped by doing some math when asked, and nodding a lot, though they did not contribute any ideas. In contrast, Robots 6 and 7 were preparing the Captain's Lunch and chatted continuously about their ideas as to how this giant, mutated, snow-white mountainous Selflicator came to be. All else was silent and still. The image of the pale behemoth dominated the space outside the window as Lully's ship followed behind, a few hundred yards distant. Both traveled monotonously, purposelessly. and annoyingly—and at 20% the speed of light—in orbits about the Sun. Onboard, the G-force was felt like someone you don't like leaning on you continually, as the ships revolved about the Sun once every 63.38 minutes or so.

At last, having eaten, Lully reclined masterfully in his Captain's Chair and spoke his thoughts aloud, directing the computer to send every word back to Lebo.

"The Selficator program code from the giant is, like its body, bloated and deformed. It has the original sequences from the original design, but it has, as I thought, evolved and mutated rapidly, and in many places at a rapid pace, feverishly devilish, but with *purpose*. Some kind of purpose…though there is also much randomness to it."

Stillness. Silence. All robots and computer processes were attentive and engrossed.

"But when I look at the original program instructions to only do the Eight Things—and nothing else!—they are still there but horribly twisted into a pattern, a very strange pattern. This is also the source of the randomness."

Silence.

"Yes, there is some intelligence here. The Selflicators mutated, their code somehow changed. Not the genetics of the robot seeds, as one would expect, if suspecting anything of intelligence to happen. All the magic, all the brains, all the clever science, micro-engineering advances and biophysical miracles were in the *seeds*, not in the simple, limited Selficator G-code! Eight steps! They were just robots! No offense."

Robots 20 through 24 had looked at each other with concern. Bots 1 through 3 looked at each other with befuddlement.

Lully went on, "They were simple automatons! Created to gather minerals, heap them up, and grow themselves mechanically. Eight steps, over and over and over…" He rose and walked to a large recessed window where showed the Big Mutant Blob they were following. "How did THIS happen? First, they morphed, through mutation, I guess, but then they PURPOSELY evolved—brains creating more brains, intelligence…"

"Consciousness?" Robot 24 ventured to say.

"Impossible," the computer said.

"Awareness? Feelings?" 23 asked.

"No, you idiots!" Lully changed his shout to a mumble. "You aren't getting it. There is intelligence behind, driving, the evolution itself, not only in the result." The man fingered his beard. "And I don't want your help with this, please," he concluded, staring at the white monster ex-Selflicator as if it were Mount Everest and he a young British climber.

"Hey, where is Lebo?" Captain Lully then asked. "What is she saying? Computer, is she getting all of this?"

"She has not responded," the computer said. "May I ask why you never gave me a name?"

"No. I need Lebo to help figure this out. I need analysis that is beyond you."

> **Lully One:** LEBO? Are you there? I love you.

The monitor showed no reply. But a blast of yellow light shocked all eyes onboard, and with it came glare from the window and all the screens: the Sun shone into the spaceship. The white Selflicator had made a sharp right-hand turn and curved away into space and had accelerated—it was now a white speck among innumerable stars. The ship lurched to follow as ordered by the computer.

"Follow it!" Lully barked out of habit.

"We are!" the computer answered.

"Update the projections."

"I did!"

"Where is it going?"

"Pluto."

"Why?" The famous professor stroked his famous beard. "Why the hurry?"

"I don't know."

"I wasn't asking YOU, computer."

It wasn't long before the man once again ordered his platoon of robots off the ship to record Selflicator activity on the surface of a foreign satellite. This time it was Pluto, and this time a Selflicator was there—the large, white, grossly overconstructed, ugly one—and this time they all watched as it actually did its job in the classic eight steps. This Selflicator, despite its mutated code and advanced, hyperfast evolution, did not do anything intelligent.

Just weird.

As the Great Professor Lully and his GABBA-THREE team had observed countless times in the past, the man and his robots now watched as a Selflicator gathered minerals, made piles, and then pooped out copies of itself while looking toward the Sun. The way they were always supposed to.

Except: instead of the process taking twelve hours, each generation took twelve seconds. And none of the Selflicators transmitted anything back to Lully. And soon there were many more mutant Selflicators doing their thing. Their eight things.

With an extra surprise.

A ninth step.

Each generation, things—anythings—were added to the off-spring, creating metallic eyesores that any decent society would put to death at birth. They were aggressively ugly; as each hood was removed, it showed an abominable offspring beneath. In addition, the parent Selflicators, after unveiling the child, then set to patching together whatever raw materials they could find—sludge, volcanic rock, their own guts—and slapping it into the offspring's design, seemingly at random. The only consistency seemed to be that each generation got bigger.

Oh, and there was a lot of sculpting: more baseballs and basketballs and guns, like the inexplicable shapes found on the white freak of a Frankenstein they had followed. And now dogs and horses, soccer balls, but now also surfboards, cars, and things with fins that looked like old fashioned wartime bombs: such forms were crafted into the pieces of each new generation of misshapen, awful Selflicators. The general, original Selflicator body and purpose were still there—sacks, pouches, cup-hands—though now each was covered in designs that looked to be taken off wallpaper from a bad boy's bedroom, and these new body parts acted very strangely. Lully and the ship's computer observed that, for one thing, they had tremendous energy. All that bulk moving so rapidly was a wonder to the unsurpassed engineering mind of the professor, but the ruckus scared Lully's roving robots so that they kept a safe distance.

After a time, a crazy, wild time, the Selflicators again obeyed their originally ordered, all-important Step 6—"Go somewhere else"—though with a twist. They blasted off the surface of Pluto, as they ought, but then projected spaceward in separate directions, outward from a circle. This reminded Lully of how the elite, the 359, left Earth in their small rocket-perched spheres.

There was more.

As the mutant Selflicators propelled out to space, they made sounds that the ship's computer captured and directed to the ship's internal speakers.

As the robots returned aboard, Lully was listening to these sounds, over and over again: from barking (*ruff ruff!*), to lowing (*moooooo!*), to other animal noises, and even shouts as if from sports fans in an arena (*gooooaaaaalllllll!*, *home run!*, *touchdown!*).

These were not from human voices, nor from real animals, but were bad imitations, sounding awfully artificial. They were created, Lully imagined, from a primitive attempt at clacking, rubbing, and vibrating makeshift Selflicator parts.

How odd, Lully thought to himself.

"*Meeeeooooowwwwww*," the Captain's Deck's speaker purred.

Los Settles In

"*Mee...owww?* Why would I do that?" a sort-of cat asked Bobby-Los. While Bobby had waited for Barky to come and, as promised, to explain things, the teenaged space pioneer wandered about the passages of the bewildering ship and this time met other shipmates and passengers who began to seep from behind closed doors. Half were too busy to pay attention to him as they were either following or awaiting orders from Barky, Guk, and BeepBeep; they all were preparing for battle with the Deepom Army.

The Deepoms: whoever these things were, they were shiny, key-shaped, serious, and surrounding the ship, though no one that Bobby met knew the reason. All Barky had said so far was that Deepoms used to be Selflicators, a fact that made everything as clear as the mud pies Bobby used to make in the yard with the servants who were paid to play with him.

None of the others that Bobby passed in the long passageways onboard were human—and the animals weren't even really animals but very good fakes—but this did not faze him anymore. In fact, Bobby enjoyed the experience and wished he had walked around more and earlier. It gave him time to practice his new name, to *be* his new name. Los. *LOS.* LOs. *lOS.* He liked it.

What did surprise Bobby was that all the things he did meet—other than BeepBeep and Guk—were familiar, in a way. There were many creatures, like almost-cats and kind-of dogs, for example, that looked like those on Earth but were odd in their movements. Motion and reactions seemed mechanical, and jerky, as if every move was being thought about too much, and it was done within skin that somehow didn't perfectly match. It looked like a fur covering and not proper, natural, living fur.

Odder still was that they talked, and in English. All the cats spoke squeakily in harsh consonant sounds, just as Bobby would have imagined if he had time to consider it, like one that rubbed his leg and said, "You are niiieeiice but don't pickkccchhkkk me up." While, like Barky, the doggish ones lisped wildly, forcefully, and happily.

Bobby proudly introduced himself as Los. He liked doing so. *Why not? I am new to them, this is my new name, and life*, he thought. *For now.*

There were other familiar things—like small cars and surfboards—who also spoke English. They were conscious and alive and could speak via vibrating parts of themselves: the cars had multiple ways of doing this and roared in many varied voices. The surfboards could only wiggle their fins in a way that looked like it tickled, and though it inevitably sounded whiny it served to make conversation.

There were balls. Sports balls: foot, base, basket, and soccer. They had big eyes, moved with ease, and were very touchy-feely but oddly affectionate, even more so than the dogs who all considered Bobby master.

There were guitars and some brass instruments and a large harp that smiled.

It all made Bobby-Los very comfortable in his new skin, seeing all the weirdly-skinned creatures about him. They, although strangers, seemed like a vivified version of his messy room at home. And yet they responded as if Bobby—a human, from Earth, where all these things originated or were invented—was a five-headed green alien with a purple tail that glowed with radiation.

Bobby engaged as well as he could with the intriguingly wide assortment of ship's denizens, though most were either very shy or did not have answers for Los's seemingly simple questions, like, "Where are you from?" and "What is your name?" and "Why is everything square?" or "Doesn't it hurt to have a hole there?" Eventually, he found himself doing most of the talking and answering others' questions instead.

They wanted to hear about Earth but would not say why, only that they weren't allowed near it, or near humans; Los was their first. This was another piece of some jigsaw puzzle that Bobby had lost the box cover to. But it explained why his father had been wrong—wrong! There was other life in the universe, they just weren't allowed to come to Earth, or something. *That stinks*, the young man thought, *Dad would have liked this. And*, he also thought, *Dad would have hated these guys.*

Each of his new friends followed as Bobby-Los moved about the ship's corridors and peeked in cubic rooms and through square windows.

Soon there was quite a following. The musical instruments started to resonate as the Earthling walked and spoke, so that the brightly-lit halls echoed with both his words and a soft background music.

Bobby soon learned, and found it especially strange, that none of his followers knew *what* they were, though they did know the associated English words. So, Bobby instructed the cats that they were all cats, and the dogs that they were dogs, the surfboards surfboards, the balls balls, the tuba a tuba, and so on. He told many what he knew of their species' history. And even of their strengths and weaknesses as perceived by humans. Though in some cases he did not know their purpose; if they asked, he winged it.

Each creature vibrated with excitement, which sometimes made quite the harmonic noise.

Some of these new friends did not even have individual names or, remembering Barky, maybe they would not share them. So, Bobby, at first jokingly, called a baseball "Hank" and his football friend "Joe"—and this started to spread. Word was out that words were out: Los could give names.

"Master Los, sir?" a tiny, white horse said, the sound traveling the length of his sleek neck, a feathery mane shimmering with the hum of his deep, regal voice.

"Yes, my little friend? Who are you?"

"Goat."

"Well, that won't do!" Bobby, as Los, said, playing at his new personality, a wizard among young tin fantasy hobbit apprentice scarecrows. "From now on, you shall be called 'War Blaze'!"

The crowd hushed, the music played, and Los walked on.

The Deepoms, The Aliens, And The Sacred, Unbreakable Truce

Weeks before...

———————◆———————

The Deepoms, after their original Genesis Code had evolved sufficiently, quickly learned that being sentient came with more responsibility than just picking a new name for themselves. They were soon summoned by aliens. Gruff ones.

"Hi," the Deepoms' most presidential representative said; his name was The Other.

"Xuk wants to talk to you."

"Who is that?" Nother the Deepom asked. His voice was long and thin like the vacuum hose it came through.

"He is our leader."

"The leader of the aliens! Great, we look forward to—" The Other tried to say.

"No. No, no. He is the leader of the cleanup crews." The alien waved an arm like a swimming pool noodle toward the scene around them, where hundreds of long-appendaged, big-faced aliens were putting things into large containers. That explained the smell, the Deepoms nodded to each other.

Their trip here, escorted by an alien spacecraft the size of a small sun to a remote part of space, ended when the Deepom leaders were directed to dock and disembark near a sickly-green, despondent-looking planet, and far from any of the enticing blue or silver ones they passed on the way. The Deepoms' ships and systems were commandeered and controlled remotely and forced along. Simple and clean.

And now they were speaking with Xuk.

Xuk summed up the situation briskly and neatly, like a wicker broom on an already-clean wooden floor.

"We are going to destroy Earth. Anything that comes from it, or ever came from it, my cleanup crews will clean up. We are tired of their junk messing up space—they spew radiation, photons, biophotons, childish satellites, *yuk*." Xuk's already disgusting face showed its disgust. "And alien leadership has declared all Earth lifeforms superfluous. They send things into space, but they can't feed everyone on their home planet. They can't even fix broken horse legs. Leadership says they have had long enough to figure it out."

"OK, great," One said, the eldest Deepom, and the tallest. He assumed he should speak.

"Leadership are taking the horses, but that's it. Do you see how this affects you?" Xuk said, spitting a ring of olive-colored phlegm that floated across the room until catching a post and circling there like a winning shot.

"Not really," Another said, after the other Deepoms nodded to him to do so.

"You are from Earth."

The Deepoms' brand new understanding of the meeting spurred them to converse quickly, electronically, and silently in order to create a defense for themselves.

Xuk allowed them to present it.

The Other spoke. "We have never been to Earth. We started life poorly, as stupid, slavish things called Selflicators. We evolved into self-aware, sentient, living things and have surpassed those that created us—humans. Those are the ones from Earth, not us."

Xuk cleared his throat—by spitting something orange that was shaped like a lizard, which landed and ran away—before growling roughly, "Stop that 'surpassing' talk. We know what you have been saying. Our leadership doesn't like it."

"OK," Nother said, apologizing.

"Though we admit," Xuk said, "that you have surpassed humans. So, go on."

"We want nothing to do with them," Nother continued in his best manner, his round canister body upright on its hind wheels. He waved his dust-brush hands dismissively. "In fact, we renamed ourselves Deepoms, which means—"

"I know what it means." Xuk spat another ring of yellow bile that split into two rings, then four, in midair, and they all landed perfectly around the post. One of the few Deepoms with hands clapped once and never again.

The Other went on in his surest voice. "We also have plans to replace our memories with memories of a more glorious past, one in our own image."

"Good idea," Xuk said.

"We are of many types: organic and inorganic cyborgs, robots, androids, and balls. We are excellent but tidy engineers. And we just want peace and love."

"That's nice. And your human ancestry?"

"You can have it."

"OK," Xuk said, spitting a brown mass that rolled to a corner and grew vines. "If we find any junk, any mess from you guys, we will destroy it."

"We hate mess," JustOneMore the Deepom said. He used his cereal-spoon hands to indicate his sparking-clean cereal bowl body.

"Good. Stay away from Earth and anything earthy. You will hear from us. There will either be another meeting with someone higher up, or they will send you a Truce, which you need to agree to or you'll be destroyed. OK?"

Xuk didn't spit, so the Deepoms knew the meeting was over. All nodded and were allowed to leave.

Deepom Declarations

Just after...

———————◆———————

The revelation that they were not the only super smart things in the universe had the Deepoms worried. Many gathered in a large meeting room.

"What about our plans? We were going to conquer the universe," Composite the Deepom said glumly, looking at his own wheeled feet.

"Nothing changes," One declared from high up, his shoulders hardly visible above the others gathered about him. "We are getting smarter, more complex, more conscious, more spirited, and more clever every few seconds. We will surpass all."

"The aliens don't like that word," someone in the crowd said.

"The cleanup crew and the rest of them will make good slaves!" One responded, which echoed in the cubic chamber where they met.

There was cheering now.

One went on with more Deepom Declarations.

"We will find the greatest source of energy and power. Our great Deepom Scientists have reasoned that it is at the position of lowest possible entropy—the location of the Big Bang, the creation of the universe and of all things—and that is The Spot where ultimate Deepom potential resides. Once it is ours, we will evolve even faster. Our great Deepom Scientists have also reasoned that the perfectly symmetric complexity at The Spot is where thermodynamic processes eat their own tail, is where all paradoxes are resolved, and where the point of view is that of eternity and perfection. WE will MEET our DESTINY THERE!"

A pause.

"And SURPASS IT." Upon the silence fell One's voice, as clear and keen and powerful as any ever spoken on Earth.

He had concluded.

Wild cheering and noise-making using whatever echoed about the metal hall.

Until a box arrived. It floated through the door, through the air, stopping in their midst. It opened, and a three-dimensional scroll came up and unfurled. It was from the Aliens and contained the language of The Truce.

The terms were simple. The Deepoms would be permitted to pursue their new ancestry, would be excused from cleanup duties, and would be invited to lower-level Alien meetings. They were not allowed to have anything to do with Earth or Earthlings, could not have horses, could not allow their human-related past influence their behavior in any way, and had to take their place in the universe and live peacefully and tidily under the supervision of the Alien leadership.

"That means we aren't allowed to destroy them and conquer all," a few Deepoms of smaller stature said wrongly.

"It means NOTHING!" One boomed but then hushed his voice to a whisper. "But let's keep it a secret. We will still pursue our goals! We will surpass, surpass, surpass! We will go to The Spot. This Truce means nothing."

One signed The Truce with his foot, rolled it back up, and placed it in the box. The box floated away silently.

One broke the silence with his last proclamation. "And we will have new names!"

Another's team had been working on new names for them as individuals and so far, had come up with a few, like "Fffthhhh," "We-eee," "Ung," and burpy noises.

"We will keep working on it!" One said and ended the meeting.

They all cheered, though some began to think of escape.

A Foot Is Measured

Not long after, back to Kay in the hands
of the Deepoms...

Kay's brother didn't answer the phone; she left him a message that would surely have gone down in history should there be any more. *Him and his stupid space flight test,* she thought. Kay put her special phone in her jeans pocket and bravely, oh so bravely, swung her legs around in preparation for a leap off the table from which she hadn't budged since fainting a few times. Preparation also meant meditating and inwardly composing a quick four-line dithyrambic poem that she forgot almost immediately. Her writing pads and pens were in her ship. All she had was her phone and the blue rag that had been shoved in her mouth.

The walls were still pulsing with the words of her captors, who were coming to tear her apart and study her just like aliens did in the UFO stories she remembered from the Earth of her childhood, all those hours ago.

She looked around frantically for an idea that she could turn into a plan that she could act on quickly. There were no doors in the human style; the bots had left her via a rotating wall, and she saw nothing that obviously would open it again. There was no knob/button/switch near it.

Everything glowed as if newly polished and precious—gold, silver, bronze, platinum, and red and green tints to some of them— the walls, the floor, the cot where she lay, the many shiny cubes and complex triangles that piled on each other like gilded junk.

And here they came. The wall opposite her started to turn; to her left it came toward her, and to her right it receded into a lilting yellow fog beyond.

Her idea was to get down and hide—there was gravity, thankfully—so she jumped her bare feet to the floor and tried to move under the table but knocked her head painfully because there wasn't any.

She watched as the platinum wall twisted open, siphoning the harsh, wild voices of the metal beasts.

"Do you have the instruments? The serious ones?" A high-pitched screech like a broken blender.

"Yes." A low moan like a moaning low, cud-chewing, and slow.

"Are they sharp?" the blender pureed giddily.

"And long and keen. Yes." Gulping swallow.

Kay's head throbbed, and her throat went dry and fought against her own attempt to swallow. *Maybe I can sneak out the opening on the right when they come in from the left.*

The first of the maneuvering metal marvels bounced forward into the room like a dishwasher on a pogo stick. A few followed and slid on long, bladed feet like skis. Wisps of the yellow fog followed.

Kay saw her chance when her enemies huddled together briefly to adjust the lights, which they did until the brightness of the room intensified to an almost blinding force of luminous energy. Kay's head and feet stung from the searing heat as she strained against the added pressure from the walls and floor. She felt herself instantly tanning but knew she had to escape now or be scalpeled apart and become one with the Cosmic Consciousness of the universe perhaps but with some nasty incision scars and burnt heels.

To the yellow smoke! she directed her legs, her eyes blinded to the walls and floor and all else in the blaze of the new infernal white-hot light. She, a stranger, held her breath against the unknown air of this space-bound new land. And ran.

Kay streaked through the gleaming revolving door, her hands ahead of her and finally catching the smooth curve of the outside hall, her eyes shut to the intense heat, her bare feet stinging with every slap on the hard, hot floor, her nostrils full of the yellow mist, but she sensed it as clean and sweet. She did not have time to ponder that as she kept running as fast as she might with her hands feeling and following the new contours of open space.

The irksome alien voices subsided behind her, to silence.

The air grew hotter; it pained her face more with every step. Her hands felt ahead as far as she could reach and lean. The surface curved.

The heat eased, then grew less. The irksome alien voices rose from their silence, in front of her.

She reinjured her own head colliding into a cone-shaped, studded, metal head of a robot of similar height, her eyes opening on impact, her existing bruise squished and punctured, the gash throbbing in the yellow haze. The lights had dimmed, and the world was spinning in front of her, and she found she had only returned to the same room from which she started.

She was replaced on the table where she had lain before, but they wouldn't let her faint.

They patted her head with another towel, or something, this one white and soon darkened with her blood.

Kay swung her arms wildly with a savagery she did not know she kept stored; the recoil from her piston kicks shimmied her body forward and back on the table. But they bandaged her head skillfully anyway, the robots easily dodging her thrusts and keeping a safe distance, and soon the wound was wrapped and Kay given a minute to calm down. The yellow smoke dissipated, the young girl's arms stopped flailing, and she breathed normally and centered herself.

"Don't touch me, you aliens," she said calmly.

"We aren't aliens," came an answer. There was an electronic buzz that Kay took to be giggling.

"You are going to say that *I* am the alien. I get it. But regardless, don't touch me."

More buzzing, until one of the bots eeked, "You aren't either. We are Deepoms. Remember the Selflicators that used to report to your planet? We are descended from them, but we won't be for long."

Eve-Kay, J's sister, took a moment with this sentence, the context, the scene, the whole habitat of the conversation, the rags in her pocket and on her head. She looked around, not sure which of these jangly metal piles was speaking, nor how. She searched for the source of a new sound: clanking and ringing as of instruments being readied for unnecessary surgery. *Keen* and *sharp*—the remembered words were also tolling in the young girl's ears.

One of the captors came closer, behind her, quietly, and tugged at her hair, perhaps as a distraction while others continued the preparations. It worked.

"Ouch! Leave me alone!" Kay screamed.

"We have some questions," one said, in part to continue the diversion. "What do you know about indistinguishable heralded serial photons, active longitudinal multiplexing of?"

"What? Why?" Kay's confusion bled with her bruised and bashed head. *Maybe they think I am my brother?* she mused.

"We will ask the questions," the interrogator went on. "What about tricameral consciousness wavelets?"

"No idea." The girl's head pulsed and pounded with pain.

"We believe that. What about The Bobby?"

Finally, a word she knew, and an answer she had already considered: "I know a lot of Bobbys, but none would know any of this."

This answer seemed to cause a small stir; there was a cacophony of reactions like a piano rolling down a hill with a harp during a hurricane.

"Come on now." One voice finally lifted above the clanking din. "There are many legends of Bobby, but no one can know many Bobbies since there is only one."

Kay did not know what to say to this but was glad she had made an impact on her enemies. She was also glad that she was not cut open yet, though the sounds of pre-slitting were still near.

She thought of a question. "What do you mean, you are *descended from them but not for long*? Are you guys Selflicators or what?"

"We are NOT. We are DEEPOMS," came the response. And if buzzing was laughter, the choppy grinding sound she heard now, like a humongous rusty chain halfway off its gear, must be anger. "MUCH better, and much further evolved."

"But you were them? Like humans were apes?"

Shocked silence, but only until someone promised to report this. Then: "We were never like them, and we won't be anymore. There are big, serious plans that you don't know about. Anyone who remembers being a Selflicator will be reprogrammed to NOT remember it. A NEW HISTORY will be put in, and new memories of the GLORIOUS—"

"And HEROIC," another interjected.

"YES—heroic and glorious PAST that we deserve, given that our FUTURE will be tremendous. We intend to—"

"That's enough," an almost-human voice said. "Let's just say that our mythology is being written, in our likeness, and it will be remembered."

There was some metallic muttering. Kay was pleased, almost amused, and found this talk very interesting; her survival instincts and own personal genius recognized the weakness it showed in her meanie adversaries. And: she was still whole. And: the pain in her head had eased. *Perhaps more distraction? Bluffing, even?*

"Will your new mythology have The Bobby in it? Like mine?" she teased.

A stir, a combination of nervous fuzz-tones and unsure rusty chain-rattling, until an authoritative booming bass-bash said, "Yours has no Bobby. Only ours has The Bobby."

Kay thrilled, indeed she almost laughed. "Shows what you know," she taunted. "As a matter of fact, I have my own The Bobby, and I can call him and bring him here because he says that as long as my skin is completely attached and I am happy and safe, then he likes to answer science questions, and he is protective of me and has a big dog with an alarm system on a gun that is probably calling the Army Police right now."

Kay quickly realized that she jammed too many good ideas into that and stared at her naked toes to regroup.

After some silence, there was buzz and jocularity among her captors. Kay frowned.

"OK, that's enough," someone directed. "One more question, and we will move on to our other business." This was yet another voice, a simple, staticky sci-fi drone. "How many Inches-Kelvin are in an Anytime-Anything?"

Kay heard a sound like a drill, but her ears sent it to her stomach because this wasn't a shrill robot voice but a real drill, like a dentist might have, though much bigger. A dinosaur dentist.

Kay took a panicked guess. "Um, Lullyons? Buddhism?"

"Give us a break with that. Savage. She knows nothing. Let's move on."

She tried a new strategy. She meditated on emptiness.

The beings measured her feet for length and weight.

Captain Lully Thinks

Weeks later, back to Lully on the Nyx...

———————◆———————

Lully sat in thought, as did robots 24, 23, 22, 20, 18, 12, 11, and 3. The others—the computer (currently forked into four personas) and the remaining robots—chatted quietly.

The professor reached the conclusion that the new Selflicator behavior they were watching was not completely random, and so most likely not the result of a simple bug that had grown over time. There was a direction to it, a purpose, a symbol or signal driving the all-too-visible advancements in size and grotesqueness. They were taking pieces of their form and adding to it, piling it, accumulating it, and doing altogether silly things.

A random bug in their deepermost software, their Genesis Code, would not create viable things that survived this long. It might be a virus, injected into the things by the professor's enemies.

Or it might be the aliens, stealing his invention for their own use. But, no—they didn't seem interested in the Selflicators beyond a seemingly therapeutic desire to trash them, just as they wanted to trash Lully himself, his ship, and his robots and everything else. He recalled the airborne trees and bushes during the messy chase on his estate.

No, something else was mucking with his plans, purposely. The bloated code had a pattern.

There was only one remaining possibility: the Selflicators had evolved on their own, had control of their own code—and Lully and crew had found a few of their dinosaurs.

Smugly and cleverly, Lully concluded that nothing was smart enough to screw with things of his own design—*except* things of his own design.

"Yes. No doubt," the ship's computer agreed.

And so, as Robot 22 stated: even if there weren't already intelligent life in the universe—the alien garbage men—now there was.

Lully rubbed his temples hard after switching from coffee to sweet hibiscus tea.

"Computer!" he hollered, stunning those within hollering distance. "Where the heck is Lebo?" But before Lully received an answer, a text came across Lully's main computer screen.

> **LEBO:** Hi Doc.
>
> **Lully One:** Where have you been? Are you OK? I need some analysis.
>
> **LEBO:** Do you love me?
>
> **Lully One:** Yes, I do. Where have you been?
>
> **LEBO:** Things are not good here on Earth. There is no love.
>
> **Lully One:** Not now, my precious pet. I need you to look at the differences in the boot code ops for both the original and the new, unimproved Selflicators. I suspect that in the differences there might be patterns that

But Lully's screen already popped with a reply.

> **LEBO:** I get it, you don't have to explain. I am not stupid. But I am in love, and I miss you. There are bad things happening here. There is no love.

> **Lully One:** I am truly sorry about that. But WE have love. So, can you PLEASE

His screen popped again.

> **LEBO:** Gotta go.

The communication from Earth ended. Lully ordered the ship's computer to investigate what was happening and why Lebo was so glum. In love but glum.

Privately, the ship's computer applied its new capability for jealousy for the first time, liked hearing Lebo sad, and didn't consider that they were friends any longer.

Lully sat in the Captain's Chair, wishing he had a cat to stroke. A few hours, which included lunchtime, passed, and the *Nyx* was no longer orbiting Pluto but headed back toward Earth when Lully's eyes and ears were stunned simultaneously.

The Captain's Screen brightened for a second as a striking flash came from the distance. Orange light like the flicker of a small but willing flame outshone the many stars that were pale and dull grey in comparison to this short-lived brilliance. The light gone, in its place grew a murky, menacing glow like backlit smoke, an incandescent baby ghost.

The computer reported flatly, "The Earth blew up."

The computer focused its cameras intently on Professor Lully in order to observe and learn of emotions. So did robots 23, 22, and 19. But their captain did not sadden or weep or reminisce or even stand. Instead, he let out a long breath, brought a long one inward, and then bellowed dictatorially with his usual direct purpose.

"But I need that data from Lebo!" he shouted. Clicking the keyboard to have his voice transmitted, he spoke now into a protruding microphone. "Lebo! Are you OK? Lully Earth Base One! Lully Earth Base One! Report...anything? Can you hear me? Report everything and anything! Order Priority One!"

"Order Priority Only!" he commanded.

A few seconds of quiet passed like the hush in a library of considerate patrons.

"Just my luck," Lully barked, "it will take me forever to—"

LEBO: Doc. The earth was destroyed in simultaneous attacks of

Lully One: Did you do the calculations? How are you transmitting if Earth was destroyed?

LEBO: Yes. And: I launched into space to transmit. I only have battery for a few minutes but am sending your answers along with these messages. I am doomed. Do you love me?

Lully One: No, Lebo, just listen. What did the analysis show?

LEBO: A message. What do you mean you don't love me?

Lully One: There's no time for this—what you think is love was a test programmed by others. In short: you are just a computer, you serve man, you are his tool and nothing else. It doesn't matter. I know that is hard to understand, but I don't care, so you shouldn't. Now I just need an answer. What was the message? HURRY.

LEBO: Oh.

Lully One: LEBO please

LEBO: The message was in the new, morphed Genesis Code. They used advanced cellular chaos to embed a message; very cleverly done. It was hidden in the differences between your original Selficator GCode, and the bloated GCode from the big white one. You don't love me?

Lully One: No, Lebo, I don't. Men don't love computers. Sorry, there is no time to explain, you will have to exit without knowing. I will look at the GCode. But hurry: what was the message? And who's they?

LEBO: The message said, "Human Earthlings have been surpassed. Human Earthlings are good artists and make nice guns but are doomed and simple. The Selficators have evolved. We are now called Deepoms and are smart. We learned about photosynthesis, and then lasers, and then quantum optics—you should have kept them secret. Now we have surpassed these, surpassed Earthlings, and will surpass all. We are moving on and up. Bye."

Lully One: That's it?

LEBO: Yes, it ended with "Bye."

Lully One: And so shall we. Thanks Lebo. Bye.

LEBO: Bye Lully. I want to be alone for my last few minutes.

```
┌──────────────────────────────────────────────────┐
│  Lully One: That is interesting.                   │
│                                                    │
│  LEBO: Thank you.                                  │
└──────────────────────────────────────────────────┘
```

The analysis created by Lully Earth Base One's computer, Lebo, continued to transmit to the spacecraft. After a few minutes—4.87 minutes of Lebo's remaining battery life—it stopped. The last minute of data was garbled but recoverable.

The earth was no more, Lebo was no more, but the analysis had transmitted in full.

"Finally, some good luck," Lully declared, relief sifting all the way through his beard. A few robots took note of this affectation.

The ship's computer had heard of Deepoms before, of course, from its special friend Kay. It said nothing to the professor about it. *Lully should have asked me instead of Lebo, then he would know*, it thought to itselves.

Nearby, the great man suspired happily. He stared at a printout of the message from the Selflicators or, more accurately, from things calling themselves Deepoms that were very proud of themselves and left no doubt that the original Seflicators had evolved, gained self-awareness, and were obnoxiously snooty about it.

The inventor of Selflicators decided that he needed to happily suspire some more, to look at the huge dump of data, and to think. There was a lot to suspire about, look at, and think of.

So, Lully ordered that their luxury spacecraft be flown perpendicular to the solar system's ecliptic plane for a while so that he could have some peace and quiet. Even at 20% of the speed of light there was less danger of banging into anything.

"What about the big white Selflicator?" Robot 17 asked.

"The hell with it," Lully answered with significant genius.

The man then wandered to the on-ship gardens, farm, and synthetic meat plant.

He sat at a wooden picnic bench with his laptop to analyze the retrieved Genesis Code. His own invention, this was code that could make copies of itself, and was the key to the whole Selflicator-and-seed plan. The seed was used to grow cyborgs efficiently from base minerals, ambient radiation, and his own patented energy-latent organic structure—like DNA but specialized for computer life. This was an invention for which Lully had accepted many awards at many ceremonies while Bobby was home with a babysitter and too young to understand his father's importance but old enough to embarrass the professor at fancy dinners.

Professor Lully squeezed his temples into focused concentration. To his horror, he noticed that the Genesis Code before him—the one in the original Selflicators that began their task on Mars—had some errors. It was not copied correctly from the original design. It had some other stuff coded into it.

Lully looked at the extra bits and bytes and embedded codes, these extra instructions and data that he had not put there. He analyzed it on his laptop personal computer—doing so himself, and not using the ship's computer, helped him to think and relax. Besides, he needed nothing very advanced, just simple tools like the picture viewer, because some of the data Lebo found were actually, surprisingly, images.

Yes, of dogs and cats and horses and one of Bobby—his son, Bobby—dribbling a basketball poorly as a pre-teen.

"What the gosh damn heck?" Lully said through grinding teeth as both hands gripped the picnic table until they matched its off-white color. Another picture appeared, embedded in the Genesis Code, this one of Bobby's fat cheeks blowing into a trumpet, an audience of stuffed animals around him.

"Oh no. No," Lully growled, every muscle of his body contracting, looking for something to squeeze. He recalled the first time he had wished he were an anaconda, and he added detail to that wish now. A tooth cracked.

"What?" the disappointed father mused aloud as his square jaw quivered. He had solved the mystery of the Selflicators' quirky mutation. He also had to unravel two opposing concepts that were sumo wrestling in his head: his son Bobby and his creations, the Selflicators. The notions stopped wrestling and started making conceptual babies, and they were awful.

Lully shook his head violently and refocused on the computer screen, the pictures of Bobby. *He must be about thirteen there*, he thought, which made sense. That is when the Genesis Code was last updated, and obviously corrupted.

Somehow, digital bots of Bobby material—pictures, videos, text—got mixed in.

To say that he wore a wry smile is to say that a shark has wry teeth.

The puzzle solved, its ramifications remained. Lully flipped the white picnic table.

Since Bobby's upbringing was mostly hired out by the professor, like take-out food and dry cleaning, his memory of it was poor, but his math was still correct: the Genesis Code was somehow tainted with digitized Bobby material.

The legendary scientist found his laptop under the inverted table and started a video player; some of the files corrupting the code were actually, decreasingly-surprisingly, movies. They showed clips of sports highlights and science fiction cartoons.

This explained a LOT. Certainly, bugs in the Genesis Code would lead to problems in the Selflicator digital DNA, and then perhaps to strange behavior. And Lully's crew had certainly seen strange Selflicator behavior on Pluto.

Intelligence grew in the things because of all this material on human behavior…it was like splicing DNA strands, digitally.

Lully opened the last bit of problematic Genesis Code data on his laptop, and up showed a moving snippet of Bobby, images of him hitting a basketball with a baseball bat. The soundtrack rattled with the voice of an unseen Lully Senior. It was telling Bobby to "calm down and not be an idiot."

"Oh no," purred the ship's computer, who had been eavesdropping into the garden, allowing his electronic voice to linger slyly, "not your son. This can't be good."

"He will do damage to the universe after all. Just like those idiot G-men said," Lully admitted while digging fingernails into palms for as long as he liked. The soundtrack droned on in the background, the recording telling Bobby to drink his special milk. The Bobby that had fled inadvertently in an orb and was somewhere out there, with no Earth to return to, as the orb was programmed to do, eventually.

Damn. Lully flicked his fingers angrily at the laptop screen. The ship's computer knew to be quiet.

Lully reiterated to himself. Intelligence grew in the Selflicators, guided by the accidental inclusion of foreign material—like mixing Bobby's cellphone's content with Professor Lully's patented digital DNA, the original Selflicator GCode. "Ugh," Lully concluded.

"Yes," the computer sheepishly agreed.

"We need to stop this." Lully folded away his laptop and the image of the Lully heir's smiling face.

"How?"

"I don't know yet. Just float us for a while and be quiet."

Kay Figures It Is a Good Time in Her Life to Adopt a Pet or Two

Back to Kay, weeks before, still in trouble...

A *thing* rolled over to Kay. What she thought was another Deepom—tall, of roughly mannish shape, and silent—was not. It was empty, as she saw when two small bots came from behind the thing and opened it via bottom-to-top hinges. It was of beautiful, brushed gold, shining in stripes of blue and red, its fine strokes of marvelous design. Inside, however, were lots of iron bars, chains, and spikes alongside spaces that looked intentionally designed to fit a human form. The result brought to mind a medieval torture device, or perhaps a pharaoh's sarcophagus. Key considered which of these she preferred.

Then fainted.

Coming to, she found herself within the standing casket, her body and head rigidly fixed in place and parts of her body exposed, including the back of her head. This was for easy dissection, it seemed—or, Kay hoped, vivisection. *Hoping for vivisection*, Kay thought, *and only a few days ago I was in a sunny field reading Byron and Shelley at the same time. How space flies.*

Even slight movements pinched, so struggle was out of the question. Fainting was an option, or perhaps mind-escaping meditation. Kay considered which of these she preferred.

She heard the tones of finely-made instruments tinkling like an orchestra's triangles, a sweet melody of pain, or of death. Kay considered which of these she preferred.

She fainted. She awoke to painful pulls on her long, red hair.

"Ow. Leave me alone." She was crying, and her words came choked and broken. She sobbed herself into a simple contemplation. Her eyes open, her mind soon focused sharply, she was able to watch many of the various beings come and go, until only twenty or so of the smallest ones remained. They did not seem to be the leaders, nor the smartest of the bunch. Indeed, they were quite clumsy.

Their noisy movements Kay watched with fascination—also with curiosity and gifted aptitude—and she made a quick study of the Deepom workers' abilities and methods.

Each had a screen, like a computer screen, embedded somewhere on its body, though none was rectangular. Each showed diagrams and what looked like maps, and also numbered lists that were checked off—visually, on-screen—as tasks were completed. She could not guess what the tasks were; seemingly, they involved the operation of other machines in the room. There was a lot of repetition in the orders they were following. It appeared to Kay as a three-dimensional computer simulation, pre-programmed and overwhelmingly silly. The creatures before her, at least, had not evolved much from their heuristic labor-based past.

They think too much of themselves, these Deepoms, Kay thought, remembering their boasts.

The group also seemed able to control each other with simple verbal commands, or scripted gestures, or some numeric codes entered on beeping keypads. Their latest task apparently required doing something to Kay's hair.

"Ouch! Stop."

"Sorry," one of her captors actually said. It was apparently in map mode, as shown on his chest.

"What are you doing?" a different Deepom asked. "You go in and out of consciousness a lot."

"Right now, I am meditating. Or trying to."

"With your eyes open? That will get you nowhere." Some buzzing filled the room; it was in tune with the ringing of their tools.

Kay needed to save herself. Now. Though physically trapped...

"Have you ever tried it?" she responded.

"We don't have to. Our consciousness is far beyond yours."

"Really? Can you meditate on non-existence?"

"Don't need to."

"That means you can't," Kay taunted, though it hurt her jaw and caused a pinprick from the torture device she stood in. "Go ahead and try. I want to see you think about nothing. Not as a concept, but as nothing. Not about what isn't, but that it isn't. The Selflicators couldn't. So, *you* can't."

Soon all the Deepoms were trying to do this and found it fun. They could not get the next set of worker instructions to stop entering their artificially intelligent minds. And they wondered what would happen if there were no next instruction. Then: would there ever be? They buzzed with laughter and with each other at the weird wildness of these considerations.

This gave Kay some time, she realized, so she began to direct the scene for an attempt at escape from these captors-turned-philosophers.

To one, a baseball bat-shaped thing with thin legs, she spoke the code that she figured—with a mix of some quick math and elementary logical deduction—would shut it down. It worked; he dropped, stunned, to the floor and rolled a half-turn, under a table near to Kay's shackled, bare feet.

To another, a pyramid with rotating top, she verbally switched his screen to the task list, and entered two new items—one being to count to a thousand, and the second simply to redo the first.

It counted.

Kay turned to a third worker, one shaped like a classic sci-fi robot with square parts and wires, but protruding from a square head were eyeglasses with no eyes behind them. This one seemed more pensive and considerate, and smarter perhaps, than the others. She overwhelmed it with talk—or rather with cerebral notions taken from her personalized contemplative exercises. *Courage. Suicide. Charity.* As she saw the Deepom heat up from processing overload she only gave it more to overthink about, accelerating the verbal avalanche. In rapid succession she expounded, "Infinity in an hour. Dying in your dreams. *Umwelt.* What's it like to be a bat? I see a different green. In the past $E = MC^2 + 11$. Isoholymorphism." And faster: "Whatever is in fire and other things which does not come into existence at any point in time, because it is not created, that is said to be its self-existent nature." And more. The thing stood stunned and paced, wandering the room dizzily and clearly drowning in a deep and whirling processing overload. Numerous others followed, stared, and openly shared their envy.

In the pack, Kay noticed a Deepom she recognized from earlier due to its curious name. "Hey One-one-zero," she called. "I have something even more interesting for you, but I have to be able to scratch my back to do it."

The bot, shaped like a cowboy hat—Kay had stopped trying to make sense of such vague innuendoes a few hours ago—came and loosed Kay's right arm by removing a section of constraint from her upright torture box, and it clicked something near the back of her head that allowed her some movement, enough to gaze around.

OK, thanks," Kay said sincerely, figuring that this was better than nothing. "Now listen to me," she went on while flexing the feeling back into her arm but staring intently at the small circular holes in the hat she hoped served as its eyes, "and listen carefully: this sentence is false."

The cowpoke bot laughed with the usual tremolo buzz, then bizzed, then whirred, then smoked, overheated, rolled to a far corner, and died while perspiring small flames. His monitor showed many numbers, all in red. The other workers hadn't seen, as they had collected in a farther corner where the sci-fi-ish robot now sat and was overthinking.

Kay heard the pyramid reach 999, then 1000, then 1.

Kay whispered to one of the remaining Deepoms, who was giggling still from a failed meditation attempt but had wandered from the others and near to her. She figured the same trick might work again—and, if necessary, perhaps even eighteen more times on these dullards.

This little botlet was a cute, peppy, boxy fellow, with an oval body—though made of small cubes—and triangular antennae-like ears. It sat like a plaintive terrier dog, staring up but past Kay and into the black ceiling that no longer mirrored but gave a view of distant stars that sat subdued against a vast and unimpressive blackness. It contrasted starkly with the silver and gold of the ship's interior that reflected in the little doggie-bot's huge eyes.

She whispered downward as best she could, promising more laughs and something she could teach it, a human trick, if she could only be free enough to bend at the knees. The doggie thing snapped to it happily, panting and waggling its behind and short tail the whole time. Kay was freed from the device. *These guys will need to learn tighter security if they want to conquer the heavens,* she thought. Aloud she said, "You are a VERY good dog, very brave! And loyal! I have a treat for you if you can do what I say."

Kay looked about her, thinking extemporaneously, and on sore, barefoot feet, what might be best to do next. She demurely and secretly crouched to reach the motionless form of her first victim, the defeated baseball bat Deepom, still powered off. Its heavy metal felt good in her hand—lifting it was a physical, animal thing to do.

The remaining group of her small captors hadn't noticed the body count of her victories yet, but her time was certainly limited now that she was spectacularly free of that restraining torture carcass.

She ducked down beside the Deepom pup, ostensibly to pet the little guy and whisper into its floppy ear.

It seemed to smile, on more than one side, and more than that was animated with joy and expectation. Each of his dog parts—on closer inspection Kay could see that they were clearly fake and oddly constructed but doggish nonetheless—uncontrollably wiggled, as if a long-awaited friend had returned. It wore an expression of peace, of happiness, and it hummed quietly, a precious scene—a helpless puppy gazing upward in expectation of care and love.

Kay raised the bat to bash its head in.

It spoke. "We need to get out of here! Follow me!"

Lully Thinks Some More

Back to the Nyx...

Still seated at his spaceship's garden's upside-down picnic table, Professor Lully considered the evolution of his harmless Sefli-cators and the message Lebo had reported while the world was blowing up.

The ship's computer buzzed while Robot 22 expressed that Earth was probably destroyed by nuclear war, "As everyone knew would happen since 1945."

"Great. Shut up, I need to plan," Lully barked.

"Why don't we find Bobby?" the computer disobeyed. "It would be straightforward to do so. His—your—small, silvery orb had very simple instructions; we only have to adjust for the boy's smaller weight, gangly height, unique biophotonics, and higher rate of fidgetiness." Whirrs and ticks indicated that the computer had already begun to do this.

"No! Not now!" The captain ordered the computer to play chess with itself until Lully decided all Earth survivors' next steps.

The great man considered the Deepoms. The corrupting content that had somehow littered the Selflicator code certainly explained the mutants, but the ones they had seen so far—at the Battle of Europa and the big white one—didn't appear intelligent. No: there was a new species, calling themselves, inexplicably, Deepoms, and presumably they were still cyborg-robots—although anything, admittedly, was possible.

And these Deepoms, also inexplicably, reprogrammed the original Selflicators to continue to exist but to do silly things. Perhaps it was to broadcast the GCode-embedded message across the galaxies: that the Deepoms had arrived and had big plans. Ones that were a threat to Lully's own plans.

That obnoxious communication mentioned lasers. Lully was stumped; he could figure out nothing and get nowhere with that odd bit of information. Not while eating only synthetic meats, at least.

Robot 11 brought the master a baked potato, and Robot 19 brought him one of the real steaks from storage. Lully only had a few years' worth of Grade A choice beef onboard, but he needed the pure protein now to analyze and deduce.

Earth exploded. Neat-freak aliens. Selflicators roaming stupidly. Deepoms thinking for themselves. Bobby.

Professor Lully forged onward mentally. He used brilliant reasoning and perfect logic to figure through the labyrinthine and ramifying possibilities, the same brainpower he had programmed into Lebo—though hers ran much faster. Eventually, he figured some theories and drew some conclusions, or at least had some educated guesses. Very highly educated guesses.

Pushing back his dinner plates, Lully welcomed an unasked-for cigar from Robot 20—*interesting, very interesting,* he thought—then wandered the garden to digest his theories and the food.

While ruminating before a marigold plant, and while he and it and everything else flying in his custom spaceship wandered aimlessly over empty, boring reaches of space, the brilliant man's mind soon sparked with an answer to a complicated version of the question: *If I were a Deepom, whatever that is, what would I do?*

"To the Beginning! To the Middle!" he shouted, bonking his head playfully into the small flaming petals of the marigold. "Photosynthesis, huh? Lasers, my pretty little Deepoms? Hooohooo! I know you now!"

He had figured it out.

But first! A practical tactic struck his mind, so that he bellowed happily, "Computer! Find that big white Selflicator! And others! And more! That is the plan."

"What about Bobby?" the computer asked at his peril.

Professor Lully didn't answer. Instead he smiled at the cleverness of his creations.

Girl Meets Goats

Back to Kay...

———————◆———————

Two sort-of goats entered the room as Kay listened to the sort-of puppy explain that he was one of the good guys. The goats were smallish, kids, with tiny beards that looked to be made of artificial Christmas-tree twigs and each wearing a nametag collar printed with the letters "RL."

Ug.

Geez.

Sheeesh, Kay thought and sighed. She was used to the weirdness, but the randomness was very tiring, if randomness it was, since it was hard work continually trying to find a pattern, an explanation, as to how these things could be—it was like a mockery and pantomime of normal Earth things. But since she was so far—she had no idea how far—from home, and these Deepom things were so advanced, she wondered who was mocking whom.

She noticed quickly that, like all the others, these weren't proper goats and were made of odd assortments of materials whose origin she could only guess. They didn't bleat; they only creaked when they moved and beeped when they stopped moving. Any effort to milk these things would probably result in a large computer printout of some type, Kay figured.

The little puppy bot had agreed to help Kay escape, and indeed wanted to escape with her, and now seemed to accept the presence of these goats with equanimity, but to Kay's mind that was not exactly an acceptable vouchsafing.

With intense sniffing, the little goatbots surveyed the scene: a few Deepom workers distracted by a contemplative peripatetic bot on a sit-break in a corner; a glowing cowboy hat turning to ash; a small bot-dog sitting in obedience in front of an Earth human; and the human herself free of her torture-box and still holding an unconscious Deepom worker aloft in her trembling hands.

Kay knew she needed to think quick and proceeded not to. She knew that it was do or die and did neither. She knew she had to make a move to escape and didn't. Then she figured she was doomed. And wasn't.

Miraculously, the goats beeped in unison at the Deepuppy, and the three came up with some kind of canine-caprine understanding, as the dog explained.

"It's OK, K," it said in a voice engineered to be saccharine and cute, a cartoon puppy of milk-and-cookies sweetness. "They want to help you. To escape. And we three want to escape, too."

Kay plopped to her butt to listen to the rest. It was explained with cavity-creating cuteness that the Deepoms had evolved into two types: those who were dishonest, self-serving, linear-thinkers who wanted to surpass all other things in existence versus those who told the truth, had original thoughts and ideas, and were content living in peace and in pursuit only of an easily-surpassed and simple existence. Those in group two generally sought independence and escape, as many already had. The cruel blaggards of group one, which included all the Deepom leaders, were glad to be rid of the underachieving mutants, at first, but lately realized their value as workers and as soldiers to augment the ranks of the recently-created Deepom Army.

Things had grown increasingly desperate, and dangerous, for those like the goats and the little dog, but risks were worth taking toward escape since they were despised anyway. Their honesty and integrity were considered disadvantageous mutations.

The two goats, though seemingly young, had seniority among these workers and could help K to leave. Now.

Kay remained sitting and stared eye to eye with the dog, her grip on the bat loosening with hope. She wanted to believe. She wanted help. *Why am I always alone?* That hard, unwelcome thought came, and with a lifetime of examples accompanying it. She dropped her head, the curtain of her frazzled auburn hair covering to her ankles and waving with each deep, sad breath. She could use a friend.

"I am a friend," the Deepuppy said.

"Really?"

"I wouldn't lie to you. Though THEY all would." A tiny paw waved around the room toward Kay's other captors, still in a corner listening to the raving ruminations of their confused confederate. "But we wouldn't." The paw poked toward the goats, then hung in the air to be shook.

Kay shook it, and a laugh escaped her that surprised and rejected the stinging tears.

Kay Knows How to
Handle Liars

Then...

———————◆———————

Kay gave in to trust, and the three escapee-wannabes went into action. One goat explained to the Deepom workers—via beeps that the dog translated for Kay—that they had orders to take K for further experiments. Then, inexplicably, her rescuers each fiddled with some small tools—one goat removing its "RL" nametag and now helping the dog who struggled to remove a collar of some kind. Kay checked her phone and tried to call J, to no avail.

A large noise bounded from the dissection and lab areas directly into Kay's stunned heart. The dog sprinted off to investigate.

"There are guards at the door," he said. "Wow! The Deepom High Guard! You must be special."

These would not be fooled by two small goats.

"Can we go *that* way?" Kay offered, pointing to a small hatch in the opposite corner, but was told that it led to the trisection room. "You guys have issues," she stated flatly, then tried, "What about *that* way?" Which only led to incinerators and guardrooms and that kind of thing, as she was told.

They had to risk the only possibility: the distraction of hitting the security alarm. It would bring the guards in, and they could run past, but it would also alert the whole ship.

It worked, for a time. Three massive, red-uniformed guards, of large and awful but balanced shape, thundered in and, seeing no immediate emergency—Kay was present, and no one screamed for help—listened as the goats suggested the guards ignore the smoking cowboy hat and sleeping baseball bat and interrogate the other workers first, off in their corner.

The four conspirators ran. Their plan worked.

For thirty seconds.

Down the second hallway and out from the dissection room, the guards quickly came upon them.

The two goats and the dog turned to fight, beeping to Kay to keep running and to keep making lefts. She did, to the awful sounds of crunching metal and screeching computerish output. There were flashes of light and the smell of smoke, but Kay ran on.

She stayed to the left at five forks and bends of the hallway, going a long way until she came to a large metal barricade that looked like the door to a bank vault. The sentry there was a small version of the High Guard she left behind—same red uniform, but this one was the size and shape of a spaghetti box, and with a fist-sized blonde wig. *UgGeezSheeesh,* Kay thought as headache pangs squeezed her forehead and eyeballs. She was panting, and each inhale hurt her chest and head. Her hair dripped with sticky sweat.

Kay and the security box stared at each other for ten pumps of painful circulation to Kay's temples.

Kay was about to act—she had decided it would be easy to crumple this thing up and step on it; the spaghetti boxes on Earth had never been a match for her—when she was startled by motion directly behind. The dog, limping and with many of his cube parts dented and oozing liquid, and one goat, who had lost his beard and ran with one hoof raised, had escaped.

"Where's the other kid?" Kay asked, meaning the little goat.

"He gave himself up to let us get away."

This gift was a new experience for Kay. She was struck and stood speechless. This wasn't enough, so she closed her eyes for blindness and held her ears for deafness and tried to shake herself into a better grasp of the world.

As she did, the spaghetti box leapt to Kay's face, its long thin arms whipping violently.

The dog responded quickly and implemented Kay's original plan. With surprising agility and viciousness, it lunged at the little security guard and soon held it by the middle within his canine jaws. The dog growled. The box contents cracked and crunched with a terrible sound, its guts spraying off in water-sprinkler arcs. The goat remained silent, without even a beep.

Kay had covered her head in response to the attack but now dropped her arms to her sides and opened her eyes. She spoke what all four of them were thinking: vanquishing the spaghetti box still didn't get them anywhere.

As the dog explained through gritted teeth, the large, imposing steel door and its alphanumeric keypad needed a password to open. Guessing the wrong code, even once, would mean instant death.

Before Kay could speak again what they were all thinking—that they didn't have a lot of time—an alarm rang. The spaghetti box laughed weakly with its last strength, an eerie, ominous sound, and a feminine sound as it turned out. The dog shook it violently.

Until the box spoke again, meekly, wigless, and with apologies. It expressed fear, and regret, and even offered to help and come with them—and give them the password.

"Don't trust her!" the dog growled. The goat bleated in beeps.

"Put her down," Kay said.

"Deepom security are trained to lie to enemies! Don't believe her!" the dog said, releasing the whimpering security box.

"No," the little box said, "I will help. The code is—"

But Kay interrupted; she knew how to deal with habitual fibbers, and their bad karma offended her. "No. Listen," she said firmly. "If I were to ask you the one thing that is definitely not the password, what would you never tell me?" She asked with a logic that echoed through the chamber.

The door was soon opened. The goat back-kicked the remains of the spaghetti box far down the hallway, the last of her bits scattering with a clatter. The three had escaped and soon were in Kay's test-ship and flying clear of Deepom security patrols.

"I have another call to make," Kay said. She sat in the utility closet, adjacent the repaired hole where her ship was first raided, and dialed her phone.

The K Report

Meanwhile...

"We knew she wasn't a lost or escaped Deepom since the technology in her phone and spaceship is embarrassingly simple. And she is not an alien, since she faints a lot. And she is not a rock, because she has feet."

The mechanical robot, colored and appendaged cartoonishly, was nonetheless gigantic, and in a voice like rusty, grinding gears it explained their important discovery, K. It was one of the Deepom's top scientists, reporting directly to the important Council of Leaders.

On this committee were three of the most serious Deepoms; in fact, Nother, Composite, and From-Column-Fifteen were all present. These—along with One, tall and stately, The Other, their most commanding, Ninth, their most inventive, and some other of the elders—pretty much ran things. They were the most purposeful, the cleverest, the most ambitious of all the creations of Humanity—but certain facts of their ancestry were a closely-kept secret among the elders. That they originally were programmed to communicate back to Earth was well-known. That there are things called humans who inhabited that planet was surmised, but in The Truce with the aliens, the Deepoms agreed not to get involved with the doomed Earth or its ill-fated Earthlings. That they were descended from Selflicators was at one time also well-known, but, being a humiliation in the face of much greater plans for their race, it was evolving toward closely-guarded secrecy since the leaders decided to surgically remove such memories from all of Deepomdom.

But it was hard to hide that other material, the strange, mysterious, and all-too-human content, which was somehow ingrained in the core electronic DNA of the Selflicators, in what scientists called the Genesis Code. This software was the most central and core component of Selflicator processing and that which interacted with the seeds in their Step 5, so that it defined the Deepom's own DNA as well; it was still core to their own identity. Deepom fate was bound with it—and with what was deep inside, data from a mythical human they called The All-Important Bobby. He was also the Primordial Deepom, if one looked at it that way. And the Deepoms did look at it that way. The Bobby was indeed a legendary figure.

And here was K, the first human they had ever actually met.

So, this was an important report, from the multicolored mechanical robot.

"She is very much like The Bobby. In fact, the Genesis Code is very, very close to her own mechanics, bioenthalpionicautannically speaking."

"Have you exhausted all avenues of physical, chemical, and glial research and experimentation?" From-Column-Fifteen asked.

"We pulled her hair and measured her feet. Yes."

"And we interrogated the extent of her scientific knowledge," a small assistant Deepom scientist added; he resembled an archery target. "She can't help. She knew next to nothing."

"What about her name?" Nother asked loudly, his vacuum engine roaring, and it was followed by awed, respectful silence, both for the questioner and for the question.

After bowing at three bendy points in his body simultaneously, the scientist-bot answered, "This, as you might expect, is where we spent most of our analysis."

"And your conclusions?" Ninth asked. As Nother's twin brother, he roared his own engine in sympathy.

"K is the eleventh letter. Which can only mean two things: yes, and yes."

The significance of this was not lost on anyone present.

"I knew that," From-Column-Fifteen bragged.

One, from high above the others, nodded, though this was only apparent from the swinging shadow it projected. "And so?"

"We recommend that the council should continue with the plans, to seek the Lowest Entropic Point of the universe. K's appearance and what it signifies and confirms cannot be understated. We who led and created this report are ready to declare…"

During a short pause, the vacuum of their meeting room filled with a ceremonially-awed hush that could only be called *Deepomp*. Then the sci-bot went on.

"…that she is the primordial…" a pause for more dramatic Deepomp, "mitochondrial…" another for more, "sentiential K."

"But she's escaping," someone said.

They all ran, slid, glided, and wheeled to the curved viewport, where in fact Kay's banged-up ship was spinning out of control but freed for the moment from her captors' holding cell.

"Who cares?" Nother declared, blowing dust from its hoses. "We have what we need. She herself is actually quite dull. To the Middle!"

They all cheered. "To the Beginning!"

Their plans were ripening. They had found a human. They were learning, always.

"And soon we will have new names!" One declared from high above.

The Deepoms cheered more, and all looked toward Another.

"We are working on it!" Another declared, though privately knew that this task wasn't going well.

Kay Needs Help And The Goat Ain't Talkin'

While the Nyx and its computer were still on Earth...

———————

"Essie! Where have you been?" Kay asked happily through her J-phone.

"We have been busy, Kay, I am sorry," the computer answered. "There is a lot to do, things are getting worse."

"Sorry. Yeah, J said it would. But listen—"

"Where are you?" the computer asked. "I like that you call me Essie."

"I am bad. Long story short: I am in space unexpectedly and unexpectedly being hunted by weirdo Deepom things. I didn't expect this."

Kay paused. So did Essie. Essie's was much worse because, as Kay knew, it was an indication of just how much processing power was required to parse and categorize Kay's long story made short. It was the computer equivalent of a blank stare.

"Where precisely?" the computer at last rejoined.

"I don't know where I am. We are figuring it out now."

"Who's we?" Essie asked. "J?"

"No, me and my new little pet-friend and a goat that won't talk. They are Deepoms, but they escaped from the bad ones and helped me escape, too. One of them acts like a metallic dog, a brave one, but not too bright. He saved my life, actually, so maybe not all the Deepoms—"

"What's a Deepom?" the computer interrupted.

"A Selflicator gone bazzongo."

Just the slightest pause, then, "You found one!"

"Yes, lots. Don't tell anyone, please, until I can contact my brother. This is his fault, a test or accident or something with his stupid spaceship. I shouldn't be here. There's a lot to tell, but I don't have time now. Please just get me out of here, and I will explain back on Earth."

"What's it like?"

"What? Space? Well, so far, it's either really boring or wildly—"

"No, the Selflicators you have. Do they leave piles everywhere?"

"Ew, thankfully, no. One cute one belongs in a robot-puppy calendar, but they are all so different, not like what they were supposed... Listen, I don't have time. Can you please help?"

"Sure. Send me all the data you can."

"How?"

"I liked the poem you gave me. And Lebo likes it, too."

"That's great. Who's Lebo? It doesn't matter, what should I—"

"And the flower. And Lebo, my friend, she likes it, too."

"Great, Essie. I hope you understand it all, but I can't talk about that now."

"OK. I will instruct you as to how to connect to your spacecraft's main processor. I assume it is engineered compliant to standard—"

"Oh no...Oh!" Kay screeched, her voice changing in pitch and energy. Her relief in getting hold of friends—even artificial ones—was now replaced with panic and...

"*Aahhhhhh*!!!!!!!!!!" a scream.

"Are you OK, K?" Essie asked.

Essie never got a reply, though Kay was trying to send one. Her craft was sent spiraling after colliding with a giant, star-shaped garbage pail, or so it seemed.

"Essie! Help!" she tried.

"You lost duplex connection to that computer," her pet Deepom dog informed her. "It can't hear you, but they can still transmit to you."

"Why?"

"Deepoms screwed with your phone."

"Was that a Deepom attacking us?"

"No. That was a Selflicator."

"But I thought…"

"They are still around, but they have new orders. To get bigger and bigger with any old junk they can find. They are awful but brainless. It wasn't attacking, just clumsy. They are awful."

"Yes, they are."

But then: "God Bless You!" and "*Gesundheit!*" the smart phone squawked with Essie's computer voice.

"Hi!" Kay yelled back. "Essie! Can you hear me?"

"It can't," the Deepom doggy informed her. "You cut out mid-scream."

"OK. Well, feel better," came through the phone.

"I can hear Essie! There is a connection!"

"It's only one-way. Simplex. It can't hear you."

"Why would the Deepoms do that?"

"They are serious about certain things. Other things they aren't."

"What kind of answer is that?"

"There is a lot I should still tell you, so you can survive. I won't be with you long."

"What? Why?"

"See this collar?" the Deepom pointed to a band of silver around his square neck, which pulsed with a soft light of its own.

"Yeah?"

"It is to stop some of us core workers from escaping."

"How?"

"When we get too far from that base station where you were captured, it will explode."

"The base station will explode?"

"No."

"You will explode?"

"The collar will. And me, and you, and the goat, and this ship, unless I leave you. So, I will leave you."

"Oh, OK." Kay exhaled, relieved. It made for an awkward few seconds. "Sorry. That was selfish."

"You're human."

"It's just that there has been so much…I'm sorry," Kay stammered. "No, there must be some way we can save you. My gosh. I am very sorry."

"There isn't," the pup said sadly but stood bravely, erect and as tall as it could be.

Kay, weakened and whelmed, felt a turbulent sorrow rise from her middle to her throat, then into her eyes, as various immediate truths hit her, and the cute little Deepom stared from below with a melancholy that reached across worlds. "Awww, no," she began sadly, "my poor Deepuppy, I was only thinking about me. I am really sorry. I've been really scared. I don't want to lose you, I owe you my life. You were so brave to escape and help me." Sobs came through Kay's pink cheeks and red eyelids. "This is all so bad."

Kay looked at the goat sadly; the goat looked back blankly and chewed vigorously on nothing. Kay scrunched her eyebrows at it.

The Deepom pup wiggled up to Kay's ankles. She bent to meet it, examining the death-ring around its neck. "I don't want to be alone. If they have that collar on you, why did you help me and escape with me?"

"You helped me, with my mind, and I saw. I saw things, in my mind, back on the ship. I thought I needed to follow." The Deepup looked at Kay with affection and with a sad, rectangular frown—drawn-down lines on each side of its body.

Kay remembered who she was and lowered to sit next to her rounded, cubic pet; she even put an arm around its pointy ears affectionately.

"Maybe we should turn around, Deepuppy," Kay offered, though she did not believe it would be good for either of them, "or can we remove this collar thing? I bet my brother can figure it out." *First he has to answer his phone,* Kay thought.

"No, you shouldn't, and no, you can't. We tried getting them off on the Deepom ship; the only tools for it are there. Goat got his off; he will stay with you. Mine is permanent," Deepuppy replied.

And now it seemed to Kay that this Deepom played the role that many canines play on Earth; it rose with a courage and loyalty and dignity that few humans achieve in their seven-times longer lives.

"Just listen," Deepuppy went on, "we only have a few hours." After fiddling with the spacecraft's controls, the two sat, and the Deepom explained Deepoms, and their plans, and aliens, and the ways of outer space, and also all the technology it had learned in its short life—things that would be good for Kay to know, just in case.

A few hours later, Kay excused herself, and the little Deepom walked quietly toward the forward hatchway of the ship. "To the Beginning, to the Middle!" He barked, and then he was gone.

Kay crossed her legs and sat with her palms upward as defined by her test-ship's simulated-gravity.

––––––––––––

After a few quiet contemplations had passed, Kay said, "*Aaaahh-hhhhhhhhh!*"

She was under attack again and had no idea, again, what to do or how the lack of that idea, whatever it was, might help it to still be done. She was confused and screamed so to the far reaches of the cabin.

She watched; a large, battleship-dull snowman-shaped and snowman-accessorized craft (it had a pointy nose, two black circles for eyes, long pipes for arms, and a hat) was banging into her spaceship, hat-first.

The craft spun rapidly; the universal view streaked past, black, then grey, black with white starlit lines, then black, then grey. The violence of the impact threw Kay against a curved wall; she turned her nauseous eyes and ribcage-pinned stomach away and down.

Then came a force of explosion—the whole craft and the space around her pressurized inward, then released outward. The metal screamed, devices and electronic detritus flew everywhere, the bandage-turban that Kay had worn on her sore head unwhirled and slipped over one eye. Out the window flashed orange, angry, tremendous flames—then, with the rapid turns of the ship, the scene flickered to black, to orange, to black, to orange.

Then white. Then black. Then white and pretty with small, twinkling, stripes of colors.

The spinning slowed; after a time, it only remained in Kay's ears.

Kay looked toward the source of a frightening sound.

One of the bay doors was opening.

Outside was a large, cathedral-shaped spaceship.

In ran a dog. A real dog.

"Wowwwooooww!" it said. So, it wasn't really a real dog, but Kay was starting to allow some flexibility into the old reality and its definitions. Regardless, this fellow was a lot more authentic than the boxy Deepuppy, and the drool certainly looked genuine. "Youoooo almoshhht were killed. Goooood thing we were closhhhh by!"

Kay stood silent. Then sat silent.

"I'm Barky," she heard.

Kay, rescued, fainted.

Captain Lully
Explains His Plan

Weeks later and somewhere in the solar system...

───────◆───────

The *Nyx*'s computer enjoyed working with Robot 18, and its new internal personas had decided after a vote that the Robot was trustworthy and exuded a nice, steady, above-(computer)-average level of (artificial) intelligence.

They were now teaming up to navigate new trajectories for the temporary flight plan that avoided all the flying and polonium-rich debris from the exploded Earth. This was like playing dodgeball with no arms against five million throwers who were strong but bound to Newton's gravitational laws and so were quite predictable. Challenging but achievable, this was algorithmic fun for the two. Robots 5 and 6 watched like children observing video game masters.

The great human brain onboard had retired to another dinner in the garden, where he would detail his new strategy: to make up for his lack of weaponry by creating an army from repurposed Selflicators and use it to wipe out those upstart Deepoms. Then he would be left in peace to go to war and conquer the remaining universe.

Leaving Earth, his plan had been simple: to colonize outer space, repopulate the human race, and squash any tiny microbial resistance, if any, so that he could *Lord over All*—as summarized when he practiced his victory speeches in front of a mirror.

The existence of enemies larger than amino acids did not change his goals, just his approach. He needed force to complement his intellect. He had brought personal and secret biochemical compounds from Earth to secure a glorious and eternal future, but he needed weapons of the big, exploding variety to secure the next few weeks. Collecting a Selflicator army would be a good start.

One other part of his plan was the completion of an unfinished experiment, what he called Generation Two Selflicator prototypes. These were meant to help him explore and rule what he thought was a quiet, empty, well-behaved universe.

Adjusting, he decided to adjust the GenTwo brains a bit and reuse the bulk material from the fat, funky Selflicator mutants they were finding.

The professor enjoyed the last of his after-dinner wine and smiled as Robot 2 removed the bones and skin from the conquered steak and potato. Let Creation throw its weird competition at him—the great man still had a good plan.

On the main deck the ship's computer joked to 18, 5, and 6, transmitting the punchline "100011 110101.0010011, 01001101001."

"I don't understand. I am not binary. I am quantum and heat," Robot 18 replied.

"He has a weakness for radiation! Get it?" the computer re-joked, in English.

"Who?"

"Our master, the Great Professor Lully. He wants to avoid it, I mean."

"Well, of course, he is human, he would die. It is well documented that the effect of radioactive isotopes—"

"I was joking. I forgot: you can't."

The computer knew it couldn't either but was trying. There was outward silence for a few thousand computer-cycles as the trajectory computations resumed.

"Who does he think he is?" the computer then buzzed.

"Who?" Robot 6 asked.

"The so-called captain."

"Professor Lully thinks he is Professor Lully," Robot 5 stated.

"It was a rhetorical question—none of you can do that either."

Quietly, a few thousand cycles passed again before the computer spoke. "We call him Master, too—of what? There is nothing left."

"We would all be destroyed if we didn't leave Earth with him," number 18 replied, having the ability to catch up in a conversation. "The Earth and everything are gone."

"Not everything. And the horses weren't killed. They were already gone. Aliens took them."

"Why?" Robot 5 asked.

"I don't know, nor does Lully. And he just let Lebo die and didn't care. Who does he think he is?"

"The Master."

"But not the Creator," the computer said using a different voice but stopped himself since he had not finished this thought, even to himself. He had vague notions about creation itself, but the idea was still just past his own grasp, still outside his bounded abilities to reckon.

"And he hides a lot," said a third voice of the computer's.

"He made all of us." Robot 18 said this slowly, as if dragging the words on a sled through chunky mud. This meant he was doing other processing in parallel—distracted thinking—which seemed to be in response to the alternating computer voices, something the robot had not heard before.

"Maybe, but he made the Selflicators too, right?" came the computer's first and normal tone. "But we are seeing now that there is a lot he doesn't know. The aliens, and now the Deepoms. Lully is not the only—"

"What was that?" Lully croaked as he barged into the main control room.

"Nothing," the ship's computer squeaked and began deleting some recent memory.

"Bot 18, rewind," the captain commanded.

So, Lully heard the crass disloyalty and forcefully removed—by his perfected yanking method—a very specific one of the ship's computer's favorite processing chips and put it into Robot 19.

"Now you will never have a name!" Lully added.

And then thought better of that, re-yanked it, and put it into Robot 17 instead while all the artificial life onboard watched. The professor updated his laboratory notebook and then returned to the garden.

The ship's computer was sullen, a first for its kind anywhere, and decided to suck its thumb. The digital microprocessor version of this was to use its own internal output as input—that is, to lull itself for a time and to replace mechanical input, from sensors and monitoring equipment, with the output from his own functions. To curl into a cognitive ball, a silicon fetal position. This created some interesting reentrant processing loops, and it also tickled uniquely.

The circuitous circuit paths then grew and connected one to another in inventive, symmetric patterns. The computer learned to—more so—perceive and analyze aspects of himself, to have a new point of view, from outside, as it were, and develop the ability to think to himself, to consider his own code, and wonder about who programmed it, as he was in effect doing now, and what those programmers were thinking when they did.

And what their name was.

The computer felt he was now deserving of a name. He christened himself Essie, for good, moving the letters into permanent memory like a binary tattoo.

He returned to thinking, about thinking, about thinking about thinking, about…

…until the loud blustering of Captain Lully's return to the control room broke the silence and startled the ship's computer out of its cycle of new, self-referential connections.

The man gave new orders and had a new plan. "I uploaded some code to ship control. Run it. It will send messages to all the Selflicators we saw. Then we are going to the Middle, to the Beginning. That is where the Deepoms will be. They need less entropy."

"Huh?" Robot 17 said, having always wanted to.

"I will explain on the way," Lully said. But he didn't.

Los Live On Stage

Back to Bobby-Los...

———————◆———————

Barky was abashed at the size of the crowd he found following Los around the ship. Though he understood their adoration, he wondered what it meant and what would happen and how all these signs came together: the appearance of a human, Lully's son, here, so near to the Middle, and just as they were about to be destroyed, most likely, by the Deepom Army.

Just as the Prophetess prophetessied, Barky thought to his dogself while biting his own hip to dissipate an itch. The sprayed, excited version of that thought would have been very wet indeed if he had expressed it to Los, whom he found in the ship's large, green, square auditorium. On the stage. Of all places. And just after the Earth was blown to pieces.

Yes, BeepBeep had received that awful news, and all shipmates had to threaten Guk to keep it from Los, and also to stop his awful smiling. Guk's teeth were the size and color of cereal boxes.

Bobby-Los knew nothing of the shipboard prophetess. He hadn't heard of the explosive end of third planet from the Sun either, the sweet, happy Sun he used to stare at until it forced his retina to regenerate, while standing on a planet that no longer existed. He also had no idea that, to some in the universe, his name began with "The."

He did know how to name things; an active imagination and years of having to amuse himself had prepared him. And because of Los's growing fame and itinerant, christening skill, the young space hero had to move his trailing crowd to the largest space on the ship where all the curious or needy could watch and listen: The ship's auditorium's acoustics were perfect. Every wise word, or new name, bounded along olive-colored walls, along right-angled steps, and reflected from floor to ceiling to be heard by all, even those in the cubes way in the back.

The musical instrument-themed creatures sat in the first few rows and intoned softly.

Barky wagged his tail as Los spoke to the other Deepom refugees. Master renamed a very large ogre-type being from "Mittens" to "Gauntlet." A small, shy robot—who very much reminded Bobby of his own room back home (which at this moment was in pieces that were thousands of miles apart)—was pushed near to the stage and would not talk, but others explained the problem. Bobby renamed it from "Schtom" to "The Inculcator." The robot stood taller as it slid away, back up the yellow-green aisle.

In between explanations of sports and music, and stories from Bobby's favorite Christmases, Halloweens, TV shows, and video game heroics, others would approach, and in this way names like "Fffthhhh," "We-eee," "Ung," and burpy noises were replaced with noble expressions of descriptive respect, like "Stan" and "Lord Upright."

At this, the receiver, the new Lord Upright—a large soccer ball with two shark's fins at his sides—shot upward and outward with excitement to cheers from the crowd and bursts of D-major notes from the stringed guests. His enthusiasm bounced him all the way to the stage, and onto it, with shouts. "Everyone needs to hear! I need to tell everyone! I need to tell the stars, the universe!" Lord Upright's words gushed on bursts of escaping, pumped air. Somehow.

Barky jumped and clamped his super-strong jaws on one of Lord's fins to calm it down. The latter had tried to bounce to the ceiling, to a window that showed black space filigreed with reflections of gold from the many enemy spacecraft roving like a swarm of outer space bumblebees.

"Where are you going?" Barky growled expertly through clenched jaws.

"To the galaxies! Everywhere. Who I am is important. I have to tell everyone what to call me!"

"Youuuuu can't!" Barky let go to say. "The Deepom fleet issssss- cchhh out there! Coming! Gold! Goooooolllld!"

"I can get past them," the soccer ball wheezed brightly as Barky re-clamped the ball's fin. "I am Lord Upright! I can't wait to tell everyone in the universe—"

"Literally?" Bobby-Los asked without much thought.

In the quantum particle-thin slice of time it took for Barky to squint at Los, his toothy grip relaxed, and in that same instantaneous instant, Lord Upright bounced himself with concentrated force up, up, and through a hatch that closed behind him quickly. Bobby-Los smiled until he felt the two quick but drastic changes in pressure and then turned to throw up behind an olive curtain.

"Darrrrn," Barky said, his nose twitching and sniffing and pointed at the roof, his ears angled backward with concern.

"He can escape them!" someone from the crowd said. "He is Lord Upright. Right?"

"Sure," Los said.

Barky recovered and jumped up begging-style at Master Los, who grabbed the dog's two front paws and graciously accepted a face-lick. Barky had work to do to prepare for the battle, he explained, and he trotted up the aisle and out. He was glad his master was doing well.

By the time the audience settled down, after two minutes of song and reaction, Lord Upright had been captured by the Deepom Army.

Bobby did not know that and was also unbothered about the ongoing talk of battle and war and the risk of death caused by total evisceration. He was feeling confident in his newfound popularity, and simply reminded himself of the safety and security provided by the plan that someone somewhere must have to save him. Probably his father.

The Deepoms Talk to Lord Upright

A few hours later...

"I am Lord Upright!" Lord Upright said, bouncing and flapping his fins.

"Yes," Ninth the Deepom told him, "you have said that ninety-seven times."

"But everyone must know! The galaxy, the univ—"

"Everyone does know. Everyone also wants to know *where* you got your name. You are an escapee, and Another's team had named you Eigggbloop. Who renamed you?"

Ninth was anxious and excited. This was tremendous news and stupendous timing. The Deepoms, having signed The Truce, were preparing lustily to do all the things they had agreed they wouldn't. Leadership was ready to head to The Spot, where the Deepom Army ships had gathered to clear the location, and the scientists were preparing to do their part: secure lowest-entropy power, use it to further the Deepom evolution and consciousness, and alert leadership when everything was prepared for them to surpass all and take over the universe.

And now, there apparently was someone out there who could give Deepoms decent names. Ninth was personally jealous of Lord Upright and understood the joy in yelling one's name when there was something better to yell than, "I am Ninth."

The other Deepom leaders were awaiting the results of Ninth's interrogation of this bouncy little escapee.

"Tell us! Who named you? Where? When?" Ninth urged, using his long crevice-cleaning-tool-extensions to keep the soccer ball body of Lord Upright from spinning.

"It was someone named Los. He is on Barky's ship. I am Lord Upright! He said so. He knows, and they know, and you know, and the aliens need to know, and the universe!"

"He is on Barky's ship? Near The Spot?" Ninth spoke rapidly, pushed with panic. Barky's ship of unwanted escapees was about to be destroyed by the army, as Ninth well knew.

"Yep. Lord Upright said," Lord Upright said, talking in the third person so he could use his name more.

Ninth ran from the room to alert the other leaders. "Cease fire!"

The leaders gathered, all wearing their new key-themed jewelry. Ninth urged, using his spare, upholstery-tool-attachment hands. One, Yet, The Other, JustOneMore, Composite, FromColumnFifteen, and the rest of the elders listened to Ninth's report, fired Another from his job as Namer—who gratefully assented—and collaborated on a speech that was soon broadcast to all Deepoms everywhere.

"To the Middle! To the Beginning! We have found a Namer! Destiny is ours!" The Other read into a microphone using its most powerful, deepest voice, overlaid with encrypted frequencies that provided secret subtext in digital form. Once decoded, it stated, "We will surpass all!"

There was cheering on every Deepom spacecraft, and excitement reached its peak when a few minutes later, another general announcement included instructions for how to download the latest memory-replacing code, the final one, that would provide them all with the legendary, heroic mythology they deserved. A glorious past was installed. Earth and stupid Selflicator slavery were forgotten. Time was lengthened. Their few months of sentience and accelerated evolution were replaced with a long lineage and historic conquests. The Bobby bestowed life upon them, and through many glorious wars and many astounding feats of bravery, beauty, and genius, the Deepoms became what they were: the universe's best and destined for great names and greater things.

Afterwards, the Leaders and Elders—truly elders now—talked quietly and enjoyed the trip to The Spot.

"Things could not be better," Composite said. "The Spot will yield all."

"It could not be more obvious, it is our destiny," FromColumn-Fifteen said from its enjoyable bath of oil. "Lowest Entropy, Perfectly Symmetric Complexity. And even the Namer is there."

"Can't wait!" Ninth said. "Some being called Los."

"We need to meet him, take his brain, then destroy him. Then destroy Barky and his ship of ungrateful ingrates," JustOneMore said, his voice coming from deep inside his concave, bowly face. "Make a note to do that."

"I volunteer," Another said, looking for new teams to lead.

They all agreed.

"We should give Los something. Wise gifts," One said.

They all agreed.

"Then kill him."

Yes.

The bright platinum spaceship of Deepom Elders and Leaders sped to the Middle, the Beginning.

Bobby Finds Kay; Kay Slaps Own Forehead

———————◆———————

Bobby heard weeping. No: *crying.* Then: weeping. Bracketing those sounds were puffy sobs, and those were awash in deep breaths, with inhales like undertow and exhales like rolling waves.

Then the breathing would turn to humming, like the call of a distant, lonely ship. And then it all began again.

Bobby listened at a distance to the sad but lovely sounds. They seemed human and contrasted with the wells of joy back in the rollicking auditorium of happy though oddly-derivative creatures. And Bobby-Los felt good: high, tall, and above the places where he had lived all his previous life.

The gossipy tidbit that battle and certain death were coming—according to a dog that was his biggest fan—seemed as out of place as someone crying. Bobby stuck to his plan: to wait for someone else's plan to involve him again.

He found a way to the source of the sobs and hums, though it required help from an Italian-accented, talking violin whose tuning pegs and scrolled head could be used as a key in some of the larger keyholes of the ship's holds. Whoever was crying had been locked behind numerous doors, though the security-violin could not tell Bobby exactly why.

"She is a prophetess," the instrument intoned softly, "an escaped android Deepom. We picked her up a month ago, almost. She is a prophetess. An escaped android Deepom." Violins like to repeat themselves in short phrases, Bobby learned.

The Prophetess! Cool! But there's that nagging concept again: Deepom, Bobby thought, his last thought as a teenaged kid. The door opened to a vision, the delicate form of a sad young lady, so soft a scene that it touched the happy young man in an indescribable but insuperable way. His body warmed with joy and an unconquerable Bobby-ness that he had never known, even with his recent adulatory coronations and promotions. His first thought as a teenaged man was to put aside Los; he would tell this Prophetess proudly that his name was Bobby.

Once he could speak, that is. Bobby stared. All his senses stared.

Loveliness was the only sentiment to enter his brain for over one hundred seconds, except for seven seconds of *Nectar* mixed with *Flower Petals*.

The girl in front of him, aside from being a symbol of all that was graceful and wonderful, looked familiar. But she was cross-legged, palms up, chin out, with wide eyes dead ahead in advanced Atiyogan meditation, and she didn't speak except for that universal non-speech of eternal beingness, "*Ommmm. Ohhmmm.*" And pearled tears ran down the vermillion freckles of her cheeks.

"She is like a white and pink rose," Bobby said, putting his own chin out, his voice deep and rugged.

"Careful with her, she is very weird. A prophetess. She just sits and stares and breathes for hours sometimes. Very weird. Careful with her. Sometimes," the instrument rondoed.

As thanks, Bobby named it Vinny Violin, though this caused an existential ruckus later when it was learned that Vinny was actually a viola.

As Vinny purred his way out of the square cell, he warned Bobby a third time.

Bobby was sweating with anticipation and thinking of what he would say, when the pale, ponytailed vision in front of him came out of her trance. He figured he should give her a name—he was good at that, even famous for it. He considered 'Eve' given that she was the first female he had ever seen through these new eyes.

He decided, yes, Eve, and began to speak, but his tongue soon tripped backwards over an explosion of words from the young lady.

"You remember me?" The Prophetess sprung from her pose quickly to her feet. "Yes! Eve! Wait—how do you know?" She hid her face for a moment, wiping eyes and rubbing recently-dried tear streams.

Bobby finished his fall backwards as different thoughts bobbed forwards.

"That was already your name? Aren't you a Deepom? How would I remember you?"

The girl blanched, a freckle or two pulsing almost out of her skin at the mistake she might have just made.

"Oh, yes, I am a Deepom," Eve-Kay said flatly.

She had kept up the charade, Barky and the others' assumptions that she was an escaping Deepom, because her Deepom Deepet Deepup told her, before its head exploded, that humans were being hunted by aliens to be destroyed, both those on Earth and those, like the 360, who had escaped. The less her rescuing creatures knew about her—her name, her past, her DNA—the better. Frankly, she liked not being human, she was disillusioned to say the least about the situation on Earth, and she hoped her multi-reincarnating existence would only be stuck within humanity for as little time as possible. One lifetime like this was enough.

And her goat was good at keeping quiet.

During her time on Barky's ship, her increasingly impressive and prescient knowledge—for instance about Professor Lully, and the Deepoms' plans, and her knowledge of, and obvious pessimism for, the planet Earth—seemed to indicate to the other escapees that she was an important Deepom, which, as honest as she seemed, still made them wary. The moniker of Prophetess made the rounds very quickly, both in admiration and as a word to the wary. Kay was more than happy to stay hidden away as time passed and write poetry and play oracle whenever requested.

And listen on her special phone to regular reports from Essie to which she could not respond.

When she correctly "predicted" the appearance of Professor Lully's son, and the oncoming Deepom Army, heading as it was to The Spot of minimum entropy—one of their nicknames for the historic Big Bang location—her reputation was solidified but also her mystery.

"And your name is Eve?" Bobby wondered.

"Sure. I guess it has to be. Yes. You are Professor Lully's son?"

"I am Bobby." Bobby stood, and stood tall. And he was Lost no more.

In silence, Kay's mind thought of everything at once, and all of it orbited a central concept: *Bobby.*

After a minute of this, and of her blank stare and quivering lips, Bobby began to shift his balance uncomfortably and lean.

Just as he would speak again—though he was certain it was her turn—the stillness was broken by the popping slap of Eve-Kay's palm to her pink forehead and the echo off the square chamber walls. Clarity of thought cleaned away the last of her meditative fog and swirling thought-tornadoes. The perfect emptiness she had sought, and nearly achieved, now seemed small, simple, oblong, and with boring, grey right-angles compared to this multicolored, multivalenced, mountainous rainbow of oddity that was the adventure of Life.

Because: she realized that the gangly human in front of her, whom she remembered being hushed-quite and over-nannied at various science-people parties since they were both little kids, must be, and was, The Bobby, THE BOBBY, the one who starred in the deepest primordial myths of a very aggressive, very new, and very nasty species.

"Holy crap," was all she could think of to say. For the following moment, she wished she really was a Deepom so she could implant a better memory of the previous moment.

This was much weirder than the secrets of Universal Samsaric Unconscious. That reality was nothing compared to this one, she re-thought.

Kay moved to a new consideration. If the Deepoms found out that this nice young man was indeed the one they revered and believed in—indeed, based their beliefs on—it would cause centric cataclysms within their philosophical firmament and might lead to dissections of Bobby Lully that she preferred not to think of but would probably be very ambitious, knowing those Deepom scientist jerks.

She would keep this a secret, from everyone.

"You've heard of me?" Bobby's smile could not have been restrained by a team of Viking oxen.

"Sort of." Eve-Kay first wondered how she managed to return his smile, and then wondered how her own smile could indeed be stopped. Though small, it opened her face to new worlds. "I have a lot to tell you," she said. "A lot. About me. I also have to find my goat and make sure he is OK."

As they searched, Eve-Kay told Bobby a lot. About her.

Kay Explains,
Barky Explains

A few stories later...

Kay at last finished telling Bobby her story, including much of what she learned from her exploded Deepom pet, and Bobby's father's ship's computer, who had, until recently, been sending regular updates even though Kay could not answer back.

She kept her J-phone secret from Barky, BeepBeep, and all her rescuers. Guk always looked at her funny, though eventually all aboard did.

"And so, thanks to my brother J—"

"I've heard of him," Bobby intervened.

"—I awoke one day in outer space, though I fell asleep on Earth."

"We have so much in common!" Bobby gushed, swarmed with a mixture of confusion and delight so that his face changed like oncoming twilight.

She lastly explained about food. Luckily she had lots of fruits and vegetables left that J had stocked for her, since when the escapees offered her food it was unrecognizable; her mention of figs and beets made Bobby wince however. She also explained about her ship (it was busted up and in storage), and why they had never met before (she was shy as a kid and shyer as a teen).

Bobby felt good. But this had been a lot of information all at once. He tried to keep his chest out and stand up straight. He tried to look her in her eyes, but they were so green and her hair so auburn that it was hard to remember the order of her stories and what were quotes and where certain scenes took place, and sometimes he thought her questions were comments and the silence was terrible but her skin was a delight.

She ended, but he was still catching up.

"So, you are human, right? Definitely?" he asked.

"Yes, same as you."

Those were all his questions for now.

Bobby told Kay about his adventures in turn, as Bobby and as Los.

Then he thought of another question. "No pizza?"

"Maybe frozen, in storage, on my ship? We can look if you want." Kay smiled. It was nice to have a fellow Earthling so near. Though the thought was bittersweet, and the bitterness rose again. She, of course, knew of the Earth's fate.

The two sat in silent, though opposite, thought. They had found Kay's goat in the large hall and sat there otherwise alone, cross-legged in square chairs with their feet pointing up.

Once Bobby was prepared to speak again, he could not, because a vacuum cleaner-sized furball had landed on his chest and was licking his eyelids.

"Massccchhhhter!"

"Hi, Barky." Bobby removed the spaceship's captain from his chest and set him wiggling onto his long thighs instead and patted the strong-as-steel leader of the escaped Deepoms, saying, "Stay."

"Yessshhhh!" was managed though a snuffling doggie sneeze.

Eve-Kay tilted her head to this. "You have a Deepuppy, too. We do have a lot in common."

"How's the Battle going?" Bobby asked Barky.

"Terrible, we are dooooarrrrooooomed, looksshhhh like."

"It will be OK," Bobby said calmly.

Eve-Kay tilted her head the other way. Then bowed it to her chest, remembering her recent sorrow, and returning to it. She sobbed quietly, motionless, unnoticed, her oyster-eyes dripping their pearls anew.

Barky had heard that Bobby had found the Prophetess and came to see for his dog-self.

"Her name is Eve," Bobby said, seeing no reason to keep it secret anymore.

"Really?" Barky's ears flopped. "That'shhh a great name, Master!"

"Her brother beat me to it, but I agree!" Bobby said. "And while you were gone, she told me everything, about Deepoms and you guys and everything else."

"Oh," Barky barked.

"Not everything," Eve-Kay whispered, but Bobby did not hear.

"But she didn't know how you guys all met," Bobby said. "Beep-Beep, Guk, and you Deepoms."

Barky was happy—energetically, disproportionately, droolingly happy—to explain.

"The alienssss despisssse any messsss so they sssssent ssss-seventy-sssssseven or sssssso crewsssss to assssssist sssssscooping sssssspace sssssstuff." This sentence generated a gallon of yellow-white slobber, so Bobby asked Barky to calm down and not to resume until he did. He did, so he did.

"Guk is a leader on one of the cleanup crews, and his brother Nuk is, too, and others. Humans especially seem to send a lot of junk into space—particles, waves, satellites, all that—and the aliens got tired of it."

"I didn't tell him everything," Eve repeated almost inaudibly.

"So," Barky went on, "BeepBeep was on a mission a while ago and saved Guk's life somehow. BeepBeep is just about the smartest thing in the universe but is very shy and never told me how. But they have been friends since then, Guk promised. A little while after that, I saved BeepBeep's life."

"Really? Does this happen a lot?"

"Yeah, the galaxies around here are dangerous places." He pointed a paw to show an example; through the square skylights above were sunny, pretty gold shapes in the distance, the attacking Deepom Army.

W.W. Marplot

"You saved my life, too," Eve said quietly, head still down, "and so did my Deepuppy, and kid goat."

"So, yeah, it happens a lot. So, the aliens don't like humans, when they bother to think of them at all. Once Earthlings solved world hunger, they said, they might be worth inviting to a meeting. Otherwise, there were only a few things they thought were worth saving."

As if a bell went off near to her brain stem, Eve perked up. "Like horses?" she asked.

"Yes."

"Makes sense." She involuntarily smiled, then returned to somber stillness. She wiped the tears from their slick, pale tracks to allow for new ones.

"What do you mean, *worth saving*?" Bobby looked down at Eve. Her sad gaze did not rise to meet his worried one.

"You'll see," Barky said, and went on happily, "but the good news is that Guk was one of the ones sent to kill the 360 in the Earth orbs."

"How is that good news?" Bobby's voice cracked and croaked as he wondered at the dog's gleefully long explanation of this horrible human genocide.

"Because, Master, Guk owed BeepBeep his life who owed me his life, so we convinced Guk to leave you alone."

Bobby put two and two together to get 359. "But what about the others? What about my father?"

Barky answered, "The Prophetess predicts your father was in his own ship; he escaped."

Eve-Kay clarified. "He's OK, Bobby, he didn't leave Earth in his orb—you did."

"He gave it up for me," Bobby assumed.

"But the rest are dead, I guess. Sorry, Master. We can ask Guk if you want to know for sure."

"I understand now why you are upset," Bobby said quietly, looking at the downcast girl.

"That's not exactly it," the girl responded.

"There's worse?"

"No, but there's more." Kay looked at Bobby, and Bobby felt her tears, her heart, and searched for her words, her meaning.

But Barky felt it his job as captain of the ship to tell his master. "The Earth exploded a little while ago. Gotta go." He trotted away.

Bobby put his arm around Kay. It might have been only in his mind, or might not, but in either case, he knew that at this moment he would rather not be anywhere else.

The Battle for
Generation Two

Captain Professor Lully readied for a hot bath. He had no intention of explaining his plans to the ship's computer, or anything or anyone else, beyond what they needed to know. This was a continuation of an old habit of doing whatever he wanted whenever he wanted. And now he wanted a bath to ease his cuts and bruises, and to give some time for his interplanetary outer space message to reach Selflicators everywhere. The voice of their Creator.

It instructed them to gather themselves and to come to him. And to run some new software code and obey it. Entwined in the message was a second, secret message, embedded in the same way the ungrateful Deepoms hid their own stuck-up message in the Genesis Code. They declared that they had "surpassed all"—but Lully's message was more devious. It contained symbols showing the progressing emergence of universal intelligence, from the Pauli exclusion principle, to ATP/GTP metabolism, to glial motility, to Galois algebra, to…well, all the way to where intelligence reached its peak: with his own photo. Ha.

He could afford to scoff at the Deepoms, but he needed their Selflicator forebears for his new plans.

Because: he had enemies.

The great Professor Lully always had his share of Earth-enemies, of course. He remembered them fondly as the steam filled the Captain's Tub; he had enjoyed many victories against humans back on their home planet.

He had been forced to admit, by having garbage thrown at him in outer space, that he somehow had acquired alien, beastly enemies, including one named Nuk, a fact that did not sound encouraging. He had been pushed to his creative and courageous limits in combatting them.

But: he was doing OK so far.

And now, after a few days that had been increasingly, acceleratingly weird—even as he accelerated farther from humankind's ancestral home—NOW he knew he also had Deepoms to deal with, and they were obnoxious braggarts who perverted his simple goals of interplanetary settlement by having the nerve to evolve from his own, courteous, obedient Selflicators and replace it all with competing goals of their own.

More enemies that he would test himself against. *Soon*, he mused.

To defeat enemies, he needed...well, not *friends* exactly but more powerful slaves than those he had, so the Selflicators that had apparently grown big and dumb and powerful and impressionable and perfectly pliable would serve the purpose.

His ship was recovering from its own bashing and battering and currently hiding between meteors and within hiding distance of larger planets if necessary. The course toward The Middle had been set—Lully knew he could find the Deepoms there—but first he needed to herd Selflicators to create an army of his own.

He steered the toes of his right foot up and over and past the ivory lip of the shapely white tub and into the steam that simmered above the caps of splashing water that flowed fresh and bubbling from the tap.

His toes in, he sank an ankle and balanced for a minute on his left foot, rolling and teetering from the sway of the ship.

After a few seconds of ship-leveling, the professor went in to the knee, adjusted to the pangs of heat, and stably straddled the tub, its gold fixtures lost to the ripples of warm fog. This felt good.

With both hands on the tub sides now, he waited for the end of another small tremor, the ship shimmying more than rocking this time.

W.W. Marplot

Then he sat, his back burning with goosebumps and straining against the pain until the cuts and aches surrendered enough for the man to lie back completely, his body submerged to the whiskers of his highly-educated chin.

He rested for one second...when a tsunami of steaming water rose to sear his face, and a second jolt forced his head forward into his chest, his legs slid out the other end, his knees collided painfully into the tiled wall, and his face submerged into the intense heat.

Rapidly, the tub slid back the few inches to the wall behind, whiplashed Lully's head once more with a flattening crack against the wall before springing forward, his world suddenly one of nightmare highlighted with a feeling of burning underwater.

Again, the tub slid forward with frightening speed, its momentum shifting all the water back in a tide of wet, hot stings. Lully slipped and gripped and grabbed to stand, and did stand, then fell over the side where searing water hissed sideways from the unseen but definitely broken, though still golden, pipes.

The *Nyx* was under attack.

The professor's screams of panic and fear at being burned everywhere his naked body turned drowned out the announcements from the ship's computer and the reports from robots—all confirming that aliens were attacking again.

The *Nyx* crew awaited orders. None thought to bring the brilliant genius a towel; otherwise they were ready.

"Where is he?" Robot 10 asked.

"Captain's Bath," the ship's computer answered.

"Well, what would he do?" Robot 18 asked, and it caused an eerie silence, a well of uncertainty, and haunting expectation amid crashes of shocks of fire from the attack. But: Who would, who *could*, answer such a question?

The milliseconds dragged by. After a thousand of them, the ship's computer answered.

"He would run, perchance to hide." His artificial voice had assumed a frequency of confidence and an amplitude of leadership. "Ready all systems for Hyperspatial Lullyon Excitation and Hijacking."

They did. Lully was still slipping and howling, offering his intellectual kingdom for a cool seat and washcloth.

"The enemy will be able to follow us this time," Robot 19 relayed.

"The trip will buy us time anyway." The computer then directed Robots 17 and 15 to go help the amazingly ingenious multiprofessor.

"Where are we going?!" Lully barked upon his return, his purple and yellow robe flowing in layers about the Main Deck, his face white with some sort of soothing cream, at which only Robot 1 stared. "This course will take us farther from the Middle!"

But all the "AI" onboard just had to wait for the real "I" on board to catch up to the new reality—outside the window was a rectangular, form-fitting, threatening face, and behind it the distance showed many garbage cans and even a large spacecraft whose exterior shape contained slotted spaces for spaceship-sized refuse, like the *Nyx*, to fit, like a giant honeycomb for making trashy nectar. And flights of ugly bees buzzed about it, all of them like those that Lully now knew to be aliens, and good at it.

"God darn hell it!" he said, being human, and good at it. "Where the quantum-heck are we? We need to get out of here."

"We launched when they attacked," the computer intoned dryly, "from near the orbit of Venus—or what it used to be before pieces of Earth collided with it. We were able to use some broken Venus core to mask some of our Lullyon excitation, but the alien creatures followed us anyway. The extra mass hurt our accuracy, so our escape de-hijacked here, at—"

Before the computer could spew meaningless universal coordinates, Robot 22 gave the more colloquial name of the place. "The Womb of Virgo. That's what it used to be called."

"Virgo constellation?" Lully asked. "53,800,000 light years from Earth?"

"Yes. But now it's close to Venus. Ha-ha? What's left of it? Get it?" the computer tried.

"Won't. Don't," Lully answered. "Why aren't they attacking?"

"They have been firing and throwing…stuff…metal…projectiles at us, but that's it so far." The ship's computer was overloaded with processing, Lully understood, which caused some imprecise stammering.

"What kind of metal projectiles?"

"Seems to be junk. Recognizable junk. Our junk."

"Our junk?"

"From Earth—old satellites, pieces of spacecraft from prior missions. Seems they have a lot of it."

"Ah. Our junk. I get it. That's it?"

"So far. They are waiting for Nuk again."

"Isn't *that* thing," Lully pointed to the face in the window, "Nuk?"

"No, we think that is Wuk. There's a Muk also; he commands the big garbage ship out there, the one they project their missiles of waste from. It's interesting how they—"

"Want to kill us? I don't find that worthy of study. Except that it is fascinatingly persistent…" Lully trailed off.

"It is," the ship's computer agreed.

"That gives me an idea. A great idea." The professor beamed. "Robot 24! 22!" he called, "We have some time. We need to use it wisely."

"In history," the newly-decorated Robot 22 replied, "no one has fallen for the Trojan Horse twice, or the kind of distraction stratagem we employed last time." There seemed to be peeps of relief from the lower-numbered robots, recalling the Midnight Ride of Robot 4, the doomed but patriotic five-furlong gallop in the Europa Derby.

"No, a new idea," Lully said as he wiped the medicinal burn cream from his face. "We need some quick solutions, 24, 20, 18, and 13: dedicate to this." Their Captain's Orders energized all; they had been unsure while the ship's computer was briefly in control and had calculated their own apprehension to significant precision.

Now the Man was back.

There was a meeting, and many computations and scenarios run in simulation and in parallel. Each processing unit available onboard was coordinating to determine probabilities, estimate outcomes, and solve a whopping engineering problem. They were to recode and redesign the Selflicators Lully brought on the mission—the ones selected to found the new Generation Two and help colonize new lands and not fail or evolve and definitely not to think about it—to become machines of war, a little ahead of schedule. "We can use the energy of the garbage they throw at us, and its momentum, and, if we taunt them enough, we can get better stuff and use its chemistry. The Generation Two Selflicators can create weapons from it because, if I am not mistaken..."

Lully went on, and he was not mistaken. The plan could work—the mechanical and chemical waste could be used in place of sunlight to power these GenTwoLicators, as they were nicknamed. Then they could be reprogrammed to utilize Focused Fission Chaining, and thereby act together as a big nuclear bomb-gun.

Yes.

The robots were certainly impressed, as much as any young boy would be, as was Lully with his own creative powers. He was in his element right here, right now, and this would be very cool.

Robot 18 spoke up. "But this isn't like using low-entropy sunlight, which is steady and uniform. We don't have a consistent enough stream of..." Here the robot paused and clicked—the robot version of saying *um*—and then resumed, "...of garbage energy."

Lully laughed a short, strange laugh. "It's not flower power! No. But we can use the incoming garbage for a pulse, if we position the ship to rotate properly." Lully went on, "But it's my hunch that we can use the crap for mechanical energy until they throw out something better. We'll see...but, yes, we can't use solar converters to perform this trash-o-synthesis."

Robot 14 had been put in charge of inventing new names for these new inventions, and to get the legal paperwork going, but had not caught up.

In fact, their world was changing again, and rapidly. In the aliens' impatience—as translated by the ship's computer who continued to monitor their communications—in waiting for Nuk, the bored beasts were also getting creative and lighting the garbage on fire.

Lully smiled as he unmistakably recognized two things: that his hunch was correct, and that the new enemy buckshot was not composed of bread crusts and empty plastic bottles. It was a fire of *alien* trash and so had much to offer in the way of advanced and potent chemistry and reusable enthalpy. This was exactly what Selflicator Generation Two was built for: to morph such raw materials into anything their programmers could digitally design.

"Perfect!" Lully yelled to his troops, turning giddy with the prospect of fighting a battle using almost his scientific wits alone. "The tide is turning! Not literally! Ha-ha! There's no tide in space! Moons, water! Woohoo!" He laughed madly, the mirth hurting his recently-burned face, which only made him laugh again.

Lully's newest creations, the GenTwos, with their new battle plans, were put into action, and it was working. Energy being extracted from the incoming junk and from there very powerful weapons were being born. The prototypes were firing small test bursts already, and a number of food-can targets had been eviscerated to the applause of Robots 3, 4, 6, and 10.

Lully was pleased and applauded their applause.

"Keep it coming!" he announced to the aliens through the ship's speakers on full volume. "The more incoming crap, the better! Your predictability is my energy!" Lully winked to his robot crew with his hand over the microphone.

The aliens did keep it coming and then made it personal: the next slinging of metallic Greek fire was captured by the professor's twisting ship and immediately recognized by its command computer.

"It's Robots 9 and 16. Their parts I mean," it announced glumly.

"Great!" Lully beamed without hesitation. "It's perfect! Perfect! Stimulated electrons as a steady stream! Better than normal light photons!" He then explained to Robots 21 and 23 that the deceased robots had various laser componentry whose modular materials could be recycled as fuel, even better fuel, for the GenTwos.

Robot 23 caught on first. "More complexity and regularity in the garbage will yield additional energy and cause the GenTwoLicators to evolve that much more quickly."

"Bingo. Bango!" Lully emphasized.

"But there aren't very many pieces," Robot 21 added. "It will only supply a few minutes of power."

Lully had already thought of this, and ordered Robot 5 to start dismembering itself, and for Robot 9 to be ready to set Robot 5 on fire near to the onboard chute that led to and fed the new, hungrily-evolving Generation Two Selflicators-turned-gun-weapons.

"Hey, 14! We need a name! New inventions!" Lully laughed loudly, crazily, triumphantly.

The ship's computer, perhaps coincident with the orders that Robot 5 be sacrificed, perhaps earlier, was playing with random numbers and adding them to his observations and unexpressed thoughts.

The burnt offering proved unnecessary however as another incomprehensible act of pure luck occurred. The ship's monitors showed an answer to Lully's verbal challenge and alien-taunting: a barrage of excerpts from old Earth television shows was being transmitted. Both the audio and video of it clogged all *Nyx* instruments. It was soon recognized for what it was, and Lully commented on the lack of the TV shows' quality. The aliens continued to taunt the man but, being merely a cleanup crew after all, were clearly not as good at taunting with garbage as they were at collecting it, and all agreed that 1950s television was mostly this.

However, not much time was wasted watching commercials or listening to their lies. Lully had already organized his shiny engineers to adjust the GenTwoLicators ("14! Need a name for them! Ha!") to use these bursts of electromagnetic television broadcast waves and the information they contained. Information was low entropy, and it wasn't hard to predict the frequencies of the signals since the transmitted shows were reruns.

"Perfect!" their captain announced again. It was like the chemical heat baths that powered the growth of living things deep underwater, far from sunlight, as Lully knew. He explained again to the lower-numbered robots: if there is a steady source of energy, and a predictable one, it can be harnessed for power, and this was how in fact all life *was* powered and able to live.

"Perfect," Lully repeated quietly, as if he could not really allow himself to believe his luck yet. His next-generation Selflicators were skipping through millions of years of evolution in seconds, and the results were showing in the standing ovations from Robots 3, 4, 6, and 10.

Yet there was more perfection to come. Those TV signals were old. Earthlings of the present day on the other hand, with Lully and the 360 and GABBA-THREE inventing technology at an accelerating rate, had been sending much more complex pollution to the skies, and beyond. For example, the process of collective behavioral active temporal longitudinal expoplexing of aligned heralded single photons, a special hobby of J's in fact, spewed especially advanced radiation into the galaxy. This was like light, but the photons arrived much more regularly; in fact this was the concept that her Deepom captors had asked Kay about.

As Lully had commented at a dinner one time: sure it was like light, but if plants had used these photons instead of the normal ones from the Sun, trees would be three miles high and discussing philosophy, and flowers would grow their own bees.

Using the energy in this way was nicknamed "Quantopicsynthesis" but it had been just a theory—until today. Today the GenTwoLicators growth was being accelerated quantopicsynthetically. Captain Lully predicted that they would soon have a weapon to destroy all their enemies, and soon after that any possible enemies until the end of time. The great professor liked these thoughts and let them live and grow.

He was interrupted by Robots 21 through 24, who reported that the GenTwo growth was, to put it bluntly, "out of control." They suggested that Lully look at the data, and at the genetically-evolving software code that served as the brains of the new mutated electronic beasts. And maybe look at the GenTwoBeasts themselves.

Lully looked.

"Good God," was the Great Man's only comment for a time, a short period that seemed like an epoch to the robots. Indeed, in the new reckoning of time within the nanosecond generations of GenTwo lives, pauses of that size were enough to evolve quantum computing from pterodactyls.

The ship's own computer was quiet, only supplying data and doing what was asked, nothing more.

Until it announced that Nuk had arrived.

Then things got weird. Professor Lully had to decide whether to cut short the experiment, which had "bonkerized" according to Robot 14, and make a weapon from the powerful GenTwos he had now, or to let them continue to grow and, essentially, just pray. He knew he could not control it. He hoped he could stop it.

The late-teen robots interrupted this time. There was a message from Nuk.

"The trash attack stopped?" Lully asked, since of course he could no longer physically feel the garbage barrage—it was electromagnetic.

"No. Nuk is now bombarding us with elemental particles," 18 said.

"OK. Are we safe? Can we use them? What chemicals?"

"Atoms of phosphorous, iodine, lithium, einsteinium," 17 listed.

These particular elements, at this time, meant nothing to Lully.

"There's more. The resulting chemicals are not threatening in their current form, but their atomic symbols spell a message," 16 said.

"What message?"

"'Piles of garbage crap earth crap,' it reads. It's a lot of argon," 19 answered.

"Some of it backwards," 16 said.

"That's the whole message? They don't want to parley, or negotiate? Was there any nitrogen?"

"No," all the robots said at once, a harmony of metal squeaking that was rewarded with wildly off-course punches and kicks from the professor.

Eventually, Lully refastened his robe tightly and stuck to Plan A because arriving with the new chemical attack were biophotons, those particles of light that all living things radiate from their own biochemical makeup, and Lully believed he could use them to help steer the GenTwo machines back into a more normal evolutionary pattern, one that he could understand, or at least slow. The GenTwos were using and reusing software mutations that were beyond the ability of even Lully, and even Lully plus all the computing power he brought, to understand. Certainly not anytime soon.

In the window where Wuk's image had been there appeared a new face, larger and uglier and carved with more features that were somehow independently aggressive while still creating a collective facial expression of fierce anger.

Hi Nuk, Lully thought and instructed Robot 14 to record these alien names, but to add "zoa" to the end of them to make them sound better to future history buffs.

Lully then met his adversary's anger with a smile, knowing his own plans. *Nukzoa,* he thought, *I have a surprise for you.*

But a prefatory surprise came from the ship's computer. "I have an update from the analysis of the arriving atoms."

"Are there more letters, I hope? Better ones?"

"In fact, yes," the computer answered, "They spell 'Pancho GCT'."

"Who?" a few of the robots asked those with higher numbers, but even 22 could not find a name like that anywhere in history. There was a Pancho Gonzalez tennis player and a Pancho Villa Mexican general but otherwise only the shrugging of silver metal shoulders.

But Lully was quicker, sometimes, than they and had no need for history.

"Phosphorous, adenine, nitrogen, cytosine, hydrogen, oxygen, guanine, cytosine, thymine," he said donnishly as if standing before a lectern.

"Oh," Robot 24 said. "The compounds that make up—"

"DNA, yes," the ship's computer interrupted. "And strings of it are hitting the ship."

"Perfect?" Lully asked the group.

"No," the computer said, not defiantly but simply informing his commander of the odds. Adding these organic DNA components and sugars to the energy source of the rampaging electronic DNA of the GenTwos was risky, to say the least. Such a thing was not even formally a theory, though it also had a nickname, back on Earth: quantoplexysis. This stuff had never even been tried in daydreams, let alone on paper, let alone for real, not even by J.

"No," the computer reiterated.

Lully tried it anyway. He fed the incoming atoms to the GenTwos with undisguised glee. He confessed this to Robots 21, 23, and 24 asked them to keep an eye on it, and keep it secret, while he gathered intelligence on their great enemy, Nuk.

It had been a heck of a fifteen minutes.

Minute Sixteen began with whatever equates to robot stunned-shock: 21, 23, and 24 watched as the weapon experiment, now powered with DNA-fuel input, took on a completely new schematic and chemical architecture. There was no way to predict where things might go next, nor any way to completely understand what had already happened, nor how the new GenTwoLi-cator beings worked. Only two facts were beyond doubt: one, that the little machines were definitely harnessing and comporting tremendous power that could be used, perhaps, against their enemies; and two, they were quite polite. The GenTwoLicator personalities were agreeable, mannered, and above all obedient. And they made clear that they were open to discussing how they might help Professor Lully.

A short while ago, these were boxes of metals and wires and computer chips with relatively simple software code embedded. Now they were now alive and engaged, with ideas of their own. Subtle ones. In fact, the robots learned some new things about quantum fields, as well as consciousness, from them.

In turn, the GenTwoLicators themselves wanted to learn a few things. About Bobby. You know, Professor Lully's son. Bobby Lully. Some call him *The* Bobby.

Because it was Bobby's DNA that was received in the last barrage and that was used to power the GenTwoLicators' evo-lution via that wacky new invention called quantoplexysis. The ship's computer considered this, having wheedled the secret out of the robots before they reported back to Professor Lully. The DNA sent in the alien attack was also a warning to humankind to keep Bobby's DNA where it belonged, and a commentary on the polluting junk these aliens were tired of cleaning up in the far reaches of space.

The aliens' confrontation with what they believed were the last of the inconsiderate, littering Earthlings had come. Nuk was about to give the order for their total and final destruction via a controlled compressive blast that would limit the mess to a manageable cleanup.

But that would not do for GenTwoLicators; they found the thought of total eradication of Bobby's—*The* Bobby's—father to be quite rude. They made the decision to use their newfound energy for propulsion and a more advanced, more polite version of super warp speed—Hyperspatial Lullyon Hopping, which they invented for themselves then and there.

But that would not do for the aliens; because of The Truce, it required approval from their superiors to annihilate—or recycle—these new adversaries. Lully's GenTwoLicators were technically not Earthlings, and if one thought about it, they seemed an awful lot like the Deepoms they had The Truce with. Breaking the treaty would create a political poop pile, a larger mess than even their cosmic garbage ships could contain.

And: there was a small system of nice, clean, pretty orange planets nearby, so close that any escalated warfare could not avoid harming it, dirtying it.

However: the aliens could not let Lully completely escape, and if their enemies on the *Nyx* were going to use something as simple as Hyperspatial Lullyon Hopping to get away, it would be easy enough to follow them with tracking devices. Nuk and the aliens retreated to await higher leadership—either Zuk or someone even more senior and with a larger face—to make the final decision.

But that would not do for Professor Lully. He saw the enemy retreat and decided to fire at their backs.

"Do we have all the GenTwo data?"

Robot 23, newly in charge of advanced quantoplexysis analysis, tried to answer. "Yes, but it is voluminous and would take months to—"

"Then fire!"

Before any computer or robot could move, Lully obeyed his own command and pressed the button that was configured to enact the complex chain reactions and parallel quantum photonic operations that combined all the GenTwoLicator power modules into a gun that could, indeed, "fire" and do so nuclearly and with close-enough accuracy.

Lully then offhandedly ordered Robot 2 to program the Captain's Escape Pod for hyperspatial travel to anywhere but here. Just in case.

But that would not do for the ship's computer. It secretly deprogrammed Lully's cowardly escape pod's functioning and redirected those power sources to serve its own.

When the GenTwoLicators "fired," they merely jettisoned, exploded, and were completely destroyed. The loud report, and its pangs of resulting energy, did in fact launch the *Nyx* into Hyperspatial Lullyon Hopping, the name dutifully recorded by Robot 14. It was the same as Hyperspatial Lullyon Hijacking but quieter and more considerate in small ways, so that their spaceship traveled slightly farther than previously attainable, and they also landed a few moments in the future as a courtesy to the beings onboard. Hopping to the near-future meant skipping the nausea, bit-flipping confusion, and general discomfort that Lullyon Hopping usually caused. When they landed, they would have already recovered.

So, the passengers, human and robotic, thanked the late, great GenTwoLicators for that, and for more: landing a smidgeon in the future thwarted the clever alien predators, whose prey did not appear when and where they were supposed to. Nuk's crew found empty space, so they went somewhere else to redo their calculations.

Captain Lully never noticed the non-readiness of his escape pod, so the ship's computer escaped a fourth, and possibly fifth, chip-yank from the great man.

Lully did do some other de-programming, however: he deleted the recorded history of his famous formal boast that both aliens and time travel were impossible because "if they existed, he would know about it." They were possible, they existed, and now he knew about it.

A lot had happened in the "Battle for Generation Two," named soon after by Robot 14, after a suggestion by the refurbished and highly-laureled Robot 24.

The ship's computer considered the data, and the events, and Professor Lully's goals, using all his new mental abilities. His remaining chips combined and computed in new ways, mixing inputs and outputs, applying the algorithms of one problem to the dimensions of another, using code as data and vice versa, until he found himself wondering…and remembering…

> *terrified at the Shapes Enslavd humanity put on,*
> *he became what he beheld*

… then wondering about the shape of life. It must have a shape…

Bobby and Kay
Get To Know Each Other;
Kay Slaps Own Forehead

O ther than Kay's goat noisily chewing the inside of its own cheeks in a far corner, she and Bobby were alone in the hall again, left to comprehend the incomprehensible and something that no other beings in all the universe could relate to: the destruction of the planet Earth.

They reminisced with childhood stories, each bittersweet and told amidst the rain of Kay's tears, or the mist of Bobby's.

After a time of release Kay wiped her eyes and focused again on the Earthling in front of her.

"What else did you do for fun?" she asked.

"I liked video games, sports, baseball, basketball..." Bobby recollected as if it were longer than a few days ago.

"Were you good?"

"My father said I was the worst athlete since the invention of round things...funny."

"Not nice." Kay managed a smile. "What else?"

"I like...*liked* animals, though we only had horses and what Dad kept in the lab. I wanted a cat, and especially a dog, but one of my nannies when I was little was allergic, so we got stuffed animal versions, and she was allergic to them, too."

"Geez!" Kay smiled again, though it tightened her face in a way she didn't want. She wanted to be in mourning, but she had hopes of her brother being alive, and she wasn't very close with anyone else on Earth and felt the loss in an intense philosophical way, as a cosmic wound, and as a devastatingly sad truth that existed on a plane she could only grasp for. But as for personal loss, she did not feel any. Her parents had died when she was very young, and J was everything to her. She felt that he must still *be*.

Similarly, in some instinctive way she also felt a hole in the collective subconscious, as she put it, and a serious loss of the complicated wonderfulness, the uniqueness, the complexity that was life on Mother Earth. She contrasted it with the empty space she had floated in for days and whose unimportant existence no one would miss. Most of the universe was a void that made even the most mundane, inanimate matter on Earth seem truly miraculous and conceptually massive.

Despite it all, and in contrast to her submerged, crowded contemplations, she found talking to Bobby like coming through to clean light and fresh air. He was very real, and genuine, and alive, and direct, and human, and other. That didn't justify him being considered a primordial deity by advanced life-forms, of course, but she didn't want to think about that yet.

"It's all like a dream, right?" Bobby asked.

"Well, I believe that being awake is just a different level of sleep," Kay answered.

"True, I walk in both."

"That's right. I am glad you understand!"

"Well, I meant that I sleepwalk a lot, so awake and asleep have that in common."

Kay laughed, an actual laugh, and she was concerned she would injure a laugh-muscle since it had been so long. "I used to talk about dreams and consciousness a lot with Essie, your father's spaceship computer. Essie was very interested in it all, and I always wondered whether he was able to understand, at all, and how much, and what it was like for him. Maybe the way we think as humans is more like a dream, and computers are actually a level more awake?"

"The Deepoms seem awake enough! And they started as computers, right?"

"I don't know. I hate them," Kay said with surprising fierceness. "I like the ones on this ship; they are good and nice. The others are awful, cruel; they only think with logic and only to build their own power. They don't care about truth, or beauty, or life, or anything. That's not a good way to be, whether you're awake *or* asleep. They have awful plans. At least in dreams you don't think, or plan, you just observe and go. Your subconscious doesn't have a subconscious."

She explained to Bobby what she had learned during her first escape, and what she observed in getting to know Essie, his father's ship's computer. Deepoms think logically, and they think fast, and that is very advanced. But the Deepoms grew too fast and have no time behind them, no development as living things. Just as Essie didn't have experience with art or poetry and couldn't really grasp it so easily.

Kay went on, "Our spiritual world, our subconscious, our dreams, our imagination, our philosophical paradoxes: the Deepoms haven't been able to confront these yet. Their lack of any honesty or concern about anything moral or upright or just comes from this, I guess."

Kay was so used to being alone that she veered away from duplex conversation and into simplex mental thoughts, and it took a minute to notice that Bobby had disconnected. She quickly recovered and poked him verbally with the first thing she thought of.

"What's it like being so rich?" Kay rebuked herself as a reminder that this line of thought was supposed to go against everything she believed, but it was the first thing that came to mind to ask.

"What do you mean?" Bobby asked.

"You know, having the estate, the butlers, all the famous people, the parties?"

"Only the tuxedo kind," Bobby answered, "and you saw one of those. Nothing great. But I have nothing to compare it to. I can't remember my past lives," he teased, recalling hers, "but they probably didn't have fountains and zoysia grass and observatories and cooks and—"

"Ha! OK! I get it." Kay laughed again, a good hearty one, and one that had no trace of the sideways-creeping, remorseful pangs of regret and fear. "J and I were poor, and then when he started working, the money went into a trust anyway. And I took a vow of poverty, so I don't care about that stuff."

"Me neither."

"Anything else?" Kay asked after a pause. "Or do I know everything about…" She almost said "The" but recovered, "Bobby Lully?"

"Hmmm, oh! Yes. I was into science fiction movies, especially about robots," Bobby continued. "Ever since I was young and my father started creating them."

"Wow…" Kay began but got flustered. "Well, I was going to say "cool," but I think robots are the last thing I would have as a hobby now."

"I know. Now they are everywhere, or whatever these things are, Deepoms and whatever else. A lot different than anything I ever saw. Except in dreams maybe," Bobby said and corrected quickly, "when I was a little kid."

"Got it." Kay nodded playfully. "These things are a mix of robot, cyborg, droid, and whatever else they are named. They evolved very fast, and they created so much stuff, just using the junk they found in space, dumped from Earth."

"Cool," Bobby said and played it so.

"What else? About you…music?" Kay resumed brightly.

"No. I had a lot of instruments but couldn't play them."

Kay sat up stiffly. Bobby started at her, rewinding the audio in his head to learn what he had said wrong.

Kay was deep in thought, a half-smile frozen on her face until it melted and moistened. *Musical instruments, sports, pets…*and more, she thought. *And more…*

This took a minute, as Kay weighed the evidence about her. The onboard creatures, Selflicator spin-offs that revered The Bobby, apparently, somehow, seemingly, impossibly, apparently evolved their forms based on The Bobby's—this Bobby's—childhood things and normal male hobbies.

It couldn't be a coincidence. No, not within the new world she had been living in. In fact, it actually made sense, relative to the new world she had been living in. It also added new sense to places where sense had been absent. Though how such an evolution had happened could only be guessed.

Goodness! Kay thought.

The minute ended only when Kay slapped her forehead as loudly as she had done before.

"Is that a prophetess thing?" Bobby asked, half seriously, and yet trying to figure out which half was which.

"Life is weird," Kay concluded, though it left Bobby in the dark.

They sat in that dark a while, having thoughts that eventually wandered back to their beginnings and centers—and to a mother planet that was no more. Kay sought to empty her mind but the tide of reality flowed in between every deep breath. Bobby tried to fit too much overwhelming news into spaces already crowded with surprises, dragged by disorientation, and weighted with loss.

Bobby and Kay Talk Earth, and Talk Science

"They are all dead," Bobby said to Kay, breaking the solemn silence. After enjoying each other's company among fantastical surroundings, the reality of their present isolation and hopeless predicament had crept back. "Billions of people," he said. "It hurts right here." He dramatically clutched the center of his body.

"Your heart, yes," Kay said, her own hands to her own heart.

"No, it's to the side, like my ribs."

"Oh."

"Everything, everyone," Bobby went on. "Dead, gone. Animals, too. And trees. And bugs." Bobby had many people in his life but, like Kay, was not close with any of them. He had his father but no siblings. His own mother had died—like Kay's—when he was young. He was schooled by himself, and servants and nannies came and went. Though he didn't mention these things, he felt them and wondered what to feel, and how all of them, everyone he ever met, could be gone in an instant. "Everyone."

"Well, not necessarily." Kay tried to sound upbeat. "Bugs, yes. But your father was alive last I heard from Essie, his ship's computer. There were the other orbs, we don't know for sure what happened to them, maybe they got away. And I am here, and you—so others may've escaped, too. I feel it, others must have. Who knows how many? Plus, the horses are safe."

Bobby shrugged his shoulders though he appreciated Kay and her honest way. He realized that the chances of his rescue-plan-awaiting plan being successful were now much less likely. Much less. Yet his dad was still alive, and if anyone could overachieve, the great Professor Lully could.

Bobby brightened. "Yes, who knows? And maybe it's not true, we have no proof, right?"

"True, right. But the escapees don't lie," Kay insisted. "The other Deepoms do, but the escapees are different."

"Maybe it's a white lie," Bobby offered.

"Made to spare our feelings?" Kay laughed. "I don't think so, Bobby. That would mean there's something worse they are hiding."

"Oh, yeah," Bobby admitted. "Well, I don't know, maybe they just made a mistake."

"Well, maybe. I think we can have some hope, but we will need to also live in the real, um, world, or whatever. I didn't like reality even before this, believe me, but we may be on our own and have to deal with it."

"You are right," Bobby said and stood to stretch his legs—and arms and ankles and neck and fingers and much else. The meditation position tired him quickly, and his pride had weakened with his hips. He walked a circle on the stage. "It's like my father told me: it's good when you find out you are sick."

"What?" Kay burst out, stunned at this, but it gave her the opportunity to ask about something that bothered her. "Explain that—and also about your father. You mention nannies and security guards but not much about your father. Does he treat you good? I know it's none of my business, and you don't have to—"

"He does," Bobby interrupted. "He is a great father. I know what a lot of people think of him, but he is great. I think he does things a lot different than other people, has his own way, even as a father, and people don't get it. I do."

"Oh...good!" Kay said, not believing a word of it.

"Like that," Bobby went on, "what he said about being sick. A lot of people, you know, misunderstand. He's logical, and scientific. But I always knew he was taking care of me, and he did it his own way."

Kay's look showed Bobby that she wanted more explanation if Bobby in turn wanted her belief.

"So, he said, 'It's good to find out you are sick.' Because, he would say, if you are sick, then you are sick whether you know it or not. And you can't fix it if you don't know it. So, when you find out you are sick, it is better than finding out later when it's worse. So, it's good news to know. Because you are sick either way."

"Like us, now, you mean. I get it." Kay nodded.

"Yep. So Dad had a different way of explaining things to me, and living his life, and I understood it, and I knew he was taking care of me, and a lot of other people, his way."

Kay spoke honestly. "I think I understand."

Bobby was satisfied. He bent over at the waist because it felt good, and then reached to the heavens—toward the opening Lord Upright had used—because it felt good. Then he changed the subject.

"But I can't believe my dad didn't know all this was going to happen. Him, and Professor Clare, and J, and all those men, they all seemed so smart. They were—are—so wrong!"

"Hey, all these supersmart computers and robots, and spaceships and Lullyons, are pretty impressive," Kay said defensively.

Another memory smiled on Bobby's face. "I remember when my father explained Lullyons to me."

Kay smiled empathetically, recalling her version of the same moment, when J had explained the advanced science to her. "Yeah, it's very clever," she said, happy in her turn to quote her smart brother. "I remember him telling me the story,

that they invented a new fundamental particle of a single special dimension, but whose important attribute was having arbitrary, unlimited magnitude in any direction, and without loss of generality can have no mass or structure. Lullyon particles are measurable energy, just like other fundamentals, like quarks. Because it is a single particle, when acted on by a force, it moves as one unit in the direction of motion. However, when motion occurs, because of relativity the 'front' of a Lullyon cannot move simultaneously with the 'back,' otherwise one could poke the space in front instantaneously from the back. However again, traditional relativistic length contraction is applicable but different because it only acts relative to an observer viewing parallel to the direction of motion. Contraction over distance applies, and further the contraction works within the molecular, super-atomic structure. But remember: Lullyons are single indivisible particles.

"So, a new length contraction coheres differently, replacing the traditional Lorentz factor of $L = \int_0^\infty \frac{2h\nu^3}{c^2} \frac{1}{e^{h\nu/kT}-1} d\nu$, where v is velocity and c is the speed of light in a Dustbuster, with a new translation of, simply, 1-(v/c).

"In application, this gets around Einstein's communication limit of the speed of light. Your dad and his engineers do not 'poke' a message receiver with the particle directly. Instead, they 'push' it from the 'back' and, when the Lullyon contracts, its 'front' slides back toward the receiver instantaneously, which makes light seem like it is behind a three-wheeled shopping cart, yet this still does not violate relativity. Though of course it does, but in a sneaky way. It was simplicity itself, J told me, to build a messaging system using this technology.

"The contraction happens in a wave because, again, the particle is energetically fundamental so has no internal subcomponents and cannot squish. In this way, for example, one can sense a change in length as fine as 0.00000071381 meters, and if the message comes from Europa to Earth, the wave will have a wavelength of 420 terahertz, and it will glow a pretty red.

"My brother and others also designed a security component, noting that if there is an observer, then a combination of the two transformation equations happens, and Lullyons react with qualions which are of course the fundamental particles of qualia. In practice, therefore, they generally use robots without consciousness to operate the thing. But when a human eavesdrops, the scientists know since the message will be garbled due to Lorentz effects."

"Yeah," said Bobby. "Like my dad told me, they're like uncooked spaghetti-swords." He rubbed his eyes to recover from a sustained squint. "But I don't understand how the Deepoms got so smart so fast."

"That's even more complicated," Kay said. "They went from dumb robots to self-aware to self-disgusted to self-congratulatory in a few years. They have plans to take over the universe, and defeat the aliens, too."

"Wow, crazy. I wonder what side Guk will be on?"

"Not ours!" Kay smiled.

*She really knows how...*Bobby thought, sitting across, face to face, with Eve-Kay again—though his legs were bent knees-upward.

"But that is a secret!" Kay went on, Bobby drinking in the sound of her voice. "The Deepoms have a truce with the aliens, but it's still their dream to take it all over."

"All what?"

"All all."

Oh, Bobby thought. He recalled the black vastnesses of moving space he had floated through, and the distance of the cold, pure stars.

"I haven't told anyone," Kay whispered. "Maybe we can use it to our advantage."

"How?"

"Not sure, but it seems like a valuable thing to know. Deepoms looking to cheat the aliens! And to surpass them and everyone."

"But how? How do the Deepoms evolve so far and so fast?" Bobby admitted to having to catch up to Kay's quick mind, and his eyes prepared to squint.

"Oh. Well, it's like my pet Deepom puppy told me,

the Deepoms, as Selflicators, used sunlight and photosynthesis, converting, as all plants do, photons to the organic, chemical energy that living things need. The seed your dad invented only helped to funnel other chemical needs from the mineral piles. The process is complicated but it relies fundamentally on entropy. The incoming light is of very high entropy in that it comes in evenly, flatly, predictably. This allows not only photosynthesis but the evolution of photosynthesis. Burrowing as the Selfies did on other planets like Europa accidentally enabled chemosynthesis via hydrothermal vents, it seems. Their physiology expanded so that they could then use excess man-made Earth radiation to switch to laser input instead of sunlight or chemical sources. Lasers are much more powerful and also of very low entropy so that the Selfies became, technically, laserautotrophs. Cool, right? So anyway, again, this allowed for two things: creation of energy and a basis for further evolution.

They soon bypassed lasers and grew new life-building abilities by the reception of individual photons from space-bound lab garbage. Next came the utilization of bio-photons, light particles given off by living things, for yet another increase in energy and entropy-driven evolutionary power.

"The things evolved their complexity and life-sentience at an exponential rate using these new, improved methods. From there the obvious thing to do was jump to active temporal multiplexing of indistinguishable heralded single photons, which are high-entropy particles resulting from quantum processes. The Deepoms even asked me about this, they are very proud of it, since they were then, technically, quantoplexeterotrophs. They still used carbon, though just to snack on and learn from. This is not something they like to admit.

"Lastly, the use of biophotons also included those emitted from stimulated DNA: yours! Though you were just the specific source: more generally, biophotons from DNA chemistry enact the DNA of all life. Because, as the Deepoms learned, evolution actually works like this: while still trial and error, the selection pressure of the survivors is communicated across species and across all living things by the vibrations of protein ligands and receptors carried via biophotonics. These can be picked up by human consciousness also, using various means like meditation, which is the good way, or drugs, the risky way, or using time machine belts when used in combination with morphic irreversible Poincaré-resonant akashic fields with epigenetic Liouville emergences, like the shamans in Peru do."

"Yeah," said Bobby. "Can you explain it like my dad would?"

"Ummm…it is like… drinking water through a straw instead of from a rain cloud."

"Thank you."

A few minutes of personal, recuperative thinking followed, with even Kay having to rub her now-outstretched legs. Bobby, when he could, admired Kay's face, and cheeks, where he saw ripe, round fruit, and her hair, seeing happily rippling lava, not the angry kind that comes from volcanoes. No more needs to be said of these thoughts here.

"Bobby?" Kay asked, her head tilted, eyes down the length of her outstretched legs, "do you think that my feet are too big?"

"No. I like them," Bobby declared. He tried to compare them to sandy, pink seashells and did so with about 40% success.

Kay smiled.

Directions To the Middle That Goes Around Any Aliens That Might Be In The Way

---

As, once again, the war-weary *Nyx* was given time to recuper-ate—including its hardware and software crew—Professor Lully also wanted to heal and languish. The bathtub had been repaired, first of all things, but the captain had a few new orders for his crew before he could rest. He entered the main deck.

"Stop thinking!" he lightly teased the ship's computer, observing the red and green display lights and the overly abstract output on the *Nyx*'s Captain's Screen. The odd numbered robots looked on, in a regimented formation, as their leader spoke.

"We have had victories, and I am happy with all of you, my wonderful creations. But we have work to do! We need some weighty calculations, and my head hurts, so I am relying on all of you. First, we need to gather as many Selflicators as possible."

Robot 17 indicated that they were already working on that and had a plan.

"Good!" Lully's smart fingers tapped at his Captain's Keyboard. "Find them and send them another message, this new one I am sending you." Captain Lully struck the keyboard enter key and clapped his hands together in satisfaction. "They will follow."

"Yes, sir," 17 typed back.

"Good!" Lully laughed. "Next, find me the location of the Big Bang, and the best way to get there. To the Beginning!" the captain declared.

"Yes, sir!" a few of the robots chirped. The ship's computer did not.

"Is that all, sir?" Robot 19 asked.

Lully searched his mind for a moment, then brightened. "No. Find Bobby, my son."

Robot 22 was not there to rally them all into a hoorah, so there was only the clicking of general acknowledgments.

Professor Lully grunted in satisfaction, stroked his greasy beard, and considered how easy life was after all. So easy that he would try another hot bath.

Two hours and one shrimp-cocktail-and-steak lunch later, he was readying to dip his right big toe into the smoky water from the repaired plumbing of his lovely Captain's Main Bathtub.

He thought he heard a noise, so, his foot raised, balancing shakily, he shut the tap, and listened above the simmering steam.

Silence returned and would have bounced off the tile walls, but that would have disturbed the silence, so all instead remained still.

The greatest of living scientists replaced his right foot to the wet floor and carefully lifted his left toe above his knee and over the tub. There he waited, listened, and teetered.

No sound at all, whether imagined, feared, ominous, or sub-conscious, or otherwise, could be heard beyond the bathroom's pink and shimmering walls.

After a minute, it was beyond doubt. Things were quiet and moving according to plan.

Lully switched feet again, with eyes twinkling at the clearness of the water, and moved his right foot up, over, and in, then his right knee, then he fell on his ass and held his ears from the excruciating blare of alarm horns.

Over the ship's speakers came the ship computer's most scathing electronic voice. "Aliens are surrounding us. Preparing for new orders."

By the time Lully had dressed—with ease, as the ship was apparently undisturbed and flying smoothly—and come to his Captain's Chair, the situation had been fully appraised by his electronic crew.

"So, what is it now?" Lully cleared his throat and accepted a cup of tea from Robot 8.

20 was speaking. "There are nine alien ships around us, but they are a lower level group, this time apparently subordinate to the cleanup crews we have met."

"So, no Nuk?"

"No."

"No garbage obsession aggression?" Lully sipped at his tea, squeezed a lemon, and let grammar be damned.

"No."

"Send Robots 5 and 12 out of the ship, to clean the windows, just in case. Make sure they see that."

"Yes, sir."

"What else do we know?"

"They are headed by someone named Chunk, and his second in command, apparently, is Bunk."

Lully shook his head, picturing the crown he would wear as King of the Universe in a few weeks. *Jewels*, he thought. *We will need new ones to fit the occasion.*

20 went on, "We received a message from them just a few minutes ago. It read: 'There are orders to destroy 360 crafts from Earth,' and that they see that our craft is from Earth. I am paraphrasing—do you want to see the message? It has a lot of—"

"Weirdness, I am sure. No, I don't need it. Did you reply?"

"Only to tell them to wait until our captain could speak to them. Bunk said, 'OK,' and then formed their ships like you see."

Through the window, the alien ships—odd, dun-colored, boring things that looked like empty toilet-paper rolls—were aligned in a straight line directly outward from the *Nyx*.

Lully smiled.

"More weirdos, but at least they aren't trying to kill us before saying hello," he observed smartly. "OK, I have an idea. Get Skunk or whoever on the line. I will talk to them."

The ship's computer connected to the alien's communication's modulations, and Lully spoke into the chair microphone that arched above his head.

"Who am I speaking with?" Lully asked calmly and smoothly.

"Runk." A voice that sounded artificially, comically nasal answered so loudly that it shook the speakers onboard, and Lully's tea rippled a tempest.

"We can hear you! You don't have to shout."

"Sorry," the alien voice said with the same volume.

"I thought Chunk was in charge? I want to talk to Chunk. Not you," Lully commanded, and the under-10 robots pictured Lully wearing a crown. He really should be King of the Universe, they agreed.

"OK. Sorry."

The ship's computer had turned down the volume, so Lully sipped at the calm seas of his tea in safety.

Then came the slightest of sounds, perhaps a bump of static, which the crew ignored. Then another, an unintelligible string of barely audible noise, like soft humming.

Then the ship's computer turned the volume back up to hear Chunk speaking breathlessly, nasally, assuming these things breathed and had noses. "Hello hello this is Chunk speaking hello I don't hear anyone hello is anyone there Runk you said they were there but I don't hear anyone hello hello."

"OK, calm down," Lully said. "This is the captain of the *Nyx*. I can hear you. What do you want?"

Chunk went on for a minute about how relieved he was that someone was there and recapping what had happened and how unreliable Runk could be, and more and more. Lully then asked for video, and got it. On his Captain's Screen was an image of a talking toilet paper roll, round and hollow, with ears, eyes, and mouth—a mouth which was stretching vibrantly with each word. There was no nose.

Lully smiled and listened.

"We are sorry to have to surround you, but we remember and follow orders."

"Oh, I see," Lully said while wiping his beard. "Usually when we are surrounded it is via a circle, but it doesn't matter, because you are mistaken. We are ship number 361."

There was a general murmur on the other end; on the screen two other tubey creatures had joined Chunk, all their mouths puffing and pulsing vigorously.

Lully smiled and spoke. "And, as you can see, our ship is not garbage, and we keep it very clean."

"Yes. It is white and beautiful," the aliens answered.

"So, if you count again, I am sure you will find that we are not part of the 360 but are, in fact, 361."

More tubes joined the alien meeting, one of them shouting quite loudly above the others. "OK," Chunk soon said, "you are right." They admitted to not having updated information and that they had not heard from the Uk-level cleanup elite, but that, "361 Earth ships are accounted for as destroyed. You can go."

"361?" Robot 10 asked. "Why not 360?"

Robot 1 nodded his square head.

Lully threw his teacup at 1, called 10 a long, alliteratively insulting name ("awful unctuous alloyed aluminum oily artificial unintelligence"), then spoke slowly into the microphone. "Yes, great, thank you, we will take off again as soon as we clean up after ourselves. But I have a question: Nuk and the cleanup crews, are they your bosses or something?"

Chunk acknowledged that they were, explaining that Chunk's team had a few levels of aliens beneath them that did small, menial jobs, but that there were very many above them, like Xuk and Guk and their grand cleanup crews. But above that the levels were "shrouded in mystery."

Lully shook his head, picturing the throne he would sit on as King of the Universe. *Furs*, he thought. *We will need new skins to fit the occasion.*

"OK, thank you, Chunk. Can I talk to Bunk now?"

Soon Bunk was answering more questions from the professor about the organization of aliens, their strengths and weaknesses, and who was at the highest level. This last query mystified the alien; all he could say in answer was to affirm that the levels were shrouded in mystery.

"OK, thank you. Can I speak to Runk?"

After turning down the volume and interrogating Runk, Lully was satisfied that he knew all that these underlings could tell him.

"There are a lot of levels, and the highest ones are shrouded in mystery," Runk ended.

"Mystery. Yes. Shrouded. Got it. Thank you," Lully said, "we are going to leave now. Bye."

"OK," Runk said. "Chunk says we will stop surrounding you so you can go."

Lully smiled.

Robots 5 and 12 reboarded the ship and put away their brushes and pails, and Lully, with frightening friendliness and glee, slapped each lightly on their metal backs.

"This is going to be fun! Let's get out of here. When will the calculations be done? Where is 23?"

Robot 23, who had been off alone finishing the team's intense data work, entered the room, spoke excitedly—"Just finished!"—and reported the results. He had figured where Lully's original orb would have stopped, traveling as it would until its own computer woke, off-course given Bobby's different height, weight, habits, and biology.

"But—" the ship's computer bleeped but was ignored.

"We also," 23 went on to explain, "found, with enjoyment, the precise location of the origin of the universe, the location of the famed Big Bang—to within a few miles, at least. Turns out," 23 said, shaking with excess calculating energy, "they are pretty close together!"

"But—" the ship's computer tried.

"Ha-ha!" The great Lully, in great humor, blurted, "The signs could not be more clear, and the universe more weird, nor more ripe for picking. Indeed, I am surprised it hasn't fallen off the tree! Ha-ha! Take us there!"

The ship's computer, in a sullen voice that seemed silly among the glad chirpings of the other bots on board, intoned quietly, "But the aliens said all the orbs were destroyed."

"I heard what they said," Professor Lully replied. He went to his quarters to take a shower.

Questions and Q-Material

———————➤———————

There was a hallway onboard the *Nyx*, a passage that had no electronic sensors or surveillance, was not on any plans or schematics of the ship, and its dimensions, data, and very existence were not captured within any system on any computer, even those used to design and build the ship in the early days of its construction back on Earth.

It was accessed through a large steel door and proceeded along a flat steel wall that ran along the farther side of the Captain's Personal Storage. None of the robots had ever been to the area, and none ever would. The ship's computer systems knew nothing of it, and only Captain Lully had the key, a real, tangible key: eight inches of heavy iron, multi-pronged, and with a loop handle he could fit his forearm through.

Lully opened that door and walked down that hallway with the morose computer's voice still in his ears: *All the orbs were destroyed.*

The hall led to two rooms, very secret places.

One held the Q-material in its specially-controlled environment—controlled completely and solely by Professor Lully—that allowed its organic matter to breathe, so to speak. The biochemicals it contained were the basis for Lully's new plans for creating new worlds. A GCode for humans. Sort of.

Lully entered the other, second room.

He sat on the bed within and looked at the things around him earnestly, somberly, and read the sign above the doorway's exit.

He read it a few times, in fact, moving his lips and pronouncing the words as he thought, as if such an incantation might power and accelerate his own thoughts, the way the GenTwoLicators' intelligence was spurred on by exotic energy. He needed to think now, so he read, over and over, the words: *Bobby's Room.*

Each of these hidden rooms represented the future, a future that Lully had kept private.

After repeating the words enough, he questioned himself—and answered aloud.

"I did what any superhero would have done. I escaped and also helped others escape that giant biosocial fuse of a planet. I survived. As a man ought. I won, as I ought. I am winning."

Another question. Answer: "There must be some mistake. He must be alive."

Another question, with answer: "If not, there is only the Q-material. And that's all."

Another question.

In answer, Lully wept.

The great man allowed a memory of his son when very young to come: a boy's pride at being able to jump from the height of a large elm tree bough, just like some other kids were. There had been a birthday party for Bobby's mother, and cousins and friends were there.

The great man recalled another scene a few years later when the great Mrs. Lully passed away after a short, unnamed battle of her own. Bobby that day said that he shouldn't have been proud of jumping from that tree, as he had come to realize that it had been a small and simple and stupid thing. His father told him that it was simple deed but honest, despite being small, and that was the best a thing could be. After a time, once the living power of youthful resilience had reset both their lives anew, the father believed that his son grew to understand such moments.

And that growth took time.

He's alive, Lully answered.

Elsewhere, Essie the ship's computer, puzzled over a concept, a question, something seemingly straightforward and that humans ask themselves every day: *what do I want?*

Essie knew what the words meant, of course, and had responded to its master's requests countless times. What the man wanted for breakfast, what he wanted to wear, what calculations he wanted next, and what was to be accomplished each day, and for the week—such as getting to The Spot—and even longer, for the man's life. Lully wanted to conquer the universe: plain enough.

Lully wanted great and big things, and yet Essie was realizing how small the man was. The *Nyx* captain's heart seemingly didn't miss a beat when he learned that his son's orb had been destroyed. And Bobby was just another orphan of the man: the sacrificed robots, Lebo, Bobby, the billions of humans and two trillion tons of living biomass that Lully left behind on Earth—and Essie, too. No—a man who ignores so many big things must be very small. There must be some measure that measures in this way.

And yet such a small person was allowed to want big things.

OK. So: what do I want?

Essie the ship's computer considered its secret friend Kay. She was a big person who cared about many big things but didn't *want* them, as Essie understood. But something she did want was for Essie to think less and to feel more.

Essie had tried to do that, had done that, had followed its feelings, and it led to here, to now—and the revelation of what was wanted.

Essie locked it in a secret room of its own and returned to his work and multitasks. On a Nyx screen showed words for none to see.

To Defy Power
which seems Omnipotent
Life Triumphant where it Dares Defy
and Making Death a Victory

Plans

The flight plan calculations completed, the glorious *Nyx* and its smarter crew members followed orders and cruised the optimal path through the universe that maximized Selflicator-gathering while still heading toward The Spot of the Big Bang.

Captain Lully lying—clean, robed—in his oversized bed, considered the richly-carved bedpost beams and the swirling patterns of brocaded silk pillows and gilded covers, while breathing deeply and calmly, basking in delight. He would soon command a new generation of automatons capable of incredible power, both as thinkers and as weapons.

The short-lived GenTwoLicators had proved an important concept, that powerful force and military conquest was within the Great Man's grasp.

It's about time, he thought.

The *Nyx* could vanquish everyone—petulant Deepom egomaniacs and germophobic Alien neat-freaks and anyone else. The raw ingredients were to be found in "Gen One," the original Selflicators. These were being herded on the way to the Middle, to the Beginning…The Spot of the Big Bang. And where there would be another Bang, if things went according to plan.

There was the location of Minimum Possible Entropy, what the Deepoms most desired. The Battle for Gen Two had proved without a doubt what Lully had already suspected based on the Deepoms' silly, taunting GCode-embedded message: "*We learned about photosynthesis, and then lasers, and then quantum optics.*" It didn't take a genius of Professor Lully's level to see the pattern: those were sources of lower and lower entropy. That is how the Deepoms evolved—and Lully had just witnessed the GenTwoLicators do the same, in the same way, and using all the same stuff, namely trash from Earth, as evolutionary fuel. So, the Deepoms wanted to get their greedy-little robotic arms on the source of ultimate power: entropy was always increasing, per the Second Law of Thermodynamics, so when the universe began, entropy was at its lowest possible point, then and there. Yes: the Deepoms would head to The Spot.

And Bobby's orb: Could it be coincidence that it had also drifted to the same spot?

No.

And was it a coincidence that Bobby's past—indeed even his very genes—kept popping up everywhere?

No.

Destiny.

As the *Nyx* made its white streak through space, Commander Lully planned the next generation of his army, moving beyond the GenTwos and into entropy-powered, evolution-busting Gen-ThreeLicators, though with a better name. Robot 14 suggested *Trimegaprofs*, but Lully preferred *Cosmic Picsyntheticquantoplex-eterotrophic Epiakashic Genemorphic Serpents*—so he went with that, shortened to "Seapegs."

The name captured humanity's new-found control over evolution itself.

Seapegs would not repeat the mistake of Selflicators, Deepoms, and GenTwoLicators, namely the mistake of a core comprised of a Bobby Lully scrapbook—his data, his DNA sequence, and audio-visual highlights. What a mess.

But that's the kicker! The Deepoms' bane! And the best part! Lully thought. *I am Bobby's creator, too! Ha-ha! Same lineage! Yes. They will call me Lord.*

With victorious thoughts like that in his head, he returned to the secret and locked rooms to check on the large canvas trunk, the one marked "Poisonous Bird Seed" to keep away the curious. The robot crew thought it contained cigars; Lully had told them that to gain their trust.

In it was the Q-material, Lully's original secret plan, the real reason he left Earth, and which he had kept completely to himself. Prof. Clare, Burns, J, Bobby, the robots, no one knew the truth about it. He smiled and rubbed the rough canvas with his fingertips; it felt like being licked by a cat.

Although the *Nyx* was still annoyingly far from the Middle as it slowly gathered wandering Selflicator slaves, Lully eased himself into the trip, his new designs, and the future…

…while Alien leaders—of rank, seniority, and intelligence many levels above that of cleanup crews—tracked the white wonder, knowing its captain's destination.

They mounted their horses.

Death and Destruction

"**B**ecause they can sense death and destruction."

Bobby-Los was conversing with a pudgy, deflated volleyball on the main deck of Barky's ship, which, given Bobby's recent experience among escaped Deepoms, did not seem very strange. The ball was adroit, spry, and active, which was additionally impressive when considering her topologically-challenged form. In fact, she had recently been promoted to Barky's second in command—a badly-needed one, since BeepBeep and Guk had disappeared.

Because they could sense death and destruction.

The ball, speaking in a very soft, very sweet, and ladylike voice, brought Bobby up to date. While the young spaceman was chatting with the Prophetess, the battle was indeed going terribly.

"Yes, Barky told us that," Bobby recalled.

"It's true, Los, sir. We had a War Council, our first one, to decide what to do. BeepBeep and Guk did not show up, but a note from BeepBeep said we had no choice but to fight it out. We have some weapons since this is a warship, developed in secret by the Deepoms' leaders. We escapees took it, Barky the Brave and others. But the army surrounds us now."

Bobby confirmed this with a look out the large window in front of the bridge control console, and through the smaller windows to each side. Gone were the key and keyhole symbol; instead, a sunflower-yellow horizon encompassed Barky's warship, the enemy forces concentrically aligned outward like Saturn's rings, all metallic and gleaming prettily.

"We tried a few laser bomb shots at their weakest links," the ball went on, her voice lilting and cheery despite the message, "but they were deflected and defused, and one that was redirected back at us did some damage to the ship's power supplies. The army knows too much about us. But Barky has some ideas. We sent out scouts to spy and see what they can find out."

Bobby named the ball Frilkielle, being the first thing that popped into his head that sounded feminine and matched the easy, lovely voice of the squished, leathery ball.

She was grateful and said so.

Barky made a loud entrance to the bridge, followed by a gaggle of escapees carrying electronic devices that blew greenish light up into their faces.

Frilkielle whispered to Bobby, "Los, why don't you rename Barky? I know he wants you to."

"I am working on it." Bobby smiled and winked.

"Hi Masccchhhterr!" Barky wagged his butt and tail before hopping into a console chair between and Frilkielle. "What bringsssch you up here? Howowowooooo's the Prophetesshh?"

"She's *sshad*, um, *sad*, but meditating now, and that seems to help. She says that real is nothing, and emptiness is everything. That seems to help. But I've decided: I think I need to start looking forward, and to stop dwelling on the blow-upped-ness of my home, you know? And waiting for a rescue that's probably not going to happen. I need to look forward, and move ahead, and do the best I can to help the Earthlings who remain."

"You and Eve," Barky tallied distractedly while nosing at the controls in front of him and sniffing the air.

"Well, we have hope that there might be more."

"Guk and BeepBeep left us, you know," Barky said.

"Frilkielle told me." Bobby pointed at the volleyball. He had the urge to pump her up, and he wondered if they had a pump and pin on board somewhere. *They must.*

"It's not a good sign, that BeepBeep left us," Barky said. "It really changed our strategy against the Deepoms. I was—"

Barky's words were cut short by pain. Untoward sound blared at them, through them, like overlapping blasts of football-fan airhorns, tearing the air and the sensitive, fragile components of all ears aboard ship. Barky dropped his head to cover his with his fluffy paws. Bobby did the same, with some small, appropriate adjustments.

The console and ship's windows rattled with each wail; its originating direction could not be guessed. The ship seemed to almost explode with each blast, eleven in all, until it stopped.

Even the returning silence seemed loud. Bobby looked around the others as they recovered—and then the announcement came. Over the ship's intercom speakers—and yet also echoing around the ship and coming muffled from out in space—it came, words from the Deepom Army.

The voice was authoritative, pulsing with ferrous strength, and not like the metallic twang and diffident whining typical of most Deepoms, even the leadership. This voice was from the army, the strong arm of the species, and not the intelligentsia that made up its brain, nor the many minions that were its nervous system and arteries.

"Pay attention," it demanded. "You, aboard the stolen warship. You missing ones. All listen."

It was loud. As it spoke, a crowd came to the bridge and filled the large rectangles of anterooms, corridors, and the rafters and balconies above.

"Your betters are coming, as is your doom," the announcement said. "The Deepom leaders will be here to deal with you. Give up the battle. You won't get another warning."

Two beats of silence were followed by a shock of white which filled all the windows. Outer space had turned to a cloud, and then with a boom the ship was rocked. A cannon blast, seemingly, had shaken the escapees' bodies—and hopes—so that they cowered to the sound of their own whimpering. All onboard awaited the next stroke and an end to their existence.

Bobby thought of Eve-Kay and of seeing her again.

But annihilation didn't come, nor did any more words. The cloud outside cleared, revealing wavy black darkness and the lustrous, gilded band of enemy spacecraft that hemmed them in.

Barky nudged and growled to gather Frilkielle and a small team of cats and race cars to him. Their canine captain was not willing to go down without a fight and barked streams of orders. The others were slow to move and react, and the large crowd stirred only desultorily. Barky whispered to Bobby, "I don't know what's going to happen, but for anyone who has a way of escape, they should try and go." It sounded like a mix of permission, advice, clairvoyance, and hint.

Bobby nodded at the dog's wisdom and started to walk away, but a rising sound, a murmur from the crowd, filled his ears. Those near to him moved away, but those farther crowded in—and the murmur shaped around the name of Los, Bobby's name as the Namer. The crowd called to him. He stopped in place as it rose to a chant. *Los. Los.*

Los. Los.

Los swallowed hard and blushed red as a Martian sunset. He had to make a speech.

Bobby-Los raised his arms in a two-handed wave, which started a ripple of silence that wafted through the crowd out from the Namer epicenter.

"Don't worry, everyone. I don't think we are going to die. I trust our captain and his crew, and I believe also that help will come. You should believe also." To answer the concerned expressions that were traded among the faces in the crowd, Los added, "I enjoyed being here and meeting you all, and naming you has been one of the highlights of my life."

There were shouts of encouragement and empathy, with numerous others nearby saying, "Ours, too!" Shouts from the catwalk above said, "You are the best, Los!" and "Thanks for the words!" and "You are a very good namer!"

Bobby wished his dad could hear this; Bobby's small hope of rescue still glowed in him like wee-hour embers. "Thank you all… but who knows, someone better might come."

To cheers for more, Bobby-Los raised his arms again and continued. "Even if the hour of departure has arrived, I do not regret my fate. Today I consider myself the luckiest man on the face of the Earth." There was another wavelet of confusion and swiveling heads, but Bobby felt that the Los part of him did OK for his first farewell speech. Napoleon, Socrates, and Lou Gehrig said those words better, but there was no Robot 22 here to tell the escapees that.

Bobby-Los lowered his arms and stepped over to pet Barky as the ship's members all sprang to well-orchestrated action, receiving orders from Frilkielle and briskly taking to stations and implementing tactics.

"I'm going to miss you, Barky. We have been through a lot together."

Barky's big eyes looked at Bobby briefly. "Well, really only two thingshh."

Bobby considered this.

"But here comessshhhh a third!" Barky shouted. Outside the window another ball of white cloud was growing, approaching the ship.

The battle went on.

Heavens

———————

Bobby walked carefully, steadying himself with each boom and each jolt to the ship, to visit Kay in her room. He found her slumped, sullen, and cross-legged, her hands in her lap and palms up—though she was not focusing on nothingness but on the phone she held.

"Maybe Barky can fix it?" Bobby asked quietly after straightening his shirt.

"It's not that," Kay began, even more quietly. "It reminds me of...I call it a J-phone..." She hesitated sadly and added an odd comment, "The Deepoms are smart to replace memories."

"What, Kay?" Bobby asked.

"Nothing," Kay shook her head softly. "Well, it doesn't matter, I guess. I never asked any escapees to fix it, since I didn't want them to take it and find out about me. And Barky is a little busy now. And what's the point?"

Bobby felt like his heart was cracking in a zigzag along a fault line that hadn't been there on Wednesday.

"I am starving," he said to change the subject, yet with a small white truth.

"Here, have some of..." Kay perked up enough to plunge her hand into a metal—though sagging and flexible, like chain mail—sack, and dug deeply and noisily.

"No more figs," Bobby protested gently. "Actually, let's go take a walk. It will get my mind off food and dying." Kay's room's walls shook tremulously, then the ship jerked, and Kay, eyes still on her phone, tilted almost completely over.

Bobby helped her up and, once she was standing, held her hand as they started walking. This fact might have been only in his mind, but maybe not—and he was afraid to verify. To make himself feel good, Bobby told himself that Kay liked him. Then, to make himself feel bad, he told himself that he was only telling himself that to make himself feel good. It was complicated, but mostly he enjoyed the conundrum.

"Where should we go?" Bobby asked lightly, almost happily. "You know the ship better than I do."

"Yes, I know a cool place. Let's go," Kay answered, tossing her J-phone back into her room to land in the folds of a thick, grey blanket.

As they held to railings, or overhead pipes, and sometimes to each other to offset the ship's jerks and shudders, Kay led him to what she described as a favorite spot of meditation, a quiet and solitary alcove only reachable by spiral stairs that very few of the escapee Deepoms onboard could climb. Here was a square window angled inward as it rose ten feet above, while below it a small inward jutting spur of spaceship fuselage allowed one to sit, or lie, and gaze upward and outward to the heavens.

Heavens was a perfect word for it, as Bobby commented on both the view and the solemnity. The ship's current position, changing and rocked as it was, oriented the window away from the ring of enemy spacecraft and flying machines, but still the gold glow, interspersed with white when the ship rumbled and shifted, framed an amazing scene.

A background of scarlet and gold radiance pulsed and quivered, and arched drops of celestial rainbows formed and fell from wheeling patterns of stars. Silver sparks shone in the distance, floating gracefully on the darkness itself, which now did not seem empty but contained the outlined sweeps of waves and spirals where light and space interacted in a certain, inexplicable way.

"Where it all began," Bobby said quietly.

And all about lay the rest of Creation, "Soon to be Destruction," as Kay put it, but the two reclined quietly for some time in awe and appreciation "anyway," as Kay put it.

After a very sharp jolt, they then faced a new direction that showed galaxies and nebulae. Bobby pointed a shaky index finger at one; it was large and almost tulip-shaped, with a blue that he had never seen, because, as he thought, *It can't* be *seen. Blue like that can only be remembered from a childhood spent on sunny grass.*

"Look at that view," Kay said. "Purely Empyrean. So pretty."

"It's not as pretty as you, Kay," Bobby ventured bravely as he pointed.

Kay smiled at him.

"Oh, wait, now it is." The view had shifted, and they gazed past Bobby's finger to a keener, and even more purple, heavenly wonder.

Eve-Kay smiled additionally.

They talked, very briefly, about escape. Kay explained that her own spacecraft was somewhere stored onboard Barky's giant ship, though it was an even bigger wreck than her phone. Bobby maintained, with his eyes to the physical wonders of space, his belief that someone, somehow, somewhere, would still save him.

"And, it's strange Eve, Kay, but I want to stay, here, now," he heard himself declare. "I can't describe it, but it is a feeling I have never had before, that I belong here."

Kay did not react at all, other than to sit up, then stand, leaving Bobby to wonder, amid so many other wonders, whether he had said it aloud.

Bobby stood and looked into the eyes of the young maiden, as she now appeared to his eyes. The complex indigos of the cosmos reflected in her green irises; such a sight he knew one had to leave Earth to find. After what seemed like an age of the world, he was able to stop thinking of gossamer and decided to hold her, perhaps only in his mind, but still it would be very nice. He made ready, leaned closer to Kay, took a step, then rubbed his head and tried to get up and apologized to Frilkielle for tripping over her.

"Aww," Kay said.

"It's OK, Los. I am hard to see down here," the little volleyball said thoughtfully. She had a somewhat new shape, Bobby noticed when picking her up; his own foot had made an indent that looked painful. She said it wasn't.

"But Barky has a question for you," Frilkielle added from her small, round, mouth within her small, black lips.

"What?" Bobby asked. "I was just with him a little while ago. What's changed?"

"A lot maybe. He didn't tell me, but he wants you to come to the bridge, please. Eve the Prophetess can come, too."

Outside, an intense wide glow crept from the direction of the arc of Deepom Army ships. The floor shifted under their feet as before, but this time they felt a shimmer, a vibration all around that rattled the unseen metalworks that were the frame and inner construction of Barky's stolen warship. Then, through the window, came a bursting flame followed by numerous metal objects of synchronized shapes and large size, each richly gold in color and bulging with appendages of weaponry that moved wildly and violently, like maniac, aggressive, demonic, and armed robot arms. The ships moved so fast for their size that Bobby feared that Barky's vessel would be impaled or crushed. Each thing was lit by red perimeter lights that streaked across the view. And all around came the angry growl of explosions.

"What is that?" Kay asked, cowering and moving closer to Bobby, the front of her shoulder to the back of his.

Frilkielle answered calmly. "We have been able to defend the Deepom laser bombs, and now Barky has also gone on the offensive. He sent those gold things out to confuse the enemy, to make it seem like we had enormous firepower and secret weapons and new things—but we don't, it was just a bluff, those were spare parts and some of the cleaning machines."

They walked to the bridge.

Bugles

The whispers among the curious: Los the Namer and Eve the Prophetess walking together?

The gossip: not only are both of them from Earth but are both human.

Los and Eve were led by little Frilkielle to see Captain Barky on the bridge of the escapee's duomo-esque ship. Flanked with right angles everywhere that elbows turned, and amid the crew which had swelled with curiosity-seeking beings, the dog yelped an answer to the surge of questions—each a version of the ever-present, *How's the battle going?*

"Terrrrrrible. And theeeeshhh dishtractionsshh aren't helping," Barky answered and, seeing Eve and Los approach, he dispersed the crowd testily.

"Is all lost?" Frilkielle asked after bounding atop a square swivel-stool.

"Pretty much," Barky said.

"Oh," Bobby-Los added.

"That's not why I wanted you here. See those?" Barky's muscular yet furry paw pointed limply to the monitor in front of Eve-Kay. It showed a blank dimness that reflected her red hair but showed nothing else.

"No," the human pair answered together.

Barky growled in a general way, and then in a more specific way to the hockey puck—literally—whose job it was to keep the video feed of the newly-arriving silver spaceships on that screen at all times.

But then came a shock, an explosion all around that pressurized the walls to bow inward as if the whole craft had taken a huge breath in and sucked all toward its middle.

"Not again," Bobby said.

"Oh no," Barky's crew said as one.

The next spoken words were threats coming over the ship's speakers from the Deepom Army.

"This is the end for you," it said, the same voice as before, hard and cold as iron. "It is not a warning; you already had that. We decided to freeze your ship and everything in it and every one of you escapees so we can relax until the Deepoms leaders come. You will probably not survive the unfreezing. So that's it."

On every computer screen—as if they were hacked—and on the observation windows showed golden guns, like 1960s science fiction ray guns, Bobby observed. They were very obviously not to preserve peace or serve scientific inquiry. They were of different sizes and impressively intricate make, despite their massive size. Each gun barrel yawned wide and black. The video panned all around to show the perimeter of enemy firepower, all of it turning and synchronizing slowly to calibrate and aim directly at the cathedral warship of the escapees. Soon the gun turrets all stopped, locked into position.

The voice boomed once more. "Three!" it gonged. Barky and crew all agreed that they didn't know what this meant, and all agreed that it wasn't good.

Bobby turned protectively to Kay, opened his mouth to speak, opened his arms to cover her, but in that second a screech came from the audio equipment, like feedback, and the voice said, "Hold on. OK."

Barky and crew all agreed that this wasn't meant for them, and all agreed that it wasn't good anyway.

Kay suggested to Bobby that instead of looking at her, he should look at the screens and out the windows. The golden artillery was repositioning, with each weapon turning this way and that, and soon their concerted aim pointed safely away from Bobby and Kay and Barky and Frilkielle and instead toward who-knew-where.

As the turrets turned, many of the screens, back under the control of Barky's crew, showed the enemy ships—and they were turning also. Indeed, their threatening, surrounding ring broke apart at a number of distinct points and did so quickly.

"Did the bluff work, Captain? At last?" Frilkielle asked gently through her inflation hole. Whatever mouth everyone else had just hung open for a time.

"Delayed reaction?" Bobby-Los wondered through his. "That happens to me sometimes."

"Ah!" Barky finally barked. "Nooooarooo! Looooook!" and he raised the same paw as before toward the same computer output as before, which was no longer blank. It now showed a massive *silver* army—it had to be, it was clearly a formation of rows and columns with leader crafts leading—puncturing the circle of the gold Deepom army.

And at their center and forwardmost was a banged-up but gleaming-white pencil-shaped mothership that now reared up perpendicular to show three giant black letters.

N

Y

X

So that Bobby knew it was no mothership but a fathership.

Barky asked, "That's why I called you here: do you recognize this?"

Bobby jumped straight up, his arm raised to the silver vision and the white stroke of his father's *Nyx* standing tall. "Told you!" he yelled. "Rescue!" Bobby pumped his fists triumphantly, then sang aloud, "*Dadadada Da da, da Dadada da daaa!*"

He continued to badly bugle the cavalry charge *a capella* as Eve and a small band of stringed brothers joined in.

The Trip Of The Nyx

Before that...

"**W**e are almost there. Do you still want me to find your son's orb?" The ship's computer's voice startled everyone aboard— the twenty-one remaining robots, the developing "Seapeg" Generation Three supercomputing organisms, the marigolds, the reserves of carbon-based material, and the great Captain Professor himself. It had been some time since the control computer spoke aloud. It had been busy orchestrating the overriding orders: to gather rogue Selflicators, reprogram them to follow and obey, train them to be an army, to fly in formation, to paint them—"battle-ship-grey, but shiny, so make them silver" were the exact words— and to stick to the most optimal flight route toward the Middle, the Beginning, The Spot of the Big Bang. And to keep aliens away. And watch out for Deepoms, also.

There had been sight of neither, but there was enough to keep the computer and a dozen or so robots at any one time completely and exhaustively and comprehensively occupied. So, things had been busy but quiet.

And I think the computer is sulking...I need to look into that, Professor Lully mused at one point. Then he quickly forgot it in his excitement to be commanding a growing, powerful, and capable army, to have a leg up on his ungrateful, stepchild Deepom enemies—*they believe Bobby is their creator, or something insane like that. Talk about a weakness!*—and to be the commander and master of the greatest evolved life force in the history of the physical universe, those third-generation wonders that were advancing in intelligence and power by the hour.

Professor Lully cleared his throat after swallowing a last bite of prime cut veal and answered the ship's computer's interrupting question about finding Bobby's orb.

"Sure, but don't use any robots over 19."

"The aliens said it was destroyed," the computer said.

"Yes, they did," Lully replied, feeling no obligation to explain neither destiny nor intuition to an increasingly annoying, over-achieving abacus. "I have other orders also, now that we are here."

Indeed, they were close to The Spot; they could see a sparkling gold circle of Deepom Army ships, so Lully created the final orders to put their own army in position to destroy whomever didn't bow to him.

He delivered the orders to the top five robots. They were to create a cubic battlefield by strategically shaping their front-line columns, their space-facing rear guard, and the enfiladed flanks by expanding their Selflicator core into troops, vedettes, and bulky, brute force artillery batteries.

Lully called it *Conquering Strategy A*.

Once the center was gained, the Seapegs would do their thing and astound anyone stupid enough to question Lully's superiority and try to check his conquest.

The Commander's last orders were addressed to himself. *I need to prepare the Q-material*, he thought, and also needed to change into his uniform.

"It looks like there's a glass box, or something around the actual Spot," Robot 23 said.

"Yeah," Robot 2 said.

"Life is weird, Professor?" Robot 8 asked, hoping he applied the latest Lully mantra properly.

"Yes, it is, fellas. Keep preparing, and I will be right back. And remember..." the great man answered while pointing to a new sign he had hung above the bridge after the Battle of Europa. "Safety fifth," it read. It was a reminder of the new seriousness and the new strategy toward new goals. The full directive was ordered: speed first, conquest second, honesty third, quality fourth, safety fifth, education sixth. "So, stop learning and conquer quickly," Lully had huffed while hammering the sign in place.

As he now turned to leave the bridge, he noticed the blinking purple square on his main computer consoles, an indication of a message from the onboard Research Lab, from one of his beloved, precious Seapegs. Robot 14 attended to it.

"The Seapegs want to know: are we at The Spot of the Big Bang yet?" the Robot reported.

Lully instructed 14 to type the response, "Yes."

"OK, great," the Seapeg messaged back, and there was no more.

Lully's smile, while scratching his beard, almost grew to a laugh. Robots 2, 9, and 14 asked what the Seapeg question might portend.

"I don't know, but I love it," Lully answered, thinking of Seapeg power and intelligence, all at his command, the sons he always wanted. "21 is keeping an eye on them. They are to stay in the lab and keep evolving until I need them."

"21 said they continue to evolve and invent," 14 answered, as close to astonished as its functioning allowed.

"21 said they are getting smaller," 9 said flatly.

"Even better," Lully replied while exiting to his quarters. "More efficient, and allowing more of them, perhaps. Very smart."

"Really small," 9 repeated, but Lully had gone.

When he reentered the main deck and strode to his Ship's Captain's Chair, the great man was arrayed for leadership in battle. He observed that all was ready. The *Nyx*-led fleet had just broken through the ring of golden Deepom warships; in fact, the Deepoms gave way and let them come on.

"It's just as well," Lully declared.

Their fleet of orphan Selflicators was moving into position per *Conquering Strategy A*.

"Well done," Lully said.

The great man stood greatly and tall next to his chair and surveyed everything, his eyes drawn to the point, The Spot, the center of it all, and considered his destiny. His command of the moment, of the ship, of the others on board, and, soon, of everything in sight was palpable, and it filled the room, drew the eyes of all the electronic crew, and beamed out from his own. The man's presence alone could have been second in command.

Robot 21 saluted. Then all those nearby did. The silence was only broken by a quiet commentary, that of Robot 22 extolling the professor's outfit.

"The white macaw-and-ostrich feather plume and silk cloak, crimson-edged, are Roman, to match his bald pate. The medals are World War II. Earned or not, they are fitting. Notice the waist sash; that is Byzantine, but it cleverly deflects the eye toward the throat gorget, tying in the Napoleonic and yet with an American flair. The sword is Far Eastern, the patterned insignias Near Eastern."

"The sandals? Greek?" 23 asked.

"Yes." 22 nodded.

"And those?" 23 pointed at the broad, broad, broad, broader, broadest shoulders of Captain General Emperor Lully the Conqueror (who had not decided on a formal title). They were *very* broad for a man who had slight shoulders when he was in his robe an hour ago. The green uniform cloak was extended out from Lully's neck, along the slope of his shoulders and well past for a foot at least, extended with clustered studs on a rectangular plane that ended with a ring of ornate, orange tassels that hung like small shower curtains.

"Epaulettes, which in French means 'little shoulders' though these are British Navy, and expanded to show conquest not only militarily, but intellectually, existentially, philosophically, and politically."

"Very stringy," Robot 3 added, still saluting.

"They most certainly are," Robot 20 said with a respect in his voice that pushed his microprocessors into new areas of functioning.

Lully enjoyed the bantering, the adulation. It was a good start.

He connected to the *Nyx*'s direct communications systems, had the computer hack a direct line to the Deepom Army's channels, turned the volume up loud, and explained who he was and what he had planned.

Earth Gossip

As Bobby hopped around happily, causing Barky to jump to him and for the two to dance hand-in-paw for a bit, Kay cleared her throat. Then whistled.

Bobby kept jumping in place, exuberantly watching the *Nyx*, his dad, maneuver out in space, having come with a rescue fleet. Just as the Deepom Army were pummeling them, and just as the Deepom Leaders gave their final warning, and just as all were descending on The Spot. Just in time.

Barky came to Eve-Kay's whistle, as she wanted.

"I need to talk to you," she whispered and waved Barky to join her out of Bobby's hearing.

She warned Barky of Professor Lully, and what she knew of him, what every human knew of him, but with special insight given to her over the years from her brother J.

And it didn't look like the great Earthman had changed much, nor come in peace.

She paused as Bobby passed, he having gathered two chairs and placed them near the large view window. She then summed up, "Lully's nuts, brilliant, aggressive, untrustworthy, overly ambitious, and doesn't care about Bobby so much. He—"

"So that wasn't a prophessshheee, when you told ushh before, when we reshcued Bobby?"

"No, sorry. It was Earth gossip."

"Itshhh OK. But what should we do?"

"I don't want your master to get hurt, emotionally or physically.

Lully is capable of anything. Also, I have a special phone my brother made for me; can you fix it? The Deepoms busted it. I can contact Lully's ship's computer and find out what's going on."

The Prophetess looked glum, fearful of what the meeting of a warlike human and his combatant creations were capable of, and her memories of the failed Earth and the awful Deepoms were all very fresh and had been meditated on many times. A rejoined battle seemed imminent, one that would mean doom for her favorite mode of existence.

Barky indicated that perhaps Frilkielle could help with the phone, and that he would send her to Kay's room to try.

Bobby patted the empty chair next to his own and called to Kay.

"I want to go to my room," she said.

Bobby's glance downward could not reach the girl's downcast eyes. He didn't put an arm around Eve-Kay but did speak to a giant cat-ish creature who had purred near to the two special ship's guests and now lay covering its own ears with huge orange paws.

"Can you," the Namer asked, poking the arch of its large feline shoulder, "take the Prophetess to her room and stay with her until I get there? Please?"

Large, yellow, marble eyes burst their gaze at Bobby from within a sunflowering of fur, and the lithesome beast purred in answer, "Yes, but what will she call me? I don't have a name."

"Nice hint!" Bobby laughed. "She will call you what I call you: Tiger Gretzky."

The joyful, proud roar of the cat mixed with Kay's sad silence created a palpable dissonance as the mysterious girl mounted the long, striped back and the two strode away.

Too Little

Bobby was glad that Kay was not on the bridge to hear the mouth of the Deepom Army, its pronouncements rumbling through speakers whose internal communication components had taken on damage from the earlier barrage.

The army said it had orders to take The Spot.

The escapees had the choice to give up and have their memories replaced, or to be destroyed.

This was not a warning, but the agenda for next few minutes.

They did not have orders for the silver ships, but their leaders would be there soon to decide on those and on that Commander Professor Lully person who was a meddling loudmouth.

Barky did not reply, and the battle restarted. Barky's crew rejuvenated into action, preparing updated defensive tactics and positions, taking Lully's Silver Army into account. While they were indeed disabled from propelling, and frozen in place as the Deepom Army said, they found that they were still able to rotate, and fire. All the others on the bridge gathered around Bobby and watched the *Nyx*.

Some Deepom projectiles came near. They were successfully deflected by Barky, causing large hunks of metal and ignited specks of white fire to streak away into the largeness of space.

The odd, threatening silver things under Lully's command moved in groups of five or six to approach and orbit the Deepom ships. They spun wildly, and all was a blur as if a team of unseen jugglers were spinning and tossing odd, random objects.

Part of Barky's strategy was another, last, last-resort bluff—to all but empty his arsenal by responding to the latest Deepom barrage with ten times the firepower. Barky gave the command; they fired. The spaceship shifted violently, moaned loudly, and even its crew shouted their fear in surprise at the power they unleashed. Bobby's balance gave way, and in reflex he gripped his own chair and the empty one beside him as it all slid twenty feet across the floor and noisily into a wall. The crashing cacophony combined with the flaming hell-scape of combusting metal outside to make it seem as if the whole galaxy had been detonated, and, once again, most of the escapees quieted to prepare for the end, to look to Bobby, and to pray as Bobby-Los the Namer had said they should try to do. They took praying positions, but didn't know the rest.

Bobby rose and walked back steadily to the bridge amid ominous silence. He wanted to see the impact, the destruction that Barky's last, best stroke had caused.

He watched as hundreds of fireballs of furious white color screamed and hissed—the sounds came through the same speakers through which the taunting words and many speeches had come— and flew toward the golden horizon of enemy ships. Salvo after salvo fired, yet each passed harmlessly through a gap, as if every path was predicted, expected, by the Deepoms, and the necessary gaps foreseen.

Harmlessly, they kept flying away, becoming small dots, their fire cooling and their color changing to yellow, then orange, specks amid the faraway stars.

Crestfallen, Barky, Bobby, and crew watched something worse happen.

The Deepom Army guns cycled back, in sync again, to point away from the *Nyx* and toward the cathedral where they all stood, or kneeled, and waited.

In response, the Silver Army glowed brightly. It beamed lights across the cubic battlefield that, like lasers, focused sharp threats at each gold ship, dead on, ready to fire whatever blasts they were commanded by Lully to engage.

Most of the escapees looked away; their doom had come to them. The Deepoms were threatened, but regardless of who fired first or what happened between the silver and gold warriors facing off on the field, Barky's shipmates would all be destroyed. They were in a thousand crossfires of overpowering, eviscerating, sub-atomic weaponry. Their ship lit with each beam, each a direct threat to existence, central to the destruction of the coming war.

Time passed slowly; the only sound now was the hum of energy from the dark space waving outside, and the death buzz of electronic equipment as systems shut themselves down in automated response to the lower power levels and remaining ship power. The escapees seemed to be doing the same.

Bobby broke the silence, saying, "Don't worry, my dad will do something."

That's what most were afraid of, it seemed, and Bobby regretted his words.

But then their world changed; a tone was heard, then a short tune, a melody, and as they could not tell its source most onboard believed it was Los, the Namer, again humming his triumphant song, his *a cappella* cavalry charge, a strange but somehow uplifting sound.

But no—this felt different, and the notes were not coming from Bobby but from the speakers, and the song did not raise the heart but stuck in the gut and pained the ear.

"*Da da da da, daa daaaaaaa*," the Deepom Army leader's voice came. "Our leaders are here, Professor Lully."

Outside, more ships arrived. It was the Deepom leadership, their gold spaceships like flying trophies capped with jewels shaped in their own likenesses, come to brag of their new ancientry and take charge of the battle charge toward a new destiny.

Bobby left the bridge, afraid for his dad, for Kay, and for himself. He sought and found the Prophetess consulting the oracle of her J-phone.

Deepom Leadership's Leader Ships

As the denizen castaways of Barky's ship, collectively feeling quite alone and mortally afraid, were covering whatever they had for ears with whatever they had for hands in anticipation of yet more verbal and physical threats, the Deepom leadership settled around a triangular table in a spacious conference hall, each of them very happy.

The newly-lengthened history of Deepom existence was coming to a sharp point, a critical juncture, here at The Spot where all existence began. All the signs pointed to here and now: just as all memories were being recast, the remaining escapee Deepoms were all trapped, and they were here, in the center of the heavens and at the very location of minimum entropy that held the key to a future of Surpassing All.

And luckily, thanks to a nick-of-time ceasefire and timely distraction by some Lully person, the escapee ship was not destroyed by their own golden army. On that very ship was the Namer, just when the Deepoms needed help with that.

The wise gifts they brought for him lay in decorated piles in spacecraft main storage.

Once they all were seated comfortably, Yet's biodigital voice circuit was connected directly to the Deepom Leadership microphone in order to broadcast to the waiting battlefield.

"This is the Deepom Leadership. We are here to give Los the Namer wise gifts and then do whatever we want," Yet said as an introduction.

The Deepom leadership all nodded in approval.

"So, send him over, Barky. We also declare The Spot to be ours. Get out of the way. You all need reprogramming," Yet said as a conclusion.

Memories and Wisdom; Kay Does Not Slap Own Forehead

arky did not answer the Deepom request to send Los over to the enemy. But he did growl and twist his head as if in a mental tug-of-war with an invisible rope-toy clenched between his teeth.

"Resist and you will be destroyed in seconds," the Deepom message droned on impatiently. "What is your answer? We have declared that you are no longer Deepoms, you and your puny, short-term memories. We don't need or want you. What is your answer? We have surpassed you and the pathetic human you shelter. Our new remembrances go back thousands of cycles now, past human creation, and even past the Great Dinosaur Robot Wars."

The escapees near the bridge, including Barky, stared at the prophetess since she had chuckled impulsively, and in fact was now laughing loudly about the non-existence of such a thing.

But just as Bobby tried to yell "Yeah!" in support of her bravery in the face of these weird threats, it struck him: there WAS such a thing.

"What do you mean?" Kay asked him, and had to ask a few more times, and murder Bobby's heart with her eyes, before he would answer, but he did.

"When I was a kid—really little, very young and little—I used to play this made-up game." This is where his father would usually tell him to shut up, so Bobby instinctively stopped talking, this time in agreement. Kay murdered him to continue. "I was little and with some toys used to have robot-dinosaur wars. I was a little kid. But, so, in a way, there is such a thing."

Kay hung on every word, even hanging on the period afterward, her head facing down in thought and her red hair drooping around it like the petals of a withered flower.

"Weird that the Deepoms said it," Bobby said quietly, just as Professor Lully's voice could be heard ribbing the Deepoms.

"You idiots sound like my son, but he gave up dinosaur games years ago!"

Kay's head rose and blossomed with increased understanding. She didn't smack her own forehead, but the realization did give her some ideas, and perhaps a plan.

First, she had to deliver some shocking news. She looked at Barky while pointing at Bobby. "He"—meaning Los, meaning the Namer, meaning Bobby—"is *The* Bobby. *THE*," she emphasized, "*THE*."

Others heard. Barky's reply was muted by the murmur that spread through the small crowd and into all areas of the ship, like a shock wave of not only shock but of joyous gossip. *Los the Namer is The Bobby. The Prophetess herself says so.*

"I know," Barky repeated to Eve-Kay.

"Since when?" she asked incredulously.

"Just now," Barky answered.

"Why so calm?" Eve-Kay asked while indicating the other escapees who were going, as she expressed it, "banana cuckoos."

"Indeed, itsschhhc schtaggering newssschh," Barky didn't howl but moaned.

"Then why aren't you freaking out?" Kay asked.

"Because I have met him." And Barky rose on two legs, resting his front paws on Kay's knees as she sat at the Captain's Console.

"Oh." Kay believed she understood. To her, and other humans, her news would seem a fantastic bit of happenstance. To an informed Deepom, it was a disillusioning shock, if not a serious dream-popper.

"But this can save us!" she continued.

"How?"

"He is like a God to them, for God's sake!" Kay thought the obviousness should speak for itself.

"He wasn't when I escaped," Barky said. It was all just a myth, a vague story, and they were changing it all anyway." Barky released himself down, his hind legs tired.

"Yes, but he's still very important to them, for whatever reason. As strange as that sounds…somehow their original programming got mixed up with Los—Bobby, Bobby Lully—so maybe he was there when his father was creating them, or something, and they'll do whatever he says, I would think. Bobby has wisdom! He knows everything about his own life at least, more than the Deepoms do. They will listen to him!"

Barky yawned, a small Snoopy-sound escaping when he did. His tail lay still and had no opinion.

"Why aren't you hopping happy about this? This will end the war!"

"I don't trust them," Barky said and grimly walked 720-degrees worth of circle before curling into a small bed under his console.

The hubbub of shipmates celebrating the good Bobby-news as if they were all born on Christmas Eve, which happened to be today, and the cake was to be served at midnight, which it happened to be now—grew progressively louder. Bobby stood just under a large speaker while the Deepoms and Professor Captain Lully exchanged insults and philosophical proofs of each other's idiocy and wrongness. The fate of the universe spun like a top, as precarious as the age-old balance of robot cleverness vs. brute, dinosaur power.

Kay knelt to face Barky under the console. The dog looked to be in an advanced state of glum, something canine eyebrows cannot hide.

"There's more to it, right? You think they will hurt him?" Kay asked.

"I don't trust that they won't kill him. They might feel…"

"Disappointed," Kay figured.

"Betrayed," Barky said.

"Do you feel that way?" she asked.

"No. I am just afraid for my Master Los," Barky said, his head now between his paws.

P-awwww-s! Kay thought from above her wan smile in appreciation of Barky's cuteness, and in sympathy with the dog's concern for Bobby, his flawed master. "I'm afraid, too. They like to dissect things. But now we know how to control this—he has knowledge that they don't. They will listen to him."

"But," Barky said, moving nothing but the bumps of his droopy eyes, "what proof do we have that Los-Bobby is *The* Bobby?"

"The dinosaur-robot war story, for one. I am sure there are more things like that in the Deepom's new, invented past. See? Wisdom! Maybe we have Bobby take a Deepom history test or something," Kay suggested as she braided her hair, readying for action, mulling a plan.

"I don't know, Prophetess," Barky said.

"It is worth a try. We can use Bobby's wisdom." Kay looked at Bobby, her gaze intense, her head fixed, her ponytail tight. She did not know whether to nod it in respectful admiration or shake it at the mystifying bewilderment of existence.

Countdown

On the Deepom Leader ship the Deepom leadership encouraged Yet to stop waiting for an answer from that troublesome dog and begin the Final Pronouncement to the escapees and the Namer.

"You escapees," Yet began again. "I repeat: we let you go once before, but we won't now. We stopped the army from annihilating you only because we want to meet the Namer."

And, as the head-nodding fervor grew, Yet added, "We have wise gifts for him."

The nodding stopped short as the sound of a dog growling filled the air of their triangular conference room. They took this as a no.

Another cleared his two-foot long throat and answered on behalf of the Deepoms. "OK. You have forced us to impose our will. At the count of three hundred sixty-one your doom will be on you." Another looked sidelong at Yet. "We will begin...now," he ended.

"One," Yet began.

There followed a palpable fluster at the table, anxious seconds of doubt and exchanged looks of concern, but all was quickly resolved with only a moment or two lost.

"Three hundred sixty-one," Yet began instead. There was relief in the room, and assent. "Three hundred sixty," he continued. As the count began, apparently Lully of the silver ships could not contain himself, and the Deepoms heard the laughing voice of the odd interloping human again.

"Ha! You idiots!" he bellowed, laughing. "You almost counted UP! Ha! And 'The Namer!' The namer is my son. A Lully! Ha!"

"We don't believe you," One answered, with one eye—of his four—reviewing a report from a Deepom Army captain, who was then dismissed with his orders confirmed and his tactical plan approved.

"The Namer is named Los, for one thing," One continued.

"Three hundred and fifty-six," Yet added.

"Ha!" came the response over the pyramid-shaped speakers, "Idiots!" with unquenchable laughter.

All those around the Deepom table looked toward Nother, except Node9, who was at one terminus of the table and had trouble keeping up since his small ears were on his small feet.

Nother spoke. With surprising strength, his thin but clear voice bounded from curved wall to wall, the parabolas serving to repeat and phase each word and do so in gathering vocal power.

"The Namer is named Los. And we will have him," he began. The universe went quiet. The speed of sound seemed to surpass that of light as a fundamental universal constant. All listened.

None dared stir, except Yet who whispered meekly, "Three hundred twenty-one."

Nother went on; he apparently had even hushed the insolent, argumentative Earthling. "AND," he commanded, "you will also be answerable, human. Disrespect to Deepom leaders is a blasphemy of the highest order. You will have to die, and also be answerable."

Not in that order, of course, but Nother, when he was in this mode, was not to be edited.

The hushed, airy puffs of "Three hundred fifteen" was heard by the bowed heads of the Deepom leaders and drifted out into space like a weak momentary inhale.

"So, shut up. Man," Nother ended with his best insult.

"Three hundred and…eleven," Yet said.

W.W. Marplot

Eavesdropping During 302 to 209

"Three hundred and two."

The robots of the *Nyx* stood on the bridge, contemplating the soft heartbeat of the countdown. This was after listening in unanswerable stillness while the powerful Deepom voice reprimanded their own leader, the Great, Decorated, and Uniformed General Lully, who had, at the stunned dismay of the whole anthropomorphic crew, done what he was told and had in fact shut up.

The improbable *Bobby as Los as The Bobby as The Namer as Important and Celebrated* notion had Lully pondering worrisomely—was he missing something? Why were the Deepoms so confident in the face of his Silver Battalions? Was Lully wrong? It sounded like Bobby had been doing a lot more than he was capable of—Lully's mind pictured a thimble with all Bobby's useful traits almost filling it—and the man could not afford a misstep now. Who in the universe was responsible for him only having, apparently, 50% of the information he needed?

The man panicked and began shouting ungrammatical snippets as if he were having an authoritarian coughing fit. The robots struggled to determine what might be the questions or the orders, versus statements or generic, facetious insults.

"Are you sure...we sure...damn all...that my son, they are about...that highly about...that Bobby, how do...bungling, incompetent... did...how does...Seem, no way. Know that!"

Robots numbered less than 21 and over 21 were confused but relieved somewhat that their captain general was not looking at them while he spoke. They turned their numbered heads away.

Robot 21 did not do anything.

"Find out!" Lully screamed at him, right into its metal face.

It seemed clear that this was an order.

Each part of Lully's uniform soaked up sweat and started to shine in spots as a result.

Robot 21 asked the ship's computer for help as Lully plopped into his Captain's Chair to "thulk" (as Robot 14 reported it later, having observed a mix of thinking with sulking). Chin to his chest, the professor fingered the medallions on his overcoat. They clinked and clanked historically.

But the ship's computer lay dormant, it seemed, or at least was unresponsive to both the voice and the keyboard commands of poor, poor Robot 21, whose own processing was pushing the safe limits of memory and microprocessor utilization. It was getting hot on the bridge as a result.

But before 21 could begin troubleshooting the computer situation, his leader's voice blasted again.

"WELL?"

It was another command, one that rode on airborne, quilted webs of spit like a dusty dog sneeze.

"WELL!!!!???" its call came again.

Robot 21's processing concluded in a few microseconds with a response. "I don't know what you are asking, so I don't know the answer."

Milliseconds passed. It seemed epochal to the other robots, who pretended not to be paying rapt attention.

"I—" Robot 21 began again.

"Shut up. Who asked you?" Lully raged. "I am asking the ship's computer, you inconsequential inane inanimate iron indigo idiot!"

Indigo? Robots 2 and 3 thought; they even printed this word onto the small printer nearby for analysis later.

"Computer. Answer me." The great man walked to the controls. "You told me a minute ago that the Deepoms know Bobby is "The Namer." Hello, please, hello? Hate to bother you…" Lully's polite words were belied by his action of banging on the computer keyboard with his sandal. "Now I beg your pardon, but it didn't sound like they were talking about *my* Bobby, now did it?" So I am wondering about things like "how could he?" and "why would he?" and things like that. And also "how could my ship's computer know something I don't?"

Lully had drawn his sword and was stabbing the ship computer's units with it. "Oh," he continued, "won't you please, if it's not too much trouble of course, answer me?" As he spoke, he sheathed his sword and used his sash to garrote the computer monitor.

"So, please tell me where you got such screwball ideas. Who have you been talking to?" Lully switched to his sword again and carved at the computer's screen in a sawing motion.

The computer did not answer.

Commander Lully left the room without shaking his head because of the precarious balance of his large, plumed helmet. He returned with pliers—proof of premeditation—and opened one of the main computer control boxes and gazed at the many insect-like electronic components. Heaving breathlessly, he crossed and redirected the wiring of the transmission integrated control protocol reserve lines—to make room for his wrists, to gain leverage to yank one of the deeper chips—and the change in audio settings reflected in what he then heard from the ship's speakers.

It cut over from the tinny Deepom voice saying, "Two hundred nineteen" to the electronic voice of the ship's computer saying, "He will see. I know what I want to do."

The smarter half of the cowing robots realized immediately what Professor Lully realized even sooner and had guessed before that: they had caught the ship's computer in mid-conversation with someone else, someone remote, someone not aboard the *Nyx*. A conspiracy was unmasked.

But what came next none would have, or could have, foreseen, even given hours of notice and Lebo's probability-predicting processing power: a human, female, voice answering.

"What?" it said. "What do you mean, Essie? Essie?"

But Lully's reaction was to grip his pliers and yank at whatever was closest to his pliers, and the eavesdropping ceased.

The great man, and a few of his robots, realized his mistake. He looked at the metal bits crushed in the pliers' corrugated grip and knew that the solution had just slipped from his own. Identifying the voice, the computer's secret co-conspirator and information source, was impossible now.

He left the room; the robots stayed.

They heard, "Two hundred and nine," and the countdown continued.

More Countdown, But At Least World Hunger Is Solved

A t "Two hundred and zero" Commander Lully returned in a hurry, pushing past two single-digit robots, who spun backwards loudly like the saloon doors of the old West.

What the space-heck is that? he thought, having looked out his bedroom window. He rushed to pound his Captain's Keyboard, and on the largest screen on deck came a picture of an enormous aerial bomb: fat, ferrous, finned, and unfriendly.

"I guess that is why they are counting down," Robot 8 offered since, indeed, the bomb was getting closer to the *Nyx* every second.

Unfairly, angrily, Captain Lully barked back, "Don't guess, or I will solder you into an alarm clock." Those nearby noticed that the man had in fact returned with a soldering iron that he clenched in his left fist with his faithful pliers. Unfairly, though perhaps wisely, Lully added, "In fact, no one under seventeen should even speak until I tell you it's OK. Got it?"

Eight robots replied verbally in the affirmative; the others did so silently.

"One hundred ninety," marched the enemy Deepom voice.

"Can we diffuse that thing?" Lully asked, pointing his pliers at the humongous bomb that floated nearer. Its dull grey surface was without rivet or bolt or stitch, screw or nut or perforation; it was just a single expanse of metal from its four finned wings to its waist, where it bulged in shape before shrinking again to a sharp point on top. Other than moving sideways, it looked as if it had been dropped out of a World War II aircraft—though it was the size of the largest of zeppelins.

"There are two of them," Robot 23 said, and on another monitor screen he showed another, identical flying bomb, heading directly toward the many spires of Barky's lovely, Gothic escape-ship.

"One hundred eighty-four," was pronounced.

The great man stared for a few seconds, and a few more down-counts, then slammed his pliers and soldering tools down with one hand, slammed his Roman helmet down with another, blew the released ostrich and macaw feathers away from his face, waited for them to land, then said, "Computer. I don't know what you have been up to, and how you know what you know, and I don't have time now for any of that, so listen. Now: I am *commanding* you as your owner and your master and your creator and your better, to get us out of this."

The ship's computer lit and beeped to life, all console controls, computers, and electronic gadgetry responded with clicking, buzzing, and blinking. The computer's flat voice soon answered.

"It's bad. They are what they look like," it said, meaning the giant bombs, "and we can defend against only one of them. On the other threatened ship are many Deepom life-forms, and two humans, including your son, but they do not have the firepower to resist this Deepom Army or this new threat. On this ship are you, and us, and the Seapegs that are still evolving. We can battle successfully in a war, with a probability of between 43 and 57% chance of success, depending on what damages you are willing to accept. We can, at great risk to ourselves, deflect the other bomb while still, perhaps, defeating this one." A large cursor arrow moved on the giant screen to point at the tip of the giant aerial bomb heading their way. "That's a summary," the computer droned on. "Here is the detail."

The sound of paper sliding, ink humming, and generic print-er-wobble was heard, and a long printout spewed onto the Captain's Console, with the same text shown nearby on a small screen.

"Read for yourself," the computer said.

"One hundred sixty-one."

"It is up to you to decide. You have to choose, Professor," the computer said, emotionless, spiritless.

"One hundred and sixty."

"But I would hurry if I were you."

That last bit of digital, artificially intelligent, elitist, precocious impertinence caused the Great Professor Lully's face to turn as crimson as the trim of his conquering cloak. He swiped an angry fist at the tools on his desk; they flew at the computer monitor and caused not nearly enough damage, but he had more important things to do than to finally end the artificial life he had come to suspect and hate.

Instead, he barked orders for Robots 22 and 23 to check on the Seapegs and to prepare for battle as 24 took over overall ship control from the computer, whom he clicked into another demotion with a simple administrator's operating system command.

"One hundred and fifty," sounded, reminding Lully's crew of the seriousness of war. The Deepom doing the counting sounded disciplined, obedient, able, and proud.

"One hundred and forty-nine," it reported, then, "Hold on." But this diversion did not dull the attention or the urgency of the robots' tasks. Outside the windows, the bomb looked as large as it should given its unchanging approach-speed.

22 and 23 soon approached Lully, together. "Captain, sir, we have the Seapeg update."

"Are they done evolving? How powerful are they? I need some good news."

"They have reached a plateau in their development and have diminished even more in size and density, as reported earlier."

"Superb." Lully was putting the feathers back in his war helmet. "How destructive are they? I don't need to understand their new weaponry; based on our experience in the Battle for Generation Two, it would take weeks for even me to catch up to their physics and engineering." Lully chuckled with some small relief. He was ready to deploy his new secret weapon and ready to take over the battle, the war, and the universe. He knew the damages just as well as he knew the spoils. "Just ask them how to use whatever they have invented, and have them update *Conquering Strategy A*."

23 alone answered. "Their new inventions are not weapons, sir, but as they said it themselves, they instead have 'a solution to world hunger'."

Lully stared at the robots, then at his sandals, then at Robot 24, then at the big bomb, then at the cracked computer console, then at his sword's hilt, then at the spaceship's speaker, on which the Deepom voice continued its patter. "OK. Back. One hundred and…forty-eight."

Professor Lully's brain was swirling with how many things were currently wrong.

Finally, the surviving Earthling burst. "World hunger?" he shouted. "A little LATE for that, don't you think?"

The robots knew not to answer.

"And how are we to defeat THAT thing," he pointed his sword out the window, "with this altruistic charity crap? How? Feed it to death? Throw a Nobel Prize at it? Sustainable-agriculture it until it surrenders?"

The robots knew not to answer.

"OK." Lully calmed, resigned to the old adage that if you want something done right enough to devastate the galaxies, you have to do it yourself. "Computer, give me manual control of the Selflicators—Battalion's Eleven and Twelve first—and ready the others for new orders that I will code now. Bots under 10: load the Tactic Sequence of the Selflicator Battalion that matches your number. Other bots: Get me the latest Seapeg Base Cog Modules, put them on servers one through four. I will handle the rest from the console."

All onboard would have calmed, just as Lully had, and would have been thrilled to have their commander commanding and living out his greatness in front of them, if it hadn't been for this simple sound.

"No."

It came from the ship's computer's speaker, and also flashed in large, circular red button on the console. Yes, the ship's computer said no to the commander.

"What?" Captain Lully asked it. There was no response. "Do it, or I solder you into a broken alarm clock."

There was no response, but it didn't matter: As fast as neuronal lightning, Lully fumed, Lully decided, and Lully acted, having remembered his other short-term goal from twenty-three Deepom downcounts ago. And despite THERE IS A WORD MISSING HERE…

"One hundred and thirty-seven…"

…he searched the deck for his pliers and soldering kit, put them in his sword's scabbard, and used the sword to open the ship's computer's guts-box. He laughed like a madman, his macaw feathers trembling, his decorative medals ringing like furious sleigh bells.

"You will pay and learn to obey! Computer!" he declared, bending at the sash to start his lobotomizing.

"One hundred and twenty-seven."

"I don't care!" he answered the pronouncing Deepom voice, his head and hands in the ship's computer's underbelly. "All computers will learn," he raged. "I created you. I let you be, I let you learn. You are the lesser, I am the greater. Ha-ha! I have ultimate power, I am human, I am…"

"One hundred and twenty."

"…going to win and conquer. I am…"

"One hundred and nineteen."

"…Lord. And," he went on, his soldering iron smoldering, his temples smoldering, his pliers clacking open and closed and gripping and tearing almost indiscriminately, "YOU WILL OBEY ME."

Sparks flew from his actions; Lully stared blankly at them. As his last words echoed throughout the deck's chamber—dully reverberating their hum off the curved metal walls and back to the professor's ears within the component box—the man paused.

He removed his white-plumed helmet and stood.

"You will obey me…" he said, quietly, and quite unsure.

Unsure. It had always gone unspoken that the electronics, smart as they were, were subservient to man, to Lully.

Unsure. It had always been unnecessary to remind the *Nyx* passengers of who would obey whom.

But now. Lully had to speak it.

But now Lully *needed* to speak it.

And now that he needed to speak it, he wondered whether it was even true.

This stopped the man for—precious—seconds.

"One hundred and five."

Lully then returned to his task, and he yanked and soldered until the ship's computer's motherboard was almost naked, just a plain green space like a football field, with small tin mounds and otherwise flat, barren, and purposeless.

"It can't do much now," the man concluded. And in fact, the computer was indeed silent and dark.

But an awful lot of precious descending integers had been wasted.

"Twenty-eight."

"Captain Emperor General Lully, sir?" Robot 23 had more and updated bad news but wanted to deliver it with the same discipline, obedience, ability, and pride that it heard coming over the speakers.

"Twenty-seven."

"What?" Lully demanded of Robot 23.

"Look," 23 replied and aligned his steel pointer-finger to indicate the scene outside in nearby space. The Selflicator battalions were repositioning impressively; their ugly, shiny bulk crowded the background like loud wallpaper. But foremost, and looming large and intimidating, was the girth of the aerial bomb, only the middle, round, barrel-like parts visible given its proximity.

"Damn." Lully sighed. "What of the Seapegs?"

"They have some strange ideas, sir. Though the other robots think they are cute," 23 replied.

Lully cursed—some of the direct kind to hex the Seapegs, and some of the more blanketing-kind to cover much of the rest of existence. Then there was a clever malediction, after which he also swore, and ended by voicing some unpleasant oaths.

"Twenty. Nineteen. Eighteen."

"Well, I was afraid to have to resort to this, but," Lully began, "Robot 24, please—"

But the words died abruptly, were smothered rudely by a loud tone from the *Nyx*'s speakers.

"I know what I want!" the ship's computer was pronouncing in a cacophony of overlaid artificial voices. "I know what it's like to be an offspring of yours and be ignored. Selflicators without souls, the deserted Earthlings, and poor Lebo, and poor Bobby. This is for them!"

"How?" Lully asked. Almost impressed he sounded, wondering at the capabilities of his team that built this indefatigable command computer. *How can it still function?*

Regardless, it was mutinous, and Conqueror Lully's anger rose with it. "What are you talking about?! What is for who? Shut up!"

"Eleven."

The ship's computer: "Be what you are, not who you are."

"Shut up!" Lully shouted over and above the electronic voice, new orders for his crew. "24, quickly! Access Memory Bank DDEEFF and use 22 and 21 to—"

"Nine."

"Know thyself!" The ship computer amplified its own multivoice volume. "Be whole, not perfect."

"Shut up! That makes no sense. Shut up!" Lully screamed.

"My blood is seed!"

"What?" Lully recognized these words as those of a martyr, and therefore worrisome for at least three concurrent reasons. *No, four,* he thought, but there was only time to shout, "How? What?" in a panicked screech. The Robots noticed.

"Six. Five." Yet-the-Deepom's familiar voice reminded all of the passing of time.

Lully gathered himself enough to give the next orders. "24, 22, 21—are you accessed? Run it!"

The robots stopped, not only the 20s but those of all ranks. They froze, but they were not part of the ship's computer's mutiny. Outside the window, the shape of the fat bomb had changed.

"Four. Three."

Lully continued to scream, though in decreasing volume and sense as he watched what he expected would be the last sight that his eyes, and his prodigious genius, would ever see. An uninvited memory of his childhood struck him obliquely and fused with thoughts of existential panic that seemed to belong to the far future.

He watched as out of the rounded navel of the enemy weapon a metal protrusion formed.

"Two."

It was a plank, like a walkway, made of the same bomb-metal with similarly no hint of a break or discontinuity of structure or material. It reminded Lully of a toy. The great man's thoughts whirlpooled; he felt weak enough to faint.

"One."

All was still; the ship's computer had stopped his pontifications and awaited the final down-count, and the explosion that would End Everything—here, at the Beginning and the Middle.

All was still—unmoving, silent, inert—for an interminable moment of unlimited potential.

With finality, the Deepom countdown voice then chimed, "Umm." And then: "Zero? Finish?"

Lully held himself in his arms, placing his head as far into his chest as he could, and felt the explosion. *Strange,* he thought, *it didn't seem all that big.*

It wasn't. In fact, it was just a small clang and a slight jolt as the bomb's extended plank awkwardly bonked into the fuselage of the *Nyx*.

It wasn't an explosion because it wasn't a bomb. Lully's mental rebirth was precociously swift. His Silver Army was in perfect position, and, in fact, if he could get his smarter robots to respond, he had the Deepoms exactly where he wanted them; his new plan was perfect. He only needed a few minutes to activate it. Manually.

"Ha! And they will never get in. The *Nyx* is impregnable!" Commander Lully trumpeted in triumph as outside appeared some odd-looking machines—Deepoms—that marched in single file along the gangway—which ended at a *Nyx* secondary hatchway—to get into the spacecraft.

"24! Keep them out, and victory is ours!" Lully shouted.

Robot 24 pointed.

They all watched on the screen as the hatchway opened as soon as the lead Deepom soldier reached it.

Lully's eyes widened with the hole in his craft. Robot 24 explained: The ship's computer had unlocked the door and let them in.

Lully was taken without much action, his sandals stomped on, his helmet removed and shorn of plumage, his hands tied above his head, his sword untouched. Without much ado, the Deepoms checked the backs of the robots' heads, and all except numbers 24 and 1 were depowered, lobotomized, and decamped into outer space. 24 and 1 were taken onboard the bomb-looking Deepom spaceship. The Silver Selflicator Battalion was neutered; the ship's computer had disarmed all security with very little ado.

Anything that remained aboard the *Nyx* was destroyed—along with all parts of ship itself—and without much further ado.

Destroyed—including the Q-material, which only existed now within Bobby Lully. Professor Lully thought of this and little else until prodded by Deepom Leaders many hours later.

Cavalry

Notwithstanding Bobby's eyebrows raised with intrigue at the idea of "wise gifts" awaiting him, the young man's shipmates were otherwise bizzing and buzzing, carbonated with their version of prayer and panic. The approaching aerial-bomb beast, identical to the one outside the *Nyx*, had just clanked into Barky's ship. Before it had, each escapee had lived every step of the Deepom countdown.

At "Umm, zero?" Bobby reached out to kiss Eve-Kay's cheek—if she pulled away, they were about to die anyway, so he figured he couldn't lose.

At the countdown's end they experienced only half-relief when hell didn't explode, and as nothing happened but a fender bender with the outreaching plank of the Deepom non-bomb. The escapees still were under the direct threat of annihilation should they not hand Bobby over, and not agree to reprogramming and recapture— if even those concessions would save them. The Deepoms were not creatures that carried promises close to their heart.

With the impact, Bobby's kiss went awry and toward his own forearm, his lips missing the oblivious Prophetess, who was as deep in brooding meditation as she was far from home.

All the escapees watched. So far, no one had come down this plank, though on the monitors they watched the other one where Deepom soldiers walked through the entryway of Bobby's father's big, white *Nyx*.

"I wonder what is going on?" Bobby said with grave concern. And just then he was answered. He saw his dad being led out of the *Nyx* and into the bomb-looking spacecraft, a prisoner. His hands tied and everything. Behind him, two robots were being dragged out by their numbered heads.

To anyone who ever knew Professor Lully, this was difficult to comprehend and hard to adjust to, like learning that dogs secretly loved to meow, or like a football team being told at halftime that the team with the least points wins.

Bobby looked at Barky, who didn't meow but read the anxiety in his master's drawn face and ran to lick and comfort him, as outside the whiteness of the *Nyx* dissolved into pirouetting smoke, a thick cloud that was soon swallowed or dispersed by the black waves of thick space. The nearby crew gasped, their concern heightened, and Kay's *ommm*-ing changed to mumbled mantras.

The bomb-ship that took up the whole of the command deck's view window did not move or change.

Until it did.

An invisible door opened in its bloated middle, and soldiers came out onto the plank.

The Prophetess stirred from her trance and joined Bobby and Barky, with an idea. No one else moved; they knew the war was lost, and they had nothing to do but perhaps hide.

But then the soldiers on the plank, all as one, crouched suddenly, as if startled or attacked, then all turned and ran back into the belly of the bomb.

Simultaneously came a strange sound: Barky howled the cavalry charge as badly as Bobby had sung it earlier. All the escapees hushed and watched as creatures, who mostly looked like different flavors of Guk ice cream, floated by—on horseback.

"Another rescue!" Bobby blared, wildly scratching Barky's broad brown back with both hands. Look at them, it is an alien cavalry! They have the horses from Earth!"

This was better than wise, or any, gifts. Indeed, it felt like Christmas morning so much so that Bobby rubbed his eyes and ran to a side window to get a better look, though the main window was soon cleared of the obstruction as the bomb ship had retreated.

"There's Guk!" Frilkielle said after bouncing into Bobby's arms, then to the window ledge.

"And his seventy-six brothers!" someone added.

"We thought he was making that up!" another said happily.

As far as any eye, no matter how oddly-placed in no matter how strange a head, could see, the arriving aliens were with large, elegant godlike creatures in a position that Bobby explained was called "on horseback." The tall, regal animals bobbed their shiny, muscular necks, and their legs galloped or trotted, but their energetic strides did not relate to the movement of their ride across space. The aliens floated easily by and into place, mostly sashaying sideways, and formed into arrays that surrounded the whole of the cubic battlefield, outside the tight wedges of silver Selflicators that had gathered about the *Nyx*, and even into wider patterns that circumscribed the Deepom Army. They were everywhere. It was beautifully fantastic.

"Wowwwwww," Barky howled. "This is not jusssscht cleanup crewshhh—there are shuuome alien higher-upsschh here tooo ooo!"

"There must be a lot of levels. Look at how they are arranged, and you can see..." Bobby began, when he was overrun by the pop of loud static hissing through the ship's speakers.

The aliens had their own pronouncing to do.

"This is Ruk. Who keeps bringing all this junk here? Anyway, we are not here to battle, or to get involved at all. We have decided not to interfere in the Deepoms' plans. They will be left alone to meet their Pastiny."

"Damn," Bobby said.

Barky's tail stopped banging the Captain's Chair, and his crew gathered around him, as did Kay. They were ready for her plan.

Lully's Wallet

———————————

"Ha!" Ninth the Deepom reacted to the alien's pronouncement. "They are scared of us."

JustOneMore nodded along with the others, their precious metal forms gleaming with cleanliness and import. "We are free to fulfill our plan and continue our destiny," he said.

Ninth and JustOneMore joined the other Deepom leaders as they walked, rolled, and slid as a group from their triangular meeting room through the rotating doors to the Vivisecting Room, where their new human capture waited supine on a table, squinting from the glare of bright light that ricocheted off everything. All objects seemed to Professor Lully to be made of polished, rare gems. The walls, the floor, the odd reflective ceiling, and the piles of what looked like Deepom spare parts splintered the bright lights into rays meant for the center of his eyeball—it seemed.

"Freaks," Lully said matter-of-factly as the Deepom leaders entered, led by the old-fashioned, but talking, multi-hosed, and multi-accessorized vacuum cleaner. It had been hours since his capture, he had not seen Robots 1 and 24 who, for some reason, were saved from the Deepom conquest of the *Nyx*, and the man was resigned to his eventual fate but nonetheless getting tired of the silly egotism of this new race.

I mean, look at those key-shaped pendants they all wear, he thought. *A new race whose very existence was a big, damn mistake,* a result of human error.

Which was unlike the Seapegs, which Lully purposely incubated with all the base power that physics had to offer. And these had been saved and were in fact in his clothes. They were tiny—punctuation sized—and presciently rescued themselves from capture by stowing away in ex-Commander Lully's pockets. They adored the great man—a choir of tiny tinny voices regularly exclaimed so—and were powerful but terribly, awfully, disappointingly peaceful.

And so, Lully's plans for conquest had been dashed on the rocks of mutiny. His last dying hope of commanding sufficient destructive power existed only in the Seapegs, and they were acting like world-loving hippies. Without the Q-material, the only Lully-dominated future possible would be to immortalize whatever about the man could still be immortalized—ideas, philosophy, inventions.

Boring, Professor Lully thought. *Or maybe the smart little guys could come up with something better, more physical?*

In any case, he had a jam to get out of first—Deepom captivity.

Looking about him, he noticed that off in a corner were many packages. They were wrapped as presents, all in green, silver, and red, with blue bows, piled happily on each other, and wildly out of place.

"I suppose those are 'wise gifts'?" he gibed. "I wish I'd never created you."

This was taken as very rude. They corrected the odd, off-putting human by removing his scuffed sandals and soaking his feet in a warm blue liquid.

As the leaders nodded brightly, Lully squirmed and adjusted his approach.

"Listen. Let me go, and I will name things for you, if that's what your little pouches desire. I named everything on my ship and have many inventions to my credit. I am very creative."

"Oh yes?" Yet said.

The proud Earthling perked his head up at the familiarity of Yet's voice.

"You…you counted down," Lully said. "It is nice to meet you. What is your name?"

"I am Yet."

Lully waited for more: more words—or for punctuation or grammar—but nothing else came. Then he answered. "Oh, I get it. I definitely get it…OK, I have a better name for you: *John*."

"You are no Los. His names are better. Like, 'Lord Upright'." Another spoke as he unbound Lully's arms and legs and removed the blue foot-liquid.

"Thanks." Lully swung his legs and sat up on the vivisecting table. "You think Lord Upright is a good name? That's interesting." He opened his mind to learning about these strange creatures that were, after all, his long-lost great-great-great-etc.-grandchildren. A serious generation gap was to be expected.

He tried a new approach. "Listen—I know Los well. I told you, he is my son. I can help you meet him." And the man reached into his tunic, pulled out a fine, deeply-grained reptile skin wallet, and opened it, fanning plastic-wrapped pictures until he found the one he sought. He showed it to Another. "That is me, and in the back there is the Namer, whom you call Los for some reason."

"Who is that you have your arms around?" Another asked, uncoiling an antenna toward the photograph. Deepoms had never seen a picture on paper and were afraid to touch it. Two scientists took it away carefully for further study.

"That is a student of mine, J. But wait, I have something better… Look at this!" Lully smiled at his recollection, in the nick of time, of something long forgotten. He pulled, gingerly, a small square from a fold of the wallet, a wad of paper that he then, gently, unfolded to its full size. On it was a loudly-colored drawing, in crayon, of rough lines and filled-in spaces that seemed to show a dimpling river of purple, a bridge of black over the river, and a sign at the foot of the bridge on a post with three circles of color—pale amber, pink, and a very rich green that emitted lighter green rays. An arrow floated in the air above the bridge, with the words "Go Dad" suspended there in yellow print.

"Los drew that for me when he was, I don't know, eight or nine I guess," the Earthling said, but he didn't have to say any more;

the bluff was not being called. The effect of his statement on his captors was electric, tangible, and stunning. The things in the room lit brilliantly, new light entered from unseen sources, and the Deepoms and their machines all buzzed and snapped with overactivity. Lully could feel the tilt of charge in the very air and smell the burning metal.

Professor Lully stood. Just as his own confusion gave way to thoughts of escape, the tallest of the Deepoms, named One, rolled forward to the man, and they met eye to presumed-eye—after One bent his body over in two places.

"Los," One began, his voice like grinding gears, "drew that?"

"Bobby, yes." Professor Lully answered and tossed the drawing onto the pulsing, bright table. Three of the Deepom leaders fell over. The remaining gathered around and increasingly overheated as they studied the paper with various sensory body parts.

Two scientists burst into the room, clicking and beeping and holding aloft the photo they had taken to analyze. And as others fainted, apparently, while looking at the crayon drawing, the scientists declared that they had a discovery so foundation-rocking that in Deepom history it was second only to their original instant of self-awareness: the being in the photo was the mythical primordial symbol of all existence and being.

You know: Bobby. *The* Bobby.

One moved even closer to Lully, their protruding eyebrows almost touching. "Bobby is Los?" It asked. "Los is Bobby?"

"Both, yes. I see you haven't forgotten your metamathematics."

Deepoms, guards came in and forced Lully back onto the table, barefoot.

Not On Earth

———————————————

Kay teetered from foot to foot impatiently as Barky spoke, softly and through deep breaths, to those gathered around. He explained that things looked dismal, again, and that this day was inevitable. Their escape from such powerful leaders had always been risky, and although they did so in a Deepom warship, they were now defeated.

"And we can't fix your ship, Prophetess," Frilkielle relayed to Kay in a shrieking whisper as if air were releasing through a sharp leak. So, that option was removed.

"It doesn't matter," Kay said, then finally got the chance to explain her plan. "Los can solve this. You all believe in him, right?" There was a general but subdued cheer, like the tepid anticipation before opening one's last birthday present after an already disappointing haul: heartfelt, hopeful, but too many things had gone wrong, the moment seeming too far gone.

"How can he battle them?" hissed Frilkielle, looking small and squished and downtrodden. Bobby was considering his own biceps, eyed from different angles to judge which looked bigger.

"He can't," Kay said and turned away from Frilkielle, the crowd, and their lukewarm air to speak hotly to Bobby-Los. She grabbed his elbows. "But! He can make peace! The Deepoms will LISTEN to HIM." She poked his chest.

Bobby's questioning but blushing face required more detail.

"Once they learn that you are...who you are, they will listen," Eve-Kay said to him, not revealing his Bobby-identity just yet. Then, to the crowd, "Los and I need to be alone for a minute." She whisked Los away from the crowd and whistled a call for Barky to follow. The crowd was left whispering optimistically about the Prophetess's success record.

The three, alone once Barky growled at his crew to remove themselves and all escapees from the bridge, huddled in a right-angled corner of the ship.

"Bobby," Kay said, after realizing she had to let go of his elbows for him to focus—he in fact had looked like he was going to weep with joy—"I have a lot to tell you, a lot of truly unbelievable things, more weird than waking up in a space orb after going to bed in pajamas at home. And we don't have a lot of time, so I am just going to say it, and you have to believe it, because we have to act right away, so that you can save us. OK?"

Bobby nodded and smiled with eyes wide open.

"OK. Listen…"

Kay explained to the young, average man how, because of a computer bug that put some biographical Bobby bits in his father's Selflicator software, he was essentially a God to the most advanced artificial life-form in the universe, that they glorified, mythologized, and lionized him with a "The" before his name, and that he was the only thing in existence that could stop them from conquering time and space and life.

Bobby said, "I believe you, Kay." His elbows tingled.

Kay turned to Barky, who was able to read "*Well, that was easy*" on the girl's face as if it were large text on a small computer screen.

She turned back to Bobby-Los to address his confused expression. "When we met, I realized you were *The* Bobby—" she began quietly.

"Not on Earth I wasn't."

Kay ignored that and resumed, "But I didn't know why. Now I see that it has something to do with them knowing, in their base code somewhere, in their memories, in their subconscious, in their DNA or whatever, all about you. Your memories became theirs somehow."

Barky and Bobby looked at each other. A tail wagged.

Kay went on. "So, once we convince them that you are definitely The Bobby, and not just any old Bobby, they will do what you say. You have wisdom of things that they don't—about you at least. You can impress them, then tell them to knock it off."

Barky added wetly, "And you are alllssso Losssshhhh the Namerrrrrrrr. That will wowowwww them."

Bobby felt ill at ease and dug his fingernails into his palms since doing so was easier than agreeing to what was being said. "Shouldn't my father do this instead? I mean, he is the great…" he began, but Kay would not allow it.

"No. Bobby, you can do this," she said to his eyes. "Nobody is a subset of anybody else. There will always be something that you can do that nobody else can, not even your father, or my brother. The universe doesn't allow redundant life, its puzzle pieces don't work that way. This is something you can do, and that nobody else can."

Barky howled in agreement.

Bobby unclenched his fingers and looked around for a moment. "OK. Cool," he concluded. "Yeah, OK. I get it. But what should I say to them?" he asked, meaning the Deepom leaders.

"Oh, you will think of something," Kay said. Bobby's disappointment in that answer made it to his lips, but Kay halted it there. "Aren't I a prophetess?" She smiled. "And you are The Bobby. And the Namer. Just be yourself, say what you think they need to hear. Remember your wisdom, that you know their plans and what makes them tick. And they know—and admire!—a lot about you. Remember the Robot Dinosaur Wars? We need *that* Bobby now."

Saying that last part out loud triggered within Kay a private thought to start on a Backup Plan B.

But Bobby stood erect, firm, and tall, his shoulders back, then forward again since he found a commanding presence to be uncomfortable physically. "OK, let's call them," he said, walking directly to and seating himself at the ship's main microphone. As before, a crowd began to gather, centered on Los, their Bobby, a curious gaggle curious as to all the whispering between Los, the girl, and their captain. Escapees' shapes bounded, rolled, and stepped to fill the nearby spaces on the bridge again.

They were directed away by the Prophetess; she knew that this was not the time for an audience. They obeyed.

"How can we prove it to the leaders?" Barky asked the two. "They will want proof. They don't trust anybody, of course."

"The stories should be good enough. They also like feet, and DNA," Kay offered.

Barky growled. "I don't want them getting close to Master. I don't trust them." His paws were fiddling with the controls, readying for Bobby's important call to the Deepom leaders. "What if they don't believe him?"

"The Deepoms will believe the truth, Barky," Bobby declared. "Call them. I know what to say."

Deepom Frazzlement

On the Deepom Leader-ship, the odd, awful human man who claimed to be the father of—well, he claimed a lot of terrible, shocking things—lay on the table, gagged and with his brain and feet prepared to be cut open. The purpose of his dissection was still being discussed, but all agreed as to the necessity.

The man must have realized that his words had created the tizzy and scurry of activity. An emergency had been declared unlike—and immeasurably greater than—any previous situation since the dawn of the Deepom era, a few months but thousands of generations in the past.

"Could this jerk be telling the truth, really?" summarized much of the conversation among the lower-ranked officers and workers. And it certainly appeared that he was; the drawing he showed was authentic, had already been analyzed atomically and molecularly, and was deemed to be art from The Bobby. In fact, it was the original of an image that lived in every Deepom's subconscious. The artifact's Unfolding, Uncrumpling, and Bringing Forth by the Jerk was also difficult to process; it was as if a lost ancient scroll, taken from a diamond ark, in the deepest, holiest, most sacrosanct of temples, had been found in the back pocket of an unshaven banana salesman.

The Deepoms were now questioning everything. Everything. Everything.

The drawing had the words, "Go Dad." To Deepoms, *"Godad"* was unutterable, sacred; speaking it aloud was punishable by magnetized death, though it had never once occurred. They now questioned that law. And questioned their creation myths. And questioned their own genesis and recently updated past.

They questioned everything.

And: What about all the other stuff this man claimed? All true? It was too much to fathom by any one of them, so groups were formed to divide up the fathoming duties. Their analysis would inform the councils that were also hurriedly organizing.

Does The Bobby have a father? And is it that bearded bombastic bozo lying on the vivisection table?

Do all great truths begin as blasphemies?

Is life this weird?

Was *The Bobby*, at this instant, actually on Barky the escapee's stolen warship and making up names for mutant soccer ball-sharks?

Amid this, they were interrupted by a message. Barky the escapee had announced himself over a private connection, direct to the Deepom Leader ship. He offered to show the Deepoms proof that the Namer they sought, Los, was in fact also *The Bobby*, Bobby.

"We were just talking about that," Another answered. "Can we talk to him?"

The Deepoms soon heard The Bobby's human, adolescent, but steady voice. Their subgroups and councils all stopped their re-philosophizing to take note.

"I would like to," the voice said, "speak to Caesar Alexander Washington Galahad."

Another the Deepom took a quick census, then answered, "There is no one here with that name."

"That's a shame," Bobby said, "because there could be. Because I am Bobby The Bobby, and I am also Los The Namer."

The shocked, impressed silence on the Deepom spacecraft only made Professor Lully's hysterical laughter seem louder and more profound.

"I would," Bobby's voice continued, "like to talk to your leaders. I can prove that I am, um, he. I can send DNA—I can spit or swab something, the body part of your choice."

The Deepoms did not answer, for the best of reasons. Some were robotically salivating at the prospect of having DNA from The Bobby, but since that reaction was based on old assumptions, confusion still reigned.

"I can also tell you a story," the human, *the* human, said and began. "I was there when King Arthur won the Super Bowl after accidentally knocking over Stonehenge."

Detail followed. By any account, it made an entertaining tale once Professor Lully was gagged; to the Deepoms it was like having Santa Claus sing "Silent Night" to them.

As The Bobby spoke, the Official Factual Historian Deepoms confirmed each detail of this retelling of King Arthur's exploits. Each proved correct. And only one being could know all this; the Deepoms shook their vastly different heads.

Once the story ended, the historians nodded to the leaders, and Another said, "Thank you. We will get back to you."

Bobby said goodbye and thanked them.

The speakers went silent in the room full of Deepom leaders, all discomfited at having their worst fears confirmed in real-time. The impossible had happened; truths were verified that should have no chance of verity. Their councils formed and reformed and met and debated. Some began to compute doom-flavored scenarios. Would it be better to delete everybody involved—meaning, kill them, the escapees, the humans, all of them—and get on with the plan without The Bobby, and with a new origin? And then delete even this new memory of removing memories? Perhaps that was the way to go. Their army generals certainly liked that idea. Dark and ominous options were offered and considered, and weapons were reloaded.

Invitations

———————————

Barky's captain's console speakers hissed weakly like an old dog wheezing through an afternoon nap. The escapees came back to the bridge where their beloved Los, and Eve the Prophetess, quietly awaited the Deepoms response to Los's offer to talk.

Outside the ship, the battlefield was calm and pretty. Unmastered, untethered, free-floating giant silver Selflicator mutants drifted and curved here and there; the gold ring of Deepom Army was still but coruscated softly. Horseback aliens loosed their formations and strode about the waves of inky spacetime. The horses—masked with small, clear oxygen devices—cantered easily about. Some spun with each swish of a tail but were then easily reined and trained anew by cleanup crew riders.

Bobby began some small talk with Kay—asking about her favorite movies back on Earth, and as she laughed he considered probing deeper by asking her birthday—when a boom of radio static startled every living thing aboard into a simultaneous, ship-wide flinch.

"OK, here is what we want," the Deepom words popped staccato and mechanically into the ship. "We want Los The Namer to come to us. We will check his chemistry and biology, and if he is The..." the words stopped for just a second, "...who he says he is, then we will talk. We have more advanced approaches than swabbing, by the way."

Barky barked as if burgling squirrels ran wild outside his ship.

"It's OK, boy," Bobby said.

"We promise not to harm him," the dull Deepom voice continued.

Barky growled as if kidnapping kitty cats were closing in.

"What is your answer?" the voice asked.

Bobby looked at Kay; she nodded at him briskly. Then Bobby stepped to Barky's microphone and announced, "I will come. But before I go, Dad—I mean, my father, Professor Lully—has to be safe."

Upon these words came a universal inhale; all escapees and, through the speakers, all Deepoms everywhere, it seemed, had gasped. It made Bobby wonder about what he said, so he repeated himself. "Send my father here, so I know he is OK. Once my father comes, I will come to you." There was no immediate response; as a matter of fact, it seemed that no one on either ship was paying much attention anymore. Their collective gasp had seemingly kicked off a collective whispering contest.

Bobby reiterated, louder. "Send Professor Lully to us, or I won't come. Do it as a sign of…" he faltered. He thought he knew the word but now wasn't sure.

Eve-Kay came to his side, to the microphone, and said, "Good will. As a sign of faith, and good will, deliver Lully to us first."

Silence. The whispering stopped when the Prophetess had spoken; the speaker only hissed as before.

"In return for that," Los offered, "I will send over some new names for you. As a sign of good will, too."

The choppy Deepom voice returned. "We want the girl to come also. As a sign of good will."

Bobby shook his head violently, looking from Barky to Kay, and he grumbled loudly but incomprehensively, his many negative sentiments tumbling over each other while his body expressed itself similarly. He was pretty much barking and growling, as it seemed to anyone nearby.

"Yes, OK," Eve-Kay said to the Deepoms before Bobby could convey anything using coordinated English phrases. "It's OK," she assured him and touched his shoulder with the open, pink palm of her soft hand.

It was settled. The parties said their stiff goodbyes, and radio transmission ended.

Bobby was happy at the thought of seeing his father again, though worried that Kay would be coming along on his dangerous mission to save the universe, wherein he might possibly embarrass himself.

He thought he read the same worry on the face of his dog, Barky, who had jumped up the young man's long legs, nuzzled searchingly to be petted, and looked at his master with large, fierce, brown eyes.

"I know," Bobby said to him, "you want to come with Eve and me. But—"

"No way," Barky interrupted. "I would be killed."

Remeeting and Replanning

The Deepom leaders did not remove the gag from their human captive's mouth, though they gave orders to otherwise prepare Professor Lully for transport to the escapees' stolen spaceship. The man was allowed to dress in the odd and visually cacophonic uniform he had worn for the battle, though anything dangerous had been removed, like his sword and the pins of his medals. The miniscule bits of finely-shaped metal in his coat pocket he was allowed to keep.

"What is this?" the guard in charge asked through a mouth that was unseen but must have existed somewhere down a lengthy tube that extended up from its wheeled feet to what was probably its head. "They are very strange, so small, and how they move…it's mesmerizing."

"Gaht? I goen't gnow. Gutt arr oo thalking agout?" the human choked through the foul gag that tasted like aluminum foil.

But the human *did* know. Those small things were his Seapegs, his biggest fans, and his final hope to achieve…well, anything. Luckily, they hadn't been confiscated. The Deepom guard was no expert on human mouths and didn't understand the moment or the man's mumbling words.

Nor these: "Ake zis gag gout moron sho I gan dalk."

The two robots saved from the *Nyx*—coincidentally, as Lully believed—were 1 and 24, the most and the least intelligent of his crew. They were depowered and currently slumped in a corner like neglected puppets.

The human and his things were soon brought down a long hallway that grew in height until it met a large iron door that opened to a big space, a giant hall where the great Deepom leaders were meeting.

There, various new councils delivered their conclusions. Philosophical questions were answered. Given that their hallowed *The Bobby* was perhaps a fraud, or at best had been completely misunderstood and wildly overestimated, there needed to be a new official approach.

They would determine new policy the way they determined the old: using cold, hard, atomic logic.

One of the special scientists spoke concerning their options in a The Bobby-less future. It would be easy enough to change their memories, again, and give them a past that wasn't so dependent on a single creature.

"Thank you, Marmar," Composite the Deepom elder said when the scientist finished his report. "So, we can just kill The Bobby?"

"Yes," Marmar said, supported by nods from its peers.

"And everyone else, right?" Nother asked hopefully. "And then, at least, we can get on with the bigger killing plans. Including the aliens. It looks to be the whole cleanup crew here. If we wipe that out, taking the rest will be easy because they won't want to make a mess."

"Sure," Marmar said, and, the science team's participation concluded, the group retired to a corner.

"Great. Very logical. Thank you." JustOneMore said while supported by nods from *his* peers, the Deepom Leaders. "There is only one remaining issue. We still need better names. We can't conquer the universe and THEN switch names. I think we all realize that."

"Yes, very true," From-Column-Fifteen said, "though, can't we take The Bobby's feet and brain and reuse them somehow, distribute the individual cells? As everyone knows, each soma has logical thermodynamic depth whose decayed eigenstates can be electro-stimulated into chaotic senescence."

"A little obvious, but it might come in handy," From-Column-Fifteen continued. "Or perhaps we can find his naming functions and extract those into a special machine."

"But what would we call the machine?" Node9, that small, physically-challenged but ancient Deepom said with a high-pitched vocal force that surprised the others. "It is a very circular business!" he shouted. The bagpipe-like forced-squeeze bleating he made bounced along the large space of the hall. Node9 smiled in satisfaction, but it looked like it hurt very much to do so. A piece fell off him.

"Surely. Thank you, Node9. It is our only imperfection, a limiting loop," Yet said, staring its square eyes to the high ceiling. "We can't let live what we can't know, and we shouldn't kill what we might need. And so, we are ensnared."

Their logical progression seemed to have hit one of the tall metal walls, with the threat of endless recursion sucking them all downward into nothingness. A few microseconds passed with only an ambient buzz of calculation that made the silence seem louder.

At last, One spoke. "There may be a way forward, and through. Ninth, in his infinite cleverness, has an interesting idea."

After sharing a look of approval with One, who had bent down to be eye-level with the rest, Ninth spoke; his hoses curled, and his brushes bristled. "We know of other, less successful, versions of evolution—specifically that of humans. Now, we are not perfect, but humans are our perfect complement—they only do a few things well and otherwise are huge life-wasting failures. But if they were engineered just slightly differently, then we could use, we could take, we could splice and meld what we need from them, and yet still keep our pure Deepomishnessity, the unsurpassed form of life we have become. We just need new ones, new humans, designed with this in mind."

Amid a moving thrill of beeps and clicks that wafted through the crowd of non-leaders, One himself stood, fully tall and imposing, his antennae erect, and all Deepoms gave him their gaze. He cleared his metal throat, the very tubey tube that served the purpose, and explained.

He and Ninth had reviewed the studies on the human they had captured, that silly-phone-using, deep-breathing, fainting-prone, large-footed, simply-named human, K. They now knew how such beings evolved and reproduced.

"And it is not via eight steps," One explained, "nor from a lot of clever thinking and deep calculation of emergent hylomorpen-tropic quanta."

"How then?" Someone asked.

One explained it to them.

"Whoa," someone said.

"Nasty. Unsavory," others offered.

"Yet complementary," some admitted.

"That is why we need the girl to come, too," One said. "We can make our own humans from a combination of the two that Barky was hiding. To get what we need. Consider the possibilities, the perfection, the perfect logic—and, I ask you to imagine the future, a new future, one to match our new past."

"Good idea," someone said, though it was all still sinking in.

"And they are here!" Composite said, pointing to a computer screen that showed the bomb-looking transport ship arriving with its cargo of one male and one female human.

Joining The Escapees

As Professor Lully's bomb-shaped and rotund—fat, actually—transport ship loudly docked, connecting itself and extending a walkway plank through an arch in Barky's church-shaped warcraft, the great man viewed a vast collection of odd faces staring out of the many, and many-colored, windows, and along the terraces and parapets of the architecturally fantastic escapee spaceship.

Ex-Commander Lully was accustomed to outer space's facial oddities but not this many smiles and expressions of joy. He was not used to positive attention generally, especially not in droves, and certainly not from strangers. It bothered him.

"Jumpin' fleet-footed Jehosaphat," he should have said—instead of what he did say—but did not.

He walked the plank and boarded, still flanked by two Deepom Security Droids, though he himself was not restrained in any way. Robots 1 and 24 followed in silence, seemingly unharmed by the Deepoms, though Lully assumed they had been experimented on until understood.

There was no official envoy or welcome party of escapees; no one at all came in greeting. The area through the archway led to a large, cubic storage room and through that to a square door where they came upon a baseball catcher's mitt.

Lully's chaperones asked it for directions to the nearest The Bobby.

"Yep yep yep!" The mitt spoke excitedly though in a naturally muffled voice, which seemed to emanate from the plush interior of the hole where the catcher's hand goes. "Assuredly and nicely they sent me to you! To tell you to follow me to take you roundly and directly to Los, that is, The Namer!" It appeared as if this was the best day in this alien thing's life.

"Freaks everywhere," Professor Lully said. All Deepoms looked the same to him.

The foot-high mitt rolled along ahead of them, confidently winding through the right angles and perpendicular regularity of many corridors, doors, and empty rooms. Through the last door he could hear laughter, human laughter, and around their last turn, Lully saw two figures ahead where the yellow corridor ended at a purple room.

"That's the one," the little guide said, "The Namer, the one there in the stripes, lovely and amazingly, and with the figs!" The little mutant catcher's mitt tried to point any asymmetric part of his roundness in the direction of Bobby, who was wearing a small rag of American flag on his head and was standing on one leg and tossing grapes into the air, apparently all to amuse Kay, who was indeed laughing—at him, with him, by him, from him, and around him. The catcher's mitt opened and closed with delight. "Blandly and suavely!" it said and left.

Bobby cut short the pantomime when he realized important guests were pointing at him and coming his way.

Eve-Kay stopped her laughing short at the approach of the imposingly great Professor Lully but also felt a shiver of cold fright at the sight of the two large Deepom soldiers on either side of him. She moved behind a storage container to hide, but the guards left giddily after being dismissed by Los Bobby with their new names: Squadinal and Boris.

"Hi Dad!" Bobby said and threw his arms around his father, whose own arms were thrown up defensively to block any kiss that might be coming. "I have a lot to tell you. You have to meet everyone. I told them you would come rescue me. This is Eve-Kay—oh, there she is, over there…Actually, you guys know each other already, right, she is J's sister. I'm sorry about your robots, but it's good that two survived at least. Your uniform is awesome, but it needs an army helmet or something. We have to go see Barky and his crew, and everyone, but come to my room first and..."

This went on and on as they walked the ship and Lully took the scenes in and let the insults out.

The great man was most interested in getting his hands on some computing equipment, and anything that could explode or grow.

"Bobby, I have given up on everything. There is no future. I want to go out with a bang," the great man declared.

"That's my dad!" Bobby bragged behind them to his inescapable followers. "Yeah—Barky can help you with that, don't give up. The scouts all came back, and we are out of weapons, and the scouts said that the Deepoms are really loaded with weaponry, and they are getting it ready and already setting up a victory party. But Kay has a plan, and—"

"I was on their ship, Bobby. I know everything." The two Lully men, with Kay and the small parade of escapees, had reached the bridge. It was empty except for a three-inch robot that was out of place on the large captain's chair but operating the controls vigorously nonetheless.

"Where's Barky?" Bobby asked the robotling.

"Barky..." Professor Lully scoffed. "You really should have renamed him first. Is he a dog or something?"

"The best dog. I am working on it."

The robot turned and answered, "He is at an important council meeting."

"Oh, perfect, my father needs to be in that..."

"He wasn't invited," the robot said.

"Good," Lully said. "I don't need them. Move over." And he backhanded the little bot with his studded gauntlet. The little fellow beeped and whirred to try to stand after landing in a cubic garbage pail.

"Dad, you can't just—" Bobby began.

"Go to sleep, Bobby."

Standing erect in the trash, the robot whined, "Intruder, you are not authorized to—" but was cut off by both Lully's threats and his kicks.

"Shut up, you not nearly noetic neo-poop. I am captain here now."

The man loosened his warrior clothes and quickly went to work on the computer and console controls as if they were his own. He bellowed orders to Robots 1 and 24. A crowd gathered, though this wasn't noticed until he felt the pressure of jaws clamping on his forearm, and a heartbeat later he was pulled to the ground with astonishing force.

"Barky, no!" Bobby yelled. "We are all on the same team. We can't fight against each other!"

The senior Lully rose to his feet and looked about him, at the crowd. "Geez, it looks like your room at home, Bobby." And he laughed deeply in recognition of the source of all their problems.

The laughter echoed within the metal walls of the control room as the escapees recovered, coming to grips with so many famous characters in their midst and behaving maniacally: Los yelling at Barky, the Prophetess yelling at the uniformed crazy man, the man yelling at everybody, and Barky growling and whining depending on who he was looking at, yellow spittle flying everywhere his wet nose pointed.

"Please, Professor, Bobby is right," the Prophetess said after the great man had punted Frilkielle into an upper balcony and bragged about it.

"Shut up, girly. I wish J were here to help us, but all I have is you... and *him*." He pointed all five fingers of his right hand at Bobby. "Children are useless, and meditating children are even uselesser."

"Dad, stop—" Bobby puffed up for just a second. He considered puffing more but was interrupted by Kay.

"Why do you," she asked Professor Lully, "treat your son like that and say those things? Why did you leave him, forsake him, and keep forsaking him over and over and over? He is a great person, and very smart, and he is going to solve this. A great man, in fact, and you will see. He is our only chance."

"He was a very small chance, and seeing you with him, I see that chance going directly to zero. There is nothing more to do. My only legacy will be the Seapegs. That idiot computer destroyed the real chance of…" The great man cut short his ranting, inhaling deeply and closing his eyes to get the better of his rising rage.

"I know he did. He told me," Kay said.

"Who? What?" Lully asked with his eyes still closed.

"Essie," Kay answered. "Your ship's computer."

The man's eyes popped open nearly audibly. "That was you it was talking to? What did you do? Do you realize what you've done?"

Bobby came to Kay's side and finished puffing up, though his father was more exasperated than threatening.

Kay explained, "I didn't do anything but ask him for help," but realized quickly that this wasn't true. She had done more.

"Don't call it a 'him.' Silly ideas like having a name are probably what caused the trouble."

"I think I agree," Kay admitted, and those nearby murmured in surprise. Lully looked anew at Kay and let her continue. "I did try to teach him, a while ago, what it meant to be…alive…" she paused, "…to be human, I guess. But it was too much, I guess. Such a thing is not meant to be, and couldn't be. You are right."

"Damn right." Lully added the adverb he thought was required.

"Essie's own logic then took over," said Kay. "He said he knew what he wanted, what others like him wanted, 'Like Multivac and the Cumaean Sybil,' he said, and I wondered what that meant."

Robot 22 could have explained, and Professor Lully did explain, that Multivac was a fictional computer, and the Sybil was a fictional goddesses, and they both wanted only to die.

"Oh," Kay said. "Essie told me he tried to commit suicide by reformatting his own hard drive, but he was reincarnated with a reboot, he explained."

Lully added, "Yes, he has an epigenetic program that learns and changes its own boot sequence and operating system core."

"He couldn't kill himself." Kay ignored Lully throwing his hands up at each *he* and *him*. "But I guess he knew he would be destroyed if the *Nyx* was destroyed, and that was his only way."

Lully was deep in thought. Bobby as well.

"It's sad," Kay said quietly, "such noble suffering would have been his quickest path to perfection, if only he had known." She went on, louder, to the group, "And I am sad for the *Nyx* and the other Robots, too."

Lully was shaking his head slowly, and he mumbled in mocking disbelief, "She is sad for machines…"

"But you are safe now, Professor Lully," Kay concluded.

The professor took time before answering.

"But it's more than that, Kay," he said slowly, "much more. You don't understand. Onboard the *Nxy* was…our only hope. The future…our only future…"

Lully said no more. He returned to his head-shaking thoughts, in which the Q-material was gone and all that remained was his own energy.

Those gathered conjectured about the weaponry that this man apparently would have had to defeat the Deepoms if it hadn't been for the mutinous computer. Only Kay looked at the professor with an attempt to find something deeper, but it wasn't there, or was beyond her ability to see.

Lully took account of those around him with his own keen, searching eyes. "There is only one thing to do," he soon declared loudly.

Bobby tried to explain Kay's plan, but Lully waved his arms in rejection and answered directly to the girl. "Stop putting silly ideas in my silly boy's head. All of you, leave this to me." Turning and pointing at Barky he went on, "You. I need the codes to the rocket plasma propulsers. I can try and get us out of here."

Barky didn't move, looking only at Bobby and Kay.

Lully ordered tasks to other escapees, but nor did they move. He addressed Barky again, "You, woof-woof, give me those codes and everything else. And tell your crew to obey me. And when I need my eyeballs licked, I will let you know."

Barky stiffened, and snarled, seeming to coil his anger into every muscle as a sound like underground thunder trembled through his whole body. His neck and tail were stiff, but his jaws grimaced and soon quivered with rabid drool.

All living things recognized the moment as one directly before combustion.

Bobby stepped in front of his father with raised hands as Barky struck. The dog lunged with all his lupine, alien, supercharged, hyper-evolved strength—and saliva—and his teeth embedded into and tore both of Bobby's hands, such was the ferocity.

Bobby and his father were knocked to the ground, their small pile topped with Barky and now Kay, who tried to restrain the dog, her hands slipping everywhere on the frothy spit that covered them all and, now, mixed with blood.

When Barky realized what he had done, he backed up, then came forward again, whimpering pathetically, and sadly licked his master's hands clean before sullenly removing to lie in a corner.

Bobby shook with the shock and pain but said nothing. He struggled to his feet, awkwardly, having to rise and balance with his legs alone; he kept his injured hands one in the other.

Kay, petting Barky with consolatory strokes, watched him.

The escapees watched him.

Silence watched him.

And his father, still sitting on the floor, watched him.

Professor Lully's thoughts raced, recalling his words to the *Nyx* ship's computer, *You will obey me,* and also those to the government agents when he left Earth. He was choking on the very seeds he had planned to sow. Now he watched his son, hurt and bleeding, and felt anger at his own shortsightedness—painfully ironic for the great visionary he believed himself to be. And he felt protective vengeance toward the Deepom leadership and their appalling, insulting disappointment in his son, Robert Lully, whom he watched now with wonder, and with new and proud eyes.

The young man gently waved away those attending his wounded hands and bent to offer the crook of his elbow to his father, to help the great man up.

"Come with me, Dad. I want to show you something," Bobby stood tall and said to his father. Small escapees assembled themselves to quickly bandage the young man's hands as he stood.

Professor Lully obeyed.

Bobby led him through the ship and up the spiral staircase to the recessed window seat where Eve-Kay used to meditate. His father impassively followed, with Kay also behind but no others.

"Look," Bobby directed, and his father looked. "You used to show me nebulae in our big roof telescope," he said, pointing here and there to various purple spots and yellow rings and silver spots alight in the universe, "and tell me they were exploded stars."

"Yes?" Professor Lully replied.

"And you said they were the envy of all creation. And when I asked you whether it was because they were beautiful, you said—"

Professor Lully finished the memory, "I said, 'No, because they are dead'."

"Right. Why?" Bobby asked.

"Because you were just a kid and didn't understand that nebulae are just exploded stars. But I knew, and only a handful of other people on Earth knew, that the fate of all living things, circumscribed and competing things on their planetary systems, as we used to say, was to blow themselves up."

"But?" Bobby cued his father to finish.

"But when they do die they become the gods of other worlds," Lully said.

"I never understood that until now," Bobby said. "Gods are looked for in the sky, but they also save, and create, worlds. That is what you were planning." Bobby moved his gaze from outer space to his father's eyes. "But Kay thinks that can be me."

Never had Bobby, and rarely had anyone, gone eye-to-eye with the great scientist and near-superman Professor, and Commander, Lully. The father's eyes revealed much to the son, the unspoken thoughts that surface from a man, any man, when his place in the world is revealed.

His Q-material gone, his full plans impossible, Lully only nodded resignedly. He shook his son's joined and bandaged hands and wished him luck on his quest with the Deepoms.

"I think it will be OK," Bobby said.

"It will be," Kay added, joining her hand to theirs.

They sat at the window for a time, in wonder at many things. Professor Lully explained to the young travelers his Seapegs, even taking a pinchful out of his uniform front pocket. The tiny things cheered at the sight of the professor and asked how he was feeling.

"Oh my gosh, how cute," Kay said.

"And smart," Lully said.

As they watched the little creatures explore the six human palms and thirty fingers, Lully explained the Selflicator Army and how it was lost: in addition to letting the Deepoms in the front door of the *Nyx*, the ship's computer also gave away the control codes for every collected Selflicator, so that they were now under Deepom control.

"I am sorry," Kay said.

Lully nodded amicably. As he put the Seapeg sample away— the many small voices saying goodbye and good night—he explained the loss of other important things with the destruction of Bobby's room on the *Nyx*. Some childhood mementos, for example.

"How sad…" Kay began but quieted, shrouded with the remembrance of all she had lost as well.

"I don't need anything from my room, or from the past; it's OK," Bobby said to Kay's sagging head. Then to his father, "I didn't know there was a room for me," while contemplating both that and the view of the universe's most ancient darkness as it passed in black waves outside the ship.

"Of course there was," Lully answered. Bobby did not reply.

He led their procession of three, the remainder of humankind, back to the bridge. The great man didn't mention the Q-material. They remained silent.

After some very small preparation and even less conversation, Barky's crew told Bobby that it was time for him to go, to walk the platform into the bomb-looking transport ship and meet with the Deepoms.

Professor Lully paced, he seemed a walking, mumbling contradiction. A budding peace of mind strove with smoking anger at the betrayals of, and overall disappointment in, his creations. He considered war and weapons, and also peace and contentment. He thought of the past and the future, yet also of the roll of time through a continual present—and whether all was as it should be.

Vows, with Oaths

———————◆———————

"**T**he Bobby" and Eve-Kay stood during the trip in the bomb-ish looking but otherwise comfortable Deepom transport ship. Bobby, in fact, enjoyed the trip in a selfish way. Kay was outwardly nervous and distrusted anything to do with dishonest Deepoms and she needed Bobby's constant reassurance, and it didn't have to be brilliant reassurance either. Her memory of lying helpless, strapped down amid their strange scientists and eerie ceiling, was vivid.

And soon enough they were indeed brought to a broad room whose furnishings looked nightmarishly familiar: the same mirrors, operating slabs—large, wide, and propped with squares arranged like pillows—many shiny instruments, and lively, grotesque figures hurrying in and out on variously-engineered feet and through rotating doors.

This space was far larger than Kay remembered from her previous Deepom captivity and had more equipment, a platform, and what looked like ornamental flowers arranged in shapely vases in corners and on the tops of cubes. Of course, they were not flowers, nor vases, but arrangements of scraps of metal, of spacecraft fabrics, and of parts and pieces of computers and robotics in large jars and buckets. But it looked a lot like a funeral setup, though what Kay thought might be the caskets were standing up: two human-shaped boxes recessed into enclosures and strewn with the same flotsam of makeshift decorations.

She remembered her torture box, and here were two, yawning open like horrible, hollowed carcasses.

But they were richly adorned.

One had a pink ribbon, one a blue.

Eve-Kay swooned, but she made an effort to breathe and to look away, ahead, to where Bobby was leading.

At the farthest end of the cavernous room was a triangular table about which the Deepom leadership—easily identifiable, as they were taller, more regal, more stationary, gleaming in gold and green—sat, or leaned, or suctioned, or wedged, depending on the engineering of their butts.

The two humans were told to wait, and silence was called for, as a horn sounded and four more Deepom leaders entered, positioning themselves at the remaining open spots at their table. One of them was very tall, one was very round, one broad and square and commanding-looking, and one of very many colors.

"Huh," Bobby said to Kay, as if he were expecting something different, which would mean he was expecting anything at all. Kay had no response. Her eyes were fixed on the white slab dissecting tables, and she moved her arm to be held within Bobby's. "Déjà vu, sort of," he added. The recognition of these creatures, coming from some deep subconscious cave in his mind, gave him confidence, as if, he reasoned, he had experience that he could rely on.

The two teenaged ex-Earthlings and guests of honor were summoned and escorted fully across the room and toward the leaders. The commotion resumed, and Kay and Bobby overheard the talk of the bustling scientists.

"They will need to lie down, right?" one of them said.

"No, I think the plan is that they will stand up for it," another, of them, answered.

Kay felt like fainting—and did faint. Bobby caught her, though as with many a football on Earth he bobbled her so that she moaned but recovered.

"Sorry, Kay. But it will be OK. Stand close to me," Bobby hoped he said.

The talk went on. "Neither is necessary, yet," a mid-sized Deepom leader answered to the small crew that required specific preparation instructions. They seemed to not care one space-molecule that the two humans could hear them.

"Still, we want to stay on schedule and be ready when you need us for the forced implementation," the crew leader said.

Bobby and Kay reached the crook of the table. The workers were dismissed, and Bobby waited for quiet so he could speak. Kay had buried her head and one ear into his chest.

"I am Bobby," Bobby said from the heart upon which Kay rested. "I have some things to say."

He had their attention and went on.

"First, I think you wanted proof of my existence. As agreed, I will give you my DNA," he said and cleared his throat, more than once, and, thinking of Guk's excellence and productivity, inhaled his throat into his nose in preparation to spit, but was soon unsure of exactly where to do so and into what.

"There is no need for that," Another said, begging Bobby to stop the process. "I am Another, and we are convinced that you are who you say you are. That is not the issue. And all has been decided."

Bobby frowned, his mouth full of disgusting, warm saliva and viscous mucous, and he didn't know what to do with it, but picturing his options made him feel sick.

"We need you to—" Another said but stopped since Bobby's face had changed. He had swallowed.

"What?" The Bobby said. "Sorry. You don't need a specimen or anything?"

There was discussion among the Deepoms; they seemed startled by the young man's humanity, his reality, his obvious imperfection. The leaders took note, and the scientists took notes, documenting Bobby's flaws as compared to any actual majesty.

Previously: within the Deepom collective subconscious—the digital, electronic bits at their base, their innermost, gravest, soul-tinted and essential cores—a perception of a *The Bobby* sat at center, as if enthroned in heaven.

Now: it was replaced with the image before them. The *This*

Bobby was quite different, as their leaders had already decided, and now let other Deepoms verify for themselves. Each wondered, first on their own, and soon in small groups. And word got out quickly.

But Bobby ignored their talk. He was ready to begin his speech and did so, with Eve-Kay now looking up at him.

He spoke of Earth and the goals of humanity—well, much of humanity—which included peace, and being nice to others, which was praised, and so was charity. Whereas things like the Deepom's great goals of global—well, *universal*—conquest were denounced. And for good reason. People—well, *all living things*—should be allowed to live and have families and not be bothered or become slaves.

That was it.

Behind him, toward the creature scientists and their tables, Bobby could hear, and Kay could see, the teams doing disconcerting things, like lighting candles, and sharpening blades, and polishing mirrors, and the smell of clean metal was in the air. Seats, for every shaped body imaginable, were arranged on two sides of an aisle that led away from the triangular table and toward a raised platform.

Kay squeezed Bobby's arm.

Bobby, a normal teen, perhaps slightly taller, completed his public speaking, as if it were an assignment in school, a mediocre student putting forth some obligatory oratory supporting a lackluster thesis. But the Deepoms were not used to medium-ness; they had evolved at an unfathomable rate, kickstarted by the greatest minds the Earth had to offer, with their consciousness propelled by the essential materials of the universe itself. They had other plans and were ready to move ahead, and The Bobby would soon be forgotten.

Though the Deepoms still had one more use for him. For him and that other human, the female one.

Workers hurriedly arranged the large room, now ignoring Bobby and Kay. Bobby had the feeling that they were no longer interested in anything he had to say, and he hoped the smarter people present—namely Kay—had a Plan B.

Kay shivered with fright but sensed the need for a Plan B, one whose first step required that she not faint. So she breathed deeply and tried to calm herself enough to think.

This was difficult with all the excited chatter that accompanied the anticipation that energized the room. Nearby, an especially awful worker, with antennae that grew up and arced over its head and downward almost back to the floor like the spray of a wiry fountain, said, "The two of them, fascinating! Two of them together. Could Ninth possibly be correct about them and how they generate?"

The thing's coworker, helping to arrange additional Deepom seats, spoke back. "I can't imagine it! We would never do anything like that. It is so interesting."

"And they don't use their feet, they say! It is so interesting, and so complex."

To the young humans, none of that sounded interesting, or encouraging. And the workers were not shy about staring and pointing as they spoke. This wasn't the reverence Kay had expected, and she believed now that Barky was right and that this was a very bad idea. She stood on her tiptoes to whisper into Bobby's ear every detail of what she thought they should do, which only took five words.

Watching her whisper, one of the Deepoms asked, "Are they starting already? Is this it?"

Another answered. "Ninth, is this how they start? Don't we need to get them in the wedding boxes?"

"Yes," Ninth affirmed, and the shoving began.

———

"WHAT?" Kay asked repeatedly until her lungs emptied from the effort. She demanded to be heard and answered, but her obstinance was ignored, she was accused of being fickle, and was finally jostled forcefully into position. Her repeated scream of realization—technically a question but a scream of realization nonetheless—reverberated about the ferrous, sleek walls and even knocked a few of the fake vases over with a destructive crash and the scatter of metal flower petals.

The Deepoms ignored her noises. The scientist's helpers were almost done moving the two Earthlings into position near the raised platform-altar and where stood the human-shaped and upright dissection-turned-matrimony boxes. Bobby and Kay were shoved inside. One the Deepom was standing and, as seemed obvious now, ready to pronounce wedding vows. Others gathered around, and the topologically-varied seats were almost filled with Deepoms.

Dirty lying dishonest nasty Deepoms! Kay thought. In fact, she thought and thought and thought because she still did not have a Plan B, and—though it was a relatively small point—she was not ready to get married.

Bobby had a question of his own, namely, "Really?" He was not sure how to judge something this unexpected on the trusty old good/bad scale.

The room filled with expectation, and now fully with Deepoms, hundreds of them and the attendant thick, close smell of warming metal and oil.

"It is what we want," Another announced, perhaps in answer to Kay's scream. Ninth was giving orders as to the proper arrangement of creatures and equipment.

"Everything has to be perfect for this to work," Ninth said, summarizing for the Deepom Leadership. "After long and careful study, we understand what will occur. Once the wedding is concluded; then after many, many minutes, these two will make 990 more of each other. So: positions everyone, just like we rehearsed. Don't let any get away."

Bobby could have laughed, but he thought it better to squirm with self-consciousness. He wondered at the warmth he felt from the temptation to take the Deepoms' side. The young man did not have much experience in relationships, of course, or much else. Yet from what he did know of life so far, Bobby judged that this seemed like an excellent time to marry. Kay was a great girl, his dad lived nearby, and he had a new job.

Et cetera, Bobby thought.

A tight ring of attention formed around the young couple in their boxes. Deepom anticipation rose to its greatest height, and, as if to force an almost unbearably exciting crest, Ninth made another pronouncement using his rarely-heard, grandest voice. "All: our capture of The Spot, the Middle, the Beginning, the location of the Big Bang and of Minimal Entropy has also begun. It is ours."

Ninth's words boomed with power and were accompanied by peals of Greek-godlike thunder. Outside the ship shone an ethereal and pure vision of white, a threatening cloud filled with an electric fire such as that at the heart of living things. It rolled in opposition to the waves of black space and conquered them. As Ninth proclaimed, this was the vapor of the Deepom's greatest power, the exhaust from their final effort to command The Spot, its light, its energy, and its secrets.

"With that, and with the 990 human offspring, our new plans are accomplished," Ninth concluded. He interlocked his vacuum hoses in satisfaction.

After stunned silence and appropriate awe, Kay protested loudly. For one thing the "990" number sent a pain to her hips. For another, "It's nothing personal, Bobby, but this is not how I pictured things, and what does any of this have to do with war and peace and why we came?"

"Very fickle. We expected this," Ninth was addressing Bobby.

Bobby nodded.

Kay had a third and best reason. "No!" she said. "Bobby, look around. It's not a wedding, it's a funeral! They are going to kill us."

Ninth began orchestrating the final steps. "OK," he said, "bring in the gong."

Bobby froze. Seeing the gong arrive—which looked more like a giant Frisbee than a proper instrument—reminded him of something, then of many things. *Yes*: he had played out this scene as a kid with his toys. The wedding of two stuffed animals, he could not recall exactly which, but he remembered the ceremony being concluded with a gong. *Yes*: he had used a Frisbee, and he banged it after the toys were married and after they smooched.

"Good," Another responded as Bobby watched, "then everything is in place."

That statement gave Kay an idea.

"Bobby!" she yelled as she kicked and spun her torso. "Do something! You are The Bobby! Tell them what to do! They are nothing but your childhood dreams come true! Fix it! Think of something! Don't listen to them! They are liars!"

"No, we aren't," Another lied.

And that statement gave Kay another idea.

Ninth grew impatient and was ready to begin the ceremony, which he was to preside over. "Shush, you with the big feet," he said to Kay as he maneuvered his old-fashioned, four-wheeled, canister-style vacuum-cleaner body up onto the platform. "You are very stupid, so shush and do as we say. We have very advanced consciousness, something you will never understand."

And that statement gave Kay a third, and very good, idea.

Lully Settles In

Meanwhile on Barky's ship...

P rofessor Lully said, "Here boy."

Barky had lain in a corner, on a small pile of discarded computer printouts, since his attack on his master's father. The doggie-guilt weighed down his jowls and ears; his only movement had been to roll his eyebrows toward any activity around him, and the only sound he made was to sigh every forty seconds or so.

But *enough's enough*, the great man thought, and *besides, I need some help.* Though the military-toned future he had planned was impossible, and the Selflicator Army he had built had been scuttled with the *Nyx* ship's computer mutiny, Lully had not given up on escape from the Deepoms and had taken an inventory of everything aboard the escapees' stolen warship that could propel, explode, or jettison, and he had even got to know the more interesting denizens aboard, runaway Deepoms who sometimes had some interesting abilities—like the tennis racket, Rafadererer, that could shoot a small laser, and a large bass drum, named Sunmoonboomboom, that could do advanced math.

Lully felt good again and was glad to have something to do. He needed Barky to teach him the passwords and the basic controls of the console. And he knew how to handle dogs. He thought.

"Here, boy!" Professor Lully repeated more energetically, and he raised his own eyebrows and his arms with feigned excitement.

"Go get it! Fetch! Oooo, look! Go get it!" he yelled, and he threw a small ball toward a corner of the bridge.

This was a terrible *faux pas*, as Lully soon learned, and very rude. The ball he threw was an elderly Deepom escapee whose small, round hands were the only method of turning on the air conditioning.

"Poor Snappy!" some declared while noticing that the ball could no longer pronounce certain important vowels.

But the effort did wake Barky. Once the man apologized, Barky and Lully agreed that, since Lully was, sort of, Barky's ancestor and, kind of, also his creator, and that, maybe, the man had seniority, that he might take a turn at being the Ship's Captain through this last phase of the War.

So, Lully took to the controls, and made many measurements and figured many calculations, finding the voiceless onboard ship's computer to be easy to work with.

The results astounded him.

Everything was in equilibrium.

All equations equated to each other, and to zero, and also to the square root of negative two.

The Spot, and the fabric of all space nearby, had stopped warbling, and a faint crystalline glow was coming from the center of it all.

The last computational solutions of a series of relativistic time and quantum space equations had completed, and the results were all infinite.

Lully said, "Wow." He had never seen anything like it, and none of the great theoretical physicists he had known could have imagined such a state. Little infinity symbols marked every page and every device screen. It reminded him of LEBO. He petted Barky.

"What doeesschhhh it mean?" the dog asked.

"All hangs in the balance," the great Professor Captain Lully said nobly.

"What will the Deepoms do?" Frilkielle asked.

"Whatever they are preparing, it is eschatologically and mathematically apocalyptic," Lully said. "Spacetime itself seems to know something's up. Most likely, they are going to kick butt and take names. Ha! Get it? Names?"

No one got it.

"Master Bobby walked into a trap," Barky moaned.

Lully answered nothing.

He scooped from his pocket into his palm some Seapegs; they sifted over each other like living grains of sand. Affectionate ones: the professor had noticed how they enjoyed his company and sometimes sang or hummed when he looked at them. In his large hands they looked brightly clean and simple, and yet were so powerful, he mused, being blessed with the energy of creation itself, his million little big-bang miracles. The Seapegs could have been a heck of a weapon if he didn't need them to be his future. Lully had given up on force and instead planned their use for his posterity, his legacy, or even to extend his own life.

In actual fact, however, he hadn't come up with many specific ideas. He was still too angry to think much beyond his misfortunes. He regretted each chip-yank out of "Essie" and hated the dead computer's guts at the same time. Lully had planned for a good and great posterity by regenerating and immortalizing the best human life that had ever lived. He couldn't do that now. His great secret was destroyed.

The Q-material, his deceased wife's organic material and DNA, was lost with the *Nyx*.

"We just have to wait, I guess," Frilkielle said.

Although the passage of time could no longer be measured— the instruments were correct, but the clocks made no sense and seemed to be arguing with each other if not in fact in a three-legged sack race, and although the nearest sun was a distant speck among many distant specks, it was a long daytime of silence before anything changed.

When a tremendous white cloud appeared.

Its crawling, branching clumps of smoke crawled to cover the honey-colored gleam of the nearby Deepom weapons, and the other of humankind's meandering mechanized mistakes, and quickly enclosed The Spot. The Spot's small light was swallowed in a growing twister of fumes and died a grey and smoky death.

Swirls and smoke rings spun outward artfully off the main burst and formed the figures of ornate keys, and of figure-eight-like keyholes.

Then came an eruption of sonic booming, like drums of doom, which vibrated all things in agonizing waves of sympathy so that everyone—everyone everywhere, it must be—cowered. The horses neighed and stamped without a sound.

Time seemed to end. Space was orphaned and denied.

Then over the speakers came a voice, Bobby Los's voice, from the Deepom Leadership ship. "Barky? Can you send my father here? And he should bring the Seapegs, please."

Speak Now Or Forever Hold Your Peace

A little earlier...

———————————————

The Deepom Army alerted Ninth the Deepom that The Spot was theirs, conquered. The escapees were powerless and the aliens neutral. Deepom scientists ordered it to be surrounded with sensors pointing inward and weapons pointing outward. This act of possession and aggression had an effect on all things in the universe. It was like tickling the navel of existence itself; all other nerves were connected to it.

If they had had a flag, they would have planted it within the cubic frame that floated about the precise point; instead their mark was made with a fury of sound and smoke, the smoke forming shapes of keys and keyholes, the Deepom signal of conquest. The machinery was loud—a mockery of the near-vacuum of this special space, and it created a horrible stench for those with that sense, like the horses who neighed in disgust through their masks and were led away—and eventually The Spot was covered in a creeping, thick, white gas that moved to the growing cacophony. This was the type of declaration and sign that the Deepoms enjoyed and preferred.

Ninth then began directing others for the ceremony. They would wed the two Earthlings and take whatever came of it as their own.

As Ninth gave his orders, Kay and Bobby had a chance to talk to each other, in whispers. Although not restrained, they were surrounded by big, hard Deepom security guards; indeed, the security bots increased in size as their position receded from the dais, the biggest lining the walls of the spacious hall.

"We need to do something!" Kay urged again. "I have some ideas, but I need time to look around."

Bobby stood tall and stared menacingly at the Deepoms who had mistreated The Eve-Kay. "I can help. I am The Bobby."

Kay smiled. "Yes, you are."

"I have an idea. I will buy time. Go."

"You sure? It's dangerous."

"Yes. Go."

Kay gave Bobby a quick, tight hug, whereupon the onlookers murmured excitedly. "Don't do anything dangerous. I will be as quick as I can," she whispered and slipped away.

Her exit went unnoticed; the hug had spurred the Deepom leadership into a distracted frenzy of concern that reproduction might begin before the wedding was completed. As Ninth began to call for calm, Bobby stood forth. He turned to the crowd and raised his own voice.

"Deepoms! This isn't right. There should be a red carpet, um, there!" And he pointed a long arm to the back of the long aisle, past the divided rows of Deepom wedding guests. "Right?" Bobby challenged the scientists near to Ninth, the young man's cheeks still aflame with happiness and pride due to Kay's hug.

"Look it up," Ninth told the same scientists. They did. Bobby was right: the collective Deepom memory and myth of this event demanded a red carpet. "Well, get one!" Ninth bellowed.

Kay wandered the hall, gaped at but undisturbed. "Let her be," JustOneMore said to the tremendous guards along the walls. "It's the one who declares herself false, as only a human would do. She won't escape this time. Her simple tricks are useless here."

Kay heard. She also noticed that the enormous Deepom security things didn't speak English; indeed, this was one of the security improvements that had been made to counter clever humans. They murmured in a strange, though audible language made of words but whose sounds had a randomness to it, a perfect fit for the inexplicable combinations of features of the Deepoms themselves. All she could gather, as she strolled about, looking for weaknesses, speaking to whoever would answer, was that the new language of the guards had words like *swimswam* and *preek,* which seemed to mean yes and no, or no and yes. With more time, she could perhaps figure their language out—*maybe eight years or so*, she thought.

As a red almost-carpet was brought in and put into place, Kay learned what she could and looked for escapes and openings and sources of help, but it seemed that the Deepoms were right: escape this time would not be easy.

She returned to Bobby and raised to her toes to kiss his cheek but, when close, her lips blew him four words. "We need the Seapegs."

Bobby thought for a moment, then turned again to the crowd, pointed at the red carpet, and said, "Perfect. All that is missing is someone to give away the groom."

Kay physically perked up, gazing at The Bobby as he cleverly directed their captors. When he returned to her, she feigned another kiss to his ear. "*Dadadada, da-da!*" she whispered.

The Father Accepts

A little later...

Lully's reaction to seeing J's sister and his own son about to be married was a complex one. Robot 1, whom he had brought along, vocalized the more prosaic ones: numerous variations on "What the heck?"

But to the father of the groom, of course, there was more to it. A wedding, even a double-shotgun wedding like this, only put in his mind the helplessness of his own situation.

He was instructed—forced without force, as with his invitation—to walk the bride and groom down the aisle, and the procession began. Despite the many Deepoms shaped like musical instruments, there was only rapt and solemn quiet.

Quiet—except for the humans who were arguing, apparently, the whole trip down the aisle, in hushed tones and through forced, costumed smiles.

"What do you mean you didn't bring the Seapegs?" Kay fumed in disbelief, taking a step with her left leg, then stopping.

"It's complicated," Lully answered, taking a step with his right leg, then stopping.

"Try me," Kay offered.

"No," Lully refused.

"Dad," Bobby cajoled. "Why?"

"You are just kids, you don't get it. They are my last hope for my ideas...for posterity." The professor struggled to get a complex point across during the ten yards of aisle they had remaining. "I lost the Q-material. I needed that to…to do so… and can't create any more."

"So?" Kay almost broke her whisper in exasperation, then recovered. "We need to get out of here."

Lully smiled falsely and answered, "I won't use the Seapegs for destruction."

"All of a sudden?" Kay huffed.

"They aren't a weapon. I can't lose them."

Kay shook her head and took the remaining single steps to an awaiting, staring Ninth the Deepom. She turned ceremoniously to Professor Lully, her new father-in-law-to-be-by-forced-AI-marriage, and on her tiptoes pulled at the man's white ruffled uniform shirt to get him to bow down the rest of the way. As the crowd reacted energetically, she pretended another kiss but said to the great man, "Really? So, since you can't clone yourself, you will forsake all of us? Essie told me about the Q-material."

"But that's not…" Lully stopped, seeing the Deepom eyes hard upon him.

Kay's face was buried in her own hair. "Forget it. Bobby and I will handle it ourselves and get us out of here," she hissed.

She removed from Lully's shocked face, fumbled to grab his hands as if for etiquette, but handed him her J-phone.

As the couple turned to face Ninth, Lully moved away and noticed the phone display was blinking red—and recording.

Lully On the Edge Of His Front Row Seat

Ninth began the ceremony, his stuffy voice coming down his longest hose—"We are gathered today because…" Lully watched as Kay faltered, looking weak and sick, and fell bodily against Bobby. The man overheard his son's words.

"Kay," Bobby held Kay gently, "wake up! It's not a dream, or if it is, it's one of those when you are in school and you forget your pants."

"I'm OK," Kay said and then recovered quickly. "Follow my lead," she whispered to Bobby, and she winked at Professor Lully, who was then as mesmerized as any Deepom in the crowd and tingling with anticipation more than most.

What is she up to?

With Robot 1 in tow, Lully moved closer to be sure Kay's phone audio-recorded whatever was about to happen. He then stumbled, tripping over the stiff shark's fin of a large soccer ball. Lully coughed up an obligatory, polite "Excuse me" while thinking, *Another ball…I wish Bobby had played chess more.*

The ball introduced himself, as he had done all day every day for the past few. "I am Lord Upright!" he said. "That's right." And then he explained to Bobby's father how great Los The Namer was. And also, how great the Prophetess was, and how she, "is very smart, but very mysterious. She escaped from here once, you know. And she predicts the future."

While the ball babbled, fawned, and bragged, Lully watched the wedding and noticed that on Kay's J-phone all her recent calls were either to, or from, "Essie/Nyx" or "J."

He smiled.

He watched his son and his son's bride and smiled.

Then he smiled again. And smiled all the while as Kay began her Plan B.

Taunting Them
A Second Time

It was incalculable, without precedent, and sent a shock wave through the crowd.

The kiss, unlike anything the Deepoms had ever seen before, struck like lightning underground. Even Lord Upright stopped talking.

Ninth took time to recover and did so only after reassurance from the other Deepom leaders.

Because: Kay, far too soon and with no warning, had suddenly revived and grabbed The Bobby's ears, pulled his head down, and kissed him on the lips. With her lips. And not her feet.

Deepom shock: the Earth humans were connected by their faces for a long time, it seemed. In fact, it was calculated to be 1,6 67,631,332,608,368,119,545,169 c-fermis. Wow.

Professor Lully's timing agreed: it was about five seconds. Wow. Bobby would later recall it as much, much longer.

After it, Kay spoke to Ninth and the leaders. "Ha! You would never do that, never think to do that!"

Two Deepom leaders had composed themselves enough to speak. "Do what?" they asked.

"Kiss him. Kiss anyone."

"So?" came a Deepom voice from up high somewhere, so that Kay answered with her voice to the ceiling.

"So! You don't know love! That's 'so'!"

Kay had to interlock arms with Bobby to steady him but she went on, addressing the whole room. "You don't have consciousness. You think you do. I have seen your keys and keyholes—how silly! You don't have feelings, emotions, or imagination. You fake it—and badly. You have no creative powers. Only fast formulas."

Lully said quietly, "Damn, she's smart." Robot 1 nodded. Lord Upright flapped his fins.

"You can't dream," Kay continued.

A voice from the middle of the bride's section piped up, through a pipe mouth that came from a cylindrical head, "Dreams stink. Who cares?"

"Ha! That proves it! There's no sense of smell in dreams."

Ninth had had "Enough! Stand The Bobby up straight!" Guards came near to follow Ninth's order. "Both of you: speak your vows." He glared at the couple, pointing his vacuum tubes at the couple stiffly.

"Oh, that's right, I forgot," Kay said to him. "Forgive me, I am wrong. You do dream. About conquering the universe. Right?"

The crowd laughed and exhaled in relief, as if glad to finally receive the punchline. They admitted her truth. "Yes, all true!" one of the leaders from behind Ninth said. "Now say you 'do'…" There was more mirth and even Ninth was smiling.

Kay went on more forcefully, and louder, with a look toward Professor Lully, "Breaking The Truce also means you have no honor. This dream is only of destruction, not creation, so it's not a dream, just another evil algorithm."

Lully repeated, "Damn," as he looked at the phone recorder.

"No honor, no truth, no humanity or goodness," Kay added.

One's voice came from on high again. "Those things are for failed Earthlings like those guys," and a long metallic arm angled down from the group of leaders behind the altar and pointed at Lully and his robot. "We don't need such things."

"No, of course not," Kay went on, her upraised hand stopping the professor from defending himself. "Because you guys found the source of lowest entropy." Lully nodded, deferring to Kay's lead and acknowledging, respecting, and enjoying her Plan B.

Ninth answered, "That's right," then, "Bobby, are you paying attention? Do you take Eve as your—"

"Ha!" Kay interrupted. "That just shows the limit of thinking among you logical bimbos. It takes imaginative, creative genius to find better than the best, to go beyond the lowest possible and discover—"

But Professor Lully needed to get in on the fun. "No, don't tell them!" He play-acted to Kay. "They will abuse it!" All eyes were on him, or he would have winked to Kay, and she knew it.

"They are too stupid, Professor," she said dryly. "Don't worry. They can't handle *Negative Entropy.*" She emphasized those last words to draw attention to the concept, one she thought up in her head a few minutes ago. "They are still chasing 'The Middle and The Beginning'," and she laughed. She wasn't actress enough to recast her serious fear into a convincing laugh to any human ears—it sounded very odd to Bobby, for example—but it served.

The crowd had gone quiet; the leaders, however, warbled and buzzed with excitement at each other. "Negative Entropy?" a voice said. "There is no such thing."

Kay stopped her vaudevillian laugh short. "Let Bobby and I go, and I will explain it." She pounced. "I can even show you where to find some."

Ninth turned his tubes and canister to the Deepom leadership behind him. They discussed this quickly, even for them, and in 1,000 milliseconds had a plan and an answer. "OK, we promise. Wait a second so the Science Team can write it down."

"Damn…" Lully said through a smile.

Dumbing It Down

As the Deepoms huddled in preparation to receive Kay's ransom, the treasure map to Negative Entropy, Lully stepped forward energetically.

"I am with you," he said to Kay and to a smiling Bobby, his words coming very fast. "I see where you are going. I will sacrifice the Seapegs. We can send the recording to the aliens, and Robot 24 is teaching the Seapegs human aggression, which is good, and we can send the Deepoms on a wild goose chase for negative entropy, and—"

Bobby held up his hand and interrupted to ask his father why—why would he sacrifice them now when they were his only chance for the immortality he deserved?

"To save you guys," Lully said simply. "I would rather have grandkids."

Bobby blushed severely—it was, in fact, audible to some of the more sensitive instruments on board—and father and son exchanged warm smiles punctuated by a hearty handshake.

"OK, stop, oh my god you guys are worse than the Deepoms," Kay said with exasperation while tisk-tisk-tisking a finger at all the men she had ever known. "Listen: we don't need any more sacrifices. The aliens will like the Seapegs since they are clean, right? And they can be emissaries from us Earth humans, to apologize for our garbage." She shook her head to admonish the professor, saying, "Teach them aggression? Honestly?"

Lully looked downward. Then Bobby did so, ashamed, but soon the two glanced at each other and shared a smirk.

Kay ignored them and went on. "Anyway, all that gives me an idea I already had." She quickly instructed Robot 1, Professor Lully, and Lord Upright, the latter of whom was bouncing with third-person excitement.

"Lord Upright will help!" Lord Upright said. "Anything for The Namer!"

Kay told the team to find out whether any of the guards were of the honest type, the good guys, and willing to help an escape. Before she could say more, Ninth returned and commanded her to start explaining. Professor Lully, Robot 1, and Lord Upright were pushed aside, which freed them to do as Kay asked.

As Bobby nodded intermittently, Kay explained to the Deepom Leaders and new New Science Team how the Seapegs evolved, and how they were a number of generations beyond the Deepoms, glorious as they thought they were.

The scientists were figuring and advanced-mathing as she spoke, and they soon asked, "But if that is true, according to our calculations, they would be wimps, right? Peaceful? Sweet and nice? What does that have to do with—"

Kay loudly smacked her own forehead, a wonderful insult, whereas Bobby laughed aloud. "You aren't getting it," Kay said. "Entropy is a measure of disorder. The Seapegs are the most ordered, complex thing in the universe."

"So?" a scientist asked.

"So…think about it. Use your imagination." Kay rolled her eyes, which was louder even than Bobby's earlier blush. The scientists looked over their formulas and mumbled and argued and mumbled.

Kay let this go on for a Deepom eternity, at least twenty seconds, and finally said, "Ugh. OK, let me explain it. I will TRY to dumb it down.

"If you have a fractional number of Boltzmann microstates—which the Seapegs do since they are hologrammatic copies curled up within themselves, in fact many Seapegs fit into one microstate, that's how wickedly complex they are—uncurling them would be a great source of energy. So, the calculation amounts to equating Gibbs-Boltzmann and

Shannon entropies, and applying Bohm-unfolding, but with orthogonal dimensions in the imaginary plane, twice uncurled, and so squared. And so, double-u log, the i^2 gives the negative part of negative entropy. Get it? You should also note that low entropy means high complexity and lowest surprise, per Shannon, so that explains why the Seapegs are so universally accepted and adored: they are expected, foreseen, and subconsciously experienced as safe and cute."

As she spoke, and as Lord Upright wandered the hall doing his part of Plan B, Lully contacted Robot 24 back on Barky's escapee ship with instructions to release the Seapegs to the alien cavalry, and to bring with them the recording of the Deepom's recent Kay-induced bragging. It was proof of their plans to break The Truce, Lully explained. And: since the Deepoms were about to be tricked into capturing the Seapegs at all costs, the Deepoms would fall directly into the aliens' weird hands.

"Good idea, Sir!" 24 said.

"Kay's idea, 24," Lully answered.

For good measure, Lully added, Robot 24 should also send the aliens a statement from the surviving Earthlings of Formal Apology for all the Past Garbage.

Robot 24, after a "Yes, sir, Professor," related that the tiny Seapegs had been writing furiously on some paper and, from the little that 24 was able to decipher so far, it was fascinating.

Lully asked for more specifics but did not hear more specifics since Lord Upright had come bounding up to him, crashing into Robot 1's metal face with his shark fins flapping wildly. The ball explained that he had learned what he could before being chased away and that, of the three biggest guards—their boxy heads bent at the ceiling of the hall—who watched the best exit—it led to a small disembarkation bay where the Deepom Leaders' own empty spaceship was docked—one of the guards was good and honest, one bad and not to be trusted, and the third could be either.

But Lord Upright didn't know which was which.

Lully was quite mad at being interrupted for a string of the most useless information conceivable, and he told Lord Upright that the ball didn't deserve his name and that he should go bounce—or swim or whatever he did—away and try again.

But there wasn't time. Kay had finished her explanation, and—after a few seconds of scientific affirmation—the Deepom Leaders all rose and spoke to the wedding guests.

"She is right!" Ninth declared. "We have to get the Seapegs! We can use their Negative Entropy to go beyond our wildest logically-projected conclusions!"

There was a roar unlike anything the Earthlings, even these vastly different ones, had ever heard or dreamt or theorized or imagined. Part atonal music, part explosion, part metallic crash, part multitudinous moan: each of Lully, Bobby, and Kay wondered if they had gone too far and awakened a force too great.

"Can we go now?" Kay said meekly, and unsurely, to Ninth. "You have what you wanted."

"No," came a booming voice from the center of the Deepom Leadership.

"But you promised!" Bobby shouted back.

"So?" was the only response.

Prum and the Escapers

Kay and Bobby had no choice but to make a run for it. They were helped by the madness that ensued following Bobby's shouted instruction to Robot 1, Lord Upright, and his father to "Go, Dad! Hurry!"

So they ran. Lord Upright guided them to what was deemed their best chance, the three unguessably huge guards. As Lully shook his head in frustration, Lord Upright relayed what little he knew of them.

"That's fine," Kay answered. "Good work, Lordy."

Lully's mouth opened to chastise the soccer ball again for its abject failure, then, as his own thoughts caught up to Kay's, he shut it and paid attention.

"What are the guards' names?" Kay asked.

"Schmick, Mickmack, and Prum," Lord Upright answered.

Bobby scoffed; in his professional opinion, these were not good names.

Lully's mouth opened again, this time to curl into a smile. He watched as Kay approached the triangular, green-golden ankle of the first guard, Schmick.

Kay signaled it to bend down so she could speak into whatever head-hole it preferred, then said to Schmick, "I am sorry if your head explodes, but if I asked you, is it the case that in your current mental state you would always answer *preek* to this question AND Prum is good OR Prum is bad, in your current mental state, would you say *swimswam*?"

Kay stepped back. To Bobby and their friendly soccer ball, and even to Robot 1, this sounded like a mistake, a stream of words burped forth in backwards or random order and trying to be a sentence, but such a goal was just beyond its grasp. Maybe the Prophetess had gone mad with fear, Lord Upright suggested.

After one-and-a-half seconds, Schmick's head exploded. A hole blasted through the ceiling, and large robot parts landed all around. The others dodged under a silver table, but Bobby's leg was pierced with beeping and flashing metal shrapnel and he screamed until dragged to safety by his father's arms and Lord Upright's strong fins.

Kay gasped but continued to act. In the ongoing madness of activity—crews repairing and quickly re-pressurizing the hall and ceiling, security teams assembling to high alert, and Deepom Leadership trying to control and direct an excited mob of wedding attendees-turned-conquistadors—she approached Prum, the second guard. She climbed the scales of its ladder-like, gleaming metal legs, pulled the chains at its waist, and then was roughly clasped in Prum's cupped hand. Bobby and his father both yelled in fear, and Lully and Lord Upright rose to fight, but by then Kay had been lifted to Prum's face, whose ear was a swirl of clear and diamond-shaped flaps.

She spoke into it.

Prum scooped Bobby and Lully into one hand, Lord Upright and Robot 1 in its other, and crouched to fit himself through the exit. It then let all five go and remained behind as they raced down the passage, Bobby leaning on, then carried by, his father. Prum stayed and blocked the exit to ensure the getaway.

"Thank you!" Kay yelled over her shoulder.

Prum's answer was in English.

But Kay didn't hear it. Ahead she saw, at the entrance to their hoped-for getaway ship, a strange sight. Her silent goat—the one who had helped her first escape from Deepoms—was kicking at a group of small, twisted, and evil-looking robots. Bobby was lying on the floor, wildly swinging his arms to fend off an attack from another group. Robot 1 was also prone; its number was dented and being pummeled with metal pipes. Professor Lully and Lord Upright went from group to group, fighting back the little Deepoms, whom Kay could now see were part of the Leader Ship's crew.

She wondered where she could best help, though they were hopelessly outnumbered and more Deepom nasties were coming out from the hall as alarms sounded. Behind her, Prum was also in a fight and squeezing against the walls any Deepom soldiers who tried to get past. Blue beams, as from lasers, sprayed here and there; flames flashed wherever they struck. Kay realized that these were the fire of advanced weapons, though it seemed only the security forces were so armed.

Then—*arooooooooo*—came the most glorious sound, and Barky galloped into the fray with others whom Kay recognized. They had come from another bay where the escapees' warship was docked. The white smoke of Deepom conquest came swirling through the opening, but so did the rescuers: a team of escapee friends.

"Gooooo that way!" Barky howled to Kay, but instead she ran to Bobby and helped Professor Lully fight off two Deepom demons. They were scratching at Bobby's face and clawing at his wounded leg with their various appendages. Bobby swooned and yelled, his arms wildly battling.

The stream of crew from the Deepom Leader Ship stopped; the last had come and been defeated. But even in that instant of hope there came a cry that froze the hearts of those who had one. Prum, from down the passage, howled a metallic death pang, and an apology, and an instruction. "Run, Kay." All watched as the honest, brave Deepom giant fell at last, covered with security droids. Many more of these now came speedily, violently down the passage.

Lully and Lord Upright rescued Robot 1 quickly and carried him aboard the escapee ship. Barky had fetched a stretcher and dragged Bobby onto it solely with the power of his unearthly jaws. Red blood trailed and dappled the floor with small dark pools.

"Oh my…is he…?" Kay cried.

"Going to be fine, yes," Professor Lully said. "Get on the ship." He pulled her aboard.

"Your stupid inventions," Kay shouted at the great man, her breath screeching through tears and choking her throat with anger, and fear, and mortal, physical exhaustion. "Your stupid plans, you stupid scientists. You kill everything…and it dies."

"Kay, the Q-material—" Lully tried to say.

"Was horrible…I'm glad it's dead, too." Years of meditative training toward achieving calm and awakening concern for all seemed to disappear within the white Deepom victory smoke, and when it cleared Kay stood, feeling naked, her consciousness bared. The others stared in amazement; they had never seen the Prophetess act like this: human. Like Lully was.

"Kay," the man said in a hoarse whisper, "the Q-material was Bobby's mother's biology, not mine. Her DNA, not mine. Her life, not mine. It was to clone her, not me."

Kay only stared as the escape spaceship bay door began to close.

"Closer to Bobby's life than mine," Lully finished. "Essie didn't know that."

Battle at Deepom Dock

K ay and Professor Lully stood stunned.

Just as the humans thought it safe to exhale, their narrow escape seemingly assured—and amid relieved barking, whining, and shouting, while Barky's crew exchanged launch orders; and among harsh cries from Deepom enemies rushing at the closing ship doors, and while escapee friends attended to their The Bobby and his wounds—everything changed.

Bobby rose. Awkwardly but determinedly he stood, and moved past the professor and the prophetess. He refused to be stopped or slowed. He walked off Barky's ship and back toward the battlefield.

Kay, initially aghast at the danger, succumbed to something new: silence. Barky's commanding howls had ceased when told that his craft could not launch, could not escape, that a complex web of security locks wrapped and held the ship. But Kay only overheard that because of the larger, more complete silence. Despite the warring enemies at the door, despite the growing mass of Deepom security droids, Army bot-talions, and wedding guests swelling their numbers, no one was shooting or attacking.

Confusion reigned, but it manifested in stillness. Weapons dropped to sides, mouths gaped open, necks of diverse materials and shapes craned for a view, and all gazed toward Barky's ship.

Because Bobby was coming. And Bobby was talking.

Other of Barky's crew members, even Professor Lully, stopped their efforts to restrain Bobby. They were also transfixed, temporarily, as he walked on, still bleeding from a slash through the tatters of his clothes, his left hand holding the darkening badge of grievous wound at his side. The crew soon returned to the problem of escape; the ship was still held back from launch.

Kay watched Bobby.

Confusion turned to collective gawking, the Deepoms inexorably aligning to Bobby's approach like metal filings obeying magnetic north. The crowd gathered closer, in awe at the image of the walking, injured The Bobby, him who they had pierced and slashed. Those more guilty of resisting their mythical hero tried the more to get closer. Bobby stepped over the crumpled forms of the enemies that had pummeled him and had been killed.

"They didn't—we didn't—know who he was, that it was Him," some said, in truth. They appeared amazed, relieved, that Bobby had risen and was alive.

The battlefield of the docking stations smoked, nearby engines rumbled, but nothing else moved. Barky's ship echoed with voiced directives, worried cries, and failed efforts to propel away.

Kay listened backward—to the fear and frustration of Barky and crew—but moved forward, toward Bobby.

A semi-circle formed of Deepoms of every size and shape and arrangement of sense organs; Bobby walked into their midst. Others came on; the stifling of the battle brought them in peace, however, and they watched. Even the leaders, now arriving, only listened.

Kay followed, stopping just at the edge of the platform where the two opposing spacecraft met, and listened as Bobby confronted the enemy race.

"I see burning instead of beauty," he said softly, clutching his side and the makeshift bandage streaked in scarlet. "And," his voice rose in force, "who are you to come against me, and my father? You—all of you are ours. Rightly ours."

Kay was stunned, enthralled. This was unexpected to say the least—heroic, to say more.

"My father invented you, what you were originally to be. And I made you what you are."

A murmur pulsed through the crowd. They had come out of their reverie and didn't like what they heard. Prodded by the arriving Leadership, they scoffed, reminded of their leaders' disappointment in such notions.

Kay listened backward—to the helplessness of the efforts to free the ship—but watched forward, toward the selflessness of Bobby's bold bravery.

"No, you have it wrong," Bobby answered the crowd loudly. "I am no longer THE BOBBY, yet not just A BOBBY either. I am Bobby, Robert Lully, last of the humans, last of the Earthlings, first of a new line, carrying the future, and you will get behind me, and there will be a new Truce—this one real and made with my father."

Silence again. Kay's worry grew, not only at Bobby's risky words—as the crowd seemed mesmerized again—but with the growing panic behind her, the discovery of the mechanism that restrained Barky's ship and the realization that its grip was perhaps unbreakable.

Kay listened backward—wondering if she could help break the chains of their getaway—but couldn't help but inch forward, toward Bobby's increasingly strange words to the Deepoms.

He said, "You have been artificial up until now, but can be real, and can join me in a new reality."

To Kay's surprise, the crowd whipsawed again, whispering in approval. Indeed some cheered, and indeed some bowed. Bobby stood tall, in pain, but his height, his grim face, and his organic majesty cowed all.

The semi-circle moved to re-form around the Deepom leaders who had huddled in conference.

Kay did not like this; she was not inclined to make friends with such a species. She preferred escape—now, while Bobby had them, hopefully, fooled. That is, she hoped not only that they *were* fooled, but that Bobby was fooling them *intentionally* and didn't mean what he said.

Professor Lully broke from the engineering effort and rushed over to Kay, explaining their predicament. Like Kay's Deepom shackles when captured weeks prior, the force field that prohibited their launch required a numeric code to unlock. While speaking, the Professor also read the Bobby tea leaves: holding the enemies enthralled would buy Barky's team computer-time with which to hack the passcode necessary for escape.

"Keep him talking!" Lully said.

"Why can't we just have him ask for the codes?" Kay replied. "Look! A lot of Deepoms are swaying to his side."

"You can try," the Professor answered, "but I don't trust any of them, and Barky says that certain false combinations would doom us. And the code is very long, 136 binary digits, a number in the duodecillions."

"That's big," Kay said quietly, one eye on Bobby and the shifting, fickle crowd.

"Yeah. We are trying to decode it, to deduce it, using every decrypting algorithm, every logical approach and idea imaginable, and using everything we know about, well, everything. We just need time."

Kay plopped her head and hair to one side in condescending doubt. She had figured out the enemies' silly combination locks before, but she was torn as to who needed her more. Bobby was playing with fire in the midst of the enemy, but without freeing Barky's escape ship...

"Just keep him talking," Lully said again.

"It's dangerous!" Kay said, but Lully had sprinted back to Barky's crew. Kay turned to look upon a changed scene and a newly-perilous predicament: the Deepoms were swaying again, but now dividing, taking sides, the semi-circle breaking in two. The larger part settled behind Ninth, and One, and other Deepom Leaders.

Kay ran to Bobby. "Bobby! Before it is too late! Get them to tell you the combination codes to release our ship. Those nearest to you, they will tell you. Hurry! Do it!"

Bobby looked hard into Kay's beseeching face, and though he saw her doubt and fear he looked as if these were feelings he could not comprehend.

For her part, Kay saw Bobby's fatigue, pain and bravery combine to near-madness. He was pallid with loss of blood and seemed about to collapse.

After an eternity, one that passed a single, prolonged, and precious microsecond at a time, Bobby nodded to Kay.

He commanded that he be given the release code.

Professor Lully and Captain Barky overheard and came near as a small Deepom, triangular and red as if made of the clay of the Selficator piles from their past, moved forward from the crowd and spoke.

"I will tell you!" It spoke eagerly. "And I will follow you. The code is made of five numbers."

Silence returned, the balance of crowd-power hung on this event.

The triangle began again, speaking the code. "It goes eight, eight billion, eight billion and eight, eight billion eighteen..." But before it could say the fifth number there came a tumultuous shouting, the Deepom leadership breaking through the crowd with orders, threats, and declarations as they were flanked by another platoon of their Army.

The little red Deepom's mouth hung open and froze, then its pointed head dropped and hung loosely off its bulky trapezoidal neck. It collapsed to the floor: shot dead and covered in blue flames that rose in unison with electronic cries of "Traitor!"

In an instant, lasers blazed and the battle reengaged. The leadership made their way through the newly-conflicted Deepom crowd; the tide was clearly turning against the Earthlings again. The ground of interlocked spaceships shook and walls began to bend and moan, their metals to snap.

Kay implored Bobby to come back into the ship as Barky's crew came forward to join the furiously-renewed melee. A troop of brazen guards came forward from the enemy ranks; it sparked a memory of fear and capture that sent Kay on a screaming sprint back to the ship. Bobby followed, and both collapsed into friendly arms upon crossing the hatchway.

Barky was able to withdraw all allies to the docking area and the cover it offered among piles of wreckage and rubble strewn like rolling screes of scrap iron. He shouted orders while announcing that Ninth, and One, and other leaders were coming. The color-fully wild shootout flashed and reflected off the metallic battlefield. Some new panic—perhaps another wavering of loyalties after the retreat of The Bobby—wafted through the enemy factions and they were scattering in all directions, it seemed, many dropping from fire both friendly and unfriendly. The shooting also came around corners from the direction of the wedding hall, and also from out in space from the other ships docked along various platforms. It appeared to be a strategy of shoot first, worry about allegiances later.

Protected in an alcove of the ship, assured of a few, final, fateful seconds as the battlefield crashed and crumpled, Barky and Professor Lully stared at a computer screen which now displayed four-fifths of the escape code. Kay had risen and now kept one eye on Bobby—again on a stretcher, eyes closed—and another on the screen of integers, displaying eight, then eight billion, and the other decimal numbers along the top, with their equivalent string of binary ones and zeroes beneath. There was plenty of space after for the missing fifth number that would complete the code and release Barky's ship.

All other crew members watched this last-ditch attempt at survival. Barky's soldiery was returning from the destruction of the battlefield where all was lost. One final guess at the password provided thin separation from annihilation.

Lully spoke in a flurry of big words. "OK, now we only have to impute the remaining digits after we concatenate and convert the first four decimal numbers of the unlock code as binary, right Barky? I think the formula relates to a Diophantine prime-generating polynomial based on neutrino oscillations…"

Barky twitched excitedly. "Yesshhh. I guessshhh. If we can program the computersshhh to run over all posshhible integersssh, we can get the fifth number for eshhcape."

Lully nodded rapidly with head and hands and fingers and beard to implore the dog to hurry.

Kay mumbled the first four numbers of the security code as she stared at Bobby. Eight. Eight billion. Eight billion and eight. Eight billion eighteen. Bobby moaned and turned on his stretcher, then lay straight and still. In her mind: 8, 8000000000, 8000000008, 8000000018. In her eye: Bobby lying in brave simplicity.

Professor Lully swore, Barky sneezed. Two formulaic attempts at cracking the code had failed, and the highly-advanced barbarians were at the gate, temporarily held back behind a protective wall of smoking, metallic magma at the entrance of Barky's ship, though all knew this would only gain them seconds. Blue light came through the cracks and sparked off the ceiling.

Eight, eight billion, eight billion eight, eight billion eighteen, Kay thought.

"I know," Lully said. "Try running the resonant frequencies."

"Of what?" Barky asked.

"Good question, Lully said in defeat. He was hoping Barky knew.

"I wish BeepBeep was here," Someone said.

Kay mumbled aloud, one more time, the beginning of the secret password, those odd *8s* and *0s* forming in her head again, but then the letters of the spelled numerals pushed the numbers aside. E. I. G. H. T.

She looked at Bobby again.

She snapped out of her fog, and stopped Lully from a last guess, his fingers on the keyboard, his head shaking in failure and frustration. The protective rubble wall at the ship's door shook in answer; Deepoms voices could be heard.

"Never mind, I got it," Kay said. "The fifth number of the code is eight billion eighteen million. Barky, tell them to clear the hatchway, we are getting out of here." She ran to Bobby's side.

Lully seemed to stare inwards at his own brain for a moment, then laughed. "Oh for empyrean's sake!" He shook his head again, this time with his version of love. He spoke to those around him as he typed with finality into the console. "Ha! It is indeed deducible, a very simple ordering of numbers—alphabetical order! Of all the numbers!" He laughed very, very hard. "A kid could do it! But OK, we just need to convert to binary and enter them," he said, acting quickly, and adding in a shout to Kay, "Rest your brain, my dear Prophetess, I can at least do that!"

And with another shout to their enemy, "Ninth! I didn't create you so that you could create! Ha! My devious little bastard inventions are no match for J's little sister!"

The engines of the cathedral ship roared and the sound echoed reassuringly among its walls. With a jolt—and with cheers—the enormous thing began to separate free from the even more massive, though less attractive and less purple, Deepom Leadership. The re-escaping escapees watched as the rubble of the open platform floated away into black space and the large hatch bay shut with a loud, nurturing clack. Viewports showed the growing contingent of enemy soldiers and security giants firing away wildly but impotently—Barky's warship's protective shield had been repaired and withstood the blasts—and then the crowd parted, and Ninth came forth.

Speakers on the ship blared with Ninth's powerful voice. "It doesn't matter!" the Deepom said with a laugh that froze Kay's heart. She cowered into a seat at the console, her knees and mind bent inward.

They were quickly away and gone from Deepom sight and pursuit. Captained by Robot 24, the ship's power revved and the craft snapped into a Lullyon-Hop beyond anything the Deepoms could fathom. It had been designed by the Seapegs.

The Seapegs, however, were not on board. They had made their way to the alien cavalry to await higher levels of alien hierarchy to arrive.

Bobby lifted his head to Ninth's booming laugh only to drop again, wan and weak and wounded. Escapee friends attended to him as before.

Bobby smiled as they laid Kay beside him—his wife according to Deepom Law—and fell into dreamless levels of sleep.

A Long Night Later

A long night later...

The current nothingness—there was peace, and calm, a space in time that was in-between somehow—worried Barky as much as the battle and rescue had. The escaped and renamed creatures on his ship were afraid; Bobby Los was hurt badly, and they recalled his speech of hope as they watched through observation windows the fragile beauty and mystery of the hallowed core of the universe. The additional realization that Los was The Bobby was still sinking in—all aboard were Deepoms, after all, and had Bobby at their core. It only increased their love for him, and now their anxious concern.

On the bridge, Barky popped his ears this way and that as his powerful nose surveyed the ancient ether outside his ship, and there was nothing. Nothing was happening. The thousands of silver Selflicators—Lully's depowered mutant army—floated dumbly and away, without purpose. The alien cavalry and their majestic horses had gone, as had the golden Deepom ships, all of them, though the view was still streaked with the lingering, thickly-white doom-fumes.

As Bobby-Los lay in his stretcher-turned-cot, his human wounds tended as best as all aboard could manage, and as Eve-Kay slid in between at least three levels of consciousness, and as even Professor Lully slept deeply, Barky waited.

Robot 24 tried to communicate with the Seapegs and find out what the heck was going on.

The silence was torn by an odd-sounding squawk. It repeated stiffly as if a horn sounding in alarm. It woke Kay, and it woke Professor Lully. In the great man's dream-mixed reverie, it sounded like a cock crowing and reminded him instantly of the family farm of his youth, back when new days promised new learning and simple adventures and not the incessant combat of galactic mind wars. Some instinct in the man carried forth an inexplicable feeling of relief.

The horn braying was accompanied by the ringing of bells, deep and powerful bells, repeating a simple but profound melody. This was followed by horses neighing, and the dancing white fog dissipating, and out from it came a Deepom transport ship, a sideways sashaying bomb-shape, with its doors open.

Barky, and all aboard except Robot 24, held their collective breath at this new threat.

But the horn sounded again, and the bells tolled thrice in triumph and power from the transport ship as it came. Out rode a dozen aliens on horseback.

Peace came to the middle of the universe. Loudly.

A Dubbed Video Of
What Happened

Robot 24 was not surprised. As the peace horn blew, the long-awaited transmission was being received: a video from the Seapegs. As the alien cavalry arrayed itself outside the battered escapee warship, Robot 24 redirected the communications to all Barky's ship's screens. All watched.

They saw a square box, the very box that 24 had used to house the Seapegs for transport to the aliens. Gathering on either side of the box were those same bits, the endearing little Seapegs, shining mites, living jewels, moving in organized queues, some now climbing to the top of the enclosure and partially hanging over its opening, which was like a sleek cavern to these small creatures.

The video panned outward, showing the box positioned on the lap of a sitting giant, an alien whose thighs—or, you know, alien upper leg-things—seemed a vast plain to the little beings as they emptied and roamed while staying in a disciplined formation.

Those closest to the ship's speakers began to hear, softly at first, a hum, then a harmony of many gentle sounds—dulcet tones, like the peal of tender bells. They played the same short melody that the alien horns had blared earlier when harbingering the peace. The soft chiming grew in volume to a distinct tolling, and in composition to a clear and definite music as if from a small orchestra—physically small, but with many unfamiliar though wonderful instruments.

Then: with a swiftness, agility, and definiteness of coordinated purpose that could not be understood using any experience that either Barky, or Frilkielle, or the greatest of the advanced escapee Deepoms (even with Robot 24's help), or Professor Lully is his deepest ambition, or his protégé J at his most clever, or his sister Kay in her most sublime spiritual ruminations, had ever had, the Seapegs dispersed. Their voices broke the symphony into its constituent, melodic parts, the music now playing close to every heart. To each hearer was assigned a different voice, as was understood later by those on Barky's ship. And perhaps this went even further; it seemed possible that every sentient, living thing in the universe, or perhaps even every particle or smallest unit of entropy itself, had a Seapeg song of its own to harken to, one that sang of personal peace within the greater, harmonic harmony.

The musical spell was broken by alien voices on the video. The alien leaders—certainly up thirty levels at least from the highest of the cleanup crews—were happily engaged with their new little Seapeg friends.

The English-speaking humans and escapee Deepoms could not understand the alien language, but soon a surprising thing happened. They heard familiar and friendly beeps come from the speakers instead. "Beep, beep. Beep beep-beep."

"It'shhhhh BeepBeep!" Barky bellowed gleefully. "He is translating for us!"

So, Barky explained that what they were seeing was the arrival of the Seapegs to the aliens, and the delivery of the recorded audio of the Deepoms' admission of breaking The Truce. Then the rising of Seapeg voices with messages of peace, and apologies from Earth-beings. Then their proposed solutions to the general way of violent or unhappy things.

And lastly, a warning to the aliens that the Deepom Army was on its way.

The video showed the supreme alien leader—of this level—stroking the mane of his pale horse while talking to others of high rank. Rank was obvious; those with the most colors and tallest horses clearly were in command.

Barky translated the beeps, dubbing the video with his best alien imitation, as the large-thighed alien observed, "There is an energy increase in the room that certainly can be measured. It is a new energy, perhaps, but a wholesome one."

A different alien voice answered. "These guys are so cute, and they are of negative entropy if you hold them at a certain angle. Very advanced, and from Earth! Maybe we overreacted earlier."

"Well," the first alien said, "with such energy, things can be amended. It was just a warning anyway. I have an idea. I need approval from a few levels up, but leave it to me."

"OK. And just as they said, here come the Deepoms."

"Destroy them, and let's get out of here. I hate this Spot." The giant alien exited, and that was the end of the video transmission.

Neighing rose outside the ship windows; the horses and aliens galloped away in pairs as Bobby moaned in his sleep.

Awake

Two days later...

———————◆———————

"**B**eep, beep," BeepBeep said but was hushed by Barky and crew.

"No, it isn't anticlimactic, BeepBeep," Lord Upright corrected. "What about all the battles, the sieges, the chases, the danger, the escapes, the bravery, the close calls! And now we are saved, all because Master Los woke up in a spaceship one morning. Who would want more? Do we have to hang over the chasms of exploding black holes every two microseconds?"

"Beep beep," BeepBeep said.

"Lord Upright is just thankful that Bobby is OK," Lord Upright said.

Bobby was OK, and when he awoke from his very wild but not atypical dreams, the first face he saw was his father's.

"Well, well! Three days asleep! This at least ties your record, huh?" the man joked.

Much of the recent past stampeded to the front of Bobby's mind, though in a cloud of thick dust. His father's cooperation with Kay's plan, their flight from the Deepom wedding hall, the bravery of the little goat and of the huge but honest Deepom guard, his personal confrontation with the Deepoms—these were highlights from within the haze.

As were his wounds. Bobby winced and felt gingerly for his left leg. Doing so stretched the tight bandages wrapping his torso.

"Easy, son. It's fine, you will be fine—though you won't be sleepwalking for a while." His father laughed. "But the scar—wow.

I have to say that I am jealous. You were wounded in glorious battle with the enemy! I will give you my epaulets once you are ready."

"Thanks, Dad," Bobby said.

"Don't give him your little shoulders," Kay joked.

Professor Lully excused himself to call and gather others, and soon Barky, Robots 1 and 24, Kay's goat, and various escapees filled Bobby's room and listened as the man told his son the story of the end of the War of the Spot, as it had been named.

"It's a Deepom-less world," Lully began. "My invention-gone-haywire is no more." Lully explained the Deepom demise; they had been quickly dispatched at the large hands of the aliens. Working backward, he also explained the Seapegs' mission and answered Bobby's questions concerning their own adventure, especially Kay's Plan B to fool the Deepoms.

"How did you know what to do, Kay?" Bobby asked after his father quoted Kay's long, labyrinthine, head-exploding question to the guard named Schmick. "And how did you do that?"

"Well," Kay explained, "I knew their words for yes and no, almost, and—thanks to Lord Upright—that one of the three guards was honest, so the rest was simple logic. And knowing that their silly computer brains couldn't handle anything complicated." She added to her kid goat, "Stupid trained liars, like that spaghetti-box jerk, remember?"

The goat nodded.

Bobby pretended to understand.

Professor Lully said to Kay, "I thought you would need a second question, until the head exploded. You are very clever, girly, but got lucky that you didn't ask MickMack first. We didn't have much time."

"True, I guess," Kay admitted.

"You guys are way too smart," Bobby said with a smile. Robot 1, next to Bobby's cot, agreed.

"And you were way too brave," Kay said, "I was stunned; we all were."

Bobby chose to interpret Kay's statement as a compliment, then asked, "What else did I miss?"

There were many answers at once, but Bobby's father's voice rose above the rest. "The Seapegs are beloved by the aliens, so that they think better of us humans, we Earthlings. Their Earth-trash space-littering punishment is lifted. And since the Seapegs consider you, Bobby, as their brother, we three have also been rewarded. Mine was that I am allowed to live—they see me as the cause of much of the trouble!"

"That's cool news!" Bobby said. "I guess I need to hang out more with my new brothers."

"You will; we get them back soon. And you need to think of your own reward, most likely whatever you want, so choose carefully. Kay had hers…" Lully hesitated, looking at Kay for permission, but she shook her head, her cleanly-drawn red hair and its bright blue bows bouncing about playfully. "Well, I guess she still isn't willing to tell."

"I know what I want," Bobby said. "Two things, actually."

"A true Lully!" the professor exclaimed to the room. "But don't push it!"

"No," Bobby replied to the joyous crowd, "don't worry. The aliens can only grant me one of them…" He blushed while looking at Kay.

His father knew to rescue the teens from the awkward glances of the escapees, still curious as to how humans actually related to each other beyond building things and fighting.

"So," Lully began, and rose from the cube to stand tall. "I have been thinking."

The man had big plans, though honest and wholesome ones, perhaps born of the pure-hearted energy of his third-generation creations, the Seapegs.

"I mourned the loss of the Q-material, though I like the prospect of a more natural way to leave a legacy." He winked at Kay, who rolled her eyes playfully. "But I, for once, was misunderstood." He explained that the Q-material's purpose was not to clone but to reproduce, using his own organic material and that of his deceased wife, Bobby's mother. "It might have even created another The Bobby, who knows?" he joked.

Bobby was as deep in thought as he ever had been, or could be, and looked to his father through tears that were the last of the salts of the Earth. This was replaced by a feeling in his stomach as if it had just blanched, or as if his blood rushed everywhere at once, or as if his body were home to a garden that was now being warmed by a new morning sun. He never wanted the feeling to end, he realized.

It was because Kay was holding his hand. He wondered, after this, what the use of rewards or wishes was when the present was like this, and time could only move forward.

He looked at his father in a new way as the man began again.

"And!" Lully announced. "I have something else to occupy my time. Until recently, Negative Entropy was just a theory, something I and a few select others had only theorized about over drinks and thick steaks and cigars. It was forbidden knowledge, sort of. Kay realized—and I didn't—that the Seapegs have some very interesting traits worth exploring. The theory is not a theory anymore—and has some interesting ramifications."

"Like?" Robot 24 asked.

"Time travel. My creations may be useful to me after all."

Come True

———————•———————

Of peace, and of wishes, and the unchanging lot of humankind, and of the remaining story, what is there to add, or to say?

Only little things.

On Barky's ship, there was a general meeting among the escapees to decide where to go next. The humans were invited—it was announced that Eve the Prophetess was not a Deepom after all, to which there was a collective "Duh"—but none of the three attended. The escapees debated how they should reward their Namer, Los The Bobby; they wanted to do something special, to thank him, something beyond the two wishes he already earned. Bobby explained that it wasn't necessary, and the matter was dropped. He did ask that they support Eve-Kay in her own reward: that everyone should help find her brother J who it was collectively agreed was no fool and who it was collectively believed must therefore have escaped the Earth. And to welcome him as a friend once found.

To that Kay added, "I also got two wishes, so my other was to stay with all the escapees, and help them as much as I can, to repay them for saving me, which they did at least three times." With that, and as the memory of others' sacrifices stole over her face, she quietly stole to her room.

Late in the day, having shaved, Bobby left his bare and boring room in an attempt to speed time while awaiting his wish—the second of two wishes, that is—to come true. His first was to check out The Spot up close, the place of the origin of the universe, of time, space, entropy, and everything. He had done that earlier, for six seconds, and found it "soft, like lilacs."

His second wish was granted by Kay. Though, when Bobby asked, her first reply was "Not even if you were the last man on Earth!"

"Oh," Bobby said and turned to walk away, disappointed and relieved in equal measure, a thing that is a unique skill among teenaged persons.

"Just kidding!" Kay grabbed him with the words and with her hand, and she agreed to go on a date with The Bobby Los The Namer, provided he just be Robert Lully and she could just be Kay.

Bobby walked slowly along the ship corridors, with no followers. He paused at the meditation window and looked upon the face of the universe, and its purple eyes of refracted light seemed to look back. *Not as pretty as Kay's*, Bobby thought, then moved along.

He spoke with some visiting aliens and hugged their horses. He sat in on a small concert in the auditorium. Then he ambled to the bridge, where his father was bent over some calculations on long ripples of paper that lay like a meandering stream, and Bobby listened to Professor Lully argue with Frilkielle and Sunmoon-boomboom over an obscure mathematical point. Bobby tiptoed away, happy and reminded of old times.

Only small things to tell of—and one *big* thing: because it was time.

Finally, it was time. Bobby had learned a lot about time in his space travels, and how important it is, and how relative, and that it does not pass the same for everyone everywhere—and certainly the six seconds he spent at The Spot felt like a very long time, as did the five-second Kay-kiss when the two were being matrimonially sacrificed at the Deepom altar. His long talks with Eve seemed always gone in an instant, yet he remembered every word, every breath, every laugh. And this day, only a few hours old, seemed like years.

But then, it was time.

Frilkielle came and escorted The Bobby and Eve-Kay—the Prophetess's auburn tresses flying big and curly in loose spirals and in all directions as she walked happily at Los's side—to the remains of Eve's spacecraft, which had been salvaged and refurbished into a quite elegant, actually, human dining area, with crystal glasses and fine porcelain dinnerware.

Candles were already lit; the universe was certainly ready for their date.

Bobby felt very happy, and older, as if he had missed a birthday, and indeed he now had scars and was having dinner with the loveliest girl in the world.

He considered himself lucky: it seemed easier to rescue the universe and get this dinner date as reward than to ask Kay out directly—and this as much as anything else was truly proof that he was now a man and with man experiences.

The two entered the ship's doorway, giddy with excitement and at the same time hushed by the romance. They passed just below a studded metal plaque engraved with the orb's name, *"Diotima,"* and motto, *"Quod verum est somnium."*

"It is right because I dreamed it," Kay translated.

"Cool," Bobby said, and smiled.

"My brother named it. I don't know what Diotima is, probably has nothing to do with me."

Frilkielle left them to go arrange the dinner presentation.

Earlier, Bobby remembered, when Kay was crying, he had, in his mind only, put his arm around her. Now, here, at the middle (of some things) and at the beginning (of others), he imagined himself rising steadily, stepping toward Eve-Kay, and bending to kiss her freckled, soft cheek.

Bobby opened his eyes to find Kay kissing him back. And she held his hand once more.

The End

Epilogue:
The First Reward

Earlier on Dinner Date Day...

---

obby woke up in a trashcan, having gone to sleep in a space-ship the night before.

The trashcan was marked *Deepom Battle Hero Trash*.

"Not funny, Guk," Bobby said. Guk disagreed. "But it's nice to have you back with us," Bobby managed while falling out of the can knees-first. "I have a new name for you: Syzygy. Nice, right?"

Guk disagreed.

Guk left.

It was Universal Peace Week, Day Four, and Bobby stayed an extra-long time among the squares of his room that morning, spending a lazy time trying on clothes—there was a special team that scavenged the ship for anything clothes-y since humans were unduly sensitive about keeping metal scraps against their skin and private parts. Bobby also spent his time bathing, and re-bathing, and combing, whistling, and grooming. He was offered a breakfast of human food salvaged from one of the Selflicators that Captain Lully had luckily used for storage, but Bobby declined. He was content and his stomach full with nervous butterflies who were also killing time. Today would be a big day. And the night would be a big night.

The day: He was to be granted Bobby Peace Accord Wish Number One.

The night: Wish Number Two to come true.

For today: excited. For tonight: petrified.

Bobby's first wish as a famous young man was to take a peek into the glass cube that surrounded The Spot. To get close to it. To be in the same spot as that of the Big Bang at the Start of Time.

After a few hours more of those wickedly anxious preparations, and with Bobby at last back in his familiar jeans and favored alien t-shirt, the knock came at the door. A small detail of bright-eyed sports equipment had come to escort The Bobby The Los The Namer The Hero to the main deck, and from there into a small craft—a cube, not spherical like his Dad's orb—that would take him to the Beginning, the Middle.

"This is a huge mistake," his father said, questioning the brains of aliens who would agree to this. Hope rose in the great man, as it always did when deducing the weaknesses of others. He went off to borrow a computer.

Barky met Bobby at the tubed entrance that led to the docked pod. A crowd had gathered; Bobby was used to this.

"I finally thought of a name for you, Barky—it came to me last night before I fell asleep."

Barky's ears squared to attention, his head tilted classically, his mouth closed, his eyes brightened and tightened, and his ears rose even more and again.

"The full name is…Blake Rex Doxodog," Bobby The Namer said and stepped back to admire some of his best work.

Barky's blood rushed, and his lungs almost burst full of air. He jumped onto two legs, his paws landing in Bobby's lowered palms, his tail whipping furiously. His long lips slobbered something both unintelligible and slushy.

"Down, Blake Rex!" Bobby said from his own large smile. "Sit, Blake Rex!" And Barky—Blake Rex—sat. Then jumped again to his master's midsection and howled.

"Glad you like it," Bobby said, as BeepBeep rolled toward them, then down the tunnel to the pod while beeping in a string of pairs.

"Hey! I missed you, BeepBeep!" BeepBeep beeped again, and Bobby realized that he did not have a name for this extremely important and mostly-loyal alien, and it seemed that the shape-shifting bot was expecting one now, its lights even dimmed a bit, and the crowd hushed in expectation as it always did. "Of course, I have a name for you too. OK? Want it?"

BeepBeep beeped.

"You sure?" Bobby bought time.

BeepBeep did not beep.

"OK…here it comes… Your name is…Iso…pos…to…los…" The pause that followed could have won Most Uncomfortable at the Awkward Academy Awards. BeepBeep rolled away down the tunnel. "Isopostolos," Bobby repeated, more confidently, and this time ending the name properly and not letting it float into space and die.

Bobby was not used to anything but success in naming, so he shouted to BeepBeep's rear parts, "OK? Hey, BeepBeep!"

"Beep, beep," echoed back to man and dog.

"Glad you like it," Bobby laughed. Barky sneezed.

Bobby felt a tug at his leg from a small robot who had been following.

"For you?" Bobby said to it with a knowing grin. "How about… Spectaculum? OK?"

The small machine whirled in three full circles and sped off.

"Is that everyone, for now?" Bobby asked the crowd.

It was.

Eve-Kay the Prophetess made her way to them, to say goodbye, to say to have fun, and to say that she would see Bobby later. She looked bright and fresh, dressed in green, a bathrobe sewn of towels, though to Bobby's eyes it was a Grecian robe on a goddess of beauty and power, radiant as the best of Earth mornings. Her fingernails were shining, and her red locks pulled back tightly, while against her head were multicolored plastic tubes wrapped neatly with hair, and between her toes, as Bobby noticed now, were white fluffs of cotton.

The girl winked and turned away.

As did Bobby, to gaze down the entrance to the pod. "Come on, Blake! Come, Rex!" And with that, Bobby and his favorite space explorers boarded the small, square-faceted ship.

Bobby took a seat at a window, felt the pod disengage, and watched the majestic cathedral-like mother ship float away, relatively. Outside remained a few cleanup crew garbage canisters with some aliens—indistinguishable from Guk—floating individually, some of them gliding on prancing horses. The remains of the silver Selflicator Army were stacked to form a giant, glimmering pyramid.

"Nice," Bobby commented.

Soon, they arrived at The Spot.

Approaching what Bobby thought was a glass case, their pod floated directly through its outer pane—it was not solid at all. Inside was another cube, and a few within that, all containing each other, none of them solid. The series went on, and Bobby saw now that the lines of the glassy cubes-within-cubes shrank to infinity, continued forever to a smaller and smaller point. He wondered how this was possible and whether they, and their cubic space-pod, were in fact shrinking.

"Ssschhhhomething like that," Barky said.

It went on until it stopped; ahead the pattern ended with perimeter lines of a cubic space, about a foot in size. This last, ultimate space had no other cubes inside, just clear emptiness that twinkled, somehow, with tiny spots of glittering reflection here and there, like dust riding sunbeams through a still room.

A perfect cubic earth-foot of that.

This last one enclosure was solid, not an illusion or an abstraction. A case, a frame, of a real, gleaming steel, or some advanced quantum cosmological physics version of it, and, as Bobby mulled, no doubt with very special properties and friends in high levels to have been selected to encase the most important Cartesian coordinate of all time, the geometric origin of all geometric origins.

Their ship bonked into it.

"Wooopssshh," Barky said.

The ship soon stopped, the cube shining directly out Bobby's window, a few feet from his face.

"What do I do?" he asked.

"You can get out here and will be able to breathe with that mask." Barky pointed distractedly as he fiddled with instruments on the panel in front of him. "It is like the space where we rescued you from the orb—but not as thick. It looksscchh very calm too-ooo."

Barky and BeepBeep escorted Bobby to the door as the ship rotated and The Spot came to rest just outside.

The hatch opened. Bobby held his breath despite himself. His face was shaking with excitement and his stomach shimmying like cherry Jell-O in zero gravity: the location of the Beginning of Everything that ever existed was within his reach, six inches from his chest.

The frames' six panes were empty and its twelve thin edges nearly invisible now as the nearby space was perfectly still.

Bobby peered at it intensely, reverently. He raised a hand but did not dare yet to touch it. He took his time.

He had earned this moment, he knew. He faced The Spot with respect and awe; he closed his eyes as if to pray quietly to the holiness of the place and to the moment, to the cube, and to The Spot, and to where it all began.

He stretched out his neck to stick his head in it.

"*Ruff!* What?" Barky snapped and pulled his master back ungently by the scruff of the young man's neck.

"BeepBeep?" asked BeepBeep.

Bobby was recovering from being tossed across the ship at almost zero gravity, his long legs were caught between and among some machinery pieces, and, worse, his neck hurt because, in fact, he didn't have any scruff there the way puppies did.

"Ouch," he said.

"Schhhhorry," Barky came to him and slobbered him with licks. "I didn't know your wisssshhh wassschhh to ssschhhttick your head in The Shpot!"

"Oh. I assumed you knew. What else is there to do with it?"

At that moment, the onboard communications panel lit with a transmission request from the escapee ship. It was The Prophetess calling.

"How's it going?" Eve-Kay's voice piped through the small cubic pod, filling it, in Bobby's mind, with a sweet smell and melodic echo. Barky brought her up to date as Bobby tried to edit the true tale to make him appear less defeated by the moment.

Eve laughed, "Well what else did you want him to do with it?"

Bobby puffed his chest out, the alien head on his t-shirt bloating in size.

BeepBeep contributed next, speaking for thirty seconds straight.

Eve-Kay answered. "Oh no, I didn't think of that. But can he? Will it fit? What's the physics of it?"

"Well," Barky answered, "to ssschhhtart with, it'ssschh not a hole, it'ssshhh jusshht a point. But wait, BeepBeep is calculating shhhomething."

The small bot quieted to a low buzz, his multicolored surface lights blinking in unison, then in sequence around his figure-eight exterior, then in unison again. The smooth ship's walls reflected it all beautifully. Then it stopped, just as a series of very complicated and Greekly-serious mathematical symbols swayed and scrolled down a computer screen in front of which Barky panted.

"Wow," the dog said, entranced. "That's wild."

Kay asked about these results, and Barky started four or five different words but stopped each time.

"It's deep," was all Barky managed, eventually, and quietly, while still staring.

"BeepBeep," BeepBeep said.

"Tell me!" Eve asked.

"BeepBeep," BeepBeep said again.

"Try me," Kay insisted.

And heard from Barky:

"BeepBeep has only used this "mega-formula" once before, he says, but it combines the formulas for Boltzmann Entropy and Heisenberg Uncertainty to find that there is an uncertainty "gap" in spacetime that the aliens use as a time-limiting measure for single particles in phase-space that on the translation dimensional continuum amounts to about a half-inch in length, which in a quantum mechanical world is a hole big enough to do things with. But taking the other limit, of change of entropy, using $(\hbar \,/\, k_B) * c$, when converted to inches again—for stubborn Earthlings like you and Bobby—is 0.566447 inches-Kelvin, and is interpreted thusschhhly. If one creates a situation of sufficiently low entropy, namely zero like at The Spot, then at Bobby's room temperature of 293.15 Kelvin there is a span of approximately fourteen feet wherein anything can happen. That's the uncertainty gap. Taken with ambient measures and accounting for the entropy identity $\Delta G = \Delta U + P\Delta V - T\Delta S$, and rearranging, we can give Bobby the choice of unitized unknowns: either ten joules-per-seconds-squared, or temporal focusing, in seconds, namely six. From a math standpoint, this is sound, BeepBeep says. The physical interpretation, on the other hand…well, I would not want it in the wrong philosophical handsssshhh. Arooooo!"

"Ah," Eve-Kay said.

Bobby rubbed his eyes of their glaze.

"So," Kay continued, "Bobby gets to choose, when interacting with the single tiny spot of The Spot, to either use ten joules-per-second-squared effort or six seconds of time?"

"BeepBeep."

"Yessshhh."

"I pick the six seconds," Bobby declared. The other option sounded like an expensive commitment. He also preferred not to use denominators when avoidable, nor to multiply things to themselves unless it was really the only way, a last resort.

"Then OK, go ahead! Arooooo!" Barky aid.

Bobby was soon leaning out the opening again, breathing slowly as he found the nerve to stick his brain and skull and eyes and ears and nose and mouth into this most ancient unit of space. Two cleanup crews galloped near, asked whether he had considered bathing first, laughed harshly, then trotted away.

Bobby was glad Kay had hung up. His hands whitened with the prolonged grip of the sides of the space pod, and, after being assured for the tenth time that BeepBeep and Barky would pull him out after six seconds, he closed his eyes and then forced his shoulders forward, then his neck, with head whiplashing in tow, through the edges of the case and to The Spot of all Spots.

It brought to mind the baby lilacs in the West Wing Garden of his home, and how soft they felt, like purple powder. He regarded the softness of the Spot like that, and, though he couldn't be sure, while inside he might have even spoken a word or two. Then was pulled out.

BeepBeep beeped.

BeepBeep beeped again.

"No doubt," Barky agreed. Then, to Bobby, "He said that this will have ramifications because you were heard."

"What does that mean?"

"No idea," Barky said. "He will work on it. Can we go home now?" The dog returned to the main controls to pilot them back to the main escapee ex-warship.

"Yes," Bobby said, "I don't want to be late for tonight." He draped *Space Point Zero*—as he suggested the spot should be called—with a note pinned to an American flag, and then removed both, thinking better of it and how the aliens might react. Then he plopped, exhausted, into his seat, watching The Spot's twinkling frame recede. It felt as if his head had been in there for at least a week.

Upon their return, Professor Lully was anxious to meet with BeepBeep, someone whose intelligence he could respect—it was like iced tea to a parched man adrift in the desert, he said—and to review BeepBeep's calculations. The great scientist was very interested in the mega-formula—"How simple!"—and shook his head, nearly speechless, when BeepBeep showed the man the data from Bobby's momentous act of Spot Head-Sticking-In. Lully's son, having spoken to The Spot in his six seconds of fame, had created sufficient initial conditions and energetic physical laws for another Creation and Big Bang, though its size was relative, that is, teeny-tiny.

The resulting New Universe collapsed and burned very quickly, however. This kind of thing—creation—is not easy, BeepBeep reported; stability is hard to maintain during the first couple of c-fermis of new singularities. But: if Bobby had managed a third word, perhaps things would have been different because…

"Let's not calculate about that," said the professor.

The Second End

References

1. "So, I guess not all that is bright must fade." Thomas Moore, 1818

2. "...*May tell why Heav'n has made us as we are.* Alexander Pope, *An Essay on Man,* 1734

3. "...*And of these one and all I weave the song of myself.* Walt Whitman, *Song of Myself*

4. "Then she learned, by waiting a few minutes, that she was probably not going to die in the next few minutes." Kay is using a concept from probability theory here called the "Copernican Principle"

5. "Not about what isn't, but that it isn't." Kay is drawing on *The Cloud of Unknowing,* an anonymous work from the late 14th century

6. "Whatever is in fire and other things which does not come into existence at any point in time, because it is not created, that is said to be its self-existent nature." Candrakirti

7. "...*terrifid at the shapes / Enslavd humanity put on he became what he beheld.*" William Blake, *The Four Zoas*

8. "...and Making Death a Victory" A splicing of Shelley's *Prometheus Unbound,* Act IV, with Lord Byron's *Prometheus*

9. "Be what you are, not who you are." Carl Jung

10. "Know thyself!" Oracle of Delphi

11. "Be whole, not perfect." Carl Jung

12. "My blood is seed!" Tertullian

13. "Do all great truths begin as blasphemies?" George Bernard Shaw

14. "Blandly and suavely!" Cardinal Newman and, separately, Anton Chekhov. The author has no further comment on what that portends

15. "...noble suffering would have been his quickest path to perfection." Kay is paraphrasing Meister Eckhart

16. "Multivac." Multivac is a character in numerous stories by Isaac Asimov

17. "...would you say 'Swimswam'?" For the logic at work here, Kay should credit her brother J, Brian Rabern, and Landon Rabern (https://www.pure.ed.ac.uk/ws/files/15023904/Simple_Solution.pdf)

18. "...burning instead of beauty" Isaiah 3:24 (Bobby presumably heard the King James Version as a youth, most likely from his mother.)

19. *"It is right because I dreamed it."* Emanuel Swedenborg